Project 19

Crisis in the Desert Series, Book One

By
Matt Jackson
&
James Rosone

1

Copyright Notice

Table of Contents

Introduction

Iraq's invasion of Kuwait in 1990 was one of the greatest military blunders of the twentieth century. This supreme political and military folly led to Iraq standing alone and fighting a war against a coalition of forces that spanned the globe—a war that would have a profound impact on the affairs of the Middle East for decades and generations to come.

Iraq had just completed a war with the Islamic Republic of Iran—a war in which Iraq was ironically being supported with weapons by the United States. This eight-year war achieved little and left Iraq with billions of dollars in debt and a largely wrecked economy.

When the dust settled from the war with Iran, Iraqi President Saddam Hussein looked to his creditors for debt forgiveness. To Saddam's thinking, Iraq had fought the war to stop the Islamic Revolution in Iran from reaching their own doorsteps. This revolution saw the secular ruler of Iran deposed by fanatical Islamic zealots, a phenomenon that threatened to spread across the rest of the Middle East. From this perspective, the secular rulers of the other Arab nations in the region owed a degree of their security to Iraq, who had fought the war on their behalf. Because of this, Saddam felt his nation's debt should have been forgiven.

The Gulf states who were owed money could argue that Saddam was motivated not by the best interests of his neighbors but rather by greed. He sought to take advantage of a weakened Iran still recovering from the infighting of the revolution in order to seize the oil fields and port facilities in the oil-rich Iranian province of Khuzestan.

In the end, although several of Saddam's key creditors—including Egypt, Saudi Arabia, and Bahrain—agreed to forgive Iraq's war debt, the tiny nations of Kuwait and the UAE held firm. They wanted their money repaid. Their refusal to go along with the debt forgiveness that the other Arab nations had given Iraq led Saddam to develop plans of his own in dealing with Kuwait.

In the lead-up to the war between Kuwait and Iraq, Saddam declared that Kuwait was illegally using slant wells to siphon off Iraqi oil. Saddam also cited the older argument that Kuwait was still a part of Iraq, as the Anglo-Ottoman Convention of 1913 had never been ratified, meaning the two countries had never officially been separated.

But Saddam miscalculated the world's reaction to his attempt to seize and control the oil fields of Kuwait. Oil is the lifeblood of the world's economies. Any potential disruption of the flow of that oil could be disastrous for the United States specifically, and the West in general. This was demonstrated during the Iran-Iraq War, when fighting threatened shipping in the Persian Gulf. The United States Central Intelligence Agency reported that Gulf oil provided 40 percent of the oil in Western European markets, and 60 percent in Japan. If that flow was interrupted, that volume would have to be recovered from other sources. Such a dramatic reduction in supply without a corresponding reduction in demand would inevitably lead to drastically higher prices.

In threatening Middle Eastern oil exports, Saddam threatened the global economy. Saddam's advisors failed to impress upon him how the world would react should he try to seize Kuwait, a problem that was further compounded by the US State Department. Prior to the invasion, the US ambassador to Iraq, April Glaspie, informed the Iraqis that "we have no opinion on the Arab-Arab conflicts, like your border disagreement with Kuwait." This was in spite of the fact that the US intelligence community was already concerned that Iraq had intentions to seize Kuwait. Two years before the actual invasion, the National Intelligence Officer for Economics, Deane E. Hoffman, concluded a report on the matter by stating: "In any case, we should remember that the Iraqis are very unpredictable and could move into Kuwait quite unexpectedly."

While Saddam made some historically bad political miscalculations, he also overestimated the strength of his military forces. Although the Iraqi Army was the fourth-largest army in the world and battle-tested after an eight-year war with the Iranians, their military force was not a well-rounded one. Being a largely land-locked country, Iraq had no naval force to speak of. The port of Um Qasr was the closest thing to a port the Iraqis had, and access to the Persian Gulf could easily be controlled by Kuwait.

In the air, the equipment in the Iraqi arsenal varied in quality and quantity. A typical "surge day" for the air force in the Iran-Iraq War was forty sorties a day. At the conclusion of the Iran-Iraq War, Iraq had the largest air force in the region with over one thousand aircraft. These were primarily Soviet and French designs.

The French-designed Dassault Mirage F1 strike fighters were equipped with Exocet antiship missiles. Iraq had shown the effectiveness of these missiles in 1987, when they were used to attack and disable the frigate USS *Stark*. In addition to this maritime strike capability, an extensive number of Su-22 and Su-24 aircraft were used in a close-air support role.

Equally impressive was the number of Soviet MiG fighters. These ranged from older MiG-21s to modern interceptors like the MiG-25 and even the latest Soviet fighter, the MiG-29. All their pilots had combat training and most had combat experience.

On the ground, Iraq possessed a large number of tanks. While they were superior when fighting one of the country's neighbors, they were no match for the coalition forces despite their crews' recent combat experience, something the coalition forces did not have. While the Iraqi Army had an armor and even a mechanized force that could be supported with artillery, what they truly lacked was the ability to combine all of that along with their air and helicopter force into an effective combined-arms force.

When considering Saddam's overestimation of the Iraqi military, there has been fierce debate over whether Iraq should have continued their invasion into and through Saudi Arabia. This could have given the Iraqis a much stronger negotiating position during any peace talks with the West.

It is questionable at best whether the invasion could have succeeded to the extent that it could keep the United States and her allies from intervening (see the aforementioned state of the Iraqi military). But what would have happened if Saddam had been able to follow up on his invasion of Kuwait with an invasion of Saudi Arabia? What would have been necessary for that to happen, and how could it have changed the future of the Middle East and the world? How would things have turned out if their ally, the Soviet Union, had opted in its final years to exact its revenge on the West by providing covert support to the Iraqis?

This series will explore how things might have turned out had Saddam's army been better prepared to fight at the outset of the war and had he not stopped in Kuwait but kept on going. We hope you enjoy this short break from reality and join us in the world of "What If" things had played out differently.

MIDDLE EAST

0   300
Kilometers   N

Mediterranean Sea

Israel Jordan
Baghdad
Turaif
Iraq
Rafha
Kuwait
Iran
Tabuk
Al Jubail Dammam
King Khalid Bahrain
Buraydah Persian Gulf
Egypt Dhahran Qatar
Medina Riyadh Gulf of Oman
Jeddah Mecca United Arab Emirates Muscat

Saudi Arabia

Sudan Red Sea
Oman

Eritrea Yemen

Arabian Sea

Ethiopia

Chapter One
Highway of Death

8 August 1990
495th Tactical Fighter Squadron
Aviano, Italy

Major William "Gunslinger" Kidd looked at the briefing material and shook his head. This was going to be a tough mission. The Saudi Air Force along with several American F-14 Tomcats had already lost a handful of aircraft attacking the Republican Guard division. No matter what anyone thought, this mission wouldn't be a walk in the park.

"Major Kidd," the briefer from the operations center said, breaking into his thoughts. "Your flight will be responsible for hitting the bridge near Al Petra. It's right before the village of Thadij, here." He pointed to a spot on the map. "It crosses a large wadi that the 7th Division needs to cross. It's imperative your flight take out the bridge and then go after as many of the armor formation as you can."

Gunslinger replied, "If our primary objective is the bridge, then I'd like two of our planes equipped with a Paveway GBU-10. A five-hundred-pounder may not be enough to take it out depending on how well it was constructed."

The briefer nodded and wrote something down on his notepad. "Agreed, I'll make the change. Do you want one on your aircraft?"

Gunslinger looked at his fellow pilots and could tell from their eager expressions that each of them wanted to be the pilot to carry one of the Paveways. "Nah, put one on Joker's aircraft and one on Ricin's. We'll let the kids have fun with this one."

His joke elicited a few laughs from the other pilots and some nods of appreciation. It wasn't every day you got to drop a laser-guided bomb on a bridge. These were state-of-the-art bombs just now being introduced into the inventory.

"What kind of AA support will this Iraqi division have that we should be aware of?" asked Gunslinger. He already knew the answer; he just wanted his junior officers to hear it a second time. While he'd flown in Operation El Dorado Canyon, the air raid against Muammar Gaddafi's government in Libya, these young pups hadn't.

A captain from the 1N or intelligence shop stood up and made his way to the briefing lectern. "My name is Captain Wolf. Based on both aerial surveillance and post-mission briefings from the other squadrons, the Iraqi Army has been equipped with a wide variety of air-defense weapons, which now appear to have been provided nearly a year ago by the Soviet Union following a massive foreign military sale agreement."

"Whoa, did you just say the Soviet Union provided them with a slew of mobile SAM and AA trucks?" repeated Gunslinger, adding important details that he wanted his men to know.

Captain Wolf took a breath in before he sighed. "That's how it appears. We're hoping to have better intelligence on this in the near future. Regardless, the 7th Adnan Division has a mixture of ZSU-23-4 Shilkas, which are 23mm quad-gun mounted tracked vehicles. These weapons have seen wide use in the Arab-Israeli wars, so we're pretty familiar with how they work. The number one thing I can tell you about them is don't get too close. This division successfully shot down two F-15s and more than a handful of Saudi aircraft already.

"The division is also traveling with some mobile SAM launchers. Your flight is going to have to be extremely careful in how you attack them. You'll have a flight of Wild Weasels flying in ahead of you to take out any of the radars that try to track you, and you'll have some Spark-Varks out there to jam the enemy radars that survive the Weasels. We don't anticipate significant enemy fighter activity, but we'll have some F-15Cs providing fighter cover to keep you from getting bounced if some do show up."

Captain Wolf paused for a moment before adding, "Don't take these systems lightly, OK? We made some tactical errors at the start of the war. We falsely assumed our electronic systems could defeat them. That was a mistake on our part. Consequently, we've lost more than two dozen aircraft since the start of this campaign. Our SEAD[1] missions are starting to work, but they take time. So keep your heads on a swivel and stay frosty out there.

---

[1] Suppression of Enemy Air Defense.

"With that, I'll hand the rest of the mission over to you, Major Kidd," Captain Wolf said before returning to his seat.

Walking up to the lectern, Gunslinger announced, "Listen up, pups." He liked to refer to the pilots in his flight as pups—mostly because they were all junior captains, fresh from training, and had little experience. "The Wild Weasels are going to attract those AA guns and SAMs for us. They'll do their best to take 'em out prior to our arrival, but that doesn't mean a few won't play possum on us. Likewise, the Spark-Varks are going to do their best to jam the hell out of their radars and communication systems. Again, that's only going to slow them down, not stop them. When we go in, expect the enemy to be ready and gunning for us. This is going to be a hot-and-heavy fight we're flying into," he explained.

He then brought up the map of the target area. "Joker, you're going to hang back at a higher altitude and go for the bridge with your laser-guided bomb. Ricin, you're the alternate in case Joker gets shot down or misses. If he scores a hit and the bridge is taken out, then use the Paveway on whatever target you choose. Just make sure it's worthy of two thousand pounds of pain."

The two pilots nodded.

"Chicken and I are going to swoop in fast, roughly five hundred feet above the deck from the east, so the opposite direction from the rest of our support aircraft." Gunslinger then looked specifically at Chicken, who'd be flying as his wingman for this mission. "Chicken, once we go in, we need to time the release of our first two sticks of Mk 82s. Remember, we're carrying six sticks of six five-hundred-pound bombs. We're likely going to make three attack runs across the division, so we'll evaluate where we want to place our sticks across the areas where we'll cause the most damage."

Gunslinger surveyed his three pilots. "Just remember, our mission is to cause as much damage and destruction to this armored column as we can. Fifty or so kilometers to the southwest is the Saudi 45th Armored Brigade. They've been fighting a tactical retreat against this division since the start of the war. We need to buy these guys as much time as we can."

Joker asked, "Gunslinger, once we've taken the bridge out, do you want us to just pick our own targets to go after?"

Gunslinger thought about that for a moment. He knew it'd be better if they could link up and hit the enemy together. Then again, it was going to be pretty chaotic once they started their attack runs. "Let's do this. Once Chicken and I finish our first attack run and you guys nail that bridge, we'll see where everyone is and what the situation on the ground looks like. If it's too hot, we may need to just make this a high-altitude bombing run. Ideally, we want to get as low as we can to place our ordnance on target. High-altitude bombing just isn't as accurate unless we have the entire squadron or even wing participate in it."

"Sounds good to us, hoss," said one of the pilots carrying the new laser-guided bombs. They were excited and ginned up. This was their first combat mission. They were the first guys from their squadron and wing to get to use the new laser-guided bombs.
****

After ninety minutes of flight time, their flight of four F-111 Aardvarks was nearing the target zone. The surrounding air was abuzz with activity. Listening to the coms, Gunslinger heard the air battle managers in the Joint Surveillance and Target Attack Radar System or JSTARS aircraft; they were a hundred miles away, directing the Weasels towards the location of the enemy SAMs and AA trucks.

The high-powered airborne ground surveillance equipment was critical in helping the aircraft identify the locations of the Iraqi ground formations. Using some deductive reasoning, and based on the formations, the battle managers on the aircraft would vector in the aircraft to a specific target's most likely locations.

Not too far from the E-8 JSTARS aircraft was the E-3 Sentry AWACS, or Airborne Early Warning and Control System, plane. They were responsible for watching the skies around the area to make sure no enemy fighters vectored into the area. If the Iraqis sent some MiGs in their direction, then they'd direct the F-15Cs to go in and deal with them.

"Karma Four-One, Eagle Six. We show clear skies. Handing you off to Hawk Two. Good luck, over."

"Karma Four-One, good copy. Eagle Six, out."

Moments later, Gunslinger's radio squawked again. "Karma Four-One, Hawk Two. Wild Weasels are finishing up their attack run of known SAM sites now. Karma Four-Three is cleared to engage the bridge. Once the bridge is destroyed, we want Karma Four-One and Four-Two vectored to sector six. You're cleared to engage them as you see fit. Karma Four-Three and Four-Four will engage sector two as they see fit. Once you've expended your ordnance, you are cleared to RTB. How copy?" asked the battle manager.

Depressing the talk button, Gunslinger replied, "Hawk Two, Karma Four-One. That's a good copy." He then switched to his flight's channel. "Karma Four-Three and Four-Four, you are cleared to engage the bridge. Get it done ASAP. Then you're to move to sector two and make your attack runs. Don't dawdle, get your runs in and hit 'em hard and fast. We'll link back up at rally point Zulu and head home together. Out."

Gunslinger then looked at the map of the sectors his flight was being told to engage. He saw exactly what the battle manager was looking to do. It was a wide-open desert area along the two major highways heading towards Jeddah and Medina. They were going to plaster the motorized division in the open areas. If they played their cards right, this could turn into a turkey shoot. Collectively, his single flight of four aircraft was going to drop one hundred and twenty five-hundred-pound bombs across these guys. That was a lot of bombs for a single mission.

With that in mind, he flipped back to channel three.

"Hawk Two, Karma Four-One. I've directed my guys to engage the bridge with their Paveways. Both myself and Four-Two are carrying six sticks of five-hundred-pounders. Our intent is to make three runs, releasing two sticks on each run. How copy?"

There was a moment of silence. Presumably, the battle managers were conferring with each other.

"Karma Four-Two, that's a negative. We have hostile aircraft inbound, so new orders. We need you to position yourself for a long single run, deploying your sticks along the way. Same with Karma Four-Three and Four-Four once the bridge is out. Eagle Six is showing some hostile aircraft being scrambled out of Riyadh. We want to get you guys in and out before they get in range of you. How copy?"

Damn, hostile aircraft already. Thank God we've got some F-15s out here with us. We aren't exactly equipped to take on enemy aircraft.

"That's a good copy. Thanks for the heads-up. We're going to angle in for our attacks now. Out."

Switching back to his flight's channel, Gunslinger said, "Heads up, pups. We got inbound hostile aircraft heading towards us. Our Eagle pilots are moving to engage them as we speak. This means we need to drop our loads and get out of Dodge. Four-Three and Four-Four, I want you both to hit that bridge with your Paveway. We don't have time to make sure the first one hits and goes off. Once you've got confirmation it's down, you need to hit your sector. Because we're short on time, you need to make a single bomb run. We can't stick around to hit them twice. You guys got this. You've trained for this in the past, now it's time to put that training to work. How copy?"

"That's a good copy, Gunslinger. We'll get that bridge taken down."

Gunslinger smiled at the confidence of his pilots. He'd been training them hard since they'd arrived in his unit. It was good to see that level of training starting to kick in.

"Chicken, it's just you and me. Let's get positioned to make our run. I want us to line up along the southwestern side of sector six at an altitude of two thousand feet at four hundred and fifty miles per hour. When it comes to releasing our sticks, we're going to release them one at a time. You need to pay attention to when each stick has been released. Then and only then do you start the process of releasing the next one. By slowing ourselves down to four hundred and fifty miles per hour, we should be able to release our entire loads across three-quarters of the sector. Once we're dry on bombs, we're going to bank to our right as we look to gain altitude and put some distance between us and them. You got all this, Chicken?"

Chicken took a second before replying, "Got it, Gunslinger. I'll follow your lead."

Good, he sounds confident and ready for action, Gunslinger thought. In the distance, he saw two bright flashes of light on the ground. He knew the bridge had likely been taken out. His other two pilots would be circling back around to get in position for their own attack runs.

Within a minute after the bridge went up in smoke, his copilot and bombardier pointed to a new set of warning lights that had just turned on. They were less than twenty kilometers from starting their bombing run when their Radar Homing and Warning System or RHAW came to life. At least one SAM or radar-guided AA truck had turned on its search radar. They likely knew something was about to happen given that the bridge they needed to secure had just blown up.

"Looks like things are about to get interesting," said Captain Bud "Jugs" Barrell. He was an avid beer drinker noted for drinking large qualities and not being affected. He would be the electronic warfare officer on this mission.

"Just stay on the jamming and get those sticks ready to go. We're only going to get one pass at this," Gunslinger replied.

Jugs nodded and started the process of getting their bombs ready to drop. At their current speeds, they'd start delivering the pain in less than three minutes.

Gunslinger glanced to his left and saw Chicken. He was slightly behind him and about a hundred meters back. Although they didn't have any lights on their planes, he could still make out the soft glow of Chicken's cockpit lights against the darkness. Returning his gaze to the front, he could see the new day was starting to creep ever closer. It would be dawn in another five minutes. All the more reason to get this run completed before the sun made it easier to spot them.

"One minute out," Jugs called out just in time for them both to see the remnants of the night sky in front of them erupt in a spectacular display of red and green tracer fire.

"Whoa! That's a lot of ground fire," Jugs exclaimed as they continued to fly towards it.

"No joke. This is going to get crazy. I'm going to bring us up to three thousand feet and increase our speed to five-five-zero."

He then sent a quick message to Chicken, letting him know of the change.

"Thirty seconds," said Jugs. The volume of ground fire only seemed to increase as they got closer.

"Hang on, we're almost over the target," Gunslinger announced excitedly.
****

3rd Squadron, Iraqi Air Force

Major Vitaly Popkov kept his MiG-29 low to the ground, flying just fifty feet above the desert. The plane was flying at twelve hundred miles per hour, living up to its unofficial nickname of "Strizh," Russian for "Swift." While the others in his squadron were mixing it up with the American F-15s, he opted to see if he could nail the large, lumbering American AWACS plane and that other radar-emitting aircraft. If he could catch one or two of these bombers along the way, he'd count that as a bonus.

Flying past the 7th Motorized Division, Popkov saw the sky around the division lighting up with ground fire. He knew the American bombers must be making their attack runs. If he was lucky, he might catch one or more of them on their way out of the area.

Soon, the ground began to ripple with a long line of explosions tearing through the division. A division his squadron of pilots was supposed to be providing cover for to prevent a situation like this from happening.

Once they'd received the alert of American aircraft heading towards the division, their squadron had been ordered to get airborne and see what they could do to protect them. Unfortunately, the Iraqi ground crews were not nearly as good as their Soviet counterparts at getting an aircraft spun up for a quick mission.

By the time they were in the air, the first wave of American aircraft had already hit the division. They knew a second wave of low-level bombers was inbound and a handful of American F-15s were loitering high above to provide air cover. They should have been airborne thirty minutes ago. Had they had a Soviet ground crew, they would have been. Popkov was still fuming at the ineptitude of the ground crew servicing their aircraft and how long it had taken them to get airborne. *I hate having to work with these Iraqis*, he lamented.

Seeing more explosions continuing to ripple through the vehicles to his left, Popkov had an idea. He was still flying roughly fifty meters above the ground when he reached for his radar control button and flicked it on. In seconds, his screen showed him a flight of two aircraft less than fifteen kilometers from his position. Thirty kilometers away, he saw another two. Given their speed and heading, Popkov judged these to be additional strike fighters. Another ninety kilometers away, he could see his primary targets: the US AWACS planes.

Knowing he had to act quickly, Popkov flicked on the seeker head of his R-73 missiles and waited until he had a solid lock on the two strike planes. They were splitting up now that they knew they were in trouble.

Squirm all you want; you can't escape the Mayak, he thought as he pickled off the first heat-seeking missile.

He then turned towards the other attacker trying to flee the scene of the crime and locked it up with his second R-73. The target had gone to full afterburner, doing its best to outrun the fighter now on its tail. Popkov was not to be deterred. He accelerated his own aircraft to keep the target in range. His missile was just at the outer edge of its range, and he wanted to make sure he scored a hit.

Before the bomber could get outside his range, Popkov turned the seeker head on to let the missile acquire the target. It took only moments for the missile to lock on to the afterburners of the aircraft. Popkov smiled a wicked smile as he depressed the pickle button one more time. The missile leapt from its underwing pylon and shot off after the bomber. In seconds, the solid-fuel rocket engine reached its maximum speed of Mach 2.5, eating away at the distance to the fleeing raider.

Popkov watched as the target spat out flares and attempted to turn away from the missile. Watching the bomber's futile attempts to evade the missile, he assumed the pilot must be new and inexperienced. No veteran pilot would release flares while leaving his afterburner on. He'd turn the greatest heat source off first, then release the flares and bank away, leading the missile to believe the flares were the tailpipe of the aircraft. Instead, this pilot had not only kept his afterburner on, he'd compounded his mistake by turning away from the flares, allowing the seeker head to know which was the plane and which was not.

Three seconds later, Popkov was rewarded with a flash of light near the rear of the bomber. Moments later, he saw a streak of flame come from the side of it. Then the pilots ejected, only to see their aircraft explode into a fireball moments later.

Smiling, Popkov angled towards the two prize targets he was really after. At this point, there was no reason to leave his search radar off. The Americans knew he was here, and so did the F-15s. Glancing at his radar, he saw that the American fighters were still in a fight against the other members of his squadron. They were nearly 140 kilometers away. Too far to intercede and deny him his aerial victory.

17

Turning his aircraft towards the American AWACS, he accelerated to get in range of his R-27 missiles. Compared to the R-73s, this missile, which NATO called Alamo, had a greater range and a larger warhead, and it traveled at speeds up to Mach 4.5. It was not an easy missile to outrun or evade. He glanced at his airspeed—he was still traveling close to twelve hundred kilometers per hour. *Slow down, you're wasting fuel,* he chided himself. He wasn't too far from the big lumbering radar plane. In under a minute, he'd be able to fire off one of his R-27 missiles.

It took less than a second for his aircraft's warning systems to alert him that one of the American fighters was attempting to lock on to him. *The aircraft must've broken off its engagement to come after me.* He recalled an old adage his father used to tell him: *You're swinging your fists after the fight is over.* He chuckled to himself as he activated one of his two R-27 missiles.

Then his SPO-15 "Beryoza" radar warning receiver or RWR mounted on the top of his two rear horizontal stabilizers blared its own warning. The American fighter had just fired a missile at him. Looking at the distance between him and the fighter, he knew the missile was likely an AIM-7 Sparrow, since he was facing off against an F-15 and not a Navy F-14, which likely would have fired an AIM-54 Phoenix at much greater range. *I've got just enough time to get my missile off before I have to worry about that Sparrow and deal with that fighter.*

Turning on the first R-27, Popkov got a solid lock on the American AWACS plane. Once he had the lock, he didn't wait around. He fired the missile and watched as it began its high-speed pursuit of what was essentially a Boeing 707 airliner. With his missile away, he turned to deal with the incoming threat. The little bastard was less than ten kilometers away from him and closing fast.

Popkov dove for the ground. He angled his aircraft into a zero-g dive, allowing gravity to help him build up his airspeed. The Sparrow was now less than five kilometers from him. Reaching for his chaff dispenser, he fired off one set. This ejected a small cloud of aluminum foil strips meant to obscure the Sparrow's radar-homing seeker, tricking it into believing the fast-approaching wall of foil was in fact the target it was after.

As the chaff dispersed behind him, Popkov pulled back on the stick and angled his aircraft to the right before hitting his own afterburner. The

18

force of the g's being thrown at him pinned him to the seat and almost caused him to black out as his vision tunneled.

When his sight returned, an explosion occurred not too far from his aircraft. Checking his systems, he saw he hadn't sustained any damage—at least none that was throwing up a warning light. He'd successfully evaded the missile.

Turning his aircraft towards the American plane that was still barreling towards him, he activated the seeker head on his R-73 missile and allowed it to get a lock. He released the missile to begin its pursuit of the American F-15. When the aircraft broke away to evade the missile barreling down on it, Popkov activated his remaining R-27. Once it had also locked on to the American, he let loose with that missile as well. The American now had to contend with both a heat-seeker and an active-radar-homing missile—two missiles that engaged a target in slightly different ways.

In the distance towards Taif, a flash of light lit up the remaining darkness. Popkov smiled as his R-27 connected with the American Boeing 707. The fiery wreck of the plane fell to the ground below as the aircraft broke apart. Then he looked for the other 707. The little bastard was going all out back to Medina. If he didn't take care of this fighter on his tail now, he'd likely never catch up to the Boeing plane.

He refocused his attention on the F-15. The American was doing his best to evade the R-27 as he unloaded chaff behind him. Unlike the American bomber pilot, this guy appeared to know what he was doing. Even so, he was so busy paying attention to the missiles, he didn't realize the MiG was closing in to get within gun range.

The R-27 bit on the chaff and exploded. The F-15 banked hard to the left as it climbed to gain some altitude and speed. The R-73 was hot on its tail. The missile continued to close the gap between them. The American deployed flares, trying to break the lock.

I'm almost there, Popkov said to himself. The R-73 detonated just behind the F-15. The shrapnel burst from the missile tore into the left side of the giant American fighter plane. The pilot tried to stabilize his aircraft. It looked like he'd already used his fire extinguisher on the left engine. He was now flying with just one engine while the other trailed smoke.

Flicking the safety off his guns, Popkov watched as his targeting reticle lined up. He depressed the button, letting a string of twenty 30mm rounds rip into the body of his prey. New flashes of flame erupted in the middle of the aircraft. Popkov turned away, knowing it was likely to explode. Fractions of a second later, that was exactly what it did. The plane exploded into hundreds of pieces as it began its journey to the ground.

The sun was finally starting to rise, making it easy for him to see. He didn't spot any parachutes. The pilot likely hadn't had enough time to eject. That kind of saddened Popkov. Just because they had fought an aerial battle didn't mean he wanted to kill the pilot, just his aircraft. He supposed that was some long-lost trait he shared with the aerial knights of the past.

Checking his fuel gauge and then the distance to the remaining Boeing 707, he saw he had enough fuel to get there and take it out. He also saw a new set of American fighters heading towards the battlespace from Medina. While he had fuel, he was alone and down to a single remaining R-73. He might have fancied himself one of the best Russian fighter pilots, but he wasn't stupid enough to believe he could take on six F-15s on his own.

"It looks like you live to fight another day," he said softly to himself. He then turned his aircraft away from the American fighters and headed back to base. "Four kills is good enough for one day."

Chapter Two
Perestroika

18 Months Prior
April 1989
Kremlin
Moscow, Russia

Mikhail Gorbachev looked at Vladimir Kryuchkov, the head of the KGB, asking, "So it's true? President Bush is continuing his predecessor's pressure campaign against the Arabs to further drive down the price of oil?"

Kryuchkov nodded. "Unfortunately, yes, Mr. President. At every corner, the Americans are attempting to counter our efforts to reform our economy and country."

"To what end, Kryuchkov?" asked Ivan Silayev, the chairman of the Committee on the Operational Management of the Soviet Economy. "The Americans keep talking about peace and a normalization of relations between our two nations. Why would they then thwart our efforts at reform?" As the man charged with implementing Gorbachev's Perestroika policy efforts, Silayev was particularly annoyed with the policy.

"Why do you think, Silayev? The West has been at war with our people and way of life since the end of the Great Patriotic War. Look what they did to our forces in Afghanistan. The Americans have no love for the Afghan people or the Islamic fundamentalists. But they recruited them by the thousands from the Middle East to travel to Afghanistan to butcher our communist brothers there. President Reagan found our soft underbelly—oil. Now the Americans are going to use that to destroy us from within," chided Kryuchkov angrily.

No one in the briefing room said anything right away. They were all waiting to see what Gorbachev would say next.

Finally, Valentin Pavlov, the Minister of Finance, dared to speak. "Mr. President, I think Kryuchkov is right about the Americans finding a spot within our economy where they can attack us. Your economic program is revolutionary. If it had been implemented ten years ago, when you first raised the issues of our central planning in agricultural

21

production, we wouldn't be in such dire straits today. Be that as it may, we are here. We need time for Perestroika to work, and the Americans do not want us to have that time.

"I believe there is a way that we can get that time. Perhaps we can counter what they are doing in the Middle East. I fear if something is not done soon to address this problem, Mr. President, then it will only be a matter of time until our economy and country collapse."

General Valentin Varennikov, the head of the Russian Army, caught the eye of Kryuchkov, who nodded for him to say something. Clearing his throat to gain everyone's attention, General Varennikov offered, "There may be a solution to our problem standing before us. A way to solve the oversupply problem in the Middle East and once again tilt the balance away from the Americans and back to the middle."

Gorbachev lifted an eyebrow at the subtle comment from the head of the army. He motioned with a twist of his wrist for him to continue.

"Mr. President, Kryuchkov and I, along with some of the other military chiefs, have been talking privately about an idea to handle this problem I believe you will find agreeable," Varennikov explained.

Interrupting him before he could go further, Gorbachev countered, "It had better not be a direct confrontation with the Americans or the West. While I believe you have done a fine job working to rebuild the army after the Afghan withdrawal, we are hardly in a position to wage a war."

With his cheeks blushing slightly, Varennikov countered, "Of course not, Mr. President. The other chiefs and I also agree with that assessment. Please, if you will allow me a moment to explain. We have two prominent allies in the Middle East: Syria and Iraq. Iraq just concluded an eight-year war with Iran. During this war, Iran succeeded in causing instability in the region by attacking oil platforms and tankers as they transited through the Strait of Hormuz and in the Gulf itself. This eventually resulted in the American Navy launching its largest naval action since World War II, when they pursued and destroyed most of the Iranian Navy. That brought stability back to the oil markets, and it gave us an idea.

"At the end of the war between Iran and Iraq, Iraq was left with billions of dollars in debt. President Hussein asked his Arab debtors if they would forgive his debt, since it was his military that fought against

Iran's Islamic Revolution and kept it from spreading to their nations. Many of these nations agreed to forgive their debt, except for Kuwait and the United Arab Emirates. To further complicate this problem between Iraq and some of their oil-rich neighbors, Iraq claims to have evidence that Kuwaiti oil companies have been leveraging slant wells to siphon Iraq's own oil."

Pavlov cut him off, "What is your point, General?"

Tilting his head, Varennikov gave the Finance Minister an angry look. "My point, Minister, is we can use this dispute between Iraq, Kuwait, and their neighbors as a means to both create instability within the Middle East and drive up the price of oil. It's a legitimate border dispute between the two nations, and one that could be stoked into an actual conflict."

Foreign Minister Eduard Shevardnadze leaned forward in his chair as he entered the conversation for the first time. "Mr. President, this operation with Iraq is a solid, viable option to consider. The simmering issues between Kuwait and Iraq have gone on for generations. It would not take much to push this issue in the direction we want and engineer the kind of economic results we are looking for."

Dmitry Yazov, the Minister of Defense, added, "We could provide the Iraqis with improved weapons and military equipment to help ensure a quick victory. We could also provide the Iranians with antiship weapons and naval mines to cause problems in the Strait to further aggravate the situation for the Americans."

Gorbachev then asked, "What if the Iraqis decide they want to expand beyond Kuwait? Say they decide they want to grab the rest of Saudi Arabia. Then what?"

Shevardnadze shrugged his shoulders as he responded, "Then our oil problem goes away indefinitely. If the West tries to come to the aid of the Saudis, then that war would take them years to conclude. In either case, we will see the price of oil continue to rise as both the production of it in the Middle East is halted and the Iranians make it nearly impossible for tankers to travel freely through the Strait."

No one spoke for a few minutes as Gorbachev sat back in his chair. As he did during moments that required a big decision, he turned his chair to look out the Kremlin window at Red Square.

If we don't try something... our country is doomed.

Turning back to look at his advisors, Gorbachev announced, "Let's stir the pot. Tell the President of Iraq I would like to meet with him. Let's begin looking at what we can provide them and the Iranians in terms of military aid."

****

Lubyanka Building
Moscow, Russia

"If we are going to go this route, providing the Iraqis with the necessary military equipment to create the kind of instability and chaos you are hoping for, comrade, it is going to require substantial quantities of A-level, or at least B-level, equipment," General Valentin Varennikov said as he pulled another Ziganov cigarette out and lit it.

Blowing smoke out through his nose, Kryuchkov agreed, "*Da*, it will. But if we can make it work, Valentin, it could be the thing to save the Soviet Union. Things around us are starting to fall apart, comrade. If decisive action is not taken soon, not only will the economy implode, it will mean the downfall of the entire system."

"Things in the GDR are already starting to come unraveled. Are you sure it is not already too late to prevent the collapse of WARSAW Pact Vladimir?"

"If appropriate actions are taken sooner rather than later, then, yes, comrade—I believe our collapse can be stopped. But it will require a concerted effort on our part. What forces would you recommend transferring to the Iraqis?" the KGB Director asked.

Pulling some folders out of his briefcase, the general thumbed through them until he found the one he was looking for.

"My staff has done a complex review of the Iraqi Army, post–Iran War. Their soldiers are battle-hardened from years of war, but their equipment has been greatly depleted. Most of what they operate is extremely old Russian and Chinese surplus equipment. It may have been effective against a poorly trained and led Iranian force, but it will have a hard time holding up against the better-equipped Kuwaiti or even Saudi armies, to say nothing of the Americans should they opt to get involved at a later time," the general explained, his cigarette moving with his lips as he spoke.

24

"Are you saying this plan is outside our reach or ability to make work?" the spymaster inquired, a bit of concern showing on his face.

General Varennikov shook his head as he took another drag on his cigarette, holding the nicotine in long enough for it to be absorbed in his lungs before blowing it out. "No, it can be done. As a matter of fact, it may solve some of our financial problems in the process. Transferring some of our better-equipped units will eliminate the maintenance costs of them from our books. Once the Iraqis control the Kuwaiti oil fields, they'll be able to cut oil production to drive up the price and pay off the loans for the equipment."

Chuckling at the comment, Kryuchkov commented, "Look at you, comrade. You sound like a capitalist striking a deal to steal the labor of the proletariat."

The two of them laughed at the irony before they turned serious again.

"How soon can you begin transferring equipment and getting their people up to speed on it?" asked the spymaster as his eyes narrowed.

Sensing the change in mood, the old general replied, "As soon as the Iraqis agree to the plan. How soon do you think that'll be?"

Kryuchkov looked at the calendar on the wall, searching for some dates on it. "Soon. It has to be soon. We need to get this show moving before we run out of time."

Chapter Three
Genie in a Bottle

Late April 1989
Soviet Embassy
Baghdad, Iraq

The entourage from Moscow, led by Foreign Minister Shevardnadze and Major General Sokolov, greeted the ambassador to Iraq, Viktor Minin, who had been at the post now for nearly seven years. Standing there with the ambassador was his military advisor, Colonel Popov, and the KGB Station Chief, Colonel Chekhov.

"Hello, Minister Shevardnadze, General Sokolov. I trust your flight in from Moscow was uneventful?" the ambassador asked as he guided his boss and his entourage to a sitting room nearby.

"*Da*, it was pleasant enough, comrade. Is our meeting this evening with Saddam ready? We have much to discuss," Minister Shevardnadze replied, all business as was his personality.

The ambassador nodded. "It is. They are expecting you. There will be some photos taken when everyone arrives, just like normal. Then there will be a small dinner with just you, General Sokolov, myself and Colonel Popov. On their side, Saddam, Vice President Izzat al-Douri, General Ra'ad al-Hamdani, head of the Republican Guard, and Tariq Aziz, the Deputy Prime Minister."

"Excellent, comrade. Thank you for arranging this meeting on such short notice. There are some big changes coming to Iraq. Please, let's have some tea and discuss them briefly, Viktor," Shevardnadze said pleasantly. He knew Minin was tired of the Middle East and wanted to return to Moscow or a more pleasant posting somewhere else. The man had served well in Iraq; now he'd need to serve a bit longer.

The two of them moved to his private study to talk alone and took a seat as their tea was brought in. "Viktor, I am not going to be able to transfer you to another posting just yet. There are some big things about to happen in Iraq and the Middle East. You are our most knowledgeable ambassador and trusted diplomat in the region. I am going to need you here for what is about to come next."

Ambassador Minin sighed at the news. He knew there wasn't much he could say or do about it, so he tried to make the best of it. "My wife and I had looked forward to returning to Moscow, but perhaps you have a better assignment for us once whatever happens here is complete?"

Smiling at the man's attempt to negotiate, Shevardnadze pulled his cigarette case out and extracted one of his favorite cigarettes—a Marlboro. He loved the taste of the American tobacco. Sitting back in the chair as he crossed his left leg over his right, he looked at Minin. "Come to think of it, comrade, I think there is a posting that will be opening up in either Paris, London, or New York, once you let me know where you'd like to go after this operation has concluded."

Minin's eyes lit up at the thought of gaining such a prestigious posting after such a long career in the slums of the Middle East. "Comrade, what is it Moscow has cooked up for the Iraqis that I can assist you with?"

With their internal negotiations complete, it was now time to discuss the reason for the trip.

"As you know, comrade, the President has been pushing through a series of economic and political reforms back home. Some have been well received, some have not. While the President is facing a lot of internal pressure from the hardliners, we are also facing enormous economic pressures from the Americans. Recent intelligence has uncovered a plot by the Americans, who are pressuring the House of Saud, along with the other Gulf states, to artificially depress the price of oil to drive our own prices down. The Americans are also pushing the Arabs to cut special deals with countries who currently purchase Soviet oil to get them to purchase theirs instead. This secret oil policy the Americans are pursuing is undercutting the exports of our own domestic oil, a natural resource our nation depends on to provide for our people," Shevardnadze explained.

Minin took the information in, though he didn't appear the least bit surprised by any of it. He replied, "The Iraqis believe something like this has been going on behind their backs as well. While some of the Arab countries have agreed to forgive Iraq's war debt for fighting the Islamic Revolution, others are using that debt to keep Iraq poor and in a hard place. As if the Kuwaitis do not have enough of their own oil, during the summer, the Iraqis learned they have been using a new type of oil drilling

27

technology called slant well drilling to steal Iraq's oil while at the same time increasing daily production to further drive down the price."

Nodding at the confirmation of what he already knew, Shevardnadze then asked, "So the Iraqis are going to be pretty open to any idea we offer them about disrupting the supply of oil and raising the price?"

Almost laughing at the question, Minin countered, "Comrade, they will likely ask how soon you would like them to start. But mind you, whatever you ask them to do, we are going to need to help them economically to make it happen."

"I think we have a plan that will be to their liking."

"What about the hardliners back in Moscow? Are they going to go along with whatever Gorbachev is proposing to do with the Iraqis?"

The Foreign Minister smiled as he nodded. "At first, they did not. But when they realized how badly this would impact the Americans and how this might be the surest way to ensure the survival of the Soviet Union, they agreed to fully support it."

"Comrade, if I may. What is going on in Germany and Poland? I have a brother stationed in Germany, and he is telling me he thinks the GDR is going to collapse in the coming months. Is Moscow going to allow that to happen?"

Sighing, Shevardnadze answered, "I honestly do not know. It is a tricky situation that is going on. The hardliners of course want Moscow to intervene if it comes to that, but I am not sure what Gorbachev will do. Come, let us not worry about what is outside of our control. We have a dinner party to prepare for, comrade."
****

As the presidential guards held the door to the vehicle open, Foreign Minister Shevardnadze and his entourage exited and made their way inside the presidential palace. This was one thing Shevardnadze liked about the Middle East. Each of these leaders, no matter how big or wealthy their country was, made a point of having these massive and over-the-top opulent presidential palaces.

Upon entering the formal greeting room, the Russian delegation was greeted by their Iraqi counterparts. The Russians moved towards the Iraqi leaders and began the process of greeting them and exchanging some pleasantries. A couple of photographers and a camera crew made

28

sure to document the event. Pictures were taken of the Soviet Foreign Minister shaking hands with Saddam Hussein, Tariq Aziz, and Izzat al-Douri.

Once the required propaganda pieces had been handled, the group made their way to a sitting room, where they spent the next twenty minutes discussing nothing of real importance. When their private dinner was ready, the four Russians and four Iraqis were ushered into an exquisite dining room for a private dinner. Over the next hour, the group continued to make small talk, sharing some stories and information about their families and children before their conversation turned to politics and what was going on in the Middle East.

As they finished dinner, some desserts and coffees were brought out as they moved to another room with four couches and a table sitting in the center. The drinks and desserts were placed on the center table and then the attendants left the room, closing the doors behind them.

Minister Shevardnadze then got down to the business of why he had traveled to Iraq. "Mr. President, President Gorbachev and the people of the Soviet Union have learned something that we felt important enough that it should be shared with you immediately. This is why I was dispatched to bring it to you personally and to share with you a proposal on how best to counter it."

The Iraqi leaders shared a look but said nothing as they waited for their guest to elaborate further.

"We understand that your country has fallen on some hard economic times since the end of your war with Iran. We also believe we understand who is to blame for these hard times that have befallen you, and that this was no coincidence either. Rather, this is a well-laid-out plan by the Americans."

Now the Iraqis appeared interested. Al-Douri was the first to speak. "We know who is responsible for our economic troubles. It is our renegade province, Kuwait. Not only will they not forgive our war debt—for a war we fought on their behalf—our oil engineers have determined they are using illegal slant wells to siphon our own oil away from us."

The Iraqi field marshal was seething with anger as he spoke. The President sitting on the couch next to him looked equally angry but held his tongue for the moment.

Shevardnadze nodded in solidarity. "Yes. We have heard that as well. But our intelligence sources have also uncovered a much more elaborate plan at play. One that unfortunately uses Iraq as a disposable pawn of the West."

Saddam Hussein lifted an eyebrow at this acknowledgment, asking, "What do you mean, a plot by the West to use Iraq as a pawn?"

"Think about it, Mr. President. The Americans used Iraq as a proxy to fight the Islamic Republic after their own humiliating military defeat when attempting to free their hostages nine years ago. Instead of fighting Iran directly, they pushed you into a war they knew you were not prepared to win. They provided your military with just enough aid to make you think you could win, but ultimately, it just kept you fighting for years longer than you should have. Then, when the war ended, instead of encouraging Kuwait and the UAE to forgive your debt, they convinced these nations to increase the production of oil, which only drove the price down to such levels that you could never repay your debt. It was a ruse and a trap meant to hurt and weaken Iraq and prevent your nation from becoming the leader of the Arab world," the Foreign Minister explained as he began to spin his elaborate story.

Snorting at the yarn being spun, Izzat al-Douri countered, "We know of your own troubles with the price of oil. Now that the Americans are done using Iraq, they are sacrificing our nation along with the rest of the Arab world in their attempt to destroy the evil Soviet Empire."

Al-Douri's words dripped with contempt and venom. It was clear he had no love for the Americans or how they had used his nation in the Iraq-Iran war. Especially now that America was working with Iraq's own Arab brothers to undercut them economically.

Smiling at being partially discovered, Minister Shevardnadze elaborated, "This is how the West works. They use their economy to destabilize a nation or region. Then, when civil unrest or war erupts, they swoop in as saviors to bring peace, and their brand of freedom and democracy—capitalism to exploit the beaten-down workers, who are left as beggars in their own country. This is the way of the West. OPEC was supposed to be different. OPEC was supposed to bring stability to the world oil market, and more importantly, it was supposed to bring wealth to the Arab world and prevent it from being taken advantage of."

Saddam snorted at the reference to OPEC. "The cartel is run by the Saudis, who are under the mystical spell of the Bushes. That family has been involved with the House of Saud for generations. If the American president tells the King to jump, he only asks how high. But what is it you wanted to talk with us about, Minister Shevardnadze? I doubt you flew all the way from Moscow to talk with us about OPEC and the price of oil. We know what the Americans are up to, so tell us something we do not know," the President of Iraq said, very matter-of-fact.

Direct and to the point. I like that in a world leader, Shevardnadze thought privately.

"As a matter of fact, Mr. President, I have come to speak with you about an offer the Soviet Union would like to make to the people of Iraq."

The Iraqi leaders leaned forward in their chairs a bit, their interest piqued at the possible proposition.

"We are all ears, as the saying goes," Izzat al-Douri said, skeptical of what the Soviets would actually provide them.

Shevardnadze explained, "The Soviet Union would like to provide the people of Iraq a substantial loan to lift your economy out of its economic slump and allow you to purchase the military equipment we are going to offer you. This loan will be in deferment until you are able to stabilize the Middle East under your guiding hand and tutelage. We are making this offer to you because we want Iraq to remove the American puppets from OPEC and restore the cartel's power. We also believe the Middle East would be better served if it were managed and controlled under the leadership of a strong central leader as opposed to the smattering of feckless and spoiled monarchs as it is today."

Izzat al-Douri and Saddam Hussein looked at each other before returning their gaze to the Russian. "That is a bold statement to make, even for the Soviet Empire. Your war in Afghanistan did not exactly go over well. What makes you think we want to become your next puppet?" Saddam replied. Before Shevardnadze could speak, he added, "What you are proposing, Foreign Minister, is a war that would entangle us with the Americans. Even with your aid, I do not believe our military would be able to stand up against the Americans when they intervene, and trust me, they will intervene to help the House of Saud."

"You are correct, Mr. President. If your nation were to reclaim Kuwait as a province of Iraq, the Americans might intervene. If you move to capture Saudi Arabia and the other Gulf states, then the Americans would most likely move to intercede. However, if you move fast enough, and if the Persians can be persuaded to control the Strait and keep the West out of the Gulf, then a negotiated peace, one that would be in your favor, could likely be achieved. More importantly, this move, if successful, would make you the de facto leader of the Arab world," the Russian said, hoping to appeal to the ego of the Iraqi leader.

Tariq Aziz then entered the conversation. "You are asking us to take an enormous risk. The likelihood of our surviving this war is not very good. Especially once the Americans mobilize their forces and come to the aid of the Saudis."

"That is true. In its current state, your military would not last long. However, we are intent on giving you enough military equipment to win this war. When the Americans begin to mobilize their forces to challenge you, then our military will begin a large-scale military exercise of our own in Eastern Europe. This will cause the Americans to maintain their forces in Europe and not divert them to deal with you," the Russian countered.

Saddam then asked, "Putting aside what the Americans may or may not do, what kind of military aid are you looking to provide us with?"

Handing them each a dossier, Shevardnadze replied, "We are prepared to offer you a substantial aid package. I have a couple more packets containing the details of the military equipment we are willing to provide. Suffice it to say, we are prepared to transfer via military aid two hundred of our modern T-80 main battle tanks with thermal and night vision optics. These tanks will give your armored forces an unrivaled advantage on the battlefield.

"President Gorbachev was made aware that most of your army is currently using the Chinese T-62 Mod 1972 tanks. We feel these are terrible tanks the Chinese have sold you. They are inadequate and will not stand up against modern-day tanks the Saudis have purchased from the British and Americans. To compensate for this, the Soviet people would like to replace them with two thousand modern T-72s that will all be equipped with thermal and night vision optics for all-weather combat. This will allow you to change out all of your existing armor units with modern frontline tanks prior to this war."

The four Iraqis practically fell out of their chairs at the Foreign Minister's offer of T-80 and T-72 main battle tanks. These were the Soviets' tier-one frontline tanks.

Shevardnadze smiled as he saw their reactions. "We are going to transfer four thousand BTR-80s and 70s to replace your aging fleet of BTR-50s and 60s," he continued. "This will greatly enhance your motorized divisions' capabilities to grab and seize territory across the desert. Along with the armored personnel carriers, we'll be transferring two thousand BMP-3s and BMP-2s to assist your armor and mechanized forces. However, none of this will do you any good unless you are able to keep Kuwaiti and Saudi aircraft and helicopters off your backs. As such, three hundred and fifty 9K35 Strela-10, ZSU-23-4, 9K22 Tunguska, 9K31 Strela-1, and 2K12 Kub mobile anti-aircraft units will also be added to the aid package. This will be in addition to the six hundred various self-propelled artillery units."

Saddam shook his head in bewilderment at the paper he was holding and the information being given to him. He looked at the Russian Foreign Minister as if the man had horns growing out of his head. "This must be some kind of joke. There is no way the mighty Soviet Union would give this kind of military hardware to Iraq. No one from the USSR, China, or the West has ever sold their top-of-the-line military equipment to us before."

"I assure you, Mr. President, this is no joke. President Gorbachev is essentially offering the government of Iraq the opportunity to purchase nearly an entire Russian Army's worth of military equipment. We will provide you with all of the munitions to operate this equipment along with up to two years of military trainers and advisor support to ensure your army understands how to use it."

Izzat al-Douri cut in to add, "I suppose there is a catch to all of this?"

Smiling, Shevardnadze replied, "The only catch is that Iraq must use this equipment we are providing to take its rightful place as the leader of the Arab world and the head of OPEC. We ask that you work with us to restrict the flow of oil until we achieve a price point of forty-five US dollars. At this price, Iraq will be more than able to repay the Soviet Union's loan for this equipment, and our own economy will be saved from economic collapse caused by the West."

Saddam then asked, "By when do we need to launch this attack?"

33

"When our trainers and advisors arrive in Iraq, they will work with your people to teach them how to handle the equipment. When they can effectively use it without hurting themselves, then we will work with you on a timeline for when to launch your attack. Ideally, we would like this attack to begin next summer," the Foreign Minister offered.

"I think we should discuss the air force and our integrated air defense while we are at it," replied Saddam. "The Americans recently sold the Saudis F-15E Strike Eagles, and the British sold them several squadrons of Tornados. We unfortunately learned during our war with Iran that our air-defense network was not up to the standard it should be. What are you willing to offer us in this regard?" Saddam knew he was pressing his luck, but he hoped this would be his chance to improve his air force.

The Soviet Foreign Minister sat back in his chair for a moment. He knew right then, they had them. The Iraqis would do their bidding. They'd bring instability to the region and they'd drive up the price of oil immensely, thus saving the Motherland from economic ruin and collapse. The question now was how much instability did they want to introduce? The ground equipment was one thing, but if they made their air force too strong, that might lead the Israelis to get involved, which would complicate things. They were a wild card in all of this.

"Mr. President, this has been discussed as well. While we are going to upgrade your air force, we are going to limit the number of aircraft we'll be providing. This is largely because the training program for these aircraft is lengthy and will not fit within the current timeline. That said, the Soviet Air Force will provide Iraq with forty-eight MiG-29s, thirty-four MiG-23s, forty-eight Su-24s, thirty Su-25s, and thirty special reconnaissance and ECM aircraft. When the war has settled, we can discuss selling you additional frontline aircraft. This should be enough to help ensure you a swift victory against the Arab powers you are going to face."

The group discussed the Russian offer for several more hours. They had an agreement in principle and agreed to meet again the following day to hammer out the finer details. Shevardnadze was under orders to get this agreement signed before he returned to Moscow, and he had every confidence that he would do just that.

Chapter Four
Port of Um Qasr

July 1989

"This port is utterly worthless," Major General Sokolov commented to Colonel Chekhov as they watched the second set of freighters arrive from the Soviet Union.

Chuckling, Chekhov replied, "*Da*, that it is, comrade. The real port is down in Kuwait. You know, Kuwait used to be a province of Iraq. It was administered out of Basra, then the British split it away from Iraq."

"The damn British have a way of intentionally splitting their former colonies up along ethnic, racial, and religious lines, knowing it'll cause hundreds of years of conflicts and fighting," commented the older general.

"Why do you suppose the British do that?"

Sokolov snorted at the younger man's question. "By splitting their colonies up like this, they ensured there will never be peace among them. That means instead of building a collective future together, they will be locked in perpetual conflict, thus never a threat to Great Britain."

Colonel Chekhov shook his head in disgust. "All the more reason why I hate the West. We should have our war to end all wars and be done with them."

Sokolov thought about telling the colonel about Josef Stalin's use of the exact same tactic in Nagorno-Karabakh, where a large population of Armenians was handed over to the government of Azerbaijan. He brushed the thought aside. He had no idea how Chekhov would take the statement comparing Stalin to the Imperialist British. Instead, he said, "All in due time, Colonel. Right now, our focus is on making sure our new Iraqi allies are up to the task of using this wonderful equipment we are giving them."

As the two of them stood there looking at the roll-on, roll-off ship, a handful of ground guides helped the driver maneuver the Ural-4320 fuel truck off the ship. When the driver had gotten it off the ship, it was driven over to a nearby train yard, where it would eventually be loaded onto some flatcars and eventually transported up to Baghdad or some other military base.

35

The yard itself was packed with these heavy-duty 4x4 and 6x6 off-road refueling trucks. There were also hundreds of regular ordinary "ash-and-trash" troop-and-cargo trucks used to transport large numbers of infantry soldiers and supplies for a large army formation. Parked next to the rows of trucks were several rows of BTRs. The old 1950s and 1960s versions of the armored personnel carriers with which the Iraqi Army had been making do would be phased out in favor of these new vehicles.

"I'll tell you this, General. If the Iraqi Army is not able to win this coming war after all the equipment and training we'll be providing, then I'm not sure they're capable of winning a war," Colonel Chekhov said as they walked away from the port to head back to their waiting vehicle.

Next, they'd proceed to the Iraqi military base north of the port. They had a series of meetings with their Iraqi counterparts to discuss the organization of the new training programs. In the coming weeks, thousands of Soviet trainers would be arriving to begin the process of showing the Iraqis how to use the newer versions of the equipment being delivered each day. It was already late July, and they didn't have a lot of time to get themselves ready for this summer campaign.

****

Five Days Later
Baghdad International Airport

The large nose of the Antonov An-124 Ruslan cargo plane was opened as a group of technicians swarmed around it. The operators began the process of unloading the equipment for the new S-200 surface-to-air missile system that would become part of the Baghdad integrated air-defense system. The sophisticated radar vehicles were offloaded, along with the rest of the equipment needed to operate the system.

Every three days, six of the large An-124 Ruslan cargo planes would land at either Baghdad International Airport, the Iraqi Air Force base in Balad, some forty kilometers north of the capital, or the Tallil Air Base near Nasiriyah. The large Russian aircraft were ferrying in the sensitive air-defense equipment so it could be set up and the training of the Iraqi soldiers who would operate it could start. The actual missiles themselves would continue to arrive via the ports.

Looking out the window of their temporary office above the terminal, Colonel Chekhov remarked, "I cannot believe we are still moving forward with giving the Iraqis this missile system."

Major General Sokolov just shrugged. "If they succeed in destroying more American aircraft with them, then it will have been worth it. You did see the report on their integrated air defense? They have so many holes in it. Just providing them with a few dozen newer radar sites alone is going to more than double their air-defense capability."

"I just worry about how much we're giving them, comrade General. They are not ready for this level of sophisticated military equipment. It's like giving a young child a bicycle when they are not even ready to use a tricycle."

"I understand your concern, comrade. But remember, the drop of water wears away the stone. We need patience with our Arab friends. That is why there will be hundreds of advisors who will continue to stay behind to help them operate the equipment so that when the time comes, they will be ready. The information we glean from the coming engagements will be put to good use with our own forces should the need ever arise. For the moment, Chekhov, let's be glad the hardliners are wanting to fight this war using them as their proxy. Things are becoming more unstable back home, as you can see. There was a period of time where I really thought the hardliners would initiate a war with NATO. Let us hope this coming conflict will satisfy their war lust," said the general.

The two of them watched a little while longer as the cargo planes were unloaded. The number of Russian soldiers now in Iraq had grown to more than two thousand. By the end of October, that number would rise to upwards of eight thousand as the training program started in earnest. They were still unclear as to how many advisors would stay behind once the war started the following summer, but it was clear some would. The Iraqi Army would need continued guidance on how best to employ the new weapons they were being given.
****

August 1989
Balad Air Base
Yathib, Iraq

Major Vitaly Popkov landed one of the MiG-29s his country was apparently leasing to the Iraqi Air Force. Once on the ground, he taxied towards one of the hardened bunkers. A truck with some flashing lights on it was telling him to follow him to the correct bunker.

Once his aircraft had stopped just short of it, the ground crew signaled him to shut down his engine. The crews came forward and brought a ladder for him so he could climb down. One of the ground crew had brought a small vehicle forward that would tow his aircraft the rest of the way into the hangar.

When he stepped down onto the ground and pulled his helmet off, the air was stifling. The oppressive heat reminded him that he was thousands of kilometers from home. Looking at the ground crew, he felt a little relieved when he saw close to half of them appeared to be Soviet airmen. He'd done a few tours across the Middle East and Asia and seen his share of undertrained and undermotivated ground crews. The last thing you wanted was an unqualified crew servicing a state-of-the-art fighter like the MiG-29.

A jeep pulled up to his aircraft and a Russian lieutenant got out. "Excuse me, Major. I was told to drive you over to meet with Major General Sokolov and the other pilots."

Popkov nodded at the junior officer. He grabbed his flight bag and hopped in the Russian-built UAZ utility vehicle. As they drove away from the flight line area, he saw several more MiGs taxiing toward hardened bunkers and a few more landing. He wasn't sure how many MiGs they were "leasing" to Iraq, but it was apparently more than twenty.

When the jeep stopped in front of what appeared to be an administrative building, the lieutenant told him to go ahead on in while he returned to the flight line to pick up more pilots.

Upon entering the building, he was greeted by a sergeant, who showed him to the briefing room. When Popkov walked in, he immediately spotted a lot of faces he knew. Men he'd flown with over the years from different squadrons. Some flew the 29s like him, others the MiG-23 fighter or the Su-24 and Su-25 strike planes. Clearly something was up—the question was what.

"Look what the cat has brought us," said Major Konstantin Ayushiyev as he walked over and shook his hand.

Laughing at the sight of his old friend, Popkov said, "I see they let you out of Siberia, Kostya."

"Well, when they offered me a chance to fly to this hellhole and escape another Siberian winter, who was I to say *nyet*?" He unconsciously wiped the sweat off his neck, emphasizing the lack of ease with either of his assignments.

Popkov laughed as the two took their seats. Kostya was a fantastic fighter pilot by any measure. Unfortunately, he'd made the mistake of sleeping with the wrong general's daughter after a party and had gotten caught. The old man had walked into his private study with some friends for a cigar, only to find Kostya with his pants around his ankles and the general's daughter's legs on his shoulders. Before he could even get his pants up, the general was screaming about transferring him to Kalinka Air Base in the middle of nowhere, Siberia. By the next morning the orders were official and Kostya was on a transport out of town.

As they were settling in, the door opened and another handful of pilots filtered in. It went on like this for twenty or so minutes before the room filled up. Then Major General Sokolov walked in and the room was called to attention.

"Take your seats," bellowed the old general.

Popkov guessed the old goat had probably been around since the Great Patriotic War. Judging by his rank, either he had committed a major sin like Kostya, or his drinking had become a problem known to everyone.

"You all have been chosen to fly your aircraft to Iraq because you are being given a unique opportunity. An opportunity that only comes around once in a pilot's life. An opportunity that will require you to make a very difficult choice with virtually no information available in advance," the general explained as he surveyed the room.

"Before we continue, I need to lay out some information and you will be given a short moment to decide what you want to do. Here are the basic details. If you want to accept this new opportunity, then you will have to resign your commission from the Soviet Air Force effective immediately. Once you have done that, you will be briefed on this new opportunity along with what you will be paid. If you opt to resign, you

39

will be offered the chance to return to the air force once this opportunity has ended. You will also be given an immediate promotion to your next pay grade. If you opt not to pursue this opportunity, it will not be noted negatively in your personnel file. But you will have to let us know immediately and we will ask you to leave."

Many of the officers looked at each other, wondering what kind of opportunity he was talking about. A sergeant passed out a folder for each of them to review. Inside was a simple resignation from the Russian Air Force and a standard nondisclosure agreement.

Looking around, Popkov noticed that nobody seemed to be opting out. Not that he felt pressured to join—he did like the idea of advancing another grade in service. It was becoming harder to make the next rank. This promotion would fast-track him to general officer, something he aspired to be one day.

Taking the pen, he signed his name and closed the folder. Once the sergeant had collected all the folders, the general walked back in. This time he was flanked by an Iraqi general and a junior officer who appeared to be his interpreter.

For the next half hour, they were told they were now being hired by a local Iraqi company to work as "advisors" to the Iraqi Air Force and, if necessary, fly missions with the Iraqi Air Force. They were to be paid triple their Russian salaries, and if they had to fly in combat missions, they would be compensated for each one. If they scored an aerial victory, a separate bonus would be paid.

The more Popkov heard, the more he realized they were being hired as a proxy or mercenary force for the Iraqi Air Force. Whatever it was they were up to, they were willing to pay top dollar for the Russian pilots' expertise. The Iraqi general explained they'd spend the next seven or so months aggressively training their Iraqi counterparts to use their aircraft more effectively and in a combined-arms fashion as the Iraqi Army prepared to wage war again.

Chapter Five
Prelude to War

1 April 1990
336-Mile Orbit
Above Iraq

The KH-11 reconnaissance satellite, or Big Bird, passed over the partially destroyed and abandoned industrial site south of Baghdad. The industrial center had been damaged long ago during the Iran-Iraq War, and due to the country's economic slowdown, it had never been repaired or rebuilt.

Each time the satellite passed over, it acquired the same images it had for the past couple of years. Broken and missing windowpanes marked the outside of the buildings. These were intermixed with torn and broken pipes, leaving rust stains that streaked along the cream-colored sides of the buildings. There was nothing of significance about this industrial center. Weeds and grass had taken over the service roads, the parking lots, and the storage areas that used to house whatever it was that used to be built here. At least, that was what the Americans saw on the surface—what the Iraqi government wanted the world to see. What the American spy satellite couldn't see, however, was the immense complex built below the surface.

When the Soviets had helped the Iraqis build this complex, they'd made sure the communication nodes linking this center were spread out in various directions to throw off the Americans' ability to detect what lay beneath the surface. The complex was tied together via miles of fiber-optic cables connected to dozens of remote transmitters at different sites miles away from the new nerve center of the Iraqi military and government. To further aid the Iraqis in avoiding detection by the West, the Soviets would conveniently provide them with the overflight schedule of the American satellites. This helped ensure they didn't have any equipment or work crews nearby prior to a satellite overflight.
****

Inside the Command Center

The air was electric. A sense of energy, purpose, and excitement could be felt by everyone present. Everyone who was anyone was seated in the large conference room for this very special meeting. Tonight was the night, the unveiling of a plan that would solve Iraq's immediate financial problems and position it to become one of the dominant nations of the world.

The front two rows of seats were occupied by those closest to Saddam, while the remaining rows were held in reserve for the military leaders and their staff officers, who would undoubtably be taking copious notes for their respective bosses. The officers in attendance were those who held division and brigade command positions, the ones who'd repeatedly sworn their oaths of loyalty to Saddam, who had in turn seen their careers advance ahead of their peers'.

The room was not lacking in ambience either. The first two rows in the room contained a total of fifteen overstuffed armchairs for the VIPs who'd be sitting in the front. The room was adorned with elegant and expensive Persian rugs that covered the seating area of the marble floors, giving the room a warm feeling. Being underground, there were no windows. Still, the lighting was bright and rich as it illuminated the place from opaque glass panels built into the walls and by overhead fluorescent lights mounted in the acoustic tile ceiling. On the wall facing the chairs was a projector screen, ready to display information and maps when the time was right. Several maps also graced the walls between the opaque panels.

Standing in front of their seats before Saddam walked in was Tariq Aziz, the Deputy Prime Minister of Iraq and for all intents and purposes the "face of Iraq." He was the man all the Western media wanted to talk to when they needed someone from Iraq.

Aziz was seated to the right of Saddam. To the left of Saddam's chair was Abdul Jabbar Khalil Shanshal, the Defense Minister. Next was Ibrahim Ahmad Abd al-Sattar Muhammed al-Tikriti, the Armed Forces Chief of Staff. Al-Tikriti was in charge of the Iraqi armed forces and was the man responsible for defending the nation.

The next most important military leader was the Republican Guard Commander, Sayf al-Din Fulayyih Hassan Tahia al-Rawi, who was seated to the right of Aziz. The Republican Guard Commander and the

Army Chief of Staff were in constant competition, as the Republican Guard did not answer to the army but to Saddam directly.

Other noted attendees included the Minister of Intelligence, the Air Force Commander, the Air Defense Commander, the Presidential Secretary, and the Presidential Advisor, Ali Hassan al-Majid, commonly known as "Chemical Ali" for his actions against the Kurds and Iranians. These men had been meeting frequently since the end of the Iraq-Iran Conflict the previous year as they sought to rebuild the country and return it to its prior glory.

Their communications with each other were closely monitored by the Director of Military Intelligence, ensuring no electronic emissions were intercepted by Western powers. To further ensure that they had indeed covered their tracks, the Soviets agreed to monitor their transmissions for anything that could indicate military action, although the Soviet communications and intelligence operators monitoring the Iraqi transmissions were not told about the forthcoming operation. They were doing the Iraqis a favor by just observing their general chatter and helping to ensure they weren't making it any easier than necessary for the West to eavesdrop on them.

When Saddam walked into the room, everyone became quiet and those in the front row were accepting handshakes and bowing slightly in return. Saddam was all smiles.

A young colonel stood at attention, about to give the most important briefing of his life. He was honored that he had been selected for this task.

Saddam took his seat, accepting a glass of tea, and nodded to the colonel to begin his presentation. Saddam was very familiar with what was about to be presented as they had for the past year developed, refined, and war-gamed the plan for Project 19.

"Good morning, sir. My name is Colonel Ibrahim. Our purpose this morning is to present to you the final plan for the upcoming operation, Project 19," the young colonel said. Saddam just nodded and sipped his tea.

"First slide," Ibrahim said, and a slide appeared via the overhead projector. "This first slide is our mission statement for Project 19." He kept quiet while Saddam read the slide. Again, Saddam nodded when he finished.

43

Mission: On 1 August 1990, combined Iraqi forces attack and seize Kuwait City and secure the Saudi-Kuwait border. Simultaneously, Iraqi forces will move to and secure Wadi Al-Batin on the Saudi-Iraq border. Forces along the border will remain at alert status and be prepared to continue the attack.

"Next slide," Colonel Ibrahim said. "Sir, this is the task organization for the initial attack."

TASK ORGANIZATION

1ˢᵀ REPUBLICAN GUARD CORPS

1ˢᵗ RG Armored Division (Hammurabi)
17ᵗʰ & 18ᵗʰ Armored BDE
8ᵗʰ & 9ᵗʰ Mechanized BDE

6ᵗʰ RG Mechanized Division (Nebuchadnezzar)
19ᵗʰ, 22ⁿᵈ, 23ʳᵈ Motorized BDE

2ⁿᵈ RG Armoured Division (al-Medinah)
2ⁿᵈ & 10ᵗʰ Armored BDE
14ᵗʰ Mechanized BDE

3ʳᵈ RG Mechanized Division (Tawakalna)
9ᵗʰ Armored Bde
8ᵗʰ & 29ᵗʰ Mechanized BDE

4ᵗʰ RG Infantry Division (Al Fao)

35ᵗʰ Infantry Division

8ᵗʰ RG Special Forces Division (As Saiqa)

2ᴺᴰ REPUBLICAN GUARD CORPS

5ᵗʰ Mechanized Division (Baghdad)
4ᵗʰ, 5ᵗʰ, 6ᵗʰ Motorized BDE

7ᵗʰ Motorized Division (Adnan)
11ᵗʰ & 12ᵗʰ Motorized BDE
21ˢᵗ Armored Brigade

II Corps	III Corps	IV Corps	VII Corps	IX Corps
2ⁿᵈ Inf. Div.	7ᵗʰ Inf. Div.	16ᵗʰ Inf. Div.	25ᵗʰ Inf. Div.	1ˢᵗ Inf. Div.
7ᵗʰ Inf. Div.	8ᵗʰ Inf. Div.	20ᵗʰ Inf. Div.	26ᵗʰ Inf. Div.	45ᵗʰ Inf. Div.
37ᵗʰ Inf. Div.	11ᵗʰ Inf. Div.	21ˢᵗ Inf. Div.	27ᵗʰ Inf. Div.	49ᵗʰ Inf. Div.
51ˢᵗ Inf. Div.	15ᵗʰ Inf. Div.	30ᵗʰ Inf. Div.	28ᵗʰ Inf. Div.	10ᵗʰ Arm. Div.
14ᵗʰ Mech. Div.	18ᵗʰ Inf. Div.	34ᵗʰ Inf. Div.	31ˢᵗ Inf. Div.	17ᵗʰ Arm. Div.
	19ᵗʰ Inf. Div.	36ᵗʰ Inf. Div.	47ᵗʰ Inf. Div.	52ⁿᵈ Arm. Div.
	29ᵗʰ Inf. Div.	6ᵗʰ Arm. Div.	48ᵗʰ Inf. Div.	
	35ᵗʰ Inf. Div.	1ˢᵗ Mech. Div.	12ᵗʰ Arm. Div.	
	3ʳᵈ Arm. Div.			
	5ᵗʰ Mech. Div.			

This is going better than I thought it would. "Next slide," Ibrahim said. A map of the first phase of the operation appeared.

"Sir, the Kuwaiti forces will be on their annual holiday leave during the time of our attack. This will leave them ill prepared to confront our forces or mount any sort of effective counterattack. Their forces, consisting of the 6th Mechanized Brigade located in the north, nearest our invasion point, are equipped with M113 personnel carriers, BMP2 fighting vehicles and old Vickers tanks. The 15th Mechanized Brigade is located south of Kuwait City and has M113s and Chieftain tanks. The 80th Infantry Brigade is in Garrison in Jahra. They have some Saladin

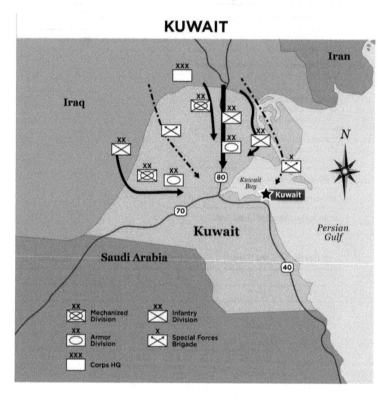

armored cars but nothing modern. The 35th Armored Brigade is west of Jahra, with their base at Ali al-Salem Military Airfield. Two companies of the 8th Battalion of the 35th Armor are in the north, currently without their equipment, guarding the oil fields. Naval vessels are in port at their main naval base located south of al-Salem. The crews are also on leave at this time, as are most of the Army forces for their annual summer leave," Ibrahim explained.

Saddam smiled. "So, no one will be there to greet us is what you are telling me."

46

Everyone chuckled at his weak humor.

"Continue, Colonel," Saddam directed.

"Sir, to execute this invasion as flawlessly as possible, we have developed an elaborate ruse. We are moving forward with a large training exercise in our southern provinces, consisting of most of our armored and mechanized infantry forces. From outward appearances, it will look like we are engaged in a very large combined-arms exercise, while in reality we will be moving the bulk of our army into position to launch a blitzkrieg assault across the Kuwaiti desert," Colonel Ibrahim exclaimed proudly as he puffed his chest out a bit.

Several of the generals and senior leaders smiled and nodded in agreement. Even Saddam smiled at the cleverness of the plan. He motioned with his hand for the colonel to continue with the briefing and bring them up to speed on the units that would be involved in the initial invasion.

"Mr. President, Generals, the 1st Republican Guard Corps will launch their attack as the main effort on 1 August with two armored divisions, two mechanized divisions, three motorized divisions, and a brigade from the 8th As Saiqa Special Forces Division. At 0100 hours, a commando company from the Airborne Brigade will seize the border crossing at Safwan." The colonel used a wooden pointer to indicate the location on the northern border between Kuwait and Iraq where Highway 80 crossed.

"The attacking unit will execute as follows. At 0300 hours, the 1st Hammurabi Armored Division, with the 17th Brigade, will attack and link up with a commando company at this point here." The colonel pointed to a small border crossing at Safwan. "These units will be the first element for the 1st Hammurabi Armored Division under the command of Major General al-Ujayli, who will lead the invasion. The 1st Hammurabi Armored Division will attack with the 17th Armored Brigade and the 8th Mechanized Brigade moving along Route 80. They will be followed by the 6th Nebuchadnezzar Mechanized Division and the 3rd Tawakalna Mechanized Division on the right flank," Ibrahim explained, pausing to allow everyone to study the map and let his words sink in.

"Simultaneously," he continued, "the 2nd al-Medinah Armored Division in a supporting role will attack from the west with the 25th

47

Infantry Division and the 35th Motorized Division following in reserve." The colonel paused to take a sip of his water and give everyone a moment to follow along. Continuing, he added, "The 4th Al Fao Infantry Division will secure the left flank of our armored thrust into the country. They'll secure objectives along the islands of Warbah and Bubiyan. The 9th Corps will follow 1st RG Corps as they move south to secure southern Kuwait."

Some of the officers talked amongst themselves, whispering something to an aide who then scribbled something down.

"And what about the VII Corps and the III Corps?" Saddam asked.

"Sir, the VII Corps remains in the north, keeping the Kurds in check. The III Corps will be our strategic reserve, maintaining vigilance along the eastern border, which we feel cannot be left unguarded."

Ibrahim observed Saddam studying the map intently. He appeared to be holding his questions for the moment, so Ibrahim pressed on. "To position our forces for this invasion, the 2nd Republican Guard Corps will move four days prior to the jumping-off point at night to a holding area in the vicinity of Wadi Al-Batin, along the neutral zone. To maintain our ruse, the 2nd Army Corps in the west will continue to conduct training exercises as part of the deception plan."

As Ibrahim continued the brief, he suddenly became aware that most of these generals and senior officers had *absolutely* no idea they had been preparing all this time to invade Kuwait. *Wait till I tell them what the second phase of the operation is. Some are liable to have heart attacks*, the colonel was thinking—and, in one or two cases, hoping.

Security had been so tight that some key players were not aware of what was being planned and was to be executed shortly. Breaking the silence, General al-Rawi, Chief of Staff of the Republican Guard, took over this part of the briefing from Ibrahim. "Sir, the Phase 1 operation will consist of a main effort along Highway 80 from Safwan south to Mutla Ridge overlooking Kuwait City.[2] There will be a heliborne assault on the pass at Mutla Ridge prior to the arrival of the 17th Armored Brigade. A supporting attack will come from the west on secondary

---

[2] Mutla Ridge is a high ridge that overlooks the coast north of Kuwait City and encircles the city to the southwest. Highway 80 comes down the ridge through a pass/choke point.

roads. To reduce the possibility of resistance, a commando heliborne assault will be executed into Kuwait City to capture the Emir, his family and senior government officials.

"The 3rd Tawakalna Division is the right flank of the main attack. Its immediate task is to seize the Ali al-Salem Air Base and link up and conduct a passage of the 2nd al-Medinah Division from the western axis. The 3rd Tawakalna Division and the 2nd al-Medinah Division will assume positions between Al-Ahmadi and the Saudi border. The 1st Hammurabi Division will then move in, seizing the area between al-Wafra and Sa'ud Port south of Kuwait City," General al-Rawi said before asking, "What are your questions, sir?"

"What is the plan for the use of the 8th As Saiqa Special Forces Brigades? If you do not include them, they will be upset," Saddam joked.

"Last week, elements of two battalions of the 8th As Saiqa Special Forces Brigade slipped into Kuwait and began inciting the protests against the Emir. At 0100 hours on G-Day, they will move along the Abdali-Jahra-Kuwait City Road with the primary mission of seizing the Emir and his family. The one battalion of the Special Forces Brigade will also be seizing the choke point at Mutla Pass. At approximately 0400, the parachute brigade of the 8th As Saiqa Division will conduct a heliborne assault to seize the Royal Compound and key government buildings in the city. Sir, if you have no questions, this completes our briefing on Phase 1 of the operation."

"And how long do you see this phase taking?" Saddam asked, shaking his glass to indicate he wanted more tea. While they paused for the tea to arrive, he pulled out a pack of Marlboros and lit up. When he was ready, General al-Rawi fielded the question.

"Sir, we see Phase 1 taking no more than forty-eight hours. Once 1st Republican Guard Corps has passed through Kuwait City and taken up positions along the Kuwait-Saudi border, the Ninth Corps will follow and can mop up any resistance in the city, which we do not anticipate will be much if anything."

"Tell me about how you are overcoming the Americans' ability to intercept our radio communications," the Iraqi leader said.

"Sir, learning from the Americans and their actions prior to the Normandy Invasion of World War II, we have established false headquarters for each of the divisions and corps. At the appointed time,

49

they will take over all communications for those elements and pass preplanned message traffic indicating administrative information typical of garrison positions," Sultan Hashim Ahmed al-Tai, the Minister of Defense, said.

"And how do we mask our movement from the satellites?" Saddam asked, attempting to cover all his bases.

"Sir, the Soviets have been good enough to provide the time schedule for the overflight of the American reconnaissance satellite. Our movement will be at night, and only when the satellites are not overhead. When they approach, we will be camouflaged and in hiding," General al-Tikriti responded.

Saddam stood and turned to face the assembled officers. As he was smiling, they all felt reassured that he was pleased, but they could not be positive. "I do not have to tell you that swift action is required. I suspect the Americans will attempt to interfere despite the words of their ambassador, who I will see in a few days. I have no doubt that we will be successful in accomplishing this exercise, but retaining our position will be the hard part. It is going to take diplomatic strength and the power of the media to rally support."

Turning to his Deputy Prime Minister, he said, "Aziz, we must use the press to our advantage for this operation. The American ambassador, April Glaspie, will, according to our sources, say that the dispute between us and Kuwait is an Arab-to-Arab dispute and of no concern to the Americans. I don't believe her for a minute, but we must push that communication. I believe the Kuwaitis are being hard-nosed because the Americans are pushing them to be so. You will meet with the Kuwaiti Foreign Minister on 30 July for a final time and ask them to agree to our terms. If the Americans were not backing them, they would have rolled over weeks ago. We need to use the press to show that the purpose of this action is to remove the Americans from the region and end their domination over our affairs. When the Arab world sees this, they will rise up with us and cast the Americans out. Get CNN, Christiane Amanpour, here when things start and let her tell our story to the world. She has credibility with the world—and besides, she is easy on the eyes, they say," Saddam said with a smile. Everyone else smiled too, as if on cue. "I am satisfied, but what are your concerns?"

General Hassan al-Rawi was the first to speak up. "I am concerned about the American fleet. They have a small flotilla of four ships in the Gulf right now. But not far away, near Oman, they have a large carrier battle group with eighty-one strike aircraft at their disposal. They also have another carrier battle group off the eastern Mediterranean Sea, and then they have their air base at Incirlik, Turkey."

General Hassan al-Tikriti fielded the comment. "First, we have sufficient anti-aircraft missiles around Baghdad and major facilities to handle their aircraft. Second, the anti-aircraft umbrella over our ground forces to include missiles and guns is sufficient to deal with those threats. And lastly, we have a fighter interceptor force of sufficient size to deal with those aircraft as well. The Americans will be reluctant to enter into a large air campaign once we have seized the major cities for fear of inflicting civilian casualties. As for those four ships currently in the Gulf, we will dispatch them in the early hours with Exocet antiship missiles if it comes down to it."

"Enough!" Saddam said. Silence fell on the room. "Do not engage those ships," he ordered. Turning to the Prime Minister, he instructed, "Once we cross the frontier, notify the Americans to remove those ships from the Gulf or they will be destroyed. We do not want to provoke a fight with the Americans, and attacking their ships first will only infuriate the American public and incite them to demand action. Tell the Americans that those ships must leave, but do not attack unless they engage any of our forces first. Tell them we do not wish for another *Stark* incident and request they move the ships out of the Gulf for the present time."

He continued, "Diplomatically, as soon as we enter Kuwait, they are going to go running to the UN Security Council. We need a strong argument to prevent any resolutions from being imposed on us. Get with the ambassador and be sure he is prepared." Saddam looked around the room. "We cannot fail," he said simply as he turned to leave. Then he paused for a moment and turned back around to survey the room. "Good, I am satisfied. We will meet again when 1st RG Division reaches the Kuwaiti-Saudi border. We execute on 1 August."

Chapter Six
National Reconnaissance Office

16 July 1990
Pentagon
Washington, D.C.

Bob Daley sat in his office cubicle in a rather plain office building in Washington, D.C. The building was known as the Pentagon and his office was on the second floor, underground. Access to his office was through a set of yellow double doors that required a code to unlock the door and a special pass. Just because you worked in the Pentagon, that didn't give you free access to every office. Bob had been in his line of work since 1975, when he was discharged from the Army after coming home from Vietnam and graduating from college. He had majored in photography in college and expected a career taking pictures of glamorous movie stars.

For the past fifteen years, he had worked in a windowless office, not knowing what the weather outside was like. In the winter, he came to work in the dark and went home in the dark to his two-story home in Alexandria, Virginia, in the Kingstown subdivision of a thousand homes. Every fourth home was identical, and although it was a civilian community, it could almost pass for a military housing area as everyone either was military or worked for the government. He found the work interesting, but nothing exciting.

Bob was a photo analyst in an organization that did not exist. He could not talk about his work, even with his wife, or tell anyone the name of his organization. At social gatherings, when asked about his job, his pat answer was, "Oh, I'm just a paper pusher in the Pentagon." His wife suspected differently.

The National Reconnaissance Office or NRO was owned by the Central Intelligence Agency. That said, it had several masters, to include the Defense Intelligence Agency (DIA), the National Security Agency (NSA), and the various services. The mission of the NRO was to manage the nation's fleet of intelligence-gathering satellites from launch to the analysis of what was sent back.

Sometimes what came back was film that had been dropped from space and retrieved by an airplane as it descended to earth on a parachute. News of this satellite had been widely published in the early years of the 1970s because someone could not keep their mouth shut and spilled the information to *Time* magazine. An article had come out in August of 1971 and let the whole world know that we had a satellite that was watching the Russians. The article even gave the code name for the satellite—Big Bird or KH-9.

As Big Bird took pictures and dropped the film, the Russians had thought it was a dead satellite as it did not transmit signals; thus, they never covered anything up when it flew over every ninety minutes. Thankfully, the article said nothing about the fact that, since 1963, the KH-7 satellite had been watching them. Prior to this, everyone had thought we were getting high-resolution photos from the U-2 or SR-71 aircraft. When Bob had joined the organization in 1975, the investigation into who had leaked the information was still ongoing.

Since Bob had joined, however, he had seen more satellites come into existence that had much higher resolutions and were capable of downlink transmissions. What used to take six to seven days to get back and be developed and then analyzed could now be done in about an hour once the satellite was over the target. The KH-11 satellites remained in orbit and used electro-optic transmissions. The recently launched current satellite had an infrared capability, which enhanced the data that Bob was receiving. Since the satellite was equipped with a hydrazine-powered propulsion system, its orbit could be adjusted. The KH-11 was serviced by the space shuttle on classified missions to keep it running well into the future.

Targeting for the satellite was the problem. Everyone thought what they wanted to look at was the most important thing in the world and should have top priority. Bob was thankful that he was not involved in the targeting process, which was handled by some high-paid government employees. He would have liked to have their pay, but not the headaches from every user always crying about how they couldn't get their pictures taken.

I come to work, I look at pictures, I write up what I see, and I go home. No headaches. What more could a guy ask for? Bob was constantly thinking. The sign on Bob's cubicle door read, "Your Priority

Is Not My Problem," and that was especially true today, as he was going home to celebrate his ten-year anniversary.

"Hey, Bob, we just got a download that I'd like you to look over. You should be able to finish that up before you leave today. Oh, happy anniversary. Where are you taking her tonight?" asked Bob's supervisor, Cliff Jeffrey. Cliff was a GS-15 and had been in the job since the early 1960s, having started in the CIA and transferred over to the NRO in the early 1970s.

"Just spending a quiet evening with Jane. Her parents are taking the kids tonight," Bob said as he slipped the floppy disk Cliff handed him into the computer. "Anything in particular I'm looking for?" he asked.

"Not sure yet. The satellite made a pass over the Middle East earlier today, looking at something for the Air Force in western Iran and these areas of Iraq and Kuwait."

"OK, let's have a look," Bob said as Cliff moved off to talk to another analyst. Bob started scrolling through the pictures. The resolution wasn't bad. These pictures were from the Crystal satellite, which offered synthetic aperture radar (SAR) imaging, producing high-resolution pictures both day and night. Because it used SAR technology, it was not adversely affected by clouds or dust.

As Bob sat there, sipping his coffee, he was almost getting bored looking at endless miles of sand. But then he sat up straight and leaned into the computer screen. *Wow, what have we here?* The picture was a night picture and clearly showed a large formation of vehicles, tanks, and combat vehicles with support vehicles, all moving towards the Basra region of Iraq. As he examined the pictures one after another, he could determine the speed and direction of movement. When he started counting vehicles, he recognized that this was no small unit move but a major deployment of an entire division. Reaching for his phone, he pressed the intercom button and asked Cliff to come take a look.

"What you got?" Cliff asked as he looked over Bob's shoulder.

"Look at this concentration of vehicles, on the move," Bob pointed out.

Studying the computer screen, Cliff asked, "That's a shitload of vehicles. Do we know where they all came from?" He was bewildered by what they were looking at. "You don't see armored formations on the move like this very often in your life," Cliff added.

54

"No, I haven't pulled up any previous pictures of Iraq to get an idea of the point of origin," Bob said. *Damn, I should have done that before I called him over here.* "I'll do that now and get back to you." *Damnit, I'm not going to get home early tonight.*

"Yeah, make a comparison to determine where they're coming from, and order up another pass to see where they went, then write it up. It's late now, so order up the pass and then take off—finish this up in the morning. It may be that they're maneuvering to go kick some Iranian ass, again," Cliff concluded as he walked off to finish up paperwork, which never ended in the Pentagon.

Bob did as instructed and ordered another pass. The results would come back in the night and he could look at them when he came in the next day. He really didn't expect to find anything. *Cliff is probably right,* he thought as he gathered his papers. Still, you didn't see a movement of vehicles like that very often, so it certainly warranted further investigation, if only to verify that it was just a training exercise. *I mean, this isn't the Fulda Gap or West Germany, but still.*

Closing shop, Bob ejected the floppy disk and removed his hard drives, placing them in the safe next to his desk. Nothing could be left out when you left your office or weren't going to be at your desk. If someone from the outside came into the room, everyone had to cover their desks and monitors with canvas covers and wait for the visitor to leave. Visitors were seldom invited into this room, largely because it meant just about everyone had to stop working and stow their classified materials until the visitor left.

Driving home that night, Bob found his mind drifting back to the photos. *If they were moving to go kick Iranian ass, why were they moving towards Basra? There's only one bridge over the river and it's on the south side of Basra, but where would they go from there? Something isn't making sense.*

When he arrived back at his house, Jane met him at the door. For a woman in her midthirties with two kids, she was still very attractive and turned heads. She also had the top three buttons on her blouse open and it was obvious she wasn't wearing a bra. Her formfitting jeans accentuated her narrow hips and tight bottom. The high-heeled shoes added to the ensemble only drove him further crazy with lust and desire.

55

Her auburn hair was shoulder-length and freshly cut, just the way he liked it.

She knew she was driving him wild with excitement and anticipation of a night alone without their kids. Worse, she kept toying with him as he entered the living room and sought to take his sport jacket off. He saw dinner was on the table, but he wasn't sure he could wait. *Fuck it, dinner can wait. I want my dessert first*, he thought as he gave her his best smile and a wink as he motioned with his head in the direction of the couch. Her face lit up like it was their honeymoon as she glided across the living room and the clothes began to fall off.

They never did eat dinner, but they had a fun romantic time. Just the two of them, no kids as they lay there naked on the couch, reminiscing about the years that had gone by and all the things they still wanted to pursue as a couple. Bob had to admit, he was one lucky man. He had a great job, a beautiful wife, and two beautiful, amazing kids. Life didn't get any better than that.

The next morning, he arrived at work while it was still dark. Such was the life of a tunnel rat in the Pentagon. He had arrived before most of the people in the office as he found he could beat the D.C. traffic and find a relatively close parking place that way. It also meant his eight-hour shift often ended before traffic picked up again later in the afternoon. Besides, he had gone to bed early last night and slept great… after a time.

Walking into the office, he saw he was, as usual, the first person there. One of the unspoken rules to opening the shop was you had to get the first pot of coffee going for the office. Most people would walk in with a cup of coffee from the coffee shop in the food court. After that first cup, they would head to the office coffeepot for round two. Considering nearly every person in the office had either been in the military or worked for the government for many years, they were all heavy coffee drinkers.

While the pot started brewing, Bob opened his safe and withdrew the floppy disks, the hard drives, and his papers and notes. Loading up the hard drives and booting up the computer took as long as it did to get that first cup of coffee. One of these days, he thought he just might wash out his coffee cup, but hell… not today. The permanent coffee stain ring showed just how much to put in.

As the computer came online, he inserted his floppy with the original photos. He studied them for a minute or two, as if something on it might have changed overnight while locked in his safe. The dinging sound alerted him to the fact that some more photos were waiting for him to download, since he'd requested another pass of the vehicle formation right before he had left for the day.

When the screen came up, he mumbled, "What the hell?" What he saw was amazing and disturbing. The unit he had tracked yesterday afternoon was now stopped, but it had doubled in size overnight. What he was looking at was a division instead of a brigade. Not only that, but it appeared that another large formation was farther north behind the first unit. On the left side of the picture, he could see elements of another formation that fell out of the span of the camera.

What am I looking at? Is this a full corps of armored vehicles, artillery, and tanks? Those appear to be T-72s and BMP-2, and they're just twelve miles north of the Kuwait border. As he sat there studying the photo and making comparisons, he zoomed in and out a few times to count some of the things he was seeing, like tanks and other vehicles of interest. Then Cliff entered the room.

"Morning, Bob, how goes it?"

"Cliff, get over here and see this."

"What you got?" Cliff asked, carrying a coffee mug with him to Bob's desk.

"I think we have an invasion force going to Kuwait," Bob said with a bit of excitement.

"Whoa, hold your horses there, General Patton. Let's not launch the missiles just yet. Let me see what you have," Cliff said, looking over his shoulder.

As Cliff looked at the images, he moved his glasses from his forehead to his face. After a minute, he nudged Bob's shoulder. "Let me sit down."

Bob got up and relinquished the chair and monitor to Cliff, who studied the photos and scrolled through the new downloads. Then he would jump back to the original photos. As Bob stood there, he suddenly felt like the world was watching. He looked up to notice that almost the entire office was standing around them, looking at the screen.

Finally, Cliff looked up at Bob. "Order up two more passes in the next orbit to the west of this last pass. I want a picture of western Iraq, Wadi Al-Batin and western Kuwait. Also, after you get those two, I want a pass over western Iran to see if anything's moving there."

As Cliff stood, he turned to the assembled group. "Folks, these next three passes are the priority, and if anyone gives you grief, you tell them to take it up with me. Bob, grab everything you have so far. We're going to see the Undersecretary of Defense for Intelligence. The rest of you, start pulling everything you have on Saddam and the Iraqi Army... any pictures, anything."

Chapter Seven
Brief Back

28 July 1990
17th Armoured Brigade
Khor Al Zubair, Iraq

Brigadier General Ra'ad al-Hamdani, commander of the 17th Armored Brigade of the 1st Hammurabi Armored Division[3], knew something big was about to happen. His earliest inkling that something was up was when his commander, General al-Ujayli, had been ordered to attend the 15 July conference with Saddam. Following that meeting, his brigade had been ordered to move from their home base in Jaykur to the northwest, crossing the river on the one bridge located in Basra and then to a position north of Khor Al Zubair. Then, on 28 July, his division and brigade had been given the order to begin Project 19.

"We cross the border on 1 August and are only just getting the order!" he said to his operations officer, who tried to shrink away from his ire.

General al-Hamdani tried to arrest his anger, declaring in a calmer manner, "OK, let's get the staff working on this, and bring in the commanders when we have a plan. As I look this over, I have some concerns that we must be sure to consider. Speed is of the utmost concern. Speed ensures surprise, and surprise ensures fewer casualties. We cannot allow ourselves to get bogged down in city fighting. Second, I am concerned about civilian safety. I have nothing against the people, and therefore I want to minimize such casualties. If we can get there fast, they will have less of a chance of putting up resistance, and thus there will be less of a requirement for us to engage them. We will not employ artillery prep fires, and I want the tanks to be uploaded only with high-explosive shells. No sabot rounds. We hit their tanks with HE and that will scare the crap out of them and not destroy the tank or kill anyone."

Thinking out loud, he added, "There is a checkpoint on the border where Highway 80 crosses. A commando unit will take that checkpoint

---

[3] In OIF, he would command an Iraqi corps at the outset.

and clear it for us. No one is to be killed. When we roll through, we will have the 6th Mechanized Brigade opposing us forward of Mutla Pass. If we are fast enough, we can get there before they get organized—hopefully before the 35th Brigade in Kuwait City can move up to close the pass. Does anyone have any questions? If not, assemble the staff and let's start putting a plan together. We don't have very long to get things ready."

****

Five days later, the battalion commanders were assembled along with company commanders. Al-Hamdani outlined the battle plan for the brigade over a sand table map of Kuwait and Kuwait City.

General al-Hamdani explained, "We will attack in two columns to this point between Abdali and Jahra on the northwest side of the city. The left column attacks to block the 6th Kuwait Brigade while the right column rushes to seize the Mutla Pass. This will prevent the 35th Brigade from coming in from the city and reaching the pass. Once both columns are through the pass, the battalions will move to their objectives."

Pausing, al-Hamdani looked up from the map in front of him and turned to the 1st Battalion commander, who would lead things off. In this case, the 1st Battalion was a tank battalion. "Colonel, your battalion will move to and seize the Fifth Circular Road and the Royal Palace, the international hotels and the Ministry of the Interior. Conduct linkup with the 8th As Saiqa Special Forces elements at the Royal Palace. Any questions?" he asked. The 1st Battalion commander looked up from the map and acknowledged he had none.

Redirecting his attention to the 2nd Battalion commander, he said, "The 2nd Battalion follows the 1st Battalion and takes the Seventh Circular Road and the Kuwait International Airport, to include the Air Forces Base. Conduct linkup with commando forces at the international airport. Any questions?" There were none.

"3rd Battalion, you are the main effort. Your armored task force will have an infantry company, an engineer company, an artillery battery, and an anti-aircraft company. You will move to seize the Sixth Circular Road and cut through the center of the city, disarming the police, the Royal Guard, and any resistance you encounter. You will advance to the water and circle back to link up with the 1st Battalion. My command post will travel with you. Any questions?" Again the commander had none.

"I cannot emphasize enough that speed in execution is paramount for our safety and the safety of the civilian population. Do not allow your lead elements to get behind the schedule, but have them bypass if necessary and have follow-on elements deal with any resistance. What are your concerns?" al-Hamdani asked.

"Sir, what about the radar balloon that the Kuwaitis have in the north overlooking our border? Will they not see us moving against them?" the 1st Battalion commander asked.

"They probably will, but it will be too late for them to sound an alarm. We will be in Kuwait City before they can react. The Kuwaiti Army is on leave at this time except for the 8th Tank Battalion, which is on guard duty in the oil fields without its tanks. We should make short work of what few forces they still have on duty. Any other questions?"

"Sir, there are British soldiers stationed in Kuwait. What if we meet them?" the 3rd Battalion commander asked.

"Yes, the British have a contingent of military personnel with their families in Kuwait. Iraqi amphibious troops of the 8th As Saiqa Special Forces Division will land at several locations on the Kuwaiti coast. Some will land near Fahaheel and secure the IBI residential camp, where a group of British servicemen working with the British Liaison Team live with their families. We will not engage them, and we will not enter that residential camp. We do not want to give the British any excuse to come to the aid of Kuwait."

"Sir, may I ask, what is our follow-on mission once we have seized the city?" the 1st Battalion commander asked. The other commanders nodded and looked to al-Hamdani for the answer. At this point, he could not divulge that information. There was a fear that if someone was captured, they might reveal the follow-on mission, which would cost them the element of surprise.

"That is a good question. Sorry I did not cover that. On order, and once we have secured our objectives, we will move from the city center to a holding area south of the city and north of the border. I will establish my command post in Al Khiran Resort," al-Hamdani said with a smile.

The battalion commanders exchanged knowing grins. "What? Shouldn't I have a comfortable place to rest my head?" he said with a sly grin. "The 18th Armored Brigade will be establishing its command post in Al Wafrah. Let's see to it that we don't crowd over into their territory. General Mustafa al-Hassan is a very jealous man and would be raising the roof if we did. Just leave them alone. Once we get settled in Al Khiran, I want all the vehicles topped off with fuel, ammo, and a three-day supply of food and water on each vehicle. I want every vehicle inspected and any required repairs to be completed within the first twenty-four hours after our arrival. Is that understood?" Hamdani concluded.

Everyone acknowledged that they understood his intent, but their facial expressions showed questions. *I know you're wondering why you're being asked to upload ammo and food for three additional days*, al-Hamdani was thinking. *Well, just wait.*

Chapter Eight
Royal Palace of Dasman

1 August 1990
3rd Special Forces Brigade
Basra International Airport

Colonel Farooq al-Basra walked the hangar floor with his senior noncommissioned officer, checking their soldiers' equipment and saying a few encouraging words to his men. These were professional soldiers, well trained for the mission at hand. Some were even sleeping while they waited for the order to load the helicopters that sat outside. As he wandered around the hangar, he came upon his three company commanders, who were sipping tea that they had found. This would be their last chance to sip tea before the mission.

The 3rd Special Forces Brigade's mission for tonight was the seizure of the Royal Palace of Dasman and several key government facilities in the center of the city. The government buildings would be the responsibility of infiltrators that had been in the city for the past week, acting as demonstrators against the Emir. Their role was part of the deception plan to convince the world that people were dissatisfied with the ruling family. As Colonel al-Basra approached the company commanders, they said in unison, "Good evening, sir." One offered his cup of tea to the colonel, who was appreciative but refused.

"How are your men tonight?" the colonel asked. Unlike many Republican Guard commanders, al-Basra had a deep love for his soldiers and concern for their welfare. Too often in his career, his survival had depended on the man on his right or left. Soldiers fought for each other, and taking care of soldiers was what it was all about for him. His soldiers saw this, and they truly loved the man for it. They would follow him anywhere in combat.

"They're all good and ready, sir," Captain al-Bishi said as the others nodded in agreement. He was the 1st Company commander and the oldest, being thirty-two years old. He was also the most decorated soldier for his actions against Iran.

"Good. And you have explained your mission to them, and they are good with what they have to do?" the colonel asked.

"Yes, sir. I explained that when our aircraft land on the north side, we move to secure the northwest access point and the northeast entrance, then link up with those elements of the brigade that infiltrated the city over the past week and allow them access while denying anyone the ability to leave," Captain al-Bishi said. Colonel al-Basra nodded his head and looked to the 2nd Company commander.

Without being asked, Captain Hafeez said, "We follow 1st Company and immediately head south, clearing any resistance as we move towards the central palace to assist 3rd Company."

"Sir, 3rd Company is the main effort," Captain Muhsin said with some pride, "and fast-ropes to the roof of the central palace to search for, then seize and secure, the Emir."

"Good, you all understand your respective missions. Do not forget, the 2nd Battalion of the brigade will be landing at the same time to the southeast and breaching the perimeter to move towards the center of the palace complex. 3rd Battalion lands to the northeast, sweeping towards the center. The Royal Guard barracks is to the northeast, so I suspect the 3rd Battalion will have a hard time of it if the Royal Guard is alerted. We do not want to get in a firefight with our own people. Understood?" al-Basra asked.

"Understood, sir," the three said in unison.

"Farooq, you understand that it is imperative that you prevent anyone from exiting or reinforcing the palace, yes?"

"No one will get in or out once we are on the ground," Captain al-Bishi said as he noticed the soldiers all starting to stand up. The battalion operations officer was standing in the open hangar doorway, rotating his right arm above his head, the universal sign that it was time to load the helicopters.

Six Mi-17 helicopters stood outside. In the next hangar down, six more Mi-17 helicopters were loading as well, and six more beyond that. He couldn't see further down the flight line, but he knew that several more groups of six aircraft were loading up with their human cargo as well.

With the three-man crews aboard each aircraft, the two Klimov VK-2500PS-03 turboshaft engines were spooling up to full power. As each soldier approached the aircraft, they were assisted by the flight engineer, who helped to pull them up into the helicopter.

While they were not carrying parachutes, they still had one hundred pounds of combat equipment on them. As the twenty-four soldiers per aircraft were loaded, each took a seat on the benches that lined the sides of the aircraft.

Colonel al-Basra took a seat in the fourth aircraft, which was the first aircraft for 2nd Company. He felt that 2nd Company was going to have the hardest fight and wanted to be with them. He had a great deal of confidence that Captain al-Bishi would not need his guidance once on the ground. As he sat there looking down the inside of the aircraft, he felt it lift off. He checked his watch. It was 0330; after a thirty-minute flight at low level over the water, they should touch down at 0400, while it was still dark out.

As Colonel al-Basra sat and stared out the open door in the side of the aircraft, all he could see was open water and blackness. There were few ships in the northern part of the Arabian Gulf. Casting an occasional glance towards the cockpit, he could see the lights of Kuwait City getting closer. The Kuwait Towers were lit up and easy to see as they were the prominent nighttime feature of the city. The three needle-shaped water towers dominated the Kuwait skyline and had been a tourist attraction since 1979.

They were now located just northeast of the palace. Looking to the south along the coastal promenade, he could see Green Island, an artificial island created in 1988 and another popular tourist attraction. Its lush gardens and central lagoon were clearly outlined in lights. The city was well lit, which provided reassurance that their mission had so far gone off undetected.

Finally, the flight engineer turned in his seat and held up two fingers. Two minutes to touchdown, and then the world as they and everyone else in the Middle East knew it would change forever. Al-Basra said a silent prayer—not for himself, but for his soldiers' safety. The helicopter's engine changed in pitch, letting him know they were near the objective. The pilot flared the nose a bit to further bleed off airspeed as the rear wheel of the giant helicopter touched down.

Al-Basra was the first out of his aircraft and sprinted to the tree line on the southeast side of the helicopter pad they had landed on. Arriving at the tree line, he took a knee and surveyed the actions of the soldiers.

He was surprised that he was hearing sporadic gunfire already. His men were under orders not to start shooting until they were fired upon.

Suddenly he realized it wasn't his men that had fired first. They were being engaged by the Royal Guard brigade protecting the palace. One of their heavy machine guns had started shooting at his troops. His soldiers didn't have any heavy machine guns.

Instead, he heard the whooshing sound of an RPG and an explosion. The reports of the heavy gun fell silent. It appeared 1st Company had silenced the gun. In the well-lit areas, he could see that men from 1st Company were fanning out to block the entrances to the palace compound. 2nd Company's soldiers were closing in all around him and quickly moving across the street to begin advancing towards the central palace, the residence of the Emir.

As the company commander gave the order to proceed down the main street, his first platoon moved out, only to be met by a hail of bullets from the residential buildings lining the street. Now Colonel al-Basra was convinced the Royal Guard must have been alerted to their arrival.

This was not going to be as easy as everyone had predicted if the guard force had been given fair warning they were coming. They'd likely called for reinforcements and had their garrison fully deployed to meet them.

As he looked in the direction of the residence, he saw one of his helicopters was in a hover. His Special Forces soldiers were fast-roping to the roof. Two more helicopters were waiting to discharge their human cargo as well.

To the northeast, more helicopters could be seen, delivering members of the brigade to their objectives around the palace. From the black night sky, two streaks of flames erupted and raced towards the barracks occupied by the Royal Guard. The explosion that followed left no doubt in the surrounding residence that the palace was under attack.

2nd Company had a fierce engagement with the Royal Guard brigade soldiers when a patrol in an armored car approached the helipad. They'd likely wanted to see who had arrived and had been summarily ambushed by 2nd Company. It was more important than ever to move quickly and secure their objectives before more reinforcements could arrive and alter the balance of power.

More gunfire erupted to the northeast, near the barracks area of the Royal Guard. 2nd Company was fully engaging them at this point. Then muffled gunfire could be heard from the vicinity of 3rd Company. They were inside the residence, and it appeared that the Emir's internal security was putting up a fight.

Why doesn't the old fool just surrender and stop this nonsense of fighting us? Colonel al-Basra thought.

As the colonel moved down the street following 2nd Company, he received a transmission from 3rd Company. The residence was secured, but it would be some time before 2nd Company could reach them. The Royal Guard was putting up a fight to prevent the linkup between the two companies. Picking up his radio handset from his radio operator, al-Basra called 3rd Company.

"Have you secured the Emir in a safe place?"

"No, we have not." That was not the response he was expecting.

"Well, why not? I thought we discussed this—search, seize, and secure. What did you not understand?"

A moment later he got his response.

"The Emir is not here in the palace," Captain Muhsin said.

"What? How do you know? Who told you?" Colonel al-Basra was beyond mad that the Emir had somehow escaped.

"Sheikh Jaber Al-Ahmad Al-Jaber Al-Sabah told me that the Emir was notified at 2200 hours that his compound was going to be attacked. His security moved him to the Ministry of Defense building. Somehow they were tipped off that we were coming."

"Did he tell you who notified them?"

"No, he did not." *Damn, this was a wasted exercise if we did not catch the slippery dog,* Colonel al-Basra thought. With the handset still in his hand, he had his RTO change to a frequency that would allow all his elements to hear him. If the Emir wasn't in the compound, then he wasn't about to waste good men on a mission with no value.

"Sir, 1st Company commander wishes to speak with you," the colonel's radioman said, holding out the second radio handset for the other radio to him.

"Bishi, what is it?" the colonel asked.

"We just intercepted a car attempting to enter the compound and engaged it. Sheikh Sa'ad Al-Abdullah Al-Salem Al-Sabah, the Emir's half brother, was in the back seat," Captain al-Bishi said.

"Excellent. Bring him to my location. Maybe we can have him convince the Royal Guard to lay down their weapons," al-Basra offered.

"Afraid he cannot help us. He was shot while his security team tried resisting. Unfortunately, he died," Captain al-Bishi said.

The colonel did not answer. *What else can go wrong in this operation?* Picking up the handset, he transmitted, "All units, proceed with your missions but do not take any unnecessary risks. If you find a pocket of resistance, contain it until the 1st Republican Guard Division arrives and let them deal with the problem." The sun was just coming up, and sporadic gunfire could be heard in other quarters of the city. It seemed the Royal Guard was attempting to conserve their resources while they waited for help to arrive.

At 1300, Captain al-Bishi reported that a tank from the 17th Brigade was at the gates. That was fine by Colonel al-Basra. *Let the Republican Guard deal with the Royal Guard. Our mission is complete. It's now the 17th Brigade's problem to deal with these holdouts.*

With his unit's objectives complete, Colonel al-Basra went looking for a comfortable place to take a long nap.

Chapter Nine
Battle of the Bridges

1 August 1990
35th Armored Brigade Headquarters
West of Al Jahra, Kuwait

Captain Khan had drawn the short stick to be the duty officer for the night shift. He had wanted to be on the day shift, where all the action was, but that wasn't to be. Then the phone rang.

"Hello, 35th Armored Brigade, Captain Khan, duty officer."

"Captain Khan, this is Colonel Al-Sorour. Put the brigade on alert and order an immediate recall." Colonel Salem Masoud Al-Sorour commanded the 35th Armored Brigade. He continued, "I want all commanders and staff in the headquarters in one hour. Tell the 7th and 8th Battalions to upload their ammunition immediately, and the 51st Artillery as well. Have the 57th Mechanized Battalion get their people back and prepare their vehicles. Do you understand?"

"Yes, sir, of course. What is happening? The 8th Battalion only has one company here, as the other companies are on guard in the northern oil fields. The 57th has one company deployed on Bubiyan Island and one on Faylaka Island. Do you want me to recall them as well?" Captain Khan asked in excitement as the adrenaline began to kick in.

"The Iraqis are preparing to invade. Get everyone you can. We may not be able to recall the deployed units, but I still want them on alert. Now get the alert orders out immediately!" Colonel al-Sorour said, almost shouting.

"Yes, sir."

As the alert went out using alert rosters, soldiers began arriving back in the unit areas. The real problem they were going to face, however, was that annual leave had started. Many people were out of town or could not be readily reached. They'd have to go with whatever soldiers they could muster in such a short time.

****

It was nearly 0300 hours when Colonel al-Sorour could finally meet with the bulk of his staff officers and commanders. He didn't waste a moment.

"Gentlemen, I want to bring you up to speed on the situation as it stands right now. It appears the Iraqi forces have officially crossed our border at 0030 hours and now occupy Al-Ratka."

Those present exchanged looks of disbelief and bewilderment.

"They are attacking down Highway 80 as we speak. It looks like they are going to try to seize Mutla Ridge with a heliborne assault, just like they seized the Dasman Palace and the international airport. Right now, I need to know the status of your units," Al-Sorour said as he looked at the 7th Battalion executive officer.

"Sir, I have not been able to contact the battalion commander as of yet," Captain Nassar said. "As soldiers report, I have been checking them in. If they have any tank experience, I am assigning them to a crew and a tank and sending them to upload the ammo. None of our tanks were previously uploaded, so right now that is what we are doing. It is going to take some time, I am afraid."

"How many tanks have you manned thus far?"

"Ten tanks, sir," Captain Nassar said, a bit dejected.

"And the status of 8th Battalion?" the colonel asked, looking at a company commander from that battalion.

"Sir, our battalion commander with two companies and some dismounted infantry is up north on guard duty. I am the only commander back here, and I have ten tanks. We are uploading ammo and fuel as we speak. Our company just came back from up there. I have all my crews either present or en route at this time," Captain al-Abdulkareem reported.

"Very good, Captain. Status of the 57th Mech?" the colonel asked, looking at another company commander.

"Sir, the antitank company is fully manned and uploaded," Captain Maloof indicated.

"Good, I want you to move out at 0430. Initially deploy in two sections. One section I want to go to the Ali al-Salem Air Base to provide security, and the second I want to secure the intersection of the Sixth Circular Road and the Salmi Road. Understood?"

"Yes, sir," Captain Maloof said.

"And the rifle company?" Colonel Al-Sorour asked, looking at the officer seated next to Captain Maloof. The colonel could not remember the captain's name as he had only recently taken command.

"Sir, my company has five BMP-2s ready, and several of our M113s are in the process of uploading their ammo. The BMPs have completed their uploads," the captain said.

"Artillery, status?"

"Sir, we have put together enough people at this point to man seven of our M109 self-propelled guns," the battalion executive officer said. He could not locate the battalion commander, so he'd taken charge for the moment.

Just then, the door opened and LTC Ahmad al-Wazan, commander of the 7th Tank Battalion, came in. "Forgive me, sir, for being late. I had difficulty getting through the city."

"I understand, Colonel. Your executive officer has been on top of the situation. Alright, at 0600 hours we depart with 7th Battalion as the lead element. We will move to block the forces coming down from Mutla Ridge. We will follow Salmi Road and take up positions along the Sixth Circular Road. Colonel al-Wazan, you are to take positions on the north side of Salmi Road. Captain al-Abdulkareem, you take 3rd Company and take up positions on the south side of Salmi Road. This will place the bridges that overpass Highway 80, Salmi Road and the Sixth Circular Road between your two forces. Any questions? If not, then let's get ready to move out," Colonel Al-Sorour said.
****

Sitting inside his vehicle, Colonel al-Sorour knew that, in five minutes, the 7th Tank Battalion would move out and head for its objective. He glanced over to the east. The sun was just starting to crest over the Arabian Gulf. The orange, yellow and pink sky announced its coming. It would be another warm day, but July was always warm here.

As he watched the sun rise, he wondered if it would set on a free Kuwait. If help did not come, he knew the answer to that question. To the west, he heard a thunderous explosion that quickly snatched his attention.

A black mushroom cloud rose above Ali al-Salem Military Airfield, where one of his two sections had moved. *I hope they were away from that,* he thought as the first Chieftain tank rolled past his position.

He counted each tank as they drove past him. A smile appeared on his face when the thirty-seventh drove past. *Good, 3rd Company of the 8th Battalion had ten, and that means that 7th Battalion was able to get twenty-seven tanks out. In a gunfight, they will be equal to the T-72. Now if the engines will just hold up.*

As the 7th rolled onto the Salmi Road, they crossed to the north side and took up a dispersed battle formation. The 3rd Company did the same on the south side. It was obvious that the days of training had paid off as each formation displayed discipline and tactical acumen. He was pleased by what he was seeing. His driver pulled out behind the last BMP of the 57th Mech and followed the formation.

"Sir," his radio operator said to get his attention, "Colonel al-Wazan reports he is pushing out his reconnaissance element to scout Highway 80 to Mutla Ridge."

"Acknowledge his report and have him keep us informed," Colonel al-Sorour replied.

As the brigade moved forward, Colonel al-Sorour could see helicopters over the city to the east. Some were Iraqi Hind gunships, and some were troop lift ships. It appeared they were concentrating on the center of the city, probably the Royal Palace and some of the downtown government buildings. It took thirty minutes for the 7th Tank Battalion to report that they had reached their battle position, which was about one kilometer off to the southwest side of Highway 80 and the Sixth Circular Road. Shortly afterwards, the 3rd Company also reported having attained their position.

"Colonel, Colonel al-Wazan reports that the lead element of a tank column is moving on the Sixth Circular Road towards his position. He is requesting permission to engage. His reconnaissance elements have also withdrawn so they don't fall behind enemy lines," the radio operator informed Colonel al-Sorour.

"Tell him to engage when he is ready. From what range is he going to engage?" al-Sorour asked.

"He said he'll look to engage them between one thousand and fifteen hundred meters."

72

"Good," al-Sorour answered, knowing that the main guns on both tanks were equally matched. The Chieftain would have the advantage of being hull defilade and therefore difficult to spot on the open roads compared to the T-72. *Now if we can just keep the attack helicopters off us...* His thoughts were broken by explosions and black smoke in the distance on both sides of the interchange bridges.

****

The 3rd Company, 8th Battalion had not been idle but had coordinated with Colonel al-Wazan on how best to attack the Iraqis.

Colonel al-Wazan allowed the first couple of Iraqi tanks to pass his position and move in front of Captain al-Abdulkareem's position. When al-Wazan was ready, he gave the command to fire, and Captain al-Abdulkareem directed his fire on this first few tanks.

The incoming rounds tore apart the first tanks, leaving behind only burning wrecks. Those tanks now blocked the road. The column stopped and rotated their turrets in the direction of the fire, seeking targets, which they quickly found from the clouds of dust caused by the concussion from the muzzle blast.

With the initial element of surprise gone, Colonel al-Wazan found it prudent to withdraw before he started to lose tanks himself. Seeing the size of the enemy force heading towards them, he realized his mission needed to change. Instead of trying to repulse the Iraqi attack, they were going to have to settle for stinging the enemy as they gave ground for time. He gave the order after discussing it with Colonel al-Sorour.

Fortunately, Colonel al-Sorour had the artillery engage the Iraqi formation to cover the withdrawal of the 7th and 3rd companies from the 8th Battalion as they withdrew to new positions further southwest along the Salmi Road. Once they were in their new positions, Colonel al-Sorour had Colonel al-Wazan and Captain al-Abdulkareem join him.

"Nice job this morning. We at least bloodied their nose," Colonel al-Wazan said.

"Yes, we did, but we have another problem now. It seems that a second front is approaching from the west on the Salmi Road, coming up behind us. The 51st Artillery spotted them and reported that one brigade is out front, with one battalion forward and a separation of a couple of kilometers between the first battalion and the second. Colonel al-Wazan, what do you think?"

"Sir, I think we can sting them again. I propose we ambush this first battalion here. Then, before any of their other units can close the distance and get us bogged down in a shooting fight, I swing my forces south and we make a run to join the 15th Mechanized Brigade down south," Colonel al-Wazan offered.

"Sir, what about helping the 80th Brigade in Jahra?" Captain al-Abdulkareem asked.

"With there being a concrete barrier dividing the road down the middle of Sixth Circular Road, I don't see a way to get to them. I am afraid they are on their own at this point. I wish I could do something for them. Maybe they can hold out until we join the 15th Mechanized Brigade and make a counterattack."

No one really had any other ideas at the moment. They were clearly feeling a bit defeated but were determined to make the Iraqis pay for every inch of Kuwait they managed to take. "OK, if you have no further questions, I suggest we get ready to meet this new threat," Colonel al-Sorour said. The others departed quickly to get back to their units and start implementing the new plan of attack.
****

Captain Khasan had left his vehicle momentarily to join one of his sergeants, who was sitting on a sand dune with a pair of binoculars. They weren't one hundred percent sure just yet what kind of unit was heading in their direction. Colonel al-Sorour was attempting to get clarification on this when the lead element appeared on Salmi Road. They appeared to be flying green flags from their antennas.

The sergeant suddenly started waving his arms, trying to get the attention of Captain Khasan and Colonel al-Sorour, who was still in the vehicle on the radio, trying to communicate with someone.

"Colonel, a column is approaching from the west, but it appears they are flying Saudi flags on their antennas. Could this be a coalition relief force coming to aid us?" the sergeant said with relief and excitement in his voice.

Colonel al-Sorour scrunched his eyebrows at the news. The fog of war was again playing havoc on his mind. Had the 51st Artillery misidentified the column approaching?

"Captain Khasan, see what this force is and who their commander is so I may speak with him," Colonel al-Sorour directed his assistant operations officer. Captain Khasan was suddenly feeling pretty good that a coalition relief force had acted so quickly and was coming to their aid.

He walked out onto the road and approached the first vehicle. The tank then stopped when the commander saw him approaching. Suddenly Captain Khasan got a terrible sick feeling in his gut. He was standing in front of a T-72 flying not a Saudi flag but the divisional flag of the al-Medinah Armored Division, which also happened to be green.

Mustering up all the courage he could, he approached the tank.

"Who are you people and where is your commander? Do you have any idea where you are and where you are going? You people are as screwed up as a goat herder. Get your commander on the radio and have him come up here. I will be right back and will speak with him personally," Captain Khasan said with all the bluster he could muster. Before the bewildered tank commander could reply, he turned on his heel and walked back toward the sand dune he'd come from. Once over the dune and out of sight, he took off at a dead run to tell Colonel al-Sorour these weren't Saudis.

"Colonel," he panted as he approached the colonel's vehicle. "We have to get out of here."

"Captain Khasan, what are you talking about? Who is the relief column and where is their commander? I must speak with him and coordinate our efforts," Colonel al-Sorour said with a bit of irritation in his voice.

Khasan was sucking in air as tankers were not exactly known for running distances. Why bother when you drove around in a tank all day? "Sir, that is not a relief column for us. It is a relief column for the Iraqis. It is the lead elements of the al-Medinah Division. We need to get out of here," Captain Khasan said, pointing in the direction of the column.

"Driver!" Colonel al-Sorour said. "Mount up, we are leaving. Now!" He grabbed the hand mike for the radio. "All elements, the lead elements of the 2nd Republican Guard Division is approaching on Salmi Road. Execute the plan as discussed. Over."

The 7th Tank Battalion had already repositioned to new locations that would allow it to engage elements as they approached the interchange between Salmi Road and the Sixth Circular Road. Captain al-Abdulkareem had also repositioned, as an infantry company from the first elements engaged on the Sixth Circular Road had dismounted and moved towards his position. That Iraqi infantry company had no antitank weapons with the range to reach his tanks but knew that his machine guns could reach them, so they were reluctant to move too close and engage. Waiting in a hide position at hull defilade while an enemy force passed in front of your guns required a great deal of patience and discipline. The engagement must be shocking and overwhelming to have its intended effect. If one undisciplined gunner fired before the enemy was in the ambush kill zone, the ambush would not achieve the desired results and could enable the enemy to flank the ambush and destroy the ambusher. Fortunately, the gunners of the 7th and 3rd Company were very disciplined.

On the order of Colonel al-Wazan, the 7th opened fire at one thousand meters. Their fire was accurate and deadly as several vehicles were hit and exploded. As the enemy turned their guns to engage the attacker to the north, 3rd Company opened fire and several more vehicles exploded.

Lieutenant Colonel al-Wazan was not about to let this element get off easy and called for artillery fire from the 51st Artillery Battalion. The 51st could not fire as the forward observers were repositioning and could not see the action. Radio communication was also failing, which only increased the fog of war, allowing the lead elements of the 2nd Republican Guard Division to escape the kill zone.

Slowly, surviving enemy elements began to turn their vehicles back out of the kill zone. Once they exited the area, they attempted to flee the Kuwaiti forces that had caught them by surprise. As they fled south and west, the forward observers of the 51st Artillery engaged them for as long as their fires could be observed and adjusted.

Against a T-72 tank, an exploding 155mm round was ineffective, unable to do serious damage unless it scored a direct hit. But the shrapnel from the exploding rounds caused antennas and any other equipment on the outside of the vehicle to be stripped off or destroyed.

Most T-72s carried extra fuel in drums on the backs of the vehicles that could be dropped when they moved into combat. Those drums were subject to shrapnel, and some caught fire when a piece of hot shrapnel penetrated the fuel drums. Several tanks continued to drive down the road with flames trailing behind as the fuel in the external fuel tanks burned.

****

As the enemy ran out of sight, Colonel al-Sorour reported their success to GHQ, which was under siege in downtown Kuwait City. GHQ was in a state of confusion at this point, with the 1st Hammurabi Armored Division moving on the Sixth Circular Road, the 2nd al-Medinah Armored Division moving east on Salmi Road, and the 3rd Special Forces Brigade assaulting Dasman Palace as well as key government buildings downtown. Adding to the confusion was a lack of communications with the 6th Mechanized Brigade, in addition to calls from the 80th Brigade trapped inside its garrison camp and attempting to fight its way out through insurgents dressed as civilians. The navy under siege at its base was also calling for assistance.

GHQ had steady communications with the 15th Mechanized Brigade south of the city, which had not been engaged yet. Colonel al-Sorour was instructed to move south and join the 15th Mechanized Brigade and prepare for further orders as a combined unit. As the 35th Brigade re-formed and began moving south, the sun had passed its apex for the day. Colonel al-Sorour was sure that the columns of black smoke rising above the city indicated that the sun would set on a Kuwait that was no longer free.

Chapter Ten
Decision Point

1 August 1990
Oval Office
White House
Washington, D.C.

"Excuse me, Mr. President, but Iraqi forces have just crossed the border and are rolling across Kuwait," Mr. Cheney, the Secretary of Defense, said as he briskly walked into the Oval Office.

He quickly added, "The situation is still a bit unclear. But it doesn't appear that Kuwait is putting up much of a fight. Most of their forces were on leave, and they did not bother to recall them within the past twenty-four hours. Only a small element of the 35th Armored Brigade is engaging with"—he checked his notes before continuing—"with thirty-six Chieftain tanks, one rifle company of M113s, an antitank company, and an artillery battery."

Cheney had been the first to get to the President after lunch, as he was on the schedule for a different discussion that had now fallen to the wayside.

"Mr. President, the National Security Advisor is here and wishes to see you," the intercom to the President's secretary announced.

"Send Mr. Scowcroft in," the President instructed.

As Brent Scowcroft came in, everyone exchanged polite greetings. As if on cue, the President's side door opened, and the steward came in with a pot of coffee and the appropriate number of cups and saucers.

How the hell does he always know the right number to bring in? wondered the President.

"Alright, I understand that Saddam has gotten ballsy and is running over Kuwait. Have the Iraqis given a reason for this? And why in the hell didn't we see this coming? What are we paying the intel weenies for anyway if they couldn't post this before it happened?" the President asked no one in particular. The steward then handed everyone a cup and proceeded to fill it to the brim with the President's favorite brand of coffee.

This is going to be a long day, President Bush thought to himself.

Brent Scowcroft took the question but really wished the Secretary of State, Jim Baker, had been present. "Mr. President, Saddam is claiming three things since initiating this attack. First, that Kuwait is stealing Iraqi oil by using slant well drilling techniques on the Rumaila oil field, far exceeding their quota, which is probably true."

"Damn little thieves. Don't they have enough of their own oil without stealing from someone else? We ought to let the Iraqis have them," the President commented harshly.

Mr. Scowcroft continued, "Second, money provided to Iraq in the war with Iran should be considered gifts between Arab brothers and not debts. The Saudis changed their loans to gifts when they signed a nonaggression pact with Saddam a few months ago. Kuwait and the UAE hold most of the debt and are demanding repayment."

"What basis does he have for thinking that?" asked Nicholas Brady, Secretary of the Treasury, who walked into the middle of the conversation.

"It's an Arab culture thing. In the Islamic religion, it's forbidden to charge interest on loans to a fellow Muslim, and Saddam has extended that notion to the money he owes," Baker answered. "The third point is that the oil policies of the Arab League are costing Iraq about one billion dollars a year, which is further hampering his ability to repay his loans and stabilize his economy. He's not happy about what he feels is a deliberate attempt to keep his nation poor. He has repeatedly asked the OPEC members to cut oil production so the price would go up on a per barrel basis, thus allowing them to repay their debts and improve their economy. OPEC is currently unwilling to do that. I might add, that's largely because we have told them to keep monthly oil production high to keep the price of oil down. This is part of our strategy to strangle the Soviet economy."

Mr. Scowcroft quickly added, "In addition, Saddam does not recognize the 1899 agreement between the British and the Ottoman Empire. That agreement is what created Kuwait. During the time of the Ottoman Empire, the Basra province included Kuwait as originally being part of Iraq. The two are only separate countries because the British were horrible at redrawing territorial borders and maps. They seem to have a penchant for creating new countries that will invariably be at war with one another for decades or more to come."

President Bush let out an audible sigh at the news. He then turned to the Secretary of Defense, Mr. Cheney. "What do you think, Dick? What are Saddam's likely intentions?"

"Sir, I think he's going to go all the way. Well beyond just seizing what he believes is a lost province. I mean, why not? The Kuwaitis are rolling over and the Saudis are ineffective. Why not seize all the oil fields of the Middle East and be king? I think he may even go all the way to Oman."

Brent Scowcroft interjected, "On the sixteenth, one of our analysts noted from satellite photos a division moving to the border. At the time, the conclusion was that the Iraqis were repositioning to hit the Iranians again. By the twenty-fourth, we noticed that he had moved five more divisions north of the border but thought it may have been an exercise to scare the Iranians. They had fought considerably in the area during the Iranian-Iraqi conflict."

The President sat sipping his coffee and thinking for a minute. When he got like this, the staff knew to just be quiet.

"Dick, see if you can get Jim Baker on the phone. He's in Siberia, meeting with the Soviet Foreign Minister, Shevardnadze."

After a few minutes, the President's intercom buzzed.

"Mr. President, the Secretary of State is on the line. Go ahead, Mr. Secretary."

"Mr. President, I just heard. I brought it up with my Soviet counterparts. They appear to be just as surprised by it as we are."

"Jim, have you communicated with April Glaspie on this? How long has she been the ambassador over there?"

"Mr. President, I have spoken with her this morning. She's been the ambassador there for six months now. She met with Saddam on 25 July, and they discussed the situation between Iraq and Kuwait. He told her that they were meeting with Mubarak and the Emir and going to work this all out. The Emir was supposedly coming to Baghdad for the past three days. She told Saddam that—and I am quoting directly from her— 'We have no opinion on your Arab-Arab conflicts, such as your dispute with Kuwait. Secretary Baker has directed me to emphasize the instruction, first given to Iraq in the 1960s, that the Kuwait issue is not associated with America.'[4] She told him the party line on this matter, Mr. President, but we never expected it to move this far."

"What are the Saudis saying about all this?" the President asked his Secretary of State.

"Sir, they're shitting bricks right now. I think we need to get some military people over there quick to talk to them and see how they view the situation and what help they may want," Mr. Cheney advised before Jim Baker could respond.

"Slow down, I don't want us running in there and getting involved in a regional dispute between Arab neighbors. This could get us entangled in a regional Arab conflict for God only knows how long," the President countered quickly.

Mr. Cheney, seemingly not having heard the President, added, "Sir, if Saddam doesn't stop in Kuwait, he could roll over the Saudis in no time at all. The Saudis only have three, maybe four brigades scattered all over the country. They've been buying the latest in equipment—M1A1 tanks, F-16 aircraft, and Black Hawk helicopters—but their level of training in the tactics and the use of that equipment is amateur at best. The Saudis have a mentality of saving face and believe if their higher commander sees them training, then they will think they are not trained, so they never go out and train. This is coming from our contacts with the civilian contractors they've hired."

The President turned to the National Security Advisor. "What do you think?"

Scowcroft recommended, "Sir, at this point, I believe we should let State handle this for right now. But we should also find out what the Saudis want and be ready to move it quickly if asked for military support. Send over someone from CENTCOM as that's their AOR."

After pausing for a few thoughtful moments, Bush announced, "Alright, State, you take the lead for now. Get everyone to condemn this action. Let's get it before the UN Security Council, for all the good that will do. When did they cross the border?"

"Mr. President, it's been about two hours. They crossed at 0200 hours their time. Initial reports say they launched airmobile assaults on

---

[4] "April Glaspie," Wikipedia, last modified April 10, 2021, https://en.wikipedia.org/wiki/April_Glaspie

Kuwait City as their armor units rolled across the border," Mr. Cheney explained.

"Alright, let's get the staff in here at 1800 hours tonight and look at the situation then. That will give us a better picture of what's going on and how far he's going to take this," the President directed.
****

At 1800 hours in the White House Situation Room, the meeting was called to order when the President walked in.

"Let's get started. I have a dinner engagement tonight and Barbara gets pissed if I'm late," the President said as he nodded to the briefing officer. Lieutenant Colonel Bob Atwell was well known to the President as he had been the White House Briefing Officer for the past year. Bob had been a warrant officer helicopter pilot in Vietnam and received a commission in 1971. He had served in aviation units in his younger years but had been sucked into the Pentagon in the late 1970s, serving in various aviation development projects that had eventually gotten him noticed by the White House Chief of Staff, John Sununu.

Sununu had tagged him to be the White House Situation Room Briefing Officer, a role Bob fit right into. Bob's longtime friend, Lieutenant Dan Cory, referred to Bob as "Slicky Boy" because of his smooth-talking ways with the brass and the ladies. Bob was a bachelor at heart.

"Good evening, sir. First slide, please." The first slide was a map of Kuwait, Iraq, and northern Saudi Arabia. "Sir, in the past twenty-four hours, the Iraqi Army has moved two corps, consisting of eight Republican Guard divisions along with several light and motorized divisions, south. On the eastern front, one corps, the 1st Republican Guard Corps, crossed into Kuwait at just after midnight on 2 August, with an airmobile assault seizing the international airport in Kuwait City and the Dasman Palace, which is the residence of the Emir. It's our understanding but not confirmed that the royal family got out and has fled to Saudi Arabia, with the exception of the Emir's younger brother, Fahad Al-Sabah, who we believe may have been killed in the initial attack.

"The 1st Republican Guard Corps reached the outskirts of the city approximately three hours ago and is moving through the city and towards the Saudi border. It is expected they will stop at the border." Colonel Atwell stopped to let what he had just said sink in and see if there were questions.

As there were none, he continued, "In the west, and outside of Kuwait, the 2nd Republican Guard Corps, consisting of one motorized infantry division and one mechanized division, has repositioned in the vicinity of Wadi Al-Batin, but outside the neutral zone." A red laser dot appeared on the map, indicating the triborder area where the wadi formed the border for the three.

"Sir," said the Chairman of the Joint Chiefs, General Colin Powell, "I need not remind you that, sixty miles south of Hafar Al-Batin, at the head of this wadi, is King Khalid Military City, the only Saudi military facility in this portion of the country aside from border outposts manned by the border police. Those Saudi forces, a mechanized brigade, have been on alert status, but there's no indication of activity above normal daily duties. It doesn't appear that they're terribly worried about the situation."

"Colin, what other military complexes do they have around the country?" asked the President.

"Sir, King Faisal Military Cantonment is in the southwest near Yemen; King Abdulaziz Military City is in Tabuk near Jordan, and there are some facilities scattered around Dhahran, such as the King Faiud Military Medical Complex."

The President just nodded his head and Powell indicated to Lieutenant Colonel Atwell to move along with the briefing.

"Next slide," Lieutenant Colonel Atwell called. This image displayed arrows indicating the direction of advance for the Iraqi forces. It mimicked what he had just said.

"Sir, Kuwaiti resistance was minimal. The Kuwaiti Army takes their annual leave at this time of year, and it appears that a recall order was not issued. Therefore, most of their frontline equipment was sitting in their bases and was seized by the Iraqi forces. The Kuwaitis had three armored brigades, one mechanized brigade, and one understrength artillery brigade for a total force of sixteen thousand soldiers. The air force has eighty aircraft and forty helicopters. It appears that the air force did get some aircraft off the ground before they were destroyed and offered token resistance."

"Where is the Kuwaiti Army now?" the President asked.

"Sir, those that have not been captured are in whatever car or truck they can find and attempting to go south to Saudi Arabia along with the royal family," Colonel Atwell said. "They're offering no organized defense or resistance."

Looking at the assembled members present, the President said, "So, gentlemen, what I just heard is that Saddam has pretty much taken Kuwait and there's nothing the Kuwaitis can do about it. Is that about it?"

Jim Baker answered for the group. "That's the picture, Mr. President. At this point, the only thing that can be done for Kuwait is a diplomatic approach starting with the UN. A proposed resolution has been drafted and will be presented in the morning to the Security Council—Resolution 660, condemning Iraq for this action and calling for their immediate withdrawal. I recommend that we think about some military action."

"I second that, Mr. President," the Vice President said. "This cannot be allowed to stand."

"If I may, Mr. President," General Powell requested, "who do we give military support to? Kuwait has fallen and has no military to support. We have no authority to send in US forces as nothing has been decided by the Security Council yet, and we're really not in a position to be tied down in a Middle East situation that doesn't have a defined outcome. Especially as the situation in Eastern Europe is very dynamic and fluid at this time, with rebellion against the Soviet Union growing. Mr. President, I recommend we do not commit any military forces at this time."

John Sununu sat there taking this all in. He enjoyed meeting with the President at the end of the day to give his thoughts and opinions outside the group in the privacy of the Oval Office over a bourbon on the rocks. *Colin has got to be the biggest anti-force general I have ever met. If we ever get in a fight, it isn't because he pushed us into it*, Sununu thought privately. *Jesus, let's at least explore some options, Colin.*

"Mr. President, before we do anything, I think we should call in the congressional leadership and give them a rundown. If we do decide to introduce a military force, we're going to need congressional approval," Sununu said.

84

"Good point, John," the President said. "Call the Hill and see if we can get the Speaker of the House and the House and Senate leaders over here tomorrow after our meeting so we can give them a rundown of the events and our options."

"Yes, Mr. President," Sununu replied as he scribbled something down on his notepad.

The President looked at his watch. "Gentlemen, good brief. As it appears the Iraqis have Kuwait for the night, let's pick this up first thing in the morning, when we have more information on what they're up to and what the Saudis are thinking. I would like to get April's opinion on what Saddam is planning. Until tomorrow, good night, gentlemen."

****

The next morning, the President headed down to the Situation Room as the first order of business.

"Good morning, gentlemen," he said as he entered.

Everyone was already standing, knowing he was an incredibly punctual individual. He was also a polite individual.

"Please, take your seats and let's get started."

Colonel Atwell had already been standing at the podium. The President nodded again in approval and took a sip of his coffee.

"Good morning, sir. First slide, please."

On the large screen to the right of Colonel Atwell appeared a map of the area with red symbols depicting the Iraqi forces. "Sir, the Iraqi forces are under the command of two Republican Guard Corps headquarters. These two Corps headquarters are the Allah Akbar Republican Guard Operations Command or 1st Republican Guard Corps and the Fat'h al-Mubayyin Republican Guard Operations Command or 2nd Republican Guard Corps. The total Iraqi force consists of thirty infantry divisions, eight armored divisions, six mechanized divisions, one motorized division, and one Special Forces division."

A few whistles could be heard from some of the advisors in the room. Clearly, a lot of soldiers and equipment were involved in this invasion.

"The attack on Kuwait was conducted by the 1st Republican Guard Corps with two Republican Guard armored divisions, two Republican Guard mechanized divisions, one Republican Guard infantry division

85

and two army infantry divisions. Commando raids were conducted by the 8th Special Forces Division using a heliborne assault on the Royal Palace and port area as well as the airport."

Colonel Atwell paused for a moment to allow the President to ask a question. When he didn't, Atwell continued. "Sir, on this blown-up image of Kuwait, you can see the deployment of Iraqi forces as of six hours ago. The 1st Republican Guard Corps, with the 1st Hammurabi Division, the 6th Nebuchadnezzar Division, and the 3rd Tawakalna Division, made the main attack across Kuwait, preceded by a heliborne assault on the city airport by elements of the 8th As Saiqa Division. The 2nd al-Medinah Division, the 35th Mechanized Division, and the 3rd Infantry Division made a supporting attack on the left flank along with the 4th Infantry Division on the right flank. The 1st Republican Guard Corps was followed by the IX Corps with the 10th, 52nd and 17th Armored Divisions. As of right now, the 45th, 49th and 1st Infantry Divisions have moved into the city, airport, refinery, and outskirts to seal off the city and further trap any military or political figures inside the country. Currently, those divisions that made the main attack are refueling and refitting just south of the city. For the moment, they appear to be taking defensive positions. Next slide, please." The next slide showed the western border of Kuwait and Iraq. Again, it was covered in red symbols depicting the Iraqi forces.

"Sir," he continued, "this slide shows the location and disposition of the 2nd Republican Guard Corps with the 7th Adnan Motorized Division and the 5th Baghdad Mechanized Division. As you can see, they've taken a defensive posture along Wadi Al-Batin, which terminates at King Khalid Military City in Saudi Arabia. North of the 2nd Republican Guard Corps, Saddam has positioned the IV Corps with the 16th, 20th, 21st, 30th, 34th, and 36th Infantry Divisions as well as the 1st

IRAQI FORCES
3 AUGUST

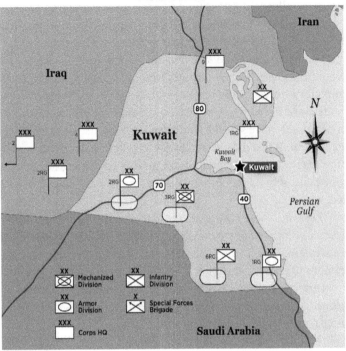

Mechanized Division and 6th Armored Division. The 2nd Army Corps is in the western desert and has been there for some time, we believe. The 7th Army Corps is in the north, where it normally is, facing Iran and the Kurds, as is the 3rd Army Corps in the area east of Baghdad. It should be noted that the 2nd, 3rd, 4th and 9th Army Corps have no Republican Guard forces. These are regular army units, which are less trained and less equipped than their Republican Guard counterparts."

Colonel Atwell saw a question forming on the President's face, so he paused. "Questions, sir?"

"Actually, yes, Colonel. What's the difference between the Republican Guard Corps and the Army Corps?" the President asked.

Before Colonel Atwell could answer, a back-row-seated general seeking face time stood up. "Sir, if I may answer that—General Andrews, sir." Andrews was a black officer that had commanded an assault helicopter company in Vietnam as his only combat experience. He was not noted for his exceptional ability, but many felt he had risen out of the military's desires for political correctness and equality.

The SecDef's eyes looked like they were boring holes into Andrews. He was here to answer questions when asked, not jump in.

Before anyone could stop him, he blurted out, "Sir, we believe the Republican Guard Corps are better trained and equipped than the Army Corps for a very specific reason. You see, these units report directly to Saddam and not to the Army Chief of Staff. We believe this was done on purpose to make sure the army didn't one day decide to launch a coup against him. If that did occur, then the Republican Guard units would be more than capable of putting it down. This competing military branch does cause some friction between the commands," General Andrews said.

Why can't these people use the first person singular and stake their reputations instead of the collective we? the President thought privately. It always irked him when people wouldn't put their name to their own opinions or observations.

Turning back to Colonel Atwell, the President directed, "Please proceed, Colonel." Andrews glanced over at the SecDef and melted into his chair from the look he received.

"Yes, sir. Next slide, please." Pausing just long enough for the President to read the slide, he explained, "Sir, this slide shows you the general organization of each of their divisions. They follow the Soviet system of task organization and tactics. These are the same systems and organizations that our ground forces train against at the National Training Center at Fort Irwin, in California, and the Joint Readiness Training Center at Fort Chaffee, in Arkansas. Of particular note is the heavy and mobile air-defense array covering their ground forces. In addition to the SA-7 shoulder-fired anti-aircraft missile, they have good mobile coverage with ZSU-23-4s and SA-6, SA-9, and SA-8 anti-air missiles."

Colonel Atwell paused for just a moment before adding, "Sir, there's something else of note that should be brought up. There are several CIA reports and satellite images to verify this. But it appears that starting in January, the Soviets began providing the Iraqi Army with a wide variety of new equipment. For example, the Republican Guard units were largely the ones equipped with modern frontline equipment. The regular army tank units were operating Chinese knock-off versions of the T-62 and T-55 tanks. The Soviets appeared to have swapped out large numbers of these tanks with newer T-72s. They also made sure that all of the Republican Guard units were using the newest Soviet tanks, infantry fighting vehicles, and armored personnel carriers. More worrisome, however, is the number of anti-aircraft track and wheeled vehicles they provided them with. These units will be able to stay on the move with the armored forces, providing them with exceptional air-defense abilities."

Atwell saw some questions forming on many of the people's faces and quickly held a hand up to forestall them. "Sorry, if you'll allow me to finish explaining, I think this may answer some of your questions. Once my portion of the brief is complete, we'll have plenty of time to take your questions." He reached down and grabbed several large folders and held them up, adding, "I also brought all the source documents with me so you can read the intelligence for yourself."

The President smiled and then laughed. "Very good, Colonel. I like it when my briefer knows to anticipate what kind of questions we're likely to have and has that information ready to go. Please, continue. This is very enlightening."

Atwell smiled at the compliment and then proceeded to give them the rest of the information. "Sir, according to three separate CIA sources in Iraq, the Soviets appeared to have struck up some sort of lend-lease or modernization program with the Iraqis. They're doing a one-for-one swap of all their older equipment for new Soviet equipment. More troublesome, though, are some of the air-defense systems they've helped the Iraqis upgrade over the last eight months. The Iraqis currently have S-200 systems. They're a reasonably decent air-defense system. But they left certain gaps in their air defense that became very apparent during the Iraq-Iran war. To solve this gap and beef up their air defense, the Soviets appear to have lent them two brigades' worth of S-300 systems. Those have the NATO code name SA-10 Grumble. This represents a remarkably potent air-defense system in the Middle East. As of yesterday's satellite overflight of Kuwait, we've seen them move one battalion of SA-10s to the Ali al-Salem Air Base. But our satellite pass also showed upwards of three more battalions moving into Kuwait. This indicates to us that they're potentially going to cross the border into Saudi, or at the very least, make Kuwait a very well defended place from the air.

"The SA-10s have the ability to engage enemy aircraft as far away as one hundred kilometers with a ceiling altitude as high as twenty kilometers, meaning they can engage not just low-flying aircraft but also high-altitude bombers and even some of our U-2s. When you couple this system with their SA-2 and SA-3 batteries, they're turning Kuwait into quite the fortress. Next slide, please."

The next slide showed multiple overlapping circles of different colors, indicating the coverage area and density of air-defense weapon systems.

He's pretty well covered his entire ground forces with dense ADA coverage, the President thought. Before the colonel could say anything further, the President asked, "What about aircraft? How is their air force faring in that department? Did the Soviets beef that up as well?"

Colonel Atwell nodded at the question and then reached for one of the folders he had with him. He took a moment to find the exact one that had the information the President asked for.

"Sir, we're a little less confident in this area than we are in the army and ADA. The Agency's sources are better placed in those groups. What little we know right now is that the Iraqis have a decent air force that has years of combat experience fighting Iran. There are rumors the Soviets did lend them additional fighters and interceptors, which would be consistent with what they've been providing the ground forces, but we don't have anything concrete to report. Sir, that concludes my portion of the briefing on the military situation in Kuwait," Lieutenant Colonel Atwell said, then waited just a moment for questions.

With no immediate questions, Atwell made his way to a row of chairs along the back wall of the room, where he'd wait silently in case someone had any additional questions they wanted him to address.

The President then took charge. "Thank you, Colonel. That was a highly informative brief. So, gentlemen, what's your assessment? It appears Saddam has moved a sizable force into Kuwait to take on just two or three brigades. It also appears the Soviets aren't done trying to make life hard on the West with this apparent lend-lease program with the Iraqis. I'd like the Agency and the DIA to spend a bit more time looking into this as well. We have been caught flat-footed on this operation. We had indications back on the sixteenth and should have been more proactive in assessing the situation."

General Colin Powell was the first to speak up. "Sir, Saddam has moved a sizable force into Kuwait. But considering that this is his first use of military force since the Iran war, he's probably a bit gun-shy about getting into a fight he cannot win. He needs a win right now within the Arab world. Also, an overwhelming use of combat power precludes getting into a slugfest. From all reports, he appears to be acting with restraint in the treatment of the civilian populace."

Brent Scowcroft appeared to challenge that assessment, asking, "Really? How do you account for the corps on the west side of Kuwait heading into Wadi Al-Batin?"

"Sir, I think that's a smart move on his part. He may be thinking that the Saudis will come to the aid of Kuwait. If they did, where would they come from? They'd come from King Khalid Military City, as it's the only thing in the northeastern part of the country. The 2nd Saudi National Guard is certainly not going to go to the rescue of Kuwait—they're scattered across the country border in little outposts."

Looking at his watch, the President stood, stretched his back and addressed them. "This was a good update. I think we've gone over a lot of information and given ourselves a lot to think about. Later this morning, the UN Security Council is going to meet"—the President looked to his SecState, who simply stared back—"and we'll wait to see what they intend to do. I feel confident that they will vote for the Iraqis to withdraw back to Iraq, which Saddam will begrudgingly do. He can't be stupid enough to think the world is going to allow him to keep Kuwait. Now if you'll excuse me, gentlemen, I have another meeting with the Education Secretary, so I have to go. Keep up the good work, and we'll talk again once we know what the UN decides and how the Iraqis respond."

Chapter Eleven
Iraqi Naval Success

3 August 1990
Dasman Palace
Kuwait City, Kuwait

Rear Admiral Gha'ib Hassan had requested an audience with Saddam earlier in the day. He had been the last commander informed of this operation and had only been notified thirty-six hours before it kicked off.

He had not been involved in any of the earlier planning sessions. Once he had been informed of what was expected from the navy, he had been unsure he could pull it off. As he waited, he reviewed his notes on what his orders had been as he wanted to be sure he covered each point with Saddam.

The orders were to liberate Faylaka Island; assume command of Kuwait's naval bases; prevent any ships from leaving or entering Kuwait's ports; not interfere with Iranian shipping or American Navy ships moving out of the Arabian Gulf; and relocate our surface-to-surface radar to more favorable terrain. We have accomplished each of those acts, he thought proudly to himself.

The meeting was not being held in Baghdad but in the Emir's palace in downtown Kuwait City, which had only been captured that day. Some gunshots could still be heard in the distance. The door to the office Saddam had taken possession of opened and Saddam himself stepped out. When he saw the admiral, he motioned for him to enter and have a seat in an overstuffed chair. Saddam took the adjacent chair and a servant poured them tea. Admiral Gha'ib was not surprised to see Sultan Hashim Ahmed al-Tai, the Defense Minister, sitting there as well.

Once the tea was poured, Saddam waved the servant away and looked to the admiral. His face showed no emotion. "Tell me, Admiral, how successful was the navy?" he asked.

"Sir, you asked me to accomplish much with little notice. I would like to address each point with you individually if I may, and you can judge how the navy did," said the admiral.

"Please continue," Saddam said, still with a poker face.

"You told me to secure Faylaka Island. We placed a battalion of naval infantry ashore after engaging the island for six hours with fire from our Osa-class patrol boats. We secured the entire island in under eight hours," the admiral said.

Saddam's only reply was a nod indicating to continue. "Our next mission was to assume responsibility of Kuwait's sole naval base, Mohammed Al-Ahmad Kuwait Naval Base, from the Republican Guard. We did not assume the responsibility of Kuwait's naval bases from the Republican Guard," the admiral said with a hint of dejection in his voice.

Saddam raised his eyebrows at this failure, but the admiral quickly added, "We seized and secured the naval bases and waited for the Republican Guard to join us," the admiral countered with a smile.

Saddam chuckled at that. "Very good, Admiral. Continue."

"We have prevented ships from entering or leaving Kuwaiti ports. We have not interfered with any Iranian-flagged ships and have not seen any American ships in the area. We are currently relocating our surface-to-surface tracking radar to a more suitable position on the Kuwaiti coast. Our Russian advisors are assisting us in this effort as well," the admiral added.

"The Russian advisors have not been involved in any of the fighting, have they?" Saddam inquired, a bit of concern in his voice.

"There were two Russian advisors on our patrol boats that seized the southern naval base. They were instructing us on the use of the SSN02A/B Styx surface-to-surface missiles, but no one was hurt. For security reasons, I did not inform them of our planned actions until we were underway," the admiral further explained. This made Saddam a lot calmer.

Saddam then leaned forward as he stared into his eyes. "So tell me, Admiral. How did you come to be so successful? You are the smallest of our forces, and yet you accomplished much. Do tell me."

"Gladly, sir," the admiral stated. He was enjoying favorable face time with Saddam. Not something you always got. "I am a student of history. I have spent much time studying both the American and Japanese naval actions in the battle of Guadalcanal. In that case, neither side had enough warships at the start of the battle. Yet both sides found ingenious ways to use what they had. The Japanese, for instance, knew they could not rush unarmed transports past the American warships, so

93

they loaded up their destroyers with troops and munitions and slipped past the Americans. Likewise, the Americans didn't have enough warships to be everywhere at once to stop the Japanese. So they made heavy use of PT boats. They are similar to the missile boats we use today. They carried four torpedo tubes. They were incredibly fast, maneuverable, and quiet. The American President John Kennedy even commanded one."

Saddam nodded his head, putting his glass of tea down. Admiral Hassan saw he had his full attention. "When you gave me the order to seize my objectives, I looked at the forces I had and the timeline I had to complete my objectives. Then I came up with a plan I felt would exceed your expectations. I broke my fleet down into two task forces. Task Force One was the main effort with our two Osa-class boats and two *Lupo*-class frigates, along with three of the Grisha-class corvettes our Russian friends lent us. Like the Japanese during World War II, we used these ships to ferry most of our naval infantry aboard."

Saddam smiled widely at the mention of how Hassan had copied the Japanese tactic.

"When our task force arrived at al-Qualayah, we captured the naval headquarters in under an hour. When they entered the harbor at first light, they moved rapidly to get our naval infantry to shore so they could rapidly capture the base and the ships tied up at the piers. We apparently caught the base commander by surprise. He initially thought this was some naval exercise that he had not been informed about. When he marched off to the hastily put-together prisoner-of-war camp, he realized it was not a training exercise."

This brought a chuckle from Saddam.

On a roll at this point, Hassan continued, "Our second element was Task Force Two. I had a battalion of naval infantry under the command of Lieutenant Colonel Said Toma. They captured the nearby islands with almost no resistance. Two of our *Lupo*-class frigates shepherded the two landing craft with the marines on board. Once they'd delivered their load of marines, they came back to the frigates and took the remaining marines ashore. Our speed and ability to get so many marines ashore to both targets at the same time completely caught the Kuwaiti defenders by surprise."

Admiral Hassan sat back and waited for Saddam's decision on how his force had done.

"What were your casualties?" Saddam asked, which surprised Hassan as Saddam had never worried about casualties in the past, just results.

"We had two sailors killed in taking the naval headquarters."

"And what of the Kuwait Navy?"

"Sir, we took two hundred and seventy-one prisoners and captured three large missile boats, three light missile boats, three supply and provision boats, and eight small utility vessels. And we seized the Kuwait radio station on Faylaka Island," the admiral proclaimed with pride.

Saddam sat for a minute, thinking. Finally he said, "You have done well, Admiral. My compliments to your men. But tell me, are the Kuwaiti vessels in good order and can your people operate them properly?"

"Yes, sir, they are in very good order. As a matter of fact, they are practically brand-new. The three large missile boats are Lussen FPB-57s that were commissioned in 1983. They are equipped with four Exocet missiles, one 76/62 compact gun, one double-barrel 40mm gun and minelaying capability. Their top speed runs at thirty-six knots."

"And the smaller missile boats?" Saddam asked next.

"They are also very new. They are Lussen TNC-45 missile boats. These were commissioned in 1984. They have a top speed of forty-one knots and are equipped with one 76/62 compact gun, one 40mm double-barrel gun, and eight surface-to-surface missiles," the admiral explained.

"Did you have to destroy any vessels during the capture of the base?"

"A few smaller vessels, yes, but we attempted to capture as many as we could," the admiral quickly explained.

"How soon could you put to sea again with these new vessels if you had to?" Saddam inquired.

What is he not telling me now? Hassan wondered.

"They are ready to put to sea now. Some of the Kuwaiti crews recognize the need for Arab unity and have pledged allegiance to us. It seems not everyone is in love with the Emir or his policies towards his people."

Saddam smiled at the news. He then leaned forward as if he was going to tell Hassan a very important secret. "This is good news, Admiral. I'm proud of what you have done. But now I have a new mission for you. A much larger and grander mission. I need you to move down the Arabian Gulf with your flotilla to include the new ships you've captured. You are to support the marine brigade of the 8th Special Forces Division. You will coordinate with them to seize the loading platform in Al-Jubail and the loading dock in Ras Tanura and bottle up the Saudi naval base at Al-Jubail. Can you accomplish that with the Kuwaiti vessels you seized and your current flotilla of ships?" Saddam asked.

Hassan wasn't sure if Saddam wanted a real answer or just to be told yes. He went with the safe answer, the one that would keep him alive, at least for a little while longer. "Yes, sir, we can do that."

"Good. Your basic orders have not changed. Do not permit any vessels to enter or depart the Saudi ports."

The admiral received this bit of news as if a wet washcloth had slapped his face. He also knew enough not to ask too many questions or question the wisdom of Saddam.

Saddam then continued his explanation. "You will avoid American naval vessels unless fired upon first. Make sure your captains know they are not to instigate a confrontation with the Yankees. You are, however, to direct any merchant ships you encounter to leave the Arabian Gulf for the time being until a safe travel route and a proper escort can be arranged.

"Admiral, I want to reiterate this to you again. We do not want to provoke the Americans or the Iranians. We have asked the Americans to withdraw their naval vessels from the Arabian Gulf, and it appears they have, with the exception of their one command ship currently tied up in Bahrain. You need to leave that ship alone for the moment. If you encounter any Saudi naval forces, request their immediate surrender and attempt to board and seize their ship. If they will not comply, then sink them. Any questions?"

Admiral Hassan had plenty of questions. Right now, he was stunned that they were not just going to war with Kuwait but also apparently going to try and seize Saudi Arabia while they were at it.

Not wanting to question their leader, and enjoying the praise he'd received thus far, Hassan asked the only question he knew it was safe to ask. "When do you wish this next phase of our operations to start, sir?"

Saddam smiled as he placed a hand on Hassan's shoulder. "As soon as you can. As a matter of fact, tomorrow morning will be fine. Take the evening to get your men and captured ships prepared. Our elite Republican Guard units will cross into Saudi Arabia early tomorrow morning. I suggest once you move, you move quickly to take the Saudi Navy by surprise, like you did the Kuwaitis. That may save more of your men's lives.

"Oh, one more important piece of information. The marine brigade will depart at 2400 hours tonight and will conduct a heliborne assault at the King Fahd Industrial Port Terminal in Al-Jubail. You are to isolate it from any naval interference that could intercede and stop the marines from capturing the site. The same for the terminal docks at Ras Tanura to the south. As to the naval base at Al-Jubail, I'll leave that up to you to handle as you see fit, but no ships must leave. Is that understood?" Saddam asked, standing to indicate that the meeting was over.

"Yes, sir, it'll be done," was all Hassan said as Saddam left the room and headed to his next meeting.

Wow, I can't believe this is really happening. We're not just invading Kuwait, we're now invading Saudi Arabia as well. This is surely going to get the Americans involved. I'm going to need to ask my Russian advisors how they think we should handle the American Navy if it comes down to it. I'm sure they've war-gamed that out a lot more than we have.

Chapter Twelve
Security Council Failure

3 August 1990
Oval Office
White House
Washington, D.C.

"Mr. President, Mr. Baker is here to see you," the intercom on the President's desk announced. The President had just started his first meeting of the day at 8:00 a.m.

"Send him in, please." The President had been in a discussion with the Secretary of Education and members of the National Teachers Union, who were attempting to impress on the President how they were all for the children and the quality of the children's education. He knew better. This gave him an opportunity to politely excuse them from the office and end the meeting early.

"You will have to excuse me for cutting our meeting a bit short. We have a situation in the Middle East that I am sure you are all aware of, and Mr. Baker is our point man on this right now," the President said as he stood. Then the door opened for Mr. Baker.

Mr. Baker paused long enough for the room to clear before he entered and closed the door behind him.

Pointing to the couch, the President asked, "How was your meeting with the Soviet Foreign Minister?"

"It went well. He appeared not to be happy that Saddam invaded Kuwait. But at the same time, he didn't appear to be all that surprised either. Almost like he knew something like this might have been in the works."

"Do you think the Soviets will attempt to intervene directly or indirectly?"

"That's a tough question, sir. It's obvious they're facing a mountain of problems at home. If there was a time when they might lash out, this would be it. But as to your question about indirectly, I think they already have. The other day during the briefing, Lieutenant Colonel Atwell brought up some of the military support the Soviets had provided them during the first part of the year. I had some of our own folks look into it.

It checked out. It appears the Soviets transferred some pretty large quantities of equipment to the Iraqis in some sort of lend-lease-style program. Our analysts at the time didn't flag it right away because it looked like the Soviets had done this more for economic reasons than to prepare the Iraqis for war. They were essentially shifting the costs and maintenance of divisions' worth of equipment to the Iraqis, thus relieving their own budgets from having to cover them. I will say this—the conflict is achieving one aim both countries have strived for," Mr. Baker explained.

Bush lifted an eyebrow at that. "Huh... let me guess. The price of oil."

Baker smiled coyly. "Exactly. The lifeline for both nations."

"OK. Then, changing subjects, how did it go at the Security Council last night? I assume Saddam received his eviction notice?" the President asked.

Baker shook his head dismissively. "Unfortunately, no, sir, he did not. The resolution failed."

"What! Let me guess. The Soviets vetoed it?" the President asked, taking a seat with a look of disbelief on his face.

"Sir, it's a bit more complicated than just the Soviets throwing cold water on the idea. It appears the Iraqi ambassador has made a compelling case that Kuwait was always a province of Iraq and the 1899 agreement that was signed with the breakup of the Ottoman Empire, created the separate state of Kuwait. They didn't even bring up their other issues with Kuwait, such as Kuwait stealing oil from the Rumaila oil field or the overproduction by Kuwait," Mr. Baker explained.

"How did the vote go?" the President asked, leaning forward in his chair.

"Sir, of the five permanent members, Britain voted with us, France, China, and Russia against the resolution. Cuba and Romania followed the Russians' lead. The African bloc of Ivory Coast, Zaire, and Ethiopia voted against, as they felt there has been enough fighting in the region and just want this to end quietly, even if that meant the Iraqis take the country. Malaysia has its own oil and sees this as a way for oil prices to increase, which is what Saddam and the Russians want. Colombia and Finland voted with us. Yemen abstained, stating the Arab League should handle the matter and not Western powers," Mr. Baker concluded.

"OK, I understand some of the votes going against us. But why the hell did the French not back us?" the President asked angrily. He was a bit surprised they would side with the Russians on this matter.

"Sir, they feel that if Saddam ensures the free flow of oil out of the Gulf, they don't care who holds the cards. They also have some very lucrative contracts with him and would like to still be paid. I need to note, Saddam's ambassador did a good job of making the rounds and giving assurances to the members that oil would not be disrupted—"

"And people bought that bullshit?" the President said in disgust.

Before Baker could reply, they were interrupted by a voice over the intercom. "Mr. President, Mrs. Thatcher is on line one and would like to speak with you. She said it's most urgent."

"Excuse me, Jim. Put her through." The President got up and went to his desk so he could pick up the phone.

"Margaret, how are you?... Yes, Jim Baker has just come in and briefed me.... Well, at this point we have to discuss this with the Saudi government as well as the Emir in exile in Riyadh and we haven't done that yet.... I suppose I'll speak to the King right after this call." While Margaret was talking, the President motioned to Jim to get a call through to the King of Saudi Arabia, pronto.

Jim nodded and left the room to set the call up.

"Margaret, our standing in the Middle East is delicate at best, with our position on Israel doing more harm than good to our cause. I would think that Great Britain would be better at pulling willing nations together for a response. After all, it was Great Britain that redrew the boundary in 1922 that has everyone's shorts in a knot.... No offense meant by that.... Yes, I suppose you would be viewed as attempting to reestablish colonial rule. We both know that's not true.... Look, let me talk to the King and I'll get back to you later today. Would that be acceptable?... Good.... Yes, I'll tell Barbara you called. Good day."

The President placed the phone in its cradle. He then made his way over to the couch to take a seat while he waited for Jim to walk back in. *This has turned into quite the mess...*

Jim Baker walked back into the Oval Office, announcing, "Mr. President, they're putting the call through now. Do you want to call a meeting for later today after the call?" he asked.

"I suppose we should. Have my secretary clear the calendar for later this afternoon and let's bring everyone in and see what we're going to do. I'll talk to the King and see what he wants and what his opinion is of this thing. Man, what the hell is Saddam thinking? Have you talked to Glaspie? Get her on the phone and see what she thinks as well. We'll talk some more later."

The intercom suddenly interrupted their conversation again. "Mr. President, Prince Saud al-Faisal is on line one."

As the President reached for the phone, Jim left to set things in motion for the afternoon meeting.

****

Situation Room

It was midafternoon when the President entered the White House Situation Room for an emergency meeting with his national security team. The group included Mr. Cheney, Mr. Baker, Mr. Scowcroft, Mr. Sununu, Mr. Watkins, and Mr. William Webster, Director CIA. Those in uniform were General Powell, Admiral Kelso, General Gray, USMC, General Dugan, USAF, and General Vuono, USA. Noticeably absent was the Vice President, Mr. Quayle, who was on the West Coast, attending a conference for the President. This was only the second time General Dugan had attended a meeting in the Situation Room, as he had only recently been appointed to the position of Chief of Staff for the Air Force.

"Alright, let's get started," the President said as Lieutenant Colonel Atwell called for the first slide. It showed the Kuwait-Saudi border with their respective forces arrayed.

Colonel Atwell cleared his throat as he began the brief. "Sir, as you can see on this slide, in the last twenty-four hours the 1st Republican Guard Corps has assumed positions along the southern Kuwait border and appears to be consolidating their positions with defensive preparations. The 2nd Republican Guard Corps, located to the west in Wadi Al-Batin, is doing the same. The 9th Corps has moved into the northern part of Kuwait and is along the Mutla Ridge. 2nd Army Corps has remained well to the southwestern part of Iraq, where it's been for a couple of weeks, and appears to be conducting a corps-level training exercise.

"Early communications intercepts of their radio traffic indicate a defensive posture. We have seen no major resupply of ammunition or petroleum products that would indicate preparations for a further attack. Some SA-2 and apparently some new S-300 missile systems the Soviets lent them have been moved to the vicinity of the Kuwait airport. This indicates to our analysts that they're looking to establish a permanent air-defense umbrella over Kuwait, not looking to invade Saudi Arabia. Furthermore, the Iraqi Air Force hasn't had any activity to indicate an offensive role such as the loading of offensive ordnance or a major repositioning of their ground-attack aircraft to Ali al-Salem Military Air Base. Sir, that concludes my update for the last sixteen hours," Colonel Atwell said before waiting for questions.

Turning to Mr. Webster, the President asked, "Bill, do you have anything to add to this?"

"No, Mr. President. We've seen no moves that would indicate a further attack. Saddam hasn't touched his chemical weapon depots, and his long-range Scud missiles are still in the depots and have not been moved. There are some reports of civil unrest in Kuwait City, but nothing of any magnitude at this point. There are, however, semitrailers at the Central Bank of Kuwait, and we estimate about one billion dollars in Kuwaiti currency is being removed."

Turning to Sununu, the President said, "Let's get Brady informed of this and see what we can do to devalue the Kuwait dinar. That should put a damper on Saddam's money grab."

"I'll talk to him right after this meeting," Sununu said, making a note.

"What do you think the Iranians are going to do about this situation?" the President asked. Everyone waited for the Secretary of State to answer, but Mr. Scowcroft took the question instead.

"Sir, I think the Iranians will sit on the sidelines and watch. As Kuwait was the bank for Saddam in his war against the Iranians, I don't think they will shed a tear for Kuwait. Kuwait is mostly Sunni Muslim, and as you know, the Iranians are Shiite, so there's no love lost there. The Iranians aren't coming to anyone's aid on this one," Mr. Scowcroft said.

The President remained silent and thought for a minute. Finally, he spoke. "Gentlemen, I spoke with Mrs. Thatcher and Prince Saud al-Faisal today. Mrs. Thatcher wants to know what we're going to do about this. She feels strongly that a response must be made, even though the UN Security Council voted against Resolution 660. She's talking an economic as well as military response to get Saddam out of Kuwait. Prince Faisal is shitting bricks over the possibility of Iraqi tanks rolling across the Kuwaiti border to gobble up his country next."

"The Saudi government placed their armed forces on alert today but haven't moved from their peacetime positions as they fear it will give Saddam an excuse to attack them. They signed a nonaggression treaty with Saddam and feel that he would see any movement of their forces as a threat," the President explained.

He looked at General Powell. "Colin, what does it mean when you put your forces on alert but don't move them?" the President asked, hoping for a better understanding of the Saudi response.

"Sir, they're probably uploading fuel and ammo, but aside from that, nothing," Powell answered, looking at the other members of the Joint Chiefs for assurance.

"Mr. President," Baker said, getting everyone's attention, "I spoke with Ambassador Glaspie before coming in here. She had a meeting with Saddam earlier today. He expressed his desire that we not take any hostile action against them. Saddam stated to her that this is an Arab-Arab dispute that should be solved by the Arab world and not a case for Western intervention. He also said that he'll keep the Persian Gulf open to commercial traffic but asks that we remove our naval forces from the area so that total neutrality of the region can be maintained and another *Stark* incident can be avoided.[5]

"We currently have four frigates in the Persian Gulf besides the flagship USS *LaSalle* at Bahrain. The Naval Support Activity on Bahrain has eight hundred naval personnel responsible for serving the ships and monitoring and inspecting merchant vessels under contract to haul oil that has been purchased for the fleet. Since the attack on the USS *Stark*

---

[5] On May 17, 1987, the USS *Stark* (FFG-31), a frigate, was on patrol when it was struck by two Iraqi Exocet missiles in the midst of the Iran-Iraq War. The Iraqi pilot mistook the *Stark* for an Iranian oil tanker.

and the incident with the USS *Vincennes*, we've attempted to maintain a lower presence in the Persian Gulf."[6]

"Admiral, how do you feel if we pull those vessels out of there, at least until this thing quiets down a bit?" the President inquired of the CNO.

"Sir, those four are there to show the flag and keep the Iranians from running wild, laying mines and generally harassing Saudi and Kuwaiti shipping as well as our own. We have recently reflagged seven Kuwaiti ships just so the Iranians would not harass them. If we pulled the frigates out but left the flagship in Bahrain, I suppose we could say that we were rotating the fleet and that might appease everyone," the admiral said. He notably had a sour look on his face indicating he did not like that idea one bit.

"Let's do that, then. We can always turn them around and run back up there if we have to," the President directed.

General Powell sat there and indicated no support for or objections to the moves.

"Yes, sir, I'll issue the order later today," the admiral said in a resigned voice.

The President then explained, "When I spoke with Prince Faisal earlier today, he said the King must seek permission for us infidels to enter the country and defend the three holy cities should it come to that. King Fahd would need to speak with Sheikh Abd al-Aziz ibn Baz and ask his permission for us to enter." The President paused for a second as he shook his head in frustration. "Who the hell is running that country?"

It was a rhetorical question, so no one answered.

The President continued recounting his call. "The Prince and the King both want to know what kind of support we can send to Saudi Arabia and how fast we can send it. I told him I would send over someone to discuss it with them and try to assess things on the ground. Who should we send for something like this?" The President looked around the table for a response.

---

[6] On July 3, 1988, the USS *Vincennes*, a missile cruiser, shot down Iran Air Flight 655 over the Strait of Hormuz, mistaking the aircraft for an Iranian fighter.

Powell leaned forward in his chair as he answered, "Sir, CENTCOM has responsibility for that AO. It should be someone from that command. General Schwarzkopf will either go himself or have someone from 3rd Army meet with the Prince as they have the best information on what can be sent and how fast it can be sent."

General Dugan spoke up next. "Sir, I would like to get an Air Force officer to attend as well. Whatever action CENTCOM takes, the Air Force is going to be heavily involved."

"Who do you have in mind?" Mr. Cheney asked.

"I would like to send Lieutenant General Horner. He knows best the capabilities the Tactical Air Command could bring to the table and how fast they could bring it."

Looking over at General Vuono, Mr. Cheney asked, "Got any idea who Norman would want to send?"

"Sir, he and I have discussed it and he wants to get General Yeosock over there as soon as possible," General Vuono answered.

"How soon do you think they could be en route to the Kingdom?" Bush asked as he placed his coffee cup down.

"Sir, both Yeosock and Horner are waiting at MacDill in Tampa right now to depart. Just say the word. We sort of anticipated that you would be sending someone over," Powell replied with a slight smile.

Turning to an aide, the President directed, "Call CENTCOM and tell them to get in the air to Saudi." Then he turned to Baker. "Jim, have someone call the Prince and give him an ETA in Riyadh. Does anyone have anything else we need to discuss? Colin, what about putting the 18th Airborne Corps on alert for this?"

"Sir, it's probably premature to do that. Right now a lot of people are on summer leave. The 101st has a battalion training in Panama and one battalion tasked up at West Point, training cadets. The 24th has a brigade out at Fort Irwin going through battalion rotations. If we put them on alert, people are going to be scrambling to get back to home stations and it may be for nothing. I would recommend we wait and see what Yeosock and Horner say," Powell indicated.

General Vuono, the Army Chief of Staff, made a note to call General Gary Luck, 18th Airborne Corps commander, right after this meeting.

Sununu looked over at Powell and shook his head. He was still a little bewildered by his apparent reticence to mobilize the military to get ready to deal with this threat after all that had transpired this past week.

President Bush nodded in agreement. He stood, which caused everyone else to stand. "Alright, then. If no one has anything else to add, I'm going to call Mrs. Thatcher and discuss a few things with her. Y'all have a good night and we'll talk tomorrow."

Chapter Thirteen
Shocker

3 August 1990
Dasman Palace
Kuwait City, Kuwait

Phase 1 had been swift and overwhelming, with few casualties. The only failure was to seize the Emir, who had escaped south to Saudi Arabia with the rest of his family. *At least his brother was brave enough to remain and die like a man*, Saddam thought.

As Saddam walked into the briefing room at the Emir's former conference room at Dasman Palace, he was pleased to see everyone standing and waiting for him. Being a bit of a Mel Brooks fan, he recalled the famous line from *History of the World Part II*—"It's good to be the king"—which put a smile on his face.

"Sit down and let's get started. But first"—he turned to Aziz—"is Ms. Amanpour going to present our side of the story to the world?"

"She is coming as we speak. I have an interview with her tomorrow in Baghdad."

"Be sure she gets it right," Saddam instructed forcefully before turning his attention to the briefer waiting to bring them up to speed. "Alright, Colonel, let's get on with it."

"Yes, sir. Our task organization has not changed. All units are reporting in excellent operational readiness as they took almost no casualties and very little vehicle damage in the execution of the mission. All units are in their positions along the Saudi border, ready to execute the next phase of the operation.

"First slide," the colonel called. Several deep breaths could be heard being sucked in as their brains began to register what was being shown.

Now they will have a heart attack, the colonel thought.

"As you can see, these are the enemy forces opposing us. The Saudi forces are the 2nd Saudi National Guard Brigade scattered in various outposts along our border and the Kuwaiti border, manned by part-time soldiers of the Fowj or militia. At the King Khalid Military City, which is located approximately one hundred and fifty kilometers from the border, is the 20th Mechanized Brigade, with some elements of the 45th

Armored Brigade. At Tabuk is the 10th Mechanized Brigade, and at Khamis Mushayt is the 8th Mechanized Brigade. The 45th Armored Brigade also has elements in the Riyadh area.

"There is also a Saudi Marine battalion located in Dhahran near their military base and some of the critical ports we'll want to seize right away. We anticipate that when the 2nd RG Corps moves across the border, the 8th Mech will move to oppose them in the vicinity of Jeddah. We also anticipate the Saudi 10th Mech will likely attempt to hit the flank of the 2nd RG in the vicinity of Buraydah." The colonel paused momentarily to check his notes before continuing.

"Sir, the Saudi National Guard is the force largely occupying many of the outposts along the border. They have a battalion at Al-Hofuf, just southwest of Dammam. They also have an infantry battalion at Al-Qasim and an infantry battalion at At-Ta'if, as well as a battalion in Buraydah and Unayzah. The Saudi National Guard headquarters, which essentially exercises total command and control for the units in the field, is located in Riyadh. All six infantry battalions are equipped with the V-100 four-wheel armored car, which has turret-mounted machine guns. Fortunately for us, they have no tanks to support them. They do, however, have artillery. They have several battalions of towed 155mm howitzers they bought from the Americans a few years back," the colonel concluded.

Saddam just waved his hand in acknowledgment. He had been familiar with the disposition of Saudi forces prior to cooking up this plan.

The colonel nodded and moved on. "Next slide. Sir, our mission statement for the next phase of the operation."

Mission: On order from the President, continue the attack to seize the Kingdom as well as the UAE and secure the Saudi-UAE-Oman border as well as the holy cities of Mecca, Medina and the seaport of Jeddah.

"Sir, Phase 2 commences on order with 1st Republican Guard Corps making the main attack south to seize Al-Jubail oil refinery, the port of Dhahran, and Dammam, destroying 2nd Saudi National Guard forces in sector, and continues to attack to seize and secure the Saudi-Oman-UAE border in the vicinity of Objective 1. Block any forces attempting to leave Qatar." Pausing briefly to allow this to register with those not in the inner circle of this plan, the colonel continued.

"Simultaneously, 2nd Republican Guard Corps makes the supporting attack to destroy King Khalid Military City and continues the attack to seize Medina, Jeddah and Mecca. 2nd Army Corps attacks to destroy forces located at King Abdulaziz Military City in Tabuk, southwest of the Jordanian border. On order turns south on the coast road to link up and follow the 2nd Republican Guard Corps. 4th Army Corps is initially in reserve and follows 2nd Republican Guard Corps. On order attacks to seize and secure Riyadh.

"As Saiqa Special Forces Division conducts waterborne assault to seize the port of Dammam and Al Jubilee; conducts infiltration to seize and destroy Saudi early-warning and air-defense control at Prince Sultan Airfield, conducts linkup with Republican Guard forces.

"9th Army Corps is initially in reserve following the 1st Republican Guard Corps and is prepared to secure Al-Jubail, Dhahran, and Dammam as well as King Fahd Airfield. Continues the attack to Al Majma'ah along Highway 50. Be prepared to seize Riyadh.

"4th Army Corps is in reserve following the 2nd Republican Guard Corps and is prepared to assume responsibility for KKMC and Buraydah. On order attacks to seize Riyadh.

"3rd Army Corps is in strategic reserve and continues to secure our eastern border with Iran.

"7th Army Corps remains in place and is a reserve," the briefing officer said, pausing to take a drink of water. "Next slide."

Interrupting the colonel, Saddam asked, "And the Air Force is prepared to support each of these attacks, I take it?" He looked over at General Shalah al-Tikriti, Air Force Commander.

"We are, sir. We have four hundred fighter interceptors at ninety-five percent operationally ready today as well as three hundred and ninety-seven strike aircraft at the same operational ready percent. We have targeted each of the five Saudi airfields for attack as soon as 1st Republican Guard Corps crosses the border. Our air commandos have reconned and are prepared to take out the Saudi early-warning ground system, which is located at Prince Sultan Military Airfield. They were inserted by infiltration five days ago and are awaiting the order to execute." A few in the room were surprised that the commandos were already in place this deep inside Saudi Arabia.

"What about their AWACS capability?" Saddam asked.

109

"Sir, we intend to fly out over the Gulf in international airspace masked as a charter flight. When he realizes we are not what we appear, it will be too late for him to send a warning, and if he did, the ground station will already have been destroyed," General Shalah al-Tikriti said.

"How long will it take 2nd RG Corps to reach King Khalid Military City?" Saddam asked no one in particular.

Quickly, General Hassan al-Rawi, Commander of the Republican Guard forces, answered, "From the border to the objective is one hundred twenty-eight kilometers and we should be there in no more than three hours," he answered. He looked to Lieutenant General Ra'ad Rashid al-Hamdani, the 2nd Republican Guard Corps commander, for reassurance that his answer was correct.

"See to it that it does not take you longer," Saddam said, looking at the general for the first time. General Muhammed al-Tikriti just chuckled to himself as there was no love lost between him and the Republican Guard Commander. The Republican Guard forces did not dance to the armed forces' tune, and this caused some resentment.

"The 2nd Army Corps is moving the longest distance over almost empty terrain with no good road system. How long before he reaches Tabuk, and will the 10th Mechanized Brigade be able to slip his grasp?" Saddam asked.

General al-Sattar al-Tikriti, the Army Chief of Staff, fielded the question. "Sir, 2nd Army Corps has the longest distance to travel, with little in the way of good roads or fuel and provision capability. However, the terrain is good, with hard-packed limestone or sand being predominant, so he will be able to travel dispersed and fast. If the 10th Mechanized Brigade should venture from Tabuk and attempt to attack the flank of the 2nd RG Corps, then 2nd Army Corps will be in a perfect position to hit the 10th in his flank. We believe the 10th will be alerted to what is happening and will either retreat to Jeddah or stay in place. The Air Force will convince the 10th that they may wish to stay where they are located rather than come out and play with the close-air support aircraft."

Saddam seemed satisfied with that answer. Looking at the colonel, he said, "Please continue with your presentation."

"Next slide," the colonel called out. "Phase 3 of the operation is on order. 4th Army Corps follows 2nd Republican Guard Corps to Az Zulfi and then turns south to seize and secure Riyadh and Prince Sultan Military Airfield. The 2nd Republican Guard Corps will continue its blitzkrieg attack to seize Buraydah, Medina, Jeddah and Mecca. IX Corps is prepared to assist from Dhahran to seize Riyadh should additional reinforcements be needed."

Jumping into the discussion, General Sultan al-Tikriti further explained, "Sir, Phase 3 will depend on the success of both the 1st and 2nd Republican Guard Corps and which one is meeting the least resistance and making the most progress. Speed is of the essence in this part of the operation. We will just have to be patient and see where we will meet strong resistance in or around Riyadh. The estimate is that the attack to seize Al-Jubail will take approximately six hours to initiate, as it is two hundred and ten kilometers from our current forces."

Saddam nodded and motioned for him to continue.

"Sir, we expect to encounter light resistance from the 2nd Saudi National Guard once we cross the border. Once across, Dhahran is another eighty kilometers and we should be there by noon of the first day. The night will also favor our operation as we have acquired a large supply of night vision goggles from a source who is providing American individual night vision devices, not the latest AN/PVS 7 version but the older PVS-5 model, which is still superior to the Russian version," the general added.

"I agree. It will be an interesting contest to see who takes Riyadh," Saddam said with a smile as he looked first at al-Tikriti, then at al-Rawi.

Changing subjects, Saddam said, "Let's talk air defense." He looked to General Hamid Raja Shalah, Commander of the Air Defense Forces. He hoped he was well prepared for this.

"Sir, as you know, each of our brigades is modeled after the Soviet organizational model, meaning each has a wide array of air-defense weapons, to include individual shoulder-fired SA-7s, ZSU-23-4 mobile anti-aircraft guns, ZSU-57 anti-aircraft guns, SA-9 anti-aircraft missiles, and SA-6 surface-to-air missiles, with each division. In addition, we are moving SA-3 launchers behind the 1st and 2nd Republican Guard Corps to increase the SAM coverage. At Ali al-Salem Air Base we've set up an S-300 system, which will provide our ground forces substantial long-range SAM coverage as they approach Riyadh," General Hassan al-Tikriti said before Saddam interrupted him.

111

"You are not stripping anything out of our home defenses, are you?"

"No, sir, these are launchers and missile systems the Russians recently lent to us, so the West and the Saudis will have no idea we have this level of air-defense capability moving with our ground forces," General Hassan al-Tikriti declared rather proudly.

"We also intend to place any captured Hawk missile batteries into operation as we have individuals who have trained on those systems," he continued. "The Americans provided some training on them back in the early 1980s, when they thought we were going to purchase them. Part of their process of showing us how easy they are to operate."

"Do you know where those batteries are located?" Saddam asked.

"We do, and the 8th has already included seizing those batteries in the Al-Jubail and Dhahran area in their plan. They are under orders to capture, not destroy the central command-and-control facility at King Fahd Military Complex or the facility at Prince Sultan Air Base, so we can continue to use them."

Saddam nodded in satisfaction, then added, "I, too, have read a lot of books about the battles and wars of the past. One thing that is always made clear is that battles and wars are won on the fighting ability of the soldiers and are lost for the lack of logistics. Tell me, how we are going to support this kind of a major attack?"

The Minister of Defense, Sultan Hashim Ahmad al-Tai, stood and stepped forward. "Sir, we are about to seize two of the largest gas stations in the world, Al-Jubail and Ras Tanura. We will seize those before they can be destroyed with the elements of the 8th As Saiqa Marine Brigade and 3rd Special Forces Brigade on waterborne and heliborne assaults. Both of these brigades are now free as they have completed their missions in Kuwait City. The marine brigade infiltrated in both locations four days ago as replacement workers when several workers came down with a mysterious case of food poisoning. We also have some individuals already in both those locations that are sympathetic to the Arab cause and will ensure nothing is damaged before our forces arrive.

"The Soviets also provided us with several hundred 4x4 and 4x6 fuel tankers and regular cargo trucks. These caravans of trucks will be used to establish the supply convoys needed to keep our mobile armies on the move and properly supplied during a battle. Our convoys will travel initially over Tapline Road.[7] As for ammunition and food, that has been planned for and will follow in the supply convoys behind each corps. If need be, 2nd Republican Guard Corps as well as follow-on forces can refuel at local gas stations along his route," he said, attempting to add humor to the presentation. No one laughed.

Saddam sat contemplating this information for a minute before he spoke. When he did, he turned to Abid al-Tikriti, his presidential secretary.

"What are your concerns at this point?" Saddam asked.

"Sir, I have none," Abid al-Tikriti responded.

No one said anything. Confidence had filled the air. After the lightning-swift seizure of Kuwait, they felt their army was primed to capture Saudi Arabia next. The Russians' lend-lease program really was playing out just like they had said it would.

Nodding in satisfaction, Saddam finally said, "Good, we launch in the morning at 0100 hours. Let's also make sure our new international wing gets to see some action. Saudi Arabia actually has a decent air force." He stood and left the room.

---

[7] Tapline Road is a two-lane paved highway that spans northern Saudi Arabia from Al-Jubail to Tabuk.

Chapter Fourteen
2nd Army Corps
3 August 1990
2nd Army Corps HQ
Western Desert, Iraq

The 2nd Army Corps had been in the desert for the past three weeks. They had arrived from several locations along the western fringe of Iraq and some units from as far north as Mosul and Ramadi. The long movement to get in position had taken a toll on their vehicles.

For the past three weeks, they had been attempting to get the vehicles repaired and serviced before they were to cross the border. Everything had to be delivered cross-country as there were no direct roads or nearby airfield they could use. This move and then keeping them supplied was proving to be a huge logistical nightmare.

Highway 1, a four-lane paved road that ran from Baghdad to Amman, was the only paved road in the area and vital to their cause. The region itself was remote, so few civilian vehicles traveled it—commercial truck traffic was dominant, when there was traffic.

The air force had cleverly figured out how to use the four-lane highway as a makeshift runway during the period of light traffic. This allowed their Antonov An-26 cargo planes to land on it so they could ferry in the most urgently needed parts and equipment to keep them running. While the cargo planes did their best to keep hauling in supplies, the Corps fuel trucks had been running nonstop to get all the vehicles fueled up in preparation for the main assault. The Corps headquarters had been located in the one town in the region, Rutba, along the Amman-Baghdad highway, Highway 1. It had a population of 28,400, most of which worked on or for the Kirkuk-Haifa oil pipeline, which paralleled Highway 1.

When the Iraqi forces had overrun Kuwait, the 2nd Army Corps Commander, General Izzat al-Douri, had assembled his division commanders in his forward command post ten miles from the Saudi border. The Saudis still hadn't been aware of what was about to happen.

In front of him sat the commanders of the 2nd Infantry Division, the 14th Mechanized Division, and the 7th, 37th and 51st Divisions. "Gentlemen, tomorrow will be a great day, for tomorrow we put to the test the last three weeks' worth of our training. Tomorrow our soldiers will be praised through the Arab world for what they are about to do." He paused to let that sink in. OPSEC was a moot point. There were no people in the area, no roads, no telephones to call home. There was nothing, so why keep everything a secret?

"Gentlemen, tomorrow morning at 0100 hours, we attack into Saudi Arabia and strike the 10th Mechanized Brigade at Tabuk," he said with a broad smile.

His division commanders sat in stunned silence, exchanging looks with each other.

Izzat al-Douri continued, "Your operations officers are being briefed at this time by the Corps operations officer and receiving your assignments. We are well prepared for this action. Our vehicles have all been inspected and repaired from their long haul to get here. Every vehicle has been fueled and our tanker trucks have all been replenished. We are fully uploaded with ammunition, and close-air support has been dedicated to our advance. What are your questions?" al-Douri asked.

The commander of the 14th Mechanized Division asked, "Sir, what will be the order of march?"

"You will be in the center of three divisions abreast with your T-72 tanks and BMPs. I want the 2nd Division on the right flank and the 7th Division on the left flank. The 37th Infantry Divisions will follow the 2nd Division, and the 51st will follow the 7th Division. If either the 2nd or the 7th is hit, then the 14th can turn and take on the attacker, with either the 37th or the 51st moving to close where the 14th was. Any other questions?"

The room was silent as they digested what they'd just been told and then examined some of the maps of Saudi Arabia they'd been given. Not coming up with any immediate questions, they simply nodded their agreement with the plan that had been given.

"Good. You all have a lot to do, so let us be about our tasks. I will personally follow the 14th Division. Now, let us all adjourn for Asr prayers."
****

At 0130, al-Douri was watching to the south. The sounds of engines began to drown out all other noises. The black night showed no civilization anywhere, just an array of millions of stars in the night sky.

The sound of thousands of vehicles was sure to raise some suspicions, but aside from some Bedouin sheepherders, he wasn't concerned about them being detected.

The units had all crossed the border on time, which his staff had happily reported to Baghdad. He knew he had the most difficult mission, even if he wasn't in heavy contact and didn't expect to be until morning of the next day. They had to drive over 480 kilometers to reach Tabuk. The T-72 tanks with their extended fuel tanks could make the trip but would be very low on fuel when they arrived. They would be the priority for refueling when they reached any gas stations along the route.

His logistics officer had briefed him on a plan that appeared sound, with each gas station identified along with the type of fuel each had. Respective units had been assigned which ones to stop at. This would still not be enough for the corps, so the tanker trucks would be critical in keeping them refueled. The first town they would come to was Hazem Aljalamid, which was along the major highway to Al Qurayyat and Jordan.

From there, the divisions would continue southwest to Sakaka. Being positioned at Sakaka, they could strike the 10th Brigade if it came east-southeast to strike the 2nd Republican Guard Corps, or al-Douri could turn west and drive right into Tabuk. By his calculations, they should be in Sakaka at about 1000 hours. It was a 198-kilometer drive. From Sakaka to Tabuk was another 376 kilometers. This made Sakaka a critical place to seize as it'd become his central supply depot to keep his corps running. If they needed additional vehicles to augment their ash-and-trash vehicles, they'd requisition whatever they needed. They would obviously pay for anything they had to seize as they wanted to win the hearts of their fellow Arabs, not drive a wedge between them.

The approach to Tabuk would be over loose sand but easy for all vehicles to handle. It was just going to be a dusty trip. Everyone would be wearing their goggles and scarves to keep the dust out. This would also cause them to travel in a wider formation, but that was OK.

"Sir," al-Douri's operations officer said, getting his attention. The look on his face in the dim glow of the lights in the command track did not foretell good news.

"What is it?" al-Douri asked.

116

"Sir, the 14th Division has reported contact. It is a Saudi National Guard unit that was quickly swept aside, but they did manage to get off several transmissions. They reported their location and approximately what they were facing."

"Very well. It was to be expected. I would have preferred that it had not happened so soon. Notify the regimental air-defense commanders to be prepared for possible enemy air strikes shortly after dawn. Do we know what type of unit our men encountered?" al-Douri quizzed.

"A reconnaissance unit. They were eliminated. No prisoners were taken."

Chapter Fifteen
Internationals

4 August 1990
1st Ground Attack Wing
Ali al-Salem Air Base

Major Nikolai Kamanin taxied his Su-25 Grach onto the runway. Looking to his right, he saw his wingman was ready. They waited for the control tower to give them permission to take off. Once the order was received, they both accelerated down the runway. Halfway down the 2,989-meter-long runway, he eased the stick back. His aircraft lifted off the ground and he began the process of clawing his way into the sky as he looked to grab more altitude.

Once he was little more than a hundred meters off the ground, he retracted his landing gear and started angling towards the Saudi border. He and his wingman settled into a cruising altitude of one thousand meters and began a lazy circle that would take them close to the border but not across it. They were waiting for the rest of their squadron to get airborne.

In the distance, he saw the MiG interceptors taking off as well. Their mission was to fly out ahead of them and clear the skies of any aircraft the Saudis might try and scramble. This would provide Kamanin and his squadron the necessary cover to carry out their surprise attack on the King Khalid Military City some 230 kilometers away. This preparatory attack would soften them up for the eventual ground invasion that would happen in less than an hour.

"Molotok One, this is Medved One. You are cleared to engage. Begin your assault," came the call from Kamanin's division commander.

They'd just been given the signal to begin their attack. This would be the first time their division had participated in this new war the Iraqis had started.

Kamanin depressed the talk button. "All Molotok elements, proceed to your assigned target boxes and engage your targets."

To minimize their radio chatter, the squadron commanders would break their target packages down into smaller engagement boxes. This way each pilot knew that he was free to attack anything in the box without having to get permission.

Fortunately for Kamanin, all the pilots in his attack squadron had one or more years of experience flying combat missions in Afghanistan. His pilots knew how to fly under fire and how to hit targets shooting back at you. They also knew how to operate their aircraft well in a combat environment, something they planned on showing their Iraqi counterparts.

Since the fighters had flown ahead of them, there was no reason to fly low to the ground or try to evade any enemy radars. They flew at an altitude of roughly one thousand meters towards their targets. Each Su-25 was equipped with four 9K121 Vikhr laser-guided antitank missiles and four UB-32A rocket pods, each carrying thirty-two 57mm antimateriel rockets. The final hardpoint had been dedicated for an external fuel tank to give them a bit more time over the target. If all went according to plan, they'd plaster the hell out of the units at the facility and pulverize a lot of the tanks before they could get into the fight.

As they got within thirty kilometers of the Saudi military base, they still hadn't detected any ground radars or aircraft in the vicinity. *These guys have to know we're about to attack*, thought Major Kamanin. The entire base was still lit up. *This is going to be easier than I thought.*

When they got within twenty kilometers of the base, the pilots of his squadron began to split up and head to their designated target boxes, where they'd look to engage the military targets within them.

Approaching ten kilometers, Kamanin started looking for his own targets. It didn't take him long to find them, either. The tank yard was fully lit up, making it easy for him to see what he was after. He spotted nicely packed rows of British Chieftain tanks, arranged like they were preparing for some sort of inspection.

A smile crept across his lips as he flicked on the targeting camera for his antitank missiles. He was going to target one tank, then flip to the next missile and get it on its way. Once he'd cycled through all four of them, he'd switch to his rockets and make a pass over the yard and anything else of value he saw. He knew his 57mm rockets likely wouldn't puncture the armor of the tank, but they'd certainly tear up the outside of it, to include its external optical sight and potentially its tracks.

Sighting in on the first tank, Kamanin depressed the pickle button, sending the first missile on its way. The missile leapt off its hardpoint, flying at Mach 1.8. It covered the distance in seconds, slamming into the tank. The HEAT charge caused a slight explosion before it caught the ammunition inside on fire, leading to a catastrophic explosion that ripped the turret completely off.

Not dwelling on the success of his first missile strike, he lined up the next missile and fired. He got into a groove and fired off his remaining three missiles before his aircraft overflew the tank yard. Explosions rippled all across the facility as the other pilots in his squadron began to hit their own targets.

Kamanin pulled up on the stick and applied more power to his engines. He gained altitude until he was around twenty-five hundred meters before he turned around to line up for his next attack. He was now going to act more like a World War II dive bomber than a modern-day tank killer as he flipped over to using his rocket pods. For this first run, he was only going to use two of the four pods.

Angling in for a row of barracks, he saw dozens of small figures running out of them, heading towards either their vehicles or some bunkers set up nearby. Lining up his aircraft, Kamanin let loose a string of antimateriel rockets across the soldiers and then into the barracks building. He then turned slightly to come back across the tank park and emptied the remainder of his rockets into the vehicles that hadn't been hit by any antitank missiles.

Pulling back on his stick again, he gave the plane more power to its engines, and it clawed its way back into the sky. Looking slightly behind him and to his right, Kamanin saw the base was getting torn apart. He also saw a couple of vehicle yards that had thus far escaped attention. He switched over to his remaining rocket pods and turned his aircraft towards them.

As he lined up for his next attack run, red tracer rounds stabbed through the night sky towards one of his pilots. They were coming from the vehicle yard he was about to hammer with his rockets. Then a second and third vehicle opened fire on his guys. A bright flash erupted to his left, and he realized one of his aircraft had been hit by either a heavy-caliber AA gun or a shoulder-fired MANPAD. In either case, the plane's right engine was in flames. The pilot looked to be angling away from the target as he sought to put some distance between himself and the enemy.

I don't think he's going to make it all the way back to base, Kamanin thought.

He then lined up his own aircraft and let loose a torrent of rockets across the vehicle park. He caught dozens of soldiers out in the open as his rockets rained down, exploding like firecrackers on the ground. Little pieces of red-hot shrapnel were thrown about the area, tearing into the soft flesh of the soldiers desperately trying to man their vehicles.

As Kamanin pulled up on his aircraft and gave his engines more power, a string of red tracers whipped across the front of his plane. He immediately kicked his rudder left while correcting right on the stick, seeking to dodge the incoming fire. He heard a handful of the rounds slam into his armored side, and he checked his gauges—it didn't appear they had punctured the thick armor or caused any serious damage.

Checking his weapons, he saw he was now dry. Well, he still had his guns. Then one of the Iraqi air traffic controllers interrupted his thoughts, alerting them that some fighters had been scrambled from an air base a little more than a hundred kilometers from them. His squadron was being recalled to Kuwait. They wanted him to rearm and prepare for the next follow-on mission.

Looking down at the King Khalid Military City, he felt pretty good about their first official combat mission since Afghanistan. His guys had done well. Now it was time to head home and get ready to repeat it a few more times throughout the day.

I wonder if it would have been like this if we had gone to war with NATO. Nah, the NATO forces actually know how to fight, he thought, then belly-laughed out loud to himself in his cockpit.
****

Major Vitaly Popkov and his flight of four MiG-29s raced towards Dhahran Air Base. The Saudis had stationed a squadron of F-15Cs and a squadron of Northrop F-5E Tigers at the air base, and Popkov's flight was assigned to cover the squadron of Su-22s and Su-25s that were going to plaster the airfield.

His sister squadron flying the MiG-23s and 25s would be flying escort duty for Iraq's only bomber assets (three Tupolev Tu-16 bombers and four Tu-22R heavy bombers). That batch of fighters and bombers was going to go after the Prince Sultan Air Base located in the closed city of Al-Kharj, south of the capital, Riyadh. Popkov wished he'd be able to see the results of that raid. The bombers were going to blanket the runways with some kind of special antirunway ordnance while at the same time plastering their E-3 Sentries and KC-135 tanker aircraft.

Suddenly his RWR warned him that a ground radar had just detected him. Popkov reached over and turned off the buzzing noise. It'd resume if a new threat was detected. He was surprised they hadn't been detected sooner. The Saudis really were arrogant in assuming the Iraqis wouldn't cross the border and invade them next.

Looking down and to his left, he knew the ground-attack planes would be going in on the air base soon. His flight of four aircraft had to just sit tight in a high loitering position and wait to see whether the Saudis managed to get any aircraft airborne to defend their kingdom.

Popkov's radio chirped, bringing him back to the here and now. "Tsaplya Six, Barusk Six. We're approaching the airfield now. It looks like some F-5 Tigers are getting airborne. We're going to try and take the runway out now before more can get off the ground. Out."

Smiling, Popkov told two of his pilots to stay in their high loitering position and go active with their radars. He and his wingman were going to splash these F-5s before they became a problem.

Once he'd turned his own radar on, he found six Tigers instead of the two he expected. He called his other flight of two fighters and told them to join the fray. They needed to down these guys before they could tear into the attack aircraft.

Spotting one pair of F-5s racing out across the desert, he maneuvered his MiG to come up behind the F-5 roughly eighteen kilometers ahead. He knew that his MiG-29 "Strizh" totally outclassed the Tiger in speed and acceleration. On the other hand, the nimble little F-5 could maneuver inside his MiG if this turned into a low-speed turning duel. He turned on the seeker head for his R-73 missile and waited until it told him it had successfully locked onto the aircraft he was painting.

Do these pilots not realize I'm targeting them? They aren't even moving to evade...

122

With a solid lock, he depressed the pickle button and let the missile fly.

While that missile took off, he switched over to his next R-73 missile to allow the seeker head to acquire its lock. Even with the Tigers running directly away from Popkov, there was a closure rate of over Mach 1. This meant it would be less than a minute before he overtook his prey if the Tiger didn't change course.

The second Tiger, however, did take evasive maneuvers. He rolled to the left, pulled hard on his stick and appeared to light up his afterburner. Popkov could recognize a panic maneuver when he saw one. With the MiG flying above and behind it, the Tiger pulled to his left. The rate of closure increased dramatically. With no time to get the missile lock, Popkov switched to guns and let loose a stream of 30mm rounds. The angry burst fell behind the turning Tiger.

Popkov knew that he didn't want to tangle with the Tiger down here. Even if he got the kill, he would put himself in a vulnerable position for the next enemy plane who decided to take on the Strizh. Instead of following the enemy, he eased the stick back and put some altitude between himself and the Tiger. He knew that his two RD-33 engines would give his MiG a major advantage in the vertical over the relatively anemic engines on the F-5.

At the apex of his climb, Popkov pulled his MiG into a gentle left-hand turn. During the entire maneuver, he never took his eyes off the enemy plane. He dipped his wing a few degrees to keep it in view so that on the descent, he could easily gauge where the enemy plane would be when he would get the lock with the infrared seeker on his R-73.

The frightened Tiger pulled out of his flat turn to the left, rolled quickly to the right and tried to dive out of Popkov's sight. It was no use. The Tiger had bled off all its speed, and with the MiG now diving on it, there was nowhere for the man to go. Once Popkov heard the tone of the missile lock, he loosed his second R-73 of the day and pulled out of his dive, being sure to keep his g-forces down to preserve his energy while he scanned the skies for any new enemy aircraft.

As he raised his nose and extended out of his run, Popkov looked around to see where the rest of his pilots were and how the aerial battle was shaking out. Judging by what he saw on his radar, three of the six F-5s looked to be down. The remaining Saudi planes appeared to be

123

running. Probably a smart move considering how outmatched they were against the MiGs. Then again, a plane is only as good as the pilot flying it, and right now, not all of these Iraqi squadrons were being flown by Iraqis.

This left Popkov with a tactical dilemma. He didn't like having those airborne threats out there, but he also didn't want to detach any of his planes to chase them down. For all he knew, the whole point of that Tiger launch was to pull the fighters away from the strike planes. No, he'd have to keep his eyes out for their return. If they came back, he'd deal with them then.

Angling his aircraft to head towards the Saudi air base, he saw columns of black smoke rising from a number of different positions on the base. A few minutes later, he got a call from the mission commander for the ground-attack planes. They were returning to base to rearm and see what the Iraqis wanted them to do next.

Popkov and his flight of four MiGs would continue to loiter over Saudi Arabia for another forty-five minutes until the next flight from their squadron arrived. Since this was the first day of the new invasion, the Iraqis were having their Russian contractors fly near-constant fighter patrols over the battlespace. They wanted their ground-attack planes to focus on taking out Saudi airfields. As far as Popkov was concerned, this was going to be easy duty unless the Americans decided to join the fray—then they'd be in for a real fight.

Chapter Sixteen
Over They Go

4 August 1990
1st Republican Guard Corps
Southern Kuwait

Brigadier General Ra'ad al-Hamdani pulled a cigarette out, and his aide struck a match. In the pitch-black night, the match was a beacon. Al-Hamdani looked south at the glow on the horizon. Al-Jubail was totally lit up with lights, as well as burning discharged gas, so that was reassuring. The Saudis still appeared not to be expecting them.

A reconnaissance team reported that Khafji, the first town across the Saudi border, was very dark except for a few lights. At 0100 hours, he did not find this particularly unusual. His headquarters was located in Al-Nuwaiseeb, with the 1st Battalion on the right, 2nd Battalion on the left and 3rd Battalion in reserve.

Somewhere overhead, he heard the sounds of jet engines. Not one or two jet engines, but a host of them. He smiled, knowing these warplanes had just crossed the border and were even now on their way to destroy the Saudi Air Force on the ground and go after some of their tank units while they were still in garrison.

Time to issue final instructions to the battalion commanders.

Turning to the 1st Battalion commander, he ordered, "I don't want you to get bogged down in Khafji, so concentrate on the highway. Any resistance we get from Khafji, the follow-on forces can address. Understood?" He added, "And keep the highway open. If you lose a vehicle, shove it off the road. We can deal with it later. We need those highways to stay clear and open."

"Yes, sir."

Speaking to his 2nd Battalion commander, General al-Hamdani explained, "You may have a problem with the ground on the right flank. The interchange at Khafji appears to have a large area of flooded ground. Our reconnaissance people say it is likely too soft for your vehicles. Avoid that by swinging out west of the power lines to this hamlet west of Khafji, then parallel the highway south." The two looked briefly at the map to see what al-Hamdani was referencing. "Understood?"

"Yes, sir. If I may, who is on our right flank?" the commander asked pensively.

"That will be 18th Armored Brigade. You must always maintain contact with them. Your forces are going to be traveling in close proximity to each other, and I do not want you accidentally shooting at each other. Also, let me know if they are falling behind or getting ahead of us. The 8th and 9th Mechanized Brigades will follow us and take care of any bypassed positions. Again, do not get bogged down in a slugfest. The Nebuchadnezzar Mechanized Division will be on their right flank, with the al-Medinah and Tawakalna divisions following behind us and the Nebuchadnezzar."

The general paused for just a moment to allow his commanders a chance to digest the information he had just given them. He then continued with their final instructions, addressing the 3rd Battalion commander. "Remember, 3rd Battalion will follow the 1st Battalion, and I want you to send one company to Ras Al-Mishab airport. We need to make sure there are no military forces there. We've also been tasked with making sure we provide a quick assessment of any airfields we overrun. The air force wants to set up more forward air bases until we capture some of the larger ones and get them operational. If your company discovers some forces at this particular field, assess if they can take them out. If they can't, then report it and we'll let a follow-on unit handle it. Any questions?"

The battalion commanders gave him a resounding "No, sir." These officers knew their jobs, and they knew what had to be done to achieve their objectives.

"Good, it appears it's time to get this show going. Return to your units and call me when you are ready. We cross at 0200 hours. *Allahu Akbar.*"

"*Allahu Akbar,*" they all shouted in unison. If God willed them to be successful in this coming war, then they would be. If not, well, then they'd try hard to convince him that they should be.
****

As the subordinate commanders returned to their respective battalions, al-Hamdani thought about his own family. He had been just a young captain when the war with Iran had broken out. For eight years,

126

he had been on the front lines. When he had seen his first human wave attack, it had truly terrified him. How the opposing generals could just throw so many of their men against fixed defenses as they had done—and, worse, suffer the kind of losses they had—had blown his mind. He'd vowed that if he ever became a general one day, he would not needlessly throw away the lives of his men like that.

The Iranians were truly fanatical fighters. Long on bravery and short on tactics or equipment. He did not think the Saudis would be anything like that. The Saudis might be rich and able to purchase the best military hardware available, but they seldom liked to get their hands dirty. They liked to use their wealth to hire others to do that kind of dirty work for them. Al-Hamdani wondered how that would work in a war.

Then his mind drifted back to the thought of home. *Maybe when we secure our objectives, it will be possible for me to get some time off and go home and see my family in Basra...*

His train of thought was broken by his operations officer.

"Sir, it's time. May I give the official order?"

Al-Hamdani could sense the man's excitement, so he nodded in the affirmative. The command track he was standing beside started its engine, as did all the other vehicles in the command post. They were ready to roll, and so was he.

Al-Hamdani went over to his command vehicle with its four radios and listened as his commanders reported in. He decided he wanted to move up closer to the front and told the driver to move out.

Although he was only five miles behind the lead elements that would charge across the border, he wanted to position himself between the 1st Battalion and 3rd Battalion. He believed that a commander should lead from the front and insisted that the commanders follow his example. As he drove past the 3rd Battalion commander, he exchanged salutes and wide grins of excitement with the tanker commanders and those standing up through the vehicle hatches. It was an exciting moment and one he wouldn't soon forget.

Soon, the first reports from the front began to come in. His lead company rolled over the Al-Khafji Customs House, with no resistance aside from the surprised looks on the customs officials' faces.

As they continued down the highway, they came to an equestrian riding facility. It seemed kind of odd and out of place in such an arid desert area, but the Saudis had money to build such niceties where they wished. The horses paid about as much attention to them as the Saudi customs officials. The College of Education, Khafji campus, was blacked out, and he suspected the students were asleep or too frightened to come out.

Looking off to his right through his night vision goggles, he could make out some tiny lights from IR chemical sticks they had acquired for this very purpose. Each vehicle had one tied to each antenna to identify the vehicle as friendly.

As they continued south, he checked his watch. They were right on schedule, and not a shot had been fired at them. *This is almost too good to be true.* Looking to the right, he wondered how things were going for the 2nd Republican Guard Corps.

****

General Ra'ad Rasjod, the 2nd Republican Guard Corps commander, had met with his division commanders earlier in the evening to discuss last-minute details for the pending attack. He'd made it very clear that no one was to enter the neutral zone before 0200 hours. Despite his orders, in their enthusiasm and vigor, a reconnaissance team had done so, going so far as to actually cross into Saudi Arabia. This matter would have to be dealt with, but now was not the time. They had returned before they had been detected by the Saudi border guards, but that did not absolve them of the consequences of disregarding his orders. Of more pressing concern was the terrain that the corps would be attacking over.

"General al-Kaab, I want you to take advantage of this four-lane highway from Tapline Road to King Khalid Military City. You are also going to have to watch that you do not get too far ahead of General al-Karawi's division. He has more difficult terrain to cover than we do, and if you get too far ahead, you'll leave your flanks exposed, which could spell disaster," General Ra'ad Rasjod explained forcefully.

Al-Kaab nodded at the logic but didn't say anything.

General Rasjod continued, "What brigade will be on your left flank?"

He was asking some of these questions about other units and their locations because he wanted to make sure they stayed abreast of what was going on around them.

128

"Sir, that will be the 4th Brigade," General al-Kaab answered quickly and confidently.

Smiling at the ready answer, Rasjod added, "It's imperative that he isolate Al Qaisumah with one of his battalions. If you want, the 6th Brigade can replace him with a battalion or however you want to do this, but I want to be sure that the left flank is protected. Nothing can be assumed or left to chance. Do you understand?"

"Yes, sir, it will be done," General al-Kaab assured him.

"I would like both of you to arrive at your final objectives at the same time, or even let him overtake it," General al-Karawi indicated.

"If he arrives a bit earlier, they will turn against him and present you with a flanking attack that your tanks and BMPs can exploit. Either way, I need both of you in the fight and not one piecemeal engagement after another. Am I clear?" General Ra'ad Rasjod emphasized before quickly adding, "I will expect updates on your progress at the appropriate phase lines, and be prepared to slow down or speed up, depending on the situation and how the enemy is reacting."

The general took a breath in and then looked off into the distance for a moment before returning his gaze to his most aggressive general. "Al-Karawi, your division is going to want to slide to the left, seeking the good road. It's smoother and faster, but do not let it happen. Hold on your axis of advance and turn to the left only when you have reached that point due west of King Khalid Military City. That will force the enemy to fight in two directions or turn towards you and present his flank to the Baghdad division." He paused as he looked at the map spread before him.

"Now one more point. I would like to take King Khalid Military City with as little damage as possible from our end. The air force is flying in as we speak to go after their tank and vehicle yards. They may even go after some of the barracks. Additionally, the air force has been told not to just outright destroy the base. They are mostly going after the tanks and armored vehicles that might challenge."

General al-Karawi smiled at the mention of the air force going in ahead of them. There had been many questions by the army about what role the air force would play. They were not exactly known for providing the best close-air support to their service. There were also rumors of a mysterious wing of pilots operating some pretty advanced aircraft that had been lent to them by the Soviets. Rasjod had his own suspicions about who was flying those planes, but he wasn't about to go asking.

"Al-Karawi, when I attended the US Army Command and General Staff College in 1979, the Saudis and we were better friends. They had even invited many of us to attend the course at King Khalid. I suspect it was meant to impress us with their army at the time. While we were there, we studied a book written by a famous Prussian general, Carl von Clausewitz. In that book, *On War*, he professed that the most successful battles are won by maneuver and not butchering each other as we did with Iran. So that is what I want us to do. I want us to show an overwhelming force to those at King Khalid Military City so that they will realize that it would be futile to oppose us. I also do not want to endanger any of their families that live there, which will just give them an incentive to fight harder. When you get within ten kilometers of your objective, I want you to stop and bring all your artillery forward for a firepower demonstration. Hopefully when they see the amount of artillery we have brought, they will surrender. Any questions?"

Al-Karawi just shook his head. He knew what was being asked of him and the trust being bestowed upon him. He wouldn't let his superiors down.

****

Hours later, as the divisions entered the neutral zone, the night was as dark as any they'd ever had. Millions of stars clearly showed where the horizon was, with the absence of light demarcating where the sky and ground touched. It symbolized a giant black hole and the unknown outcome into which their forces would be advancing.

As the divisions of the Iraqi Army advanced across Tapline Road, there was no vehicle traffic or signs of human presence anywhere. On the left, the Baghdad Mechanized Division rolled up on the highway as the 4th Brigade and the 5th Brigade moved into the Wadi Al-Batin proper. The 4th would have to take a slow approach as the 5th had to pick its way over the uneven ground. The 6th Brigade was in reserve following the 4th and was just crossing into Saudi territory when the 4th crossed the Tapline Road, right on time.

On the right flank, the Adnan Motorized Division had two brigades advancing, with one brigade acting as their reserve following slightly behind them. The 21st Armored Brigade was in reserve with their T-72 tanks while the forward brigades had the faster-moving BTR-80 vehicles. The eight-wheeled vehicle was ideal for this desert terrain. With its crew of three and fourteen soldiers, it could rush infantrymen right into the battle.

The newer BTR-80 was also equipped with a much-improved turret outfitted with both a 14.5mm KPVT heavy machine gun and a 7.62mm PKT machine gun. The additional 7.62mm PKT coaxial machine gun would handle any personnel threats while the 14.5mm could tear apart anything but a frontline tank.

General al-Hamdani knew that the 1st RG Corps would be the ones first detected once they crossed the border, and when that happened, the forces opposing his advance would be alerted. He would be in for a fight for sure. His immediate concern was not the fight for King Khalid Military City but being surprised by the 10th Mechanized Brigade hitting one of his flanks after he took King Khalid and began moving again. *I hope the 2nd Army Corps is moving.*

Chapter Seventeen
Fight for King Khalid Military City

4 August 1990
2nd Republican Guard Corps
Wadi Al-Batin

Sunrise was always glorious. Its coming was foretold with the eastern sky painted in orange and blue light reflecting off whatever clouds were present over the Arabian Gulf. Slowly the top of the red ball sun would peek over the horizon, and within minutes, the flaming ball would be completely above the horizon and then slow in its ascent, removing all color from the clouds except their natural white.

It was General al-Hamdani's favorite time of the day, especially if he'd had a good night's sleep. Last night, once they had packed up, his command post had been anything but comfortable. Traveling in a cramped armored personnel vehicle across rough terrain while trying to stay close to the front lines but not so close your vehicle might get blown up was quite the challenge.

Once his divisions had crossed the frontier, racing towards their objective, al-Hamdani had made sure his driver did his best to keep up. They were expecting a possible major clash at the King Khalid Military City, and he wanted to be nearby to help direct the units. Once they captured the facility, he wanted to get a more traditional headquarters unit set up so he could direct the next phase of the campaign from there.

As he listened to reports, he was pleased by what he was hearing. His forces had performed better than he had initially thought they would. He was appreciative of the air force going in ahead of them and disabling many of the Saudi tanks in advance. His tankers out front were reporting a lot of fires on the horizon in the direction of the Saudi base. The air force hammering the armored units ahead of their arrival would make capturing the facility a lot easier. It'd also make it easier for the Saudi commander to accept defeat if the bulk of his forces were destroyed.

When their vehicle pulled to the side of the road, everyone got out. It was a chance for them to relieve themselves and stretch their legs and backs.

As General al-Hamdani finished relieving himself, a major who was his current staff officer on duty came up behind him. "Sir, General al-Kaab just reported that their lead elements have entered Hafar Al-Batin. One battalion has moved into the area and is securing Al Qaisumah. So far, they haven't met any resistance and are pushing forward," the staff officer explained.

Zipping his trousers, al-Hamdani turned around. "Good, and what of the Adnan Division? Have we had any reports in the past hour?"

"No, sir," the staff officer responded.

He then walked over to grab some hot tea another aide had just finished brewing and stood on the side of the highway, waving his men on like General Patton used to do. He was proud to see a number of anti-aircraft wheeled and tracked vehicles moving well with the brigade. These vehicles were going to be important to ensure his guys didn't get mauled from the air if the Saudis ever managed to any fighters airborne.

Then he saw a string of those new BTR-80s the Soviets had lent them only six months ago roll on by. Behind them was a string of 4x4 and 4x6 ash-and-trash vehicles and refuelers. Behind them were the towed artillery units. He couldn't help but beam with pride as he saw this modern force roll past him.

The major, his staff officer, interrupted his thoughts with his report. "Sir, the Adnan Division's main body is twenty miles west-northwest of their objective. Their reconnaissance teams have the objective under observation and are reporting what appear to be some preparations for movement. They also report a lot of smoke and some fires spread out across the base from the air strike. We are monitoring their communications, and it appears that the reinforced brigade is issuing orders to their battalions to take up defensive positions opposing the Adnan Division."

Al-Hamdani allowed a smile to crease his face. "Good, good. Tell General al-Karawi he may engage with his long-range artillery whenever he desires, but he is not to fire into the complex itself. I want that kept intact. There are families there, and we do not want to give them an incentive to resist. We win battles by outmaneuvering the enemy and convincing him he cannot win. Our fight with Iran did not do that, and the result was a slugfest for both sides. I do not want that this time around. No one really wins in those kinds of situations.

"We want to show the Saudi commander that we have overwhelming force, and he has no chance of winning. He needs to understand that he will only get his people killed, their homes destroyed, and endanger their families. Besides, Arabs should not be fighting Arabs. We should be joining together to rid the infidels of our lands," al-Hamdani said proudly.

The major was a bit surprised, as he'd never heard the general express his views like this before. Continuing, al-Hamdani directed the major, "Contact General al-Kaab and tell him to speed up his advance. We need this Saudi brigade commander to see that he is about to be flanked and that, no matter what actions he takes, he will not save them."
****

Many miles to the southwest of General al-Hamdani sat First Lieutenant Muhammed al-Tikriti, scout platoon leader for the 1st Battalion of the 11th Motorized Brigade. His platoon had crossed the frontier a couple of hours ahead of the battalion and had laid out ChemLights as they reconned the route, ensuring that the best possible terrain was used. He had run this route several times in the past month in a civilian vehicle, both in the daytime and at night, posing as a simple shepherd looking to purchase sheep. He had never been stopped once by the Saudi border police.

Now he lay thirty meters in front of his BTR-80 scout vehicle, which was behind a low rise. He was observing the outer perimeter of King Khalid Military City. What he saw was a complete mess. Columns of smoke and flame rose from many different positions across the sprawling military base. Even the military airport had been hit hard. Still, he spotted some activity within as what remained of a mechanized battalion in M113 armored vehicles moved through the main gate. They appeared to be setting up a defensive position that would give them a good overwatch should an attacking force approach the base.

The ridge they were sitting near was only a little more than a kilometer from the edge of what appeared to a large warehouse complex that sat between him and the actual King Khalid Military City complex. Lying beside him was a sergeant who was a forward observer for the artillery battalion trailing behind them.

The sergeant had just called a fire mission for the artillery but had been told to wait as they were not in range of the position he'd just sent. As they lay there watching, they began to see some tanks moving to positions dispersed between the M113s.

I guess a few of them survived their raid...

Lieutenant Muhammed al-Tikriti turned to the forward observer. "You should notify them that some tanks have moved forward and are in hull defilade positions."

While the sergeant started making his call, Lieutenant Muhammed al-Tikriti continued to observe their activity. A couple more tanks began to exit the compound. Instead of joining their comrades, they moved to the left. Following them with his Steiner binoculars, he noticed they were heading to an ammunition storage area. Like a thunderbolt, it hit him— they were not uploaded with ammunition! Lieutenant al-Tikriti immediately reported this to his battalion commander. As he continued to watch them, his instincts were proven correct as the Saudi soldiers were opening the ammunition bunkers and attempting to upload the tanks.

Watching them, he heard thunder in the distance but saw no clouds. And then he heard what sounded like a freight train screaming overhead. All along the lower portion of the ridge where the Saudi troops were located, eruptions of dust and sand exploded into the air as the division artillery began their firepower demonstration for the benefit of the Saudi soldiers.

The message they were sending was clear. Either surrender or die.

Lieutenant Muhammed al-Tikriti observed the artillery display of unprecedented, devastating power. Slowly, his vision became obscured by the dust and dirt being kicked into the air. Turning his attention back to the tanks he'd been observing earlier, he could see the tankers really rushing to get their vehicles loaded.

Some of the Saudi soldiers not actively loading the tanks had stopped and climbed on top of the turrets to get a better idea of what was going on. After three to five minutes of a continuous bombardment, the shelling from the division artillery regiment ceased. The devastating display had been sent—now it was a matter of seeing if it would achieve the desired effect.

Still hearing explosions in the distance, he began to wonder if the Baghdad Mechanized Division was also shooting, providing an equally overpowering display of their own, or if they had just gone ahead and charged right into the Saudi base.

Lieutenant Muhammed al-Tikriti scanned to the northeast to see if he could identify the action there. Columns of dust and dirt were rising, much larger than what the artillery could be causing. Then he not only saw them but heard the loud screaming of jet engines. A flight of Sukhoi Su-25 Grach aircraft, or Frogfoots as NATO liked to call them, were diving in on the enemy. The close-air support or CAS fighters were swooping in like World War II Stuka dive-bombers, releasing their five-hundred-pound dumb bombs on some unseen force. Then a new pitch joined the battle, only this was from the rocket pods under the wings of the aircraft. The pilots were apparently laying it on thick on whoever was over there.

Higher still in the sky, Lieutenant Muhammed al-Tikriti could see several other aircraft circling above while the CAS aircraft continued to release their ordnance slowly and methodically. Although he tried to look at the circling aircraft above with his binoculars, they were too high to identify what type they were.

A flash in the circling jets suddenly appeared as an aircraft blew apart, its flaming wreckage falling to the ground. The other circling aircraft turned to the southeast and launched two missiles. Looking in the direction of where those missiles were headed, al-Tikriti saw them chase something, but he couldn't tell what. There was no sound to let him know those missiles had found their mark, and the only thing he could see was two flashes in the southeastern sky and an earthbound trail of black smoke. Lieutenant al-Tikriti could only assume this had been an air-to-air engagement.

****

General al-Hamdani had moved up behind the follow-on brigade and was sitting in a café in Hafar Al-Batin, enjoying an early lunch. His command vehicle was parked at the curb, so he could almost hear the radio. As he ate, he heard an unusual sound and looked skyward, recognizing that a plane had been lost as the burning wreckage plummeted to earth. Not giving it a second thought, he resumed eating his meal.

The duty staff officer approached him quickly, which startled him a bit. "What is it?" he bellowed, annoyed that his few minutes of alone time was being intruded upon.

"Sir, General al-Kaab is on the radio and would like to speak to you. He said it is most important," the staff officer replied.

Slowly the general rose and turned to the waiter. "Don't touch it, I'll be back," he said before walking the few feet to the vehicle. "General, you have something for me?" he said, not bothering to use his call sign.

"*Allahu Akbar*. The Saudi commander has struck a white flag. He wishes to surrender with no further bloodshed. He requests a meeting with you at your convenience. He only asks that their families and soldiers be spared any harm," General al-Kaab said.

"Tell him I am on my way as soon as I finish my lunch. Secure a place for this meeting and tell him we will go to prayers together. There will be no more fighting today," General al-Hamdani promised. He then went back to finish his lunch with a renewed sense of optimism and a wide smile on his face.

Chapter Eighteen
Iraqi Navy Engages

4 August 1990
Iraqi Flagship
Persian Gulf

Rear Admiral Gha'ib Hassan's helicopter arrived over his flagship, a *Lupo*-class frigate, while it was underway. As the helicopter approached, the admiral could see the white wake on the black sea of other vessels traveling with his flagship.

In his absence, his operations officer had received the plan and coordinated the new operation with the commander of the Marine Brigade. All was prepared, and as soon as the crews were assembled, the flotilla departed Ras al-Qualayah for the next phase of the war.

His other three *Lupo*-class frigates were behind in a trail formation, along with the other two Osa-class missile boats creating a screen for his flagship. Between the Osa missile boats and the flotilla, they had another three Lussen TNC-57 fast-attack missile boats they'd captured in Kuwait. The attack boats were mostly going to accompany two seagoing tugs that had been converted to minelayers, the *Al Raya* and the *Jumariya*. They were not as fast as the others in the flotilla. As the *Al Raya* and *Jumariya* had departed earlier, they'd arrive at the appointed time off the coast from Al-Jubail. The three Grisha-class corvettes were dispatched to the south to help close the Strait of Hormuz should any American or British vessels attempt to enter.

Once the admiral was on board, the operations officer, a Navy captain, briefed him on the plan. "Sir, we received the order just after you departed to meet with Saddam. I thought you had been briefed on the operation and took it upon myself to get things organized and depart. I hope that was alright," the seasoned naval officer said, not sure if he'd made the right move.

"Captain, it is not often we are rewarded for initiative in this land. You did right and I thank you for taking charge. Now, would you be so good as to explain to me what we are about to do?" the admiral said.

"Sir, our mission is to isolate the ports of Al-Jubail and Ras Tanura and to block the Saudi Navy at their base in Al-Jubail or capture and destroy them." He paused while the admiral absorbed his comments.

"That is basically what Saddam told me. Continue."

"To do that, I have placed a screen line with the Osa-class missile boats to scout and engage any vessels that do not surrender. They are followed by three of the captured Kuwait fast-attack boats, which are also carrying sea mines, in addition to the seagoing tugs the *Al Raya* and *Jumariya*. They've both been fully loaded with mines. Their mission is to lay their mines across the two entrances to the Saudi naval base at Al-Jubail. They will then lie offshore and engage any Saudi vessels that attempt to clear the mines or try to break out. They have one hundred and thirty-three nautical miles to travel and, at twenty knots, they should arrive at about the time the 1st Republican Guard Corps crosses the border.

"The smallest entrance is the northern entrance, at three hundred twenty meters across. The southern entrance is five hundred meters across. While they are laying mines in the northern entrance, the Osa boats will make a run at engaging the Saudi ships at the docks through the southern entrance and escape through that entrance before the last of the mines are laid."

The admiral interrupted to add, "We need to deceive the Saudis for as long as possible about our true intent or they'll look to engage us. Their coastal radar will undoubtedly detect our approach as we get closer."

"I have considered that. We will make our approach paralleling the coast just outside of Saudi waters and initially bypass the naval base with two of the Osa boats and two of the FPB-57s. I'll have one of the FPB-57 slow to a crawl and transmit that he is having engine trouble and cannot proceed to Doha for the naval exercise. I'll have them transmit in the clear. The tug *Al Raya* will respond in the clear that he is coming to assist. The Saudis may not be fooled into thinking we are running an exercise with Qatar, but they may believe we are going on a raid to one of the Iranian oil rigs further south. As the lead FPB reaches the southern entrance abeam, it will announce the code word and the Osa missile boats will turn into the southern entrance and commence engaging the Saudi ships that attempt to leave the docks. At this hour and with surprise, I doubt any will. If we can bottle them up, then later we can deal with them," the captain explained.

"What do we know of the Saudi ships in port at this right now?" the admiral asked, reaching for some tea.

"Sir, currently in port at the naval base, according to our source, is one *Badr*-class corvette, the *Al-Yarmook* 614. The second ship, the *Badr* 612, is in dry dock undergoing service. It has been there four months now. There are also three of the five Al Sadiq patrol boats at the docks—the 511 *As-Siddiq*, the 513 *Al-Farouq* and the 515 *Abdul-Aziz*. The 517 and 519 are at sea, and we believe south of Bahrain. Their one supply vessel in the eastern fleet is also at the docks, the 902 *Boraida*. Six of the twelve AS532 Cougar helicopters and twelve of the AS565 Panther helicopters are at the Jubail Naval Airfield on the northwest side of the city," the captain summarized.

"Very good. You have addressed the Saudi naval base, which is our biggest threat. Now what about the important petroleum terminals at Al-Jubail and Ras Tanura?" the admiral questioned as he removed his uniform jacket and loosened his tie.

"Sir, one of the other *Lupo*-class frigates will remain with us outside of the King Fahd Industrial Port, along with four of the TNC-45 fast-attack boats, which are carrying a contingent of Marines. The King Fahd Industrial Port Terminal sits at the end of a six-kilometer road from the mainland to the terminal. The terminal has thirty-one berths for ships varying in size from eight thousand tons to one hundred and ten thousand tons. It can also handle liquid petroleum and bulk container ships. This sounds huge, but in reality, the Special Forces Marine Brigade only needs to control a few places and then wait for the 1st Republican Guard Corps forces to arrive or someone to relieve them. The first elements of the Special Forces Marine Brigade will conduct a heliborne assault to establish a roadblock between the terminal port area and the mainland, effectively isolating the port. They will also seize the terminal control facility, which controls all the pumps and electrical systems at the facility.

"As to possible resistance, there are only a few private contractor security guards, and they are not armed. We do not expect to meet any resistance. Most workers usually work during the day. It's believed there might be one or two night shift crews, but nothing our forces won't be able to handle. Once they cut the power and pumps, they will be easily subdued. While the heliborne assault is going in, four of the TNC-45 craft will come alongside and offload their soldiers to reinforce the assault force," the captain concluded.

"Let us not forget, Captain, our mission is to isolate the port and support the Special Forces Marine elements. It is their mission to plan and execute the seizure of the terminal facilities. We will put them where they wish and isolate the terminal from the sea. The rest is their responsibility, and if they fail, that is on their heads, not ours. Are we clear?" the admiral asked. He was not about to put his head on the chopping block if things went bad. The ground plan was the responsibility of the commander of the Special Forces Marine Brigade.

"Yes, sir. I just want to be able to say we did all we could to ensure success," the captain acknowledged.

"Good, now for the plan at Ras Tanura?" the admiral asked.

"The heliborne assault will land at 0130 hours and establish a roadblock at the entrance to the six-kilometer-long road to the loading docks. As you know, this is not a large complex like the facilities at Al-Jubail. In addition to seizing the terminal, the Special Forces will also seize the refinery with the help of infiltrators that have been there for a week and are working with local sympathizers. It seems that many are dissatisfied with the current king. There are only a couple of ships docked there and we will prevent any of them from leaving."

"Good, it appears you have covered everything. I am going to retire for the time being. Wake me at 0030 hours unless you need me for something. At that time, I want a complete update on each ship's position and status. We will have communications with the ground force, right?"

"Sir, I am in communications with their operations officer. All is on track at this time," the captain responded with confidence.

"Good, until 0030 hours, then…" The captain knew when to leave the sea cabin of the admiral.

****

Promptly at 0030 hours, there was a knock on the door of the admiral's cabin. "I'm awake and will be out shortly" was heard through the door.

Fifteen minutes later, the admiral stepped onto the bridge. "Admiral on deck" was announced for all to hear, but on such a small bridge, it was also easy to see someone enter.

The admiral yawned and stretched his back. "Ops," he said, addressing his operations officer, who was standing next to the ship's captain, "what is the status of the flotilla?"

"Sir, all in order. No reported contacts by the Osa missile boats. The tugs and gunboats are approaching the northern entrance to the Saudi naval base at Al-Jubail. The current moved things along a bit faster than anticipated."

That should not have happened, Captain. The speed of the current should have been accounted for in your navigational computations and the speed adjusted accordingly, the admiral thought privately.

"Have we adjusted for this?"

"Yes, sir, a message went out a few minutes ago in the clear that the ship was having trouble and needed a tug. By transmitting in the clear, we are sure the Saudis would have intercepted the communication. They are now adrift outside Saudi territorial waters and will be ready in forty-five minutes to go into action. Two of the Osa missile boats have turned and are coming back to join the FPB-57 and tug to provide security, which would be done under normal circumstances. Our contact at the naval base reports no unusual activity."

"Good. Have you heard from the heliborne force?"

"They are in the air as we speak and anticipate landing at 0100 at the King Fahd Industrial Port."

"So everything is going according to the plan, correct?"

"Yes, sir," the captain replied with some confidence.

It was a clear night with no moon. To the east, only a few lights on offshore oil rigs could be seen, and most of those rigs were abandoned. The price of oil was so low that many had been shut down for the time being. The huge oil field and complex at Manifa in the north had been closed since 1984 due to the cratering price of oil. It was a double-edged sword. On one side, the revenue from oil had fallen off significantly, which was hurting the country overall, but on the other side, fuel was cheap, so the navy could run its ships and train more frequently. To the west, it was just the opposite—the skyline was ablaze with lights of all colors. Flames danced in the sky, burning off the gases from the

142

petroleum production. Multicolored neon signs advertised everything from appliances to cars and hotels. The petroleum plant at Al-Jubail was bathed in yellow light with a tinge of orange caused by the dust in the air. Some noise could be heard across the water, but for the most part the night was quiet.

Behind his flagship, the admiral could see the other *Lupo* frigates trailing his ship as their bow wake clearly marked their positions. Forward, he could not see the ships as their navigation lights were all off. As they were just creeping along with the current, there was very little wake.

On the bridge of his ship, only green instrument lights were visible as there was no need for white lights, which would only ruin one's night vision. The smoking lamp was out as well, as the glow of a cigarette at sea could be seen for some distance. With just the Arabian Gulf on the left side of his ship, his flotilla would not be silhouetted against the night sky the way a vessel coming from a Saudi port would be against the lighted background of the coast.

****

With one eye on the clock and one on the radar, the captain and admiral waited patiently but with apprehension. *This has got to go right*, the admiral was thinking. Saddam was not tolerant when it came to failure. Unless you were a high-ranking loyal member of the Ba'ath Party, and few in the navy were, second chances were hard to come by. The admiral's train of thought was broken by a call over the intercom system from the combat information center or CIC.

"Sir, radar has a flight of six slow-flying aircraft approaching from the north at one hundred and sixty knots and an altitude of one hundred meters. They are twenty-four kilometers out," the report said.

"That will be the flight to Ras Tanura with one hundred and forty-four soldiers. They have the longest leg to fly," the captain announced.

The admiral just acknowledged with a nod. A few minutes later, another report came over the speaker.

"Sir, radar has a second flight of twelve aircraft, fifteen miles north at one hundred meters and one hundred and sixty knots airspeed. They appear to be heading to Al-Jubail."

143

"Roger, keep me posted on both flights. Have you any surface activity?" the admiral asked the CIC over the intercom.

"No, sir, not in our vicinity. Appears to be some tanker traffic going into Bahrain, but that is all."

"Roger, keep me posted," the admiral said as he turned to his operations captain. "Tell the minelayers to move in now and the Osa missile boats to start their attack. Have the FPB-57s cover the missile boats and tugs," the admiral ordered.

These events would have happened without the order as these were preplanned actions, but he felt in control giving the orders just the same.

In the CIC, the radar operators watched on their radar screens as two blips quickly got up to speed and raced for the southern entrance to the Saudi naval base. The two Osa missile boats were quickly in the harbor, moving about at high speed for such a confined space with erratic maneuvers that guaranteed they would not be hit. One blip went into the northern entrance on the north side and started slowly and deliberately moving to the southern side of the entrance, dropping mines as he did so. The other minelaying tug entered the southern entrance on the south side and began moving north in a slow, deliberate manner just as its partner was doing. Before the southern entrance was closed with mines, the Osa missile boats raced back to the southern entrance and exited on the north side. The minelayer turned out and made a second pass southbound before heading for the open sea. The Osa missile boats took up positions around both entrances. Fortunately, or not, no Saudi vessels had moved from the docks.

As the admiral watched this naval action on the surface radar, his ear was cocked to listen to the action on the north at King Fahd Industrial Port. From what he could glean, the heliborne force went in as planned and quickly established a roadblock as well as the seizure of the master control facility, which was close by. A third element seized the central power plant and disconnected all electrical power. Suddenly, King Fahd Industrial Port was no longer bathed in light but covered in darkness. Only the lights on the ships in port were seen, and none were attempting to move.

By 0230, all missions had been accomplished and now it was a matter of time as they waited for the 1st Republican Guard Corps to arrive. The admiral's flotilla would remain on station to provide any

144

gunfire or air-defense coverage that was needed. *Ops can handle this. I am going to bed*, the admiral thought, then excused himself. He returned to his cabin, much to the pleasure of his operations officer, who wanted his chance to shine on his own.

The admiral's sleep was, sadly, short-lived.

The call to battle stations and general quarters combined with the pounding of the main gun woke the admiral from a sound sleep.

"What is happening?" he asked in a controlled tone after making his way to the bridge.

"Sir, one of the Al Sadiq patrol boats must have been returning from the open sea and was engaged by one of the Osa missile boats. They exchanged fire and then two of the Al Sadiq patrol boats at the docks departed and attempted to get out of the harbor. One hit a mine and has sunk. We are engaging the other one right now," the ship's captain explained.

"Captain, I want you to break contact and I will have the TCN-45s engage that craft. I want us ready to engage the *Badr* corvette if he should attempt to break out." Turning to the intercom, he added, "CIC, have the *Werija* and the *Jalboot* engage that patrol boat. And do it quickly."

"Aye, sir," the CIC responded.

The ship's main gun stopped shooting, but in the distance, the admiral could see an exchange between the two TCN-45s and the Saudi patrol boat. A sudden flash and explosion on the horizon to the west told the story without the report. A ship had exploded and was probably sinking rapidly, if anything was left to sink. The admiral just hoped it was an Al Sadiq patrol boat and not the Osa missile boat. A few minutes later, he was relieved when the Osa made his combat report. He was in the process of picking up survivors before the sharks could get to them.

"What have you heard from the Special Forces Marine Brigade?" the admiral asked his operations officer next.

"Sir, all appears to be quiet," the captain responded.

"And we still have the ports sealed?" It was more of a statement than a question.

"Yes, sir. No one has even attempted to depart or enter, except at the naval base." The eastern sky was beginning to show the start of a new day, a day that would shine on the admiral and the Iraqi Navy.

Chapter Nineteen
Late-Night News

4 August 1990
Presidential Residence
Camp David, Maryland

The President and his wife had no social events for the evening. Earlier in the day, they had flown up to Camp David for a relaxing stay as the President felt things might become hectic with events unfolding in the Middle East. He wanted some time to unwind before that happened. He was looking forward to a quiet evening reading the latest Tom Clancy book. He had read *Red Storm Rising* and *The Hunt for Red October* and found both to be fascinating. When the house phone rang, his thoughts suddenly turned dark.

This can't be good.

"Hello, who is this and what do you want?" he said in a tone that let the person on the other end know he was not pleased by the interruption.

"Evening, Mr. President. I hate to bother you, but we have a situation. May we come over?" He recognized the voice as Jim Baker's.

"Who is we? And, yes, by all means," the President agreed begrudgingly.

"I have Brent and Cheney with me, sir. We will be right there," Jim said before they ended the call.

Bush turned to Barbara. "Dear, can you ask the steward to put on a pot of coffee? I've got a feeling it's going to be a long night." His tone was one of resignation. He had really wanted this to be a relaxing weekend before the storm. It appeared the storm had arrived early instead.

"Sure, and then I'm going to bed. Don't need to hear you boys discussing business as I don't think this is a social call." She stood and moved to the kitchen, where their steward usually stayed with the Secret Service agent on duty.

Entering the kitchen, Barbara noticed Master Chief Sanvictores, who had served nine presidents, talking to the Secret Service agent on duty.

"Master Chief, can we get a fresh pot of coffee, please? It appears we are going to have visitors," Barbara asked.

"Certainly, ma'am, I have already been notified," the master chief said, exchanging a knowing smile with the Secret Service agent. "He told me."

When the President opened the door to the new arrivals from D.C., the looks on their faces told him all he needed to know.

"Come in and let me have it. I can tell this isn't going to be good," Bush said as he motioned to the couches that were facing each other over a coffee table. The steward had already placed the correct number of cups and saucers.

How the hell do they know every time? wondered the President.

Once everyone was seated, Jim Baker explained the purpose of their late-night visit.

"Mr. President, approximately two hours ago, Iraqi forces crossed the Saudi border and they are now moving deeper into Saudi Arabia along the highway from Kuwait to Al-Jubail. It appears their objective is the refinery at Al-Jubail. Information is still lacking, but I got a call from Charlie Freeman, our ambassador in Riyadh, who spoke with King Fahd. They're officially asking for assistance," Mr. Baker explained.

The President stared at him in shock for a minute before speaking. "What the hell is Saddam thinking? Have you spoken with Glaspie?" Bush finally asked.

"No, sir, all communications with our embassy in Baghdad have been cut off. We have not been able to contact them, nor can they contact us," Baker explained. "In addition, we've lost communications with the embassy in Kuwait City."

"The force that's invading Saudi Arabia... how big are we talking about?" the President asked as he reached for his coffee cup.

Secretary of Defense Cheney jumped at this question. "Right now it appears to be a corps-sized attack, or at least that's all we've been able to determine so far. That would be the 1st Republican Guard Corps."

"So the 2nd Republican Guard Corps is still sitting in Iraq. Well, that's good," the President indicated. Cheney looked at Scowcroft, and the President caught the look. "What... what about the 2nd Republican Guard Corps?"

"Sir, we just don't know. That part of Saudi is uninhabited until you get to Hafar Al-Batin, which is about fifty miles inside Saudi Arabia. For all we know, at this point he could be there. Our reconnaissance satellites should be able to show us something pretty soon," Cheney said.

"What have we got for satellite coverage over there now?" the President inquired. He didn't like being in the dark like he was right now.

Mr. Scowcroft explained, "Currently, Mr. President, we have Lacrosse, which is a radar-imaging satellite that can provide intel at night. There's one covering the Middle East and it makes a pass every ninety minutes. Information is downloaded to Fort Belvoir and analyzed. We have the Keyhole Spy Satellite Program with three satellites in polar orbit at this time, each taking ninety minutes to orbit, but they cannot penetrate clouds or dust. We have the KH-12 photoreconnaissance satellites, but that's not real-time data. In addition, two satellites from the Defense Support Program have been positioned over the Persian Gulf to detect any missile launches. If they detect one, after it's analyzed and the impact area determined, it'll give us roughly a two-minute window before impact if the missile is a Scud."

"Two minutes isn't much of a warning," the President mocked.

"I would agree if he was shooting a nuclear round, but the worst he can do is a chemical warhead, and that two minutes is sufficient for our people to get into a protective posture," Scowcroft reminded him.

"What about our aerial reconnaissance assets, the U-2s and the SR-71s?" the President asked.

"Sir, the U-2s have all been taken out of military service and now fly for NOAA and NASA. The SR-71s are presently going to the mothball yard in Tucson," Cheney explained.

"Like hell they are. Put a stop to that right now until we sort this out… and tell NOAA and NASA that DoD is taking those aircraft back, at least for the time being. What have you heard from General Yeosock and General Horner, our two guys on the ground?"

"Sir, they're in the air and only halfway to Riyadh. As soon as they're on the ground and have a chance to make an assessment, I'll get a report from them," Mr. Cheney said. "Sir, I recommend we place 18th Airborne Corps on alert for a possible deployment and move the 6th Fleet in the Med to the eastern portion."

"Do it. I still want those four naval vessels in the Persian Gulf out of there now. We don't need a *Stark* incident on top of this. Have we had any news on what action the Saudis are taking so far?"

"Sir, I was led to understand they're attempting to scramble some of their jets, but the central command-and-control facility at King Salman Air Base was badly damaged in a commando raid. The Iraqi Air Force has also surprisingly launched a pretty effective and complex air attack on many of the Saudi air bases. We think they caught many of their squadrons on the ground but cannot confirm that just yet. We'll know a lot more once our liaisons get on the ground and can provide us with a better assessment of things. Because of the attacks, their air force is in the process of switching their command and control over to Prince Sultan Air Force Base in Al-Kharj," Mr. Cheney informed the group. He had spoken with the Saudi Minister of Defense, Prince Sultan bin Abdulaziz, as he tried to get a better picture of what was going on.

"Alright, let's get a formal complaint before the Security Council at the UN. Spin up the 18th Airborne Corps for a possible deployment. Move the 6th Fleet into position off the eastern Med. And let's get some damn real-time looks at what's going on. How many fronts have the Iraqis opened up? How many units are involved? What's the long-range endgame they are pursuing? Lastly, I want to know what the Saudis want us to do. It's getting late and there's a lot that needs to get done, so get the balls in motion now. Let's go ahead and schedule an eight a.m. meeting in the Situation Room. It'll be midafternoon in Saudi Arabia by that time and we should have a better understanding of what's happening on the ground. Is there anything else?"

Mr. Baker looked at the two other cabinet members and shook his head. "Mr. President, I believe that's all we have to report as of right now."

The President nodded and then got up. He was going to head off to bed while the others flew back to Washington to get things moving.
****

The next morning, the President entered the White House Situation Room to a flurry of activity. He had just arrived back from Camp David on Marine One moments ago.

"Good morning, Mr. President," Mr. Cheney said, sounding perhaps a bit more chipper than the President himself felt.

"What's so damn good about it, Dick? Tell me the Iraqis came to their senses and pulled back to Kuwait," the President quipped. He was in a bit of a foul mood after having his weekend spoiled.

"I wish I could, Mr. President, but that didn't happen. I'll let Lieutenant Colonel Atwell explain. Colonel Atwell..." Mr. Cheney motioned with his hand for the briefer to start.

Colonel Atwell could see the President was in no mood for morning pleasantries, so he jumped right into his brief. "Mr. President, at approximately 0200 hours Kuwait time, the 1st Republican Guard Corps launched an attack out of southern Kuwait with five divisions. These units appear to be heading towards the Al-Jubail oil refinery along the coast. They've already seized the King Abdulaziz Naval Base at Ras Al-Khair, which had one ship in port, a *Badr*-class corvette, along with two patrol boats that couldn't escape before the base was captured.

"In addition, they captured the Jubail Naval Airport. Unfortunately, the Iraqi Army had blitzkrieged their way across the border and nabbed the base in the early hours of the morning, capturing approximately eighteen helicopters. They covered some two hundred kilometers before dawn, catching the vast majority of the Saudi armed forces by complete surprise as they slept. Judging by the latest satellite intelligence, it would appear the lead elements at this time are between Al-Jubail and Safwan north of Dammam. This means they'll likely capture King Fahd Air Force Base before noon today," Colonel Atwell explained, pausing only long enough to let the information be digested by the policy makers. When no immediate questions were raised, he continued.

"Sir, on the western side of Saudi, the 2nd Republican Guard Corps entered the Kingdom with two divisions at the same time as the 1st RG Corps in a closely coordinated effort to take the bulk of the Saudi military out on the first day of the war. Presently, the 2nd Republican Guard Corps advanced rapidly on the King Khalid Military City. This facility did have a large armored force of tanks and infantry fighting vehicles along with an air base. Had they been able to get organized, they could have blunted the Iraqis' advance," Colonel Atwell explained.

"I suppose you're going to tell us that didn't happen, though?" Bush interjected, sounding rather glum at how fast the Saudi Army appeared to be crumbling.

Atwell shook his head somberly. "Unfortunately, no. A couple of hours prior to the ground assault, the base came under a surprise air attack. A flight of Su-22s Fitters carried out an attack on the runway, disabling it before any fighters could get airborne. That attack was quickly followed by a squadron of Su-25 Frogfoot ground-attack aircraft that hammered the tank and vehicle yards on the base. They apparently destroyed much of the brigade's armored vehicles, leaving them little with which to defend the base or the nearby city.

"When the 2nd Republican Guard Corps arrived around 0900 local time, they were engaged by what remained of the Saudi brigade. At approximately 1200 local time, it appeared the fighting had finally ceased, and the Iraqis had taken complete control of the base. Our last satellite feed showed they already had combat engineers working on repairing the runways. They're probably going to move more of their aircraft and helicopters forward as their forces look to move deeper into the Kingdom." Colonel Atwell paused as he could feel the President staring daggers at him.

He's going to shit bricks after this next set of news I have to deliver, Atwell thought.

"Well, is that it, Colonel?" the President asked snarkily. When he'd gone to bed, things had seemed OK. Somehow, in the span of ten hours, the Iraqi Army had managed to capture a huge swath of the country and destroyed large portions of the Saudi military in the process.

Colonel Atwell took a deep breath in before slowly shaking his head. The President's expression changed from one of anger and frustration to a look of shock and horror that the situation could possibly be graver than what he'd already been told.

"Unfortunately, no, sir. We're waiting on confirmation, but we suspect that at 0200 hours, the 2nd Army Corps—not the Republican Guard Corps, but the regular army units out in the far western desert—crossed the Amman-Baghdad Road and are now moving to strike Tabuk. Intelligence believes if they succeed in capturing Tabuk, they'll likely move down the coastal roads and mountain passes to capture Jeddah, and then the two Islamic holy cities of Medina and Mecca."

151

"Oh jeez, you are just full of cheery news this morning, aren't you, Colonel?" Bush replied. "Go ahead, continue. We've ripped the band-aid off, let's go ahead and clean it out and get all the bad news out in the open."

Colonel Atwell gave a sheepish smile as he continued. "Sir, at dawn, the Iraqi Air Force surged across the border with three-hundred-plus aircraft and attacked the King Khalid Military City as we discussed earlier—the Dhahran Air Base, the King Faisal Air Base, King Fahd Air Base, and the King Salman Air Base. However, they really made a point of hitting the Prince Sultan Air Base in Al-Kharj incredibly hard. As a matter of fact, they hit it with their Tu-16 Badger bombers and Tu-22 Blinder bombers. They'd used these bombers during the Iran-Iraq War, so it's not entirely surprising that they would use them here. What did catch us off guard was how many were involved. At the end of the Iran-Iraq War, they had three Badgers and four Blinders left. They had sustained a few combat losses. The attack on Prince Sultan, however, was carried out by sixteen Blinders and Badgers each. Not only have the Soviets lent the Iraqis new frontline ground equipment, but it's becoming more apparent they also lent them additional modern fighters, interceptors, and now bombers."

"Jesus! How in the hell did this happen?" President Bush blurted out angrily. "How were the Soviets able to transfer what amounts to thousands of modern-day tanks, infantry fighting vehicles, anti-aircraft equipment, and now aircraft? Last I checked, we still had a Central Intelligence Agency, yes?"

Dick Cheney intervened, adding, "It's not that our intelligence agencies dropped the ball on this. It's not. What we're discovering is that these agencies and their assets have been so focused on the Soviets that they failed to see the forest for the trees. Upon further review, they're starting to find more and more evidence that the Soviets may in fact be behind Saddam's rapid arms buildup before the war. They may also have provided arms to the Iranians to further beef them up as well."

"But to what end, Dick? What are the Soviets trying to achieve by stirring up a war in the Middle East?" Bush asked as he looked at his Secretary of Defense and then the others in the room. Something wasn't adding up and he wasn't sure what it was.

James Baker came to Dick's defense, countering, "Mr. President, all of our departments have been pretty taxed with what's been going on abroad. The apparent Soviet lend-lease program took place during Operation Just Cause in Panama, so we didn't see what they were doing. Our focus has also been on pressuring the rest of OPEC to keep the price of oil low to further subvert the Soviet economy. While our people continue to unravel what happened, I propose we stay focused on what's going on here and now. We can't change the past, but we most certainly can influence the future."

Bush bit his lower lip in frustration as he turned to one side. He then let out a long sigh and appeared resigned to the idea that the past was the past and what mattered now was the future.

"Colonel Atwell, sorry for my interruption. You're doing a fine job with the brief. It's just hard to take it all in. Please continue," the President directed now that he had regained his composure.

Colonel Atwell smiled reassuringly at the President and then continued. "Sir, when the Iraqi commandos took out the command-and-control center at King Fahd Air Base, the Saudis really lost control of the air battle almost immediately. Few interceptors were able to get airborne, and the ones that could largely got shot down or flew away to another airfield that wasn't under direct attack. This meant most of the Saudi aircraft were destroyed on the ground in the early hours of the day."

The President looked like he was getting angry again as he asked, "Well, how many Iraqi aircraft did they manage to shoot down?"

"As best we can tell, sir, none."

"None! What about their Hawk batteries? Hell, they bought enough of them to cover every air base and port in the country."

"Sir, the air-defense center controlling them all was co-located with the command-and-control center. There are also reports that several of the Hawk batteries failed to respond to commands. We aren't sure why at this point."

"So let me see if I have this right, Colonel. You're telling me that the Iraqis have seven divisions running around over northern Saudi Arabia, who have already, in the first twelve hours of the war, had one brigade destroyed along with the Saudi Air Force and a portion of the Saudi fleet? Do I have that about right?" the President asked. It was obvious that his blood pressure was on the rise.

153

"That's about right, sir," Colonel Atwell said. "The 1st Republican Guard Corps has four divisions, the 2nd Republican Guard Corps has two divisions, and the 2nd Army Corps has five divisions. All told, sir, the Iraqi Army has fifty divisions on the books."

"Thank you, Colonel," the President said, deflating his emotions. He turned to the assembled group. "Dick, have we heard from Yeosock or Horner?"

"Yes, sir, I spoke to both of them just before I came in here. The picture's as bleak as Colonel Atwell has outlined. The only unit that could respond was the brigade at King Khalid Military City, and their response couldn't be much as they were just overwhelmed by two divisions with supporting artillery and attack helicopters, and they got mauled at the outset of the war by Su-25s. The attack on the left to Al-Jubail has been very tempered in the use of their artillery as the Iraqis appear to be showing some restraint in not wanting to hit civilian targets. Both corps are respecting the civilian population, which honestly is a huge relief. They're trying to appear as liberators who free the people from a tyrannical king—at least that's what both our and the Saudi psyops guys believe."

Bush snorted at that last assessment. It was a good ploy on Saddam's part. "OK, so what are the Saudis asking for from us?" the President asked, already in his mind knowing the answer.

"Sir, everything and anything right now," Mr. Cheney answered swiftly.

"Gentlemen, your opinions. General Powell, you first."

"Mr. President, it's obvious that the Saudis were ill prepared for this attack, even though the Iraqis had just invaded Kuwait with an overwhelming force. If we sent equipment to them, I doubt that they could effectively use it, which would only result in it falling into the hands of the Iraqi forces."

"Jesus, Powell, you're talking about sending over equipment when they're screaming for combat troops," Sununu snapped. He'd had it with the Chairman's lack of resolve to use military force.

General Powell turned to the President's Chief of Staff. "The President has asked for my military advice and I'm providing it. Thank you very much."

Bush placed a hand on Sununu's arm. "It's OK, John. He's doing his job. Please continue, General."

Powell nodded slightly to the President, then stared daggers at his Chief of Staff. "As I was saying, I would recommend we have air from the fleet provide air support to replace the Saudi Air Force and we go ahead and put several wings of fighters and bombers from England on alert while we pursue some basing rights for them to operate out of."

"General Vuono, what is your recommendation?" the President asked his Army Chief of Staff.

"Sir, after our last meeting, I called Gary Luck at the XVIII Airborne Corps and gave him a warning order. 1st Brigade of the 82nd can be airborne in six hours with the rest of the division following on. 101st has been given an eighteen-hour notice for their attack helicopters and the rest of the division to follow. 24th Mech in Savannah can have their heavy equipment at the port and begin loading the pre-positioned ships in twelve hours. If the Air Force can lend them some C-5s, they can airlift the division and most of their non-heavyweight equipment with them. All told, we can probably have boots on the ground in twenty-four hours with their heavy armor and equipment showing up roughly nine days later. The 101st still has a battalion down in Panama training that they have to get back and one battalion up at West Point, but you say the word and they'll get them pulled back home and spun up to deploy within a few days," the Army Chief of Staff explained.

The President smiled at the news. He was starting to see a plan coming into view.

Looking at Admiral Kelso, the CNO who'd have to make a lot of things happen, Bush asked, "Admiral, where do things stand on your end?"

Admiral Kelso cleared his throat. "Sir, last night we ordered the Carrier Battle Group *Eisenhower* to proceed to a position in the eastern Med. In addition, the Carrier Battle Group *Independence* is holding its position in the Gulf of Oman. Both groups have an MEU with them that we can put ashore at any time."

Turning to General Dugan next, the President asked, "What have we got for Air Force assets in the area?"

"Sir, we can self-deploy the 1st Fighter Wing, out of Langley AFB, Virginia. The wing consists of forty-eight F-15 aircraft: the 36th Tactical

Fighter Wing, from Bitburg, Germany, with thirty-six F-15s, and the 7440 Composite Wing from Incirlik, Turkey, as well as some AC-130 aircraft from Hulbert Field. It just depends on what CENTCOM wants. We also have the 48th Fighter Wing out of RAF Lakenheath. They've got sixty-six F-111F medium-range tactical attack aircraft and ten EF-111 electronic countermeasure aircraft from the 42nd and 390th Electronic Combat Squadrons. If we send a squadron of refueling aircraft, we could run sustained air operations over much of Saudi Arabia if ordered," General Dugan explained.

Satisfied with the response, Bush turned to the Commandant. "General Gray, what about the Marines? What kind of support could we quickly provide?"

"Sir, the MEU with the *Eisenhower* is the slowest vessel of the fleet. If we're considering moving the *Eisenhower* to the Gulf, then I'd recommend we move the MEU now. By the time they get to the Gulf, the *Eisenhower* would have caught up. They can move now through the Suez Canal, as long as the Egyptians don't close it to traffic."

"Jim, what has Mubarak said about this?"

Baker snorted at the question before replying, "He is not happy, Mr. President. He views this as a slap in the face, as he tried to broker a compromise that would have prevented something like this from happening. He really thought he had a deal worked out between Saddam and the Kuwaiti Emir. If you want, I'll get back to him, but for now I don't think that's going to be a problem after how embarrassed he feels by Saddam's actions."

"Sir, if I may," Powell interjected politely.

"Sure, go ahead."

"Sir, we may be able to get Saddam to back down without getting into a shooting war with him. After all, he controls the fourth-largest army in the world."

"And how do we do that," asked Cheney, in genuine shock as he looked at Powell.

"Sir, if we put the 82nd in right away someplace that hasn't fallen into Iraqi hands, that will plant the flag. Saddam is going to think twice before he attacks an American unit. That might be enough to have him stop in place and call for a cease-fire and allow negotiations to begin," Powell offered.

156

"Gentlemen, your opinions?" the President asked. It took only seconds for everyone to be in agreement.

Sununu added, "Mr. President, if we take this course of action, I want to get the press on the scene and show the world—and more importantly, Saddam—that we mean business. That we're readying and deploying the force. That might help convince him that we aren't bluffing and he needs to think really hard about whether he wants to wage war against the United States also."

The President smiled at that. "Good idea, do it. Alright, General Powell, get the 82nd moving and the 101st. Coordinate with the embassy on where these boys are going in, and make sure it isn't someplace that may be overrun before they even get there. I don't want to push them into a fight as soon as they get off the plane. General Gray, Admiral Kelso, get the MEU moving and let's see what port the Saudis think the MEU should dock at and figure out how soon we can get them there. Admiral, let's also move the *Eisenhower* into position to support the MEU and join the *Independence*. Powell, let's see what CENTCOM wants and how soon we can get it to them. We have a lot to get ready and not a lot of time. Let's put all these decades of planning and training into practice and make it happen. That'll be all."

"Mr. President, I would recommend you address the nation tonight and explain what has happened and what actions we're taking. This would reassure the people and give you an opportunity to let Saddam see that you're not bluffing," Sununu said.

"Good idea, set it up. I'll go live and lay out what's happened and what we're planning to do about it at this point," the President responded.

With that, he got up to handle some domestic affairs. He had a solid team, and they knew what to do. He just needed to stay out of the way once the decision to act had been made.

Chapter Twenty
Attack South

4 August 1990
1st Hammurabi Armoured Division
Al-Jubail, Saudi Arabia

The sun was well above the horizon as the 1st RG Corps continued to move south. Al-Jubail had easily been bypassed by the 17th Armored Brigade, who had met little to no resistance.

As they approached the refineries, they appeared to be intact. The 18th Armored Brigade on the right flank had met no resistance except for desert sand dunes. These natural obstacles had broken up the terrain and prevented an orderly spread-out move by the armored vehicles. Instead, they ended up bunching up on each other until they got past some of the terrain features. Many of the 18th Armored Brigade's vehicles had to follow in a trail formation, with those following eating the dust of those leading. Meanwhile, the 17th Armored Brigade traveled on a four-lane road and for the most part did not suffer the dust.

Lieutenant General Majid al-Dulaymi, the 1st Republican Guard Corps Commander, was pleased with the progress. He hadn't needed to call for close-air support so far. But in the distance, he could see black smoke, indicating that King Fahd Military Airport had been put out of action. Sitting in his command vehicle behind the 1st Hammurabi Armored Division, he was not eating dust. He also had good communications with his various units and could easily watch the events unfolding before him.

Turing to his driver, General Majid al-Dulaymi directed, "Let's move up and find General al-Ujayli. He should be up ahead not far on this road."

General al-Ujayli commanded the 1st Hammurabi Armored Division and would normally travel behind the lead brigades and in front of the reserve brigade. In this case, he was following the 17th Armored Brigade.

As General al-Dulaymi moved up, passing vehicles of the attacking brigades, he could see the enthusiasm in the faces of his soldiers. *No longer are we the beggars of the Arab world, but the victors,* he thought with pride. But he did have some growing concerns for their equipment.

Our T-72 tanks have undergone some modernization with laser range finders and sabot rounds thanks to the Russians. Still, I wish we had better range than the Saudi M1 tank. We are just going to have to use the terrain better and be inside their range when we engage. "First shot, first kill" is what we have taught our tank commanders. Our training has improved our performance as well since the conflict with Iran. We learned a lot in that fight—learned what not *to do.*

Pulling up alongside General al-Ujayli's vehicle, he motioned for al-Ujayli to pull over to the side of the road. Getting out of their vehicles, they exchanged salutes.

"How is the 1st Division doing?" al-Dulaymi asked.

"We are meeting our schedule, sir. We have met almost no resistance except a small contingent at the Jubail Naval Airport, but it surrendered quickly. They only had a few Saudi Marines guarding the place. The 17th is just now securing the refinery at Al-Jubail. The Special Forces elements from the 8th As Saiqa Division did well in securing the refinery before any destructive charges could have done damaged or destroyed it," General al-Ujayli reported.

"Good, don't get bogged down in the refinery. You must keep moving. Let the Special Forces elements secure the refinery and get the 17th moving again. I will talk to the IX Corps commander and have one of his divisions swing in to secure the refinery. That is not your job. Your job is to press home the attack and keep the Saudis off-balance and on the backs of their heels. Understood?"

General al-Ujayli got the message loud and clear. "Yes, sir, I will get the 17th moving right away." He turned and started to bark out a set of new orders to one of his aides.

"One other thing, General. Don't let your brigade or battalion commands get bogged down in Dammam or Dhahran either. We have follow-on forces ready to secure those places. Your mission needs to press the attack to the Saudi-Omani border. The quicker you do that, the faster we can bring this action to a conclusion. I do not think it will be long before we see American aircraft attack us from above as they try to prevent us from achieving our goals. The Americans have too much invested with the Saudi king to just stand by and watch us take over his kingdom. Now get your people moving."

"Yes, sir," General al-Ujayli said as he moved to head back to his vehicle while still facing General al-Dulaymi. The last thing he wanted was to get into a pissing contest with al-Dulaymi.

****

Climbing into his command vehicle, General al-Ujayli thought it best to get face-to-face with General Ra'ad al-Hamdani. He felt relatively secure as there had been no contact with any Saudi forces to speak of and he did not expect any resistance either. His driver moved them down the highway until he finally spotted the pennant on the antenna of al-Hamdani's vehicle sitting on the side of the road. He directed his driver to pull in behind it and saw al-Hamdani was standing next to the vehicle.

As his own vehicle came to a stop, al-Hamdani approached.

"Good morning, sir," al-Hamdani said as he saluted.

"Good morning. Why are you stopped?" al-Ujayli asked with a quizzical look.

"Sir, we are refueling some vehicles at the refinery before we move on," al-Hamdani said.

"Why are you needing to refuel tanks? The range on the T-72 is four hundred and sixty-four kilometers without the exterior fuel drums and six hundred and eighty-eight kilometers with the drums, and you have drums. Get your attack moving now. The fuel trucks can refuel you on the road if needed, but we need to get moving."

Holding a hand up in surrender, al-Hamdani said he'd order his units to get back on the road and skip the pit stop. Before he could get away from the ire of his superior, General al-Ujayli added, "When you get to Dammam and Dhahran, do not let your units get bogged down there. Bypass them and let the follow-on forces deal with it. I need you to attack south with all haste and keep the Saudis on the backs of their heels. Is that understood?"

"Sir, we are on schedule, and bypassing those major cities leaves our follow-on supplies in peril," al-Hamdani said with a bit of concern and surprise.

160

"The 8th Mechanized Brigade will secure your rear until the arrival of the IX Corps. Two of their divisions will seize and occupy those two cities. There is another division of this corps following you to protect your supply line, and the IX Corps is coming in behind them. Let the army dogs bark at Dhahran and Dammam. I need you to get to the Saudi-Omani border ahead of schedule if possible."

"What about cutting over to seize Riyadh? I thought—" al-Hamdani started to say.

"That is not your problem any longer. Your orders are to attack south. Understood?" Al-Hamdani could see that al-Ujayli was becoming irritated.

"Yes, sir, we will get moving right away. If you will excuse me, I will give the order." Al-Hamdani saluted, then turned and walked back to his vehicle.

Why can't he be following the 18th and stay off my back? al-Ujayli thought privately.

The 18th Armored Brigade was moving southward under very different conditions. Since leaving Kuwait, the brigade had encountered only small farm settlements with no resistance at all. What few people they came across just stood and looked at them as they rolled by. Those following the lead elements wore goggles and face masks to protect them from the dust.

With few roads and open desert, the 18th Brigade was well dispersed into four columns. As they rolled south, they would be able to pick up a paved road, Highway 75 in the vicinity of Shifiyah, fifty-four miles west of Al-Jubail. Shifiyah was a small farming compound consisting of three or four homes and not much more. The brigade would turn further south and strike out for Urayarah, twenty-nine miles to the south or Shifiyah. Seizing Urayarah would allow the brigade to cut the main highway from Dhahran to Riyadh. Once that was done, a decision was going to have to be made as to who would get to capture the prize, Riyadh.
****

Brigadier General Mustafa al-Hassan had commanded the brigade for over two years. He knew his commanders and most of the individual tank commanders, of which there were over a hundred and fifty. He had

161

handpicked each one of them. In his eyes, they were all lions. All had fought the Iranians, so they didn't lack for combat experience either.

Still, al-Hassan had felt slighted when the main attack for the division had been given to al-Hamdani. If he seized the Riyadh highway, he would be in an excellent position to lead the division attack into Riyadh with al-Hamdani following.

To al-Hassan, it was all about speed, and therefore he ordered his commanders to stop for nothing. When they reached Urayarah, they could refuel their vehicles there if they needed. If a vehicle ran out of fuel, then a fuel truck would come along and handle it.

However, the tank commander that ran out of fuel had best have a good reason for doing so. Each tank should have enough fuel to make it to Urayarah easily. Any fuel they came across in the Saudi farms went into replenishing the fuel trucks. Time was not on their side. Speed was life at this point, and they needed to cripple the Saudis now, before the Americans looked to intervene.

Chapter Twenty-One
My Fellow Americans

4 August 1990
Oval Office
White House
Washington, D.C.

The producer held up three fingers. "Three, two, one," he counted, pointing at the President, who was seated behind the Resolute Desk.

"Good evening, my fellow Americans. I come before you tonight to explain a grave situation that has developed in the Middle East. As you know, Iraq sent forces into Kuwait on the first of August and overran that tiny nation in one day. We presented a strong case to the Security Council along with Great Britain to force the Iraqi Army out of Kuwait and reestablish the legitimate government. The Security Council, led by the Soviet Union and China as well as France, refused to condemn this action. The festering argument between Iraq and Kuwait is over the debts Iraq incurred during the Iran-Iraq War and Iraqi insistence that it did not have to pay those debts back. Several nations, to include Saudi Arabia and Egypt, forgave the debt and attempted to present a negotiated peace settlement, but Iraq refused and launched an attack. The brother of the Emir was killed in this action, and we extended to His Highness our deepest sympathy.

"This morning while we slept, Iraq, not satisfied with the results it achieved in Kuwait, launched a surprise attack into Saudi Arabia on three fronts with overwhelming forces. In addition, air strikes have hit most airports and military facilities. It appears that they will quickly overrun the country resulting in Iraq controling the majority of the world's oil supply, and that cannot be allowed.

"Therefore, I have ordered that US naval forces in the region provide support to the Saudi armed forces. In addition, I have placed the 18th Airborne Corps on alert for immediate deployment to the region. It is my sincere hope that Iraq will recognize the sovereign rights of Saudi Arabia and withdraw its forces as quickly as possible. We are asking the nations of the world to join us, if necessary, in forcing Iraq out of Saudi Arabia and Kuwait. In the days to follow, you will see our service members from

163

across the country moving to embarkation ports and airfields. It is my sincere hope that their presence in the region will be sufficient to convince the Iraqi forces to return to Iraq without bloodshed. But Iraq must understand that, one way or the other, Iraqi forces will return to Iraqi soil.

"I ask all of you for your prayers for our service members and their families as we undertake this endeavor. Good night and God bless."

Chapter Twenty-Two
Air Superiority

5 August 1990
CENTCOM Headquarters
MacDill Air Force Base
Tampa, Florida

"John, Norm here. What's the situation?" General Norman Schwarzkopf asked.

Lieutenant General John Yeosock was his deputy and commander of the 3rd Army, the ground component of CENTCOM. Yeosock and Horner had arrived in Riyadh after an eighteen-hour flight from MacDill AFB in Tampa. Their plane had done a couple of in-flight refuels.

"Norm, it isn't good. The Iraqis have punched across the border and are attacking on three fronts. One just took the King Khalid Military City, and another's driving towards Dhahran. The Iraqi 2nd Corps is heading for Tabuk and meeting little to no opposition. The Iraqis have taken the refinery at Al-Jubail intact and the Royal Saudi Navy base just north of there. The Iraqi Air Force hit almost every Saudi airfield pretty hard at dawn after their commandos took out the central air-defense command and several of the Hawk batteries."

There was a slight pause in the report before he continued, "There's an armored brigade minus here in Riyadh, but the King is reluctant to move them as they don't know which front offers the greatest threat. Like an armored brigade is going to stop this juggernaut. Either of two fronts could turn towards the capital. I think the King will probably be bugging out for his home in Spain now that the brigade at King Khalid Military City has fallen. Right now, he is asking if we could send in jets from the carrier task force to assist. I told him I would have to clear that with the President, and we would need to get an ANGLICO team with the Saudis to coordinate the strikes. Many of the royals are at the airport getting on their private jets and beating feet out of the country at this point," General Yeosock concluded.

"John, we need to move fast if we're going to do anything. I'm ordering that we execute the force package in OPLAN 1002-88 right away. I've spoken to Powell, and he's in agreement. His staff is cutting the orders now. I've also spoken to Gary Luck at 18th Airborne Corps, and he anticipated this going down and already put his ready brigade on alert, so they'll have a wheels-up in about four hours instead of dead start eighteen hours. McCaffrey is ready to move tanks to the port of Savannah. Where should they send them?"

"At this point, and as long as it's going to take to get them here from the States, I cannot say with any certainty—by the time they get here, Dammam and Dhahran will have been captured. As for the ready brigade of the 82nd, the airfields will probably be overrun except for Prince Sultan Military Airfield south of Riyadh and Riyadh International, but they'll be totally isolated shortly if things keep going this poorly. Hell, it would be another Bastogne. I would recommend that we get an MEU to Jeddah on the Red Sea in case we need to evacuate people or want to get a force in-country and put the 82nd in there to help hold that port. If things get really bad, we can evacuate them," Yeosock explained, trying to convey the direness of the situation.

"Sounds good. Is Horner there with you?" Schwarzkopf asked.

"Yeah."

"Put him on," Schwarzkopf directed.

General Yeosock handed the phone to General Horner. "He wants to talk to you."

"Norm, the Saudi Air Force got caught with their pants around their ankles. The early-warning command center at Prince Sultan Military Airfield was taken out by commandos before dawn and just before the air strikes came in. The one AWACS aircraft the Saudis had in the air was taken out just about the same time. Hawk batteries were hesitant to fire, so they were ineffective because no one knew what was going on."

"Has the Navy launched any aircraft in support of the Saudi ground forces?" Schwarzkopf asked, hopeful that maybe US and Saudi forces were working together to stop this invasion.

"I don't believe so. They have a problem right now of not knowing who the naval air wings should talk with, and they're unfortunately really lacking any kind of big-picture awareness of what's going on. Honestly, Norm, the Iraqis really did a hell of a job knocking out the Saudis' initial ability to respond to the invasion. The Iraqis are masterfully using this confusion to rush their units all across the country, gobbling up as much of it as they can, as quickly as they can."

General Horner audibly sighed for a moment before adding, "Right now, Norm, the Iraqis have air superiority over Saudi. The Iraqi Su-25s have been hammering any sort of defense the Saudis even try to organize. At this point, if the Saudis want to retain any control of their country, we need to get the Navy in an air interdiction role as well as getting fighters out of Incirlik to hit Iraq from the north."

"To do that, we have to clear it with Turkey to use that base for that purpose. I'll speak with Colin and have him get State on that," explained Schwarzkopf.

"Well, we can start moving stuff this way. I think we should alert the 71st out of Langley and the 42nd Bomb out of Loring and get them over here quick. We can stage the 42nd out of Diego Garcia, and the 71st I would send to Muscat or someplace in Oman, but not Saudi. Can we get them into Oman... or Egypt?" Horner asked.

"You get them moving and I'll get the clearance for someplace over there. I'll call you back in a few hours and let you know where we're moving CENTCOM headquarters, as I'm not going to sit in Tampa and play this from here. Pass on to John that I'm going to order the prepackaged loads at Diego Garcia to head to the area. You guys think the ports would be overrun before the ships could get there?" General Schwarzkopf asked. "It's only a four-day sail."

"Right now, I'd bet those ports will be in Iraqi hands in twenty-four hours. There's nothing to stop their advance in the east, or the west right now," explained Horner.

"OK, well, at least they'll be en route. The Marines at Camp Lejeune have been alerted for deployment along with 18th Airborne Corps, whose rapid reaction force should be arriving soon. Let me get cracking on the other things and I'll call you back in about four hours. We should have some decisions by then."

With that, General Schwarzkopf turned to his aide, who'd been taking notes, and directed, "Get General Powell on the phone."

A few minutes later, Schwarzkopf was connected to the Chairman of the Joint Chiefs. "Colin, I just got off the phone with Yeosock and Horner. We're going to need some immediate diplomatic support. My guys on the ground in Saudi are saying things are not only bad, they're going to get a lot worse in the next forty-eight to ninety-six hours."

Schwarzkopf heard an audible sigh from Powell before he asked, "The situation has gotten that dire that quick, then?"

"Unfortunately, yes. They're telling me that the Iraqis are attacking on three fronts as they roll across the country. By tomorrow, they'll have captured Dammam, Dhahran and the major port and refinery facilities in the Gulf. They're likely looking to capture all the way down to the Omani border in a day or two. Right now, the only port the Saudis think they'll be able to control in a week's time is Jeddah on the Red Sea. Same with airfields, as the Iraqi Air Force took out most of the Saudi Air Force in a predawn strike. Prince Sultan Military Airfield is operational, as are the international airports at Jeddah and Riyadh, but that's it. Right now I'm looking at putting the rapid reaction force for the 82nd in at Jeddah as well as an MEU. That will give us a toehold. What I need is a port on the eastern side of the country that won't be overrun in the next thirty days—it's going to take that long to get some heavy forces to the area. What I would like is to see if the Oman government will allow us to use their port facilities and staging areas. The ports can handle offloads, although they're not great and the terrain between Saudi and there is pretty rugged and not conducive to armor—"

"I don't want to expand this and involve Oman unless we really have to go that route," Colin interrupted.

"Well, damnit, Colin, you could at least ask Baker to ask them, couldn't you? Horner wants to see if we can land our fighters there in Oman as well as Turkey, or Egypt if the Turks give him shit. He's looking at bringing the 42nd out of Loring and landing them at Diego Garcia, but the fighters need a base closer, unless you think the Navy with eighty-some aircraft can take on the Iraqi Air Force with over four hundred fighters," Schwarzkopf pointed out.

"No, we're going to need to get air assets in the area. I'll talk to Baker about basing in Egypt and Oman," Powell said reluctantly.

"Thank you. Oh, wait one. We only have one carrier with the 5th Fleet in the Arabian Sea. Can we get the *Eisenhower* out of the Med and reposition to the Red Sea? That would provide some protection to the 82nd boys and MEU."

"I'll talk to Kelso and get an update on the availability of carriers," Powell said in a resigned voice.

168

"Excellent, I'll wait for your call." When Stormin' Norman hung up, he had a satisfied smile on his face—something his aide took notice of and smiled himself.

Chapter Twenty-Three
US Air Force to the Fight

6 August 1990
Langley Air Force Base
Newport, Virginia

Captain Willis Tate packed a deployment bag as soon as he heard the Iraqis had crossed into Kuwait. He had a sixth sense about this, or maybe he was a little more intelligent than most about what was going to happen. Or maybe he was just hoping he'd have a chance to get into some real aerial dogfighting.

Tate was an F-15C fighter pilot, and a damn good one at that. He'd been with the 71st Fighter Squadron for four years, and not only did he love the squadron, he also loved the area. Living in Newport, Virginia, with all the area had to offer his family, made this posting a dream come true. As an avid fisherman, he found that the Chesapeake Bay offered every kind of good eating fish a man could seek, not to mention the crabs.

When he went to bed, he had the weekend all figured out. He and his wife were going to take the munchkins out on their thirty-foot fishing boat to cruise the gunk holes of the Chesapeake. That was until he heard the phone ringing next to his bed. As he reached for the receiver, his eyes caught sight of the alarm clock: 0300 hours.

Damn, this had better be good.

"Captain Tate here," he said in an obvious sleep voice.

"Sir, sorry to wake you, but we have a recall. You have a flight briefing at 0500. Oh, and, sir, don't expect to be going home afterwards," the voice on the other end said.

"Where are we going and for how long?" Tate asked as he rolled out of the bed, knowing full well what the answer was and that it would not be said over the phone.

"Can't say, sir. Just told to contact you and provide the information," the man said.

"OK, I'm up. I got it. Thanks."

His wife groggily rolled over and asked, "What's going on, Willis?"

Being an Air Force fighter pilot's wife, she had gotten used to the early-morning recalls the base would initiate from time to time.

170

Turning a light on so he could see her face, he said, "I have to go, hon."

Now she sat up, a startled look on her face. They'd talked about what was going on in the Middle East and how one day he might get called to head over there.

"This is it, isn't it? That thing you said that might happen?" she said, a bit of fear in her voice and uncertainty spreading across her face.

Tate didn't say anything for a moment. It just hit him that this probably really was it. He was about to leave for war, a war he might not come home from. In that moment, he turned and faced her. He placed both hands on her face and kissed her deep and long. Without saying anything more, they made love for what might be the last time. They didn't spend long in bed but made sure it was a memorable experience before he jumped in the shower while she got a pot of coffee going and readied his thermos.

When he walked into the kitchen, he asked, "Do you want to drive me to the Ops building or do you want me to leave the car there?"

"No, I'll drive you. Let me get the kids up," she said, heading down the hall to wake the little monsters up.

"You don't need to wake them. You'll only be gone, what... fifteen minutes?" he said before taking his first sip of coffee.

"Willis, don't be a fool. I'm not leaving the kids here. They'll want to see you. God only knows when you'll be back."

As she walked down the hall in her formfitting jeans, he smirked. *Damn, I'm going to miss that ass.*

They loaded the kids and his deployment bag into the car and made the short ten-minute drive to Flight Ops. It seemed that everyone in the squadron had been called, to include pilots and ground personnel. Husbands and wives stood close to each other, exchanging kisses, while young children held Daddy's or Mommy's leg. Slowly, the folks in uniform all moved into the building, and even more slowly, those left behind began to leave the parking lot.

Once everyone was in the squadron briefing room, Lieutenant Colonel Keith Roberts stepped up the podium. He was the squadron commander and had been for a year. Like most lieutenant colonels in the Air Force, he'd caught the end of the Vietnam War and had some combat experience over the skies of Hanoi in those closing days.

171

"Alright, listen up. Sorry to drag you out of your beds, but we received a deployment order around midnight. The ground personnel were called in first and have been here readying your planes. Once you guys are airborne, they'll be off themselves to follow behind in some C-141s."

This sudden deluge of news caught everyone by surprise, especially with how fast things were happening. Once Lieutenant Colonel Roberts had gotten everyone to quiet down again, he continued.

"You all know the Iraqi forces crossed into Saudi Arabia two days ago. Apparently they're gobbling up the country a hell of a lot faster than the brass at the Pentagon thought possible. They also hit every Saudi airfield ahead of the ground attack and appear to have destroyed most of the Saudi Air Force before it had a chance to get off the ground or even relocate to an airfield further away from the fighting.

"Right now, it appears the only operational airfields are Prince Sultan Air Base near Riyadh, though it was hit pretty hard during the opening day of the war, and a couple of air bases around Jeddah and Medina. The runways for the bases in and around the Jeddah and Medina area are intact from what we've been told, but the Prince Sultan Air Base only has one operational runway until the others can be patched up. This means we're going to be flying into some airfields that are currently under enemy air attack, so we'll need to be flexible on where we land." Roberts paused for a moment to let that sink in.

"This will be a deployment to Mildenhall with an RON[8] and then a continuation to the Middle East." Moans and groans could be heard from the pilots. "We'll launch at 0700 this morning, with twenty-four aircraft departing in groups of four in one-hour intervals. Until you launch, you will remain here, and there will be no outside phone calls. I'll be flight leader for the first flight. Major Goodall will be flight leader for the last flight. He'll assign flight leader positions later. If there are no questions, Major Goodall will give the mission brief," Colonel Roberts said and stepped down.

Major Goodall, the squadron operations officer, outlined the flight, to include headings, altitude, frequencies and refuel points where they'd

---

[8] RON means Remain Over Night.

172

rendezvous with tanker aircraft from the 91st Aerial Refueling Squadron. Each fighter would need in-flight refueling to make the hop across the Atlantic. Everyone prayed for a tailwind as they all knew it was going to be a long flight sitting in the single-seat aircraft. A few had stuffed a paperback book in their flight suit to read along the way as the aircraft flew on autopilot. Anything to stay awake and keep the mind engaged.
****

Captain Tate, Iron One-Two, sat in his aircraft with the engine at flight idle and the canopy open. He was number two in the first flight, flying with Lieutenant Colonel Roberts's wing. He was waiting for the other two aircraft to notify the flight leader they were ready.

"Iron One-One, Iron One-Three, I'm up."

"Roger," Colonel Roberts, Iron One-One, replied.

"Iron One-One, Iron One-Four, all systems up." Iron One-Four had applied for astronaut training and was attempting to add some humor to the flight.

"Roger. Iron One-Two, get us clearance for the runway."

"Roger, Iron One-One," Captain Tate replied excitedly. "Langley Ground Control, Iron One-Two. Flight of four for the active."

"Iron One-Two, roger. You are cleared from present location and proceed to runway 26. Contact Langley Tower on two-three-six-six, over."

"Roger, Langley Ground Control." Colonel Roberts had monitored the conversation and began taxiing his aircraft after exchanging a salute with the crew chief, who would fly over the on a C-141 aircraft with the rest of the maintenance crews of the squadron. As the aircraft taxied forward, following the leader, each lowered his canopy and made sure the air conditioners were working and positioned themselves just short of the runway.

"Langley Tower, Iron One-Two, flight of four for takeoff."

"Iron One-Two, you are cleared to take the active and hold while I get your clearance from Norfolk Departure."

"Roger, Langley Tower, Iron One-Two flight of four holding." As the four aircraft rolled out and looked down the eleven-thousand-foot runway, they assumed a staggered formation with flight leader in the front and Captain Tate behind and off his right wing. Iron One-Three was lined up behind the flight leader, with Iron One-Four behind and off his right wing.

"Iron One-Two, Langley Tower."

"Langley Tower, go ahead."

"Iron One-Two, you are clear for departure. Contact Norfolk Departure Control on climb-out on two-seven-three. Good hunting. Langley Tower out."

Langley Tower knows where they're going. Can't keep a secret long on this base, Colonel Roberts thought as he pushed forward on his throttles.

"Iron One-Two flight of four is on the go." And with that, the four F-15C fighters departed down the runway with a fifteen-second interval between the first two aircraft and the next two. The scene would be replayed five more times that day—the largest air campaign since the beginning of the Vietnam War.

******

At Loring Air Force Base, pilots with the 42nd Bombardment Wing had been called into the squadron briefing room. Those crews that flew the nuclear-capable bombers were used to spending seven days in the ready alert building and being called out at all times of the day or night. They were used to these unannounced exercises, especially as they were assigned to Strategic Air Command or SAC, who routinely ran a lot of alert drills.

The 42nd was the only squadron with all its B-52G bombers being conventional bombers not capable of using nuclear weapons, as agreed upon in the SALT II treaty talks. Therefore, they seldom had a no-notice exercise. Generally, the wives would know of a planned no-notice exercise before their husbands did. They had all gotten the phone call at 0100 hours and were told to be seated by 0300 hours. Colonel Doug McClure came to the front and everyone quieted down.

Colonel McClure was an Academy graduate and had been in B-52s his entire career. He had flown nuclear-armed planes as well as the "G" model that was modified for conventional bombs only. He had cut his teeth flying in Operation Linebacker over North Vietnam in the late 1960s. He knew what it was like to watch a B-52 being hit by a surface-to-air missile. He also knew that the chance of getting out of the crippled plane was small.

"The situation is this. Iraqi forces that crossed over into Saudi Arabia are driving on two fronts towards the port of Dhahran and the capital of Riyadh," Colonel McClure said. This previously unknown news had caused a few surprised looks on the faces of the pilots and confirmed some murmurs they had been hearing.

"The Saudi government has officially requested our assistance, and the President has obliged. We've been assigned to the 7th Air Division out of Diego Garcia as part of AFCENT. General Horner is commanding AFCENT and is currently in Riyadh." Again there were murmurs and looks exchanged, some smiling, some not so happy. "Gentlemen, you will depart here and fly nonstop to Diego Garcia. It's a twenty-hour flight. We'll be getting some in-flight refueling along the way. Refuelers will be coming out of Clark Air Base and Diego Garcia as well as from here and will join you in Diego Garcia." The crews were used to long flights as part of SAC.

"Each of your aircraft departs here with a full load of seven-hundred-and-fifty-pound bombs. We will depart starting today and have the entire wing deployed in seventy-two hours. Aircraft and crew assignments are posted on the board. I'll be flight leader on the first flight departing today. Flight Operations has your flight plans for each flight, to include routes, altitude, and planned refuel points. Any questions?" the operations officer asked.

One of the junior pilots poked his hand up. "Sir, why are we leaving with full bomb loads? If we load up in Diego Garcia, we won't need so many in-flight refueling points."

"Did you ever consider, Captain, that you may be making a bomb run en route to Diego Garcia? This is a fluid situation right now, so be prepared if you get a change of mission and route change in flight." It still hadn't registered with some that they were going to war. The colonel's last statement quickly snapped them out of that momentary fog.
****

The sky was clear, and turbulence was being felt. Perfect day for a CORNET across the ocean. The 91st Aerial Refueling Tanker had pre-positioned to Gander to meet a flight of four F-15 fighters as they came up the Eastern Seaboard en route to Mildenhall, England, for an overnight stop prior to leaving for their final destination in the Middle East. Captain Kyle Haydel had flown the route several times and was also a maintenance officer for the KC-135. Lieutenant Thibeaux-Moore was flying left seat with him on this trip. Moore was fresh out of flight school and transition training in the KC-135. This was his first operational mission. Master Sergeant Lamar Daniel was the boom operator and busy filling out the mound of paperwork required at the beginning of each trip. Weight and balance tables, flight logs, and maintenance logs all had to be up to date, and that fell on Daniel's shoulders as there was no flight engineer on the KC-135.

Daniel had joined the Air Force right out of high school and had been a boom operator for the past fifteen years. He loved his job. At the rate he was going, he would be able to retire from the Air Force after twenty years of service and still only be thirty-eight years old. Still young enough to pursue another career and have a nice retirement check from Uncle Sam. Not enough to live on, but enough to make life comfortable with another job.

Once in flight, Captain Haydel would start shifting fuel to meet the requirements of the fuel plan for the respective fighters they would be meeting. Once the refueling process began, the pilots would be responsible for transferring the fuel. Daniel would be responsible for flying the boom.

The flight was as expected, almost boring. Captain Tate sat in the cockpit of his F-15 Fighter with the autopilot on, reading a book about helicopter pilots in Vietnam. *Undaunted Valor: An Assault Helicopter Unit in Vietnam* had been making the rounds in the squadron, and now it was about to make the rounds in the Middle East. Everyone in the Ironman flight was on autopilot. These fighter pilots were used to short flights—they weren't the ferry pilots that typically made the over-big-water flights to deliver an aircraft to some distant airfield. The seats were comfortable for short flights, but for seven-hour flights, even a La-Z-Boy would be uncomfortable. Tate was just thankful he hadn't filled up on coffee before takeoff, as there was no relief tube in the F-15 and meals consisted of a candy bar that one could pull out of one's pocket.

When they'd first departed, the usual banter between aircraft had taken place, but things had quieted down for the past four hours. The only excitement was about to unfold as they were approaching a rendezvous point with a KC-135 flying gas station out of MacDill Air Force Base in Tampa, Florida. The KC-135 from the 91st Air Refueling Squadron was on station and just waiting for them to drain their fuel bladders, which contained 202,800 pounds of JP-5 fuel. Each F-15 would take up to five thousand gallons of fuel if need be. The 91st was part of the 6th Wing, which had three refueling squadrons, the 91st and 50th Air Refueling squadrons and the 99th Air National Guard squadron out of Sumpter Smith Air National Guard Base, Alabama. The crews had been briefed earlier and were launched long before the fighters departed so they could be in position to meet the fighters as they made their way across the ocean to England.

"Flight, Ironman One-One, over," Lieutenant Colonel Roberts radioed on the UHF radio. That got everyone's attention.

"Ironman One-Two, up."

"Ironman One-Three, over."

"Ironman One-Four has you loud and clear."

"Flight, we should be seeing the flying gas station soon—I have him on radar. I suspect we all have the same fuel status. Anyone low and needs to go first?" Ironman One-One asked.

"One-Two is good."

"One-Three good."

"Mission Control, One-Four is A-OK."

"Roger let's step up in chalk order," Lieutenant Colonel Roberts instructed as he commenced to contact the flying gas station.

"Bolt One-Five, Ironman One-One, over," Lieutenant Colonel Roberts transmitted, attempting to contact the KC-135 from the 91st Aerial Refueling Squadron.

"Ironman One-One, Bolt One-Five, over," Captain Kyle Haydel, pilot of the KC-135, transmitted after a brief pause.

"Bolt One-Five, Ironman is a flight of four looking to fill up, over."

"Roger, Ironman One-One, we've been expecting you. We are at angels two-four-zero and airspeed of three-five-zero. Altimeter setting two-nine-nine-five, over," Bolt One-Five reported.

"Roger, two-four-zero at three-five-zero, two-nine-nine-five, we should be ready in about thirty minutes. Order for refuel will be One-One, One-Two, One-Three and One-Four."

177

"Roger, Ironman One-One. We are standing by," Bolt One-Five transmitted, then switched frequencies. "Newfoundland Center, Bolt One-Five, MARSA, over."

"Roger, Bolt One-Five, understand MARSA," Newfoundland Center responded, acknowledging that Bolt One-Five would now take responsibility for aircraft separation with the cluster of jets around his aircraft that Newfoundland Center was seeing on their radar screen.

Captain Haydel was familiar with the 71st as it was his first assignment on graduating from flight school and the maintenance officers' course. After four years, he'd switched over to flying the KC-135. He had been in the Air Force for the past eight years.

As the Ironman flight of four approached Bolt One-Five, two aircraft came up and stood off the right wing and two off the left wing, creating a large V formation if observed from the ground.

"Daniel, visual," Haydel reported, indicating that he saw the F-15s forming up on them. Daniel now knew he would be talking to the fighters for the remainder of the refueling operation.

"Bolt One-Five, order of refuel will be Ironman One-One followed by One-Two, One-Three and One-Four. How copy?" Ironman One-One transmitted.

"Roger, good copy," Daniel said.

One-One approached from behind and slightly below. Lieutenant Colonel Roberts could look up and see the boom operator, Master Sergeant Daniel, peering down at him from the boom pit. A door with a small window covered a much larger fixed window in the boom pit through which the operator could observe the fighters below and behind. Once the door was raised, the boom pit operator was provided a panoramic view of the earth passing behind them. Slowly the boom started to lower from behind the KC-135 like the stinger of some giant insect. Daniel controlled the lowering and extending of the boom with his left hand on two levers. In front of him, the console showed him the elevation of the boom, and he strove to maintain that elevation at between twenty and fifty degrees. Another instrument showed him how many feet out the fuel probe was extended or telescoped, and he wanted to keep that at less than eighteen feet. Once the boom was lowered, it slowly began to extend. Under the telescoping gauge were three lights that Daniel monitored, the Signal System Status. The first was a ready

178

light indicating the system was armed and ready to receive an aircraft. Second was a green light indicating that the fighter was connected to the fuel probe, and lastly a red light indicating the probe was disconnected. Daniel controlled the movement of the boom with his right hand on a control stick similar to the flight control stick of the fighter. On the console, he had an azimuth indicator that showed him whether the boom was centered on the aircraft or was drifting off to the side and outside the boom envelope. Daniel would fly the boom through that control stick to the fuel intake, maintaining the boom in the refueling envelope. Roberts focused on the boom and the yellow strip down the belly of the KC-135, indicating he was lined up with the centerline of the refueler. Roberts had to maneuver his aircraft in the envelope of the boom in order for it to connect with his fuel port. In the cockpit of the KC-135, Haydel dialed in thirty thousand pounds of fuel to be sent to Ironman One-One. Master Sergeant Daniel was lying on his stomach with his head resting on the neck support, watching Ironman One-One approach. At the appropriate time, Daniel would call out the distance of the jet to the end of the boom.

"Twenty feet... fifteen feet... ten feet... reaching... contact." A green light lit up on Daniel's console to show that the boom was securely attached to the hungry jet. Haydel had a similar light, and immediately, thirty thousand pounds of jet fuel began flowing at a rate of two thousand pounds a minute into the jet fighter.

"Daniel, coming up on complete," Haydel indicated as he controlled the fuel flow in accordance with the fuel plan.

"Offload complete," Haydel said.

"Roger."

"Ironman One-One, fuel complete. Disconnect."

"Roger, disconnect," Ironman One-One transmitted, and as the boom was extracted, he throttled back and began to descend. The red light on Daniel's console indicated that the boom was disconnected from the fighter. As he pulled away and took up a position off the wing, Ironman One-Two moved into position and completed the same process. Once all the fighters were refueled, they resumed their positions off Bolt One-Five's wings and tagged along until the next time they needed to take on more fuel.

A boring hour passed, and then Bolt One-Four transmitted, "Hey, Bolt One-Five."

179

"Bolt One-Five here, go ahead."

"Bolt One-Five, watch this." And Bolt One-Four executed a barrel roll, stopping upside down and maintaining his position. Finally, he rolled back upright.

"How was that, Bolt One-Five?"

Daniel had been watching this demonstration of flying ability. "One-Four, that was pretty awesome, but I can do some pretty amazing stuff too," Daniel said.

"Oh, yeah? Show me," Ironman One-Four responded.

"OK, here goes," Daniel said.

Ironman One-Four waited in great anticipation for this demonstration. And he waited.

"Hey, Ironman One-Four, did you see that?"

"No, Bolt One-Five, I didn't see anything. What did you do?"

"Oh, I got up and went to the bathroom and then made a sandwich and got a cup of coffee. Pretty amazing and I bet you can't do that," Daniel transmitted. The other Ironman aircraft knew what was coming at Ironman One-Four's expense and could be heard laughing over the radio. Ironman One-Four wasn't heard from until the next refueling point.

Chapter Twenty-Four
Readjust

6 August 1990
CENTCOM Headquarters
Macdill Air Force Base
Tampa, Florida

"Norm, John here," came the gruff voice from across the globe.

"John, what's the situation like there? My staff is briefing that the Iraqis are moving across the north like shit through a goose," General Schwarzkopf exclaimed in an urgent tone.

"They're not far off the mark, Norm. It's official. We got word the King Khalid Military City surrendered without a fight. What's killing me is it took nearly two days to finally get confirmation of that. God only knows where that Iraqi division that took 'em out is right now. As if that wasn't bad enough, the refinery at Al-Jubail was seized intact, as was the navy base, and the Ras Tanura oil terminal. King Fahd Military Airfield has been seized, and most of the other airfields have been badly damaged. The Saudi Air Force at this point doesn't exist. It was either destroyed on the ground or the remnants of it have flown across the country to bases along the Red Sea."

General Schwarzkopf could hear John pause long enough to catch his breath, then he continued, "The Iraqi attack is a juggernaut at this point and there's nothing really left to stop it. They've got a brigade of M-60A1 tanks here in Riyadh, and from the sounds of things, they're staying here to defend the city. There's some talk they may also push them out to support a battalion to the north in the vicinity of Buraydah. They've got a battalion of light infantry from the Saudi National Guard trying to prepare a last-ditch defense of the capital."

"Jesus, John. It sounds like the Saudi military has completely fallen apart. I don't want you stuck in Riyadh if it's going to be overrun. State has talked to the Sultan of Oman, and he's offered for us to establish a headquarters there and begin stationing fighter aircraft and ground forces in his country. I'm sending a plane to get you and Horner out of there and into Muscat to set up the headquarters. Our advance party will be airborne in about six hours to meet you there and set up shop. The

Brigade Rapid Reaction Force from the 82nd is en route. The big question I need answered right now is where do you think we should put them?" questioned General Schwarzkopf.

"Jeddah. It's four hundred miles from Riyadh, with some really nasty rugged terrain between there and here. Good infantry country. It won't be easy to move a mechanized/armor force through there. We have an MEU securing the airport. They've got solid air cover from the carrier until we can get more units brought over. That's my recommendation, sir. Have them link up with the Marines."

Jokingly, Schwarzkopf asked, "Do you think Marines and soldiers together will get along long enough to fight Iraqis and not each other?"

Yeosock laughed over the phone. "Oh, there'll be a few bloody noses, I'm sure, but they'll come together when the Iraqis show up."

"OK, we'll notify MARCENT that the 82nd is coming and is under their control until the division is established ashore. Then the MEU will fall under the 82nd's control until we move them back aboard. We'll likely see about moving a battle group to the Red Sea, but it'll be a while as both are in port right now on the East Coast. I understand the *Eisenhower* will be replaced shortly by the *Saratoga*," Schwarzkopf explained. "What do we do about the 24th ID? You know they have a rapid reaction force company team ready to deploy. McCaffrey is chomping at the bit and has already rolled some stock to the port. No ships are there yet, but he and his equipment are."

General Yeosock offered, "At this point, the best I could recommend is fly the rapid reaction force team into Jeddah to reinforce the 82nd. The 82nd has no tanks or heavy combat vehicles except the Sheridans, and we can only fly a couple of those in at a time. The 24th Rapid Reaction Force is only a company team, but it may be able to help out."

"Where do we send McCaffrey?" Schwarzkopf asked.

"Where I would like to send him and where we need to send him are two different places," Yeosock said sarcastically. "Look, he won't arrive here for at least two, probably three weeks. We can let this situation work itself out and decide then where it would be best to land the 24th. Those ships have got to cross the Atlantic, come through the Med and refuel, then go through the Suez Canal and down the Red Sea. We have time to make that decision."

"What's the situation in Riyadh?"

182

"The King is leaving in the next couple of hours for his home in Spain. Most of the royals have already left as well. Those in the military are talking to the Sultan of Oman about setting up a government in exile and a command headquarters there. We should get State to support that position with the Sultan."

"Alright, I'll get that 82nd brigade diverted to Jeddah along with the rest of the division. Also, where do you recommend we put in the 101st?"

"Send the 101st to Jeddah. Their attack helicopters will have a field day if the Iraqis attempt to move against Jeddah... and their attack helicopters should be the first to arrive. Oh, if McCaffrey is adamant about knowing where he's going, then tell him Muscat. We can start to build a heavy force around him there. If we have to send him elsewhere, we can change that at sea. Don't bring his people over until we say the word. A heavy force won't do much good in the Jeddah area. It's just too mountainous for an armored force to effectively navigate and fight through. If the Iraqis attempt it themselves, they'll learn a hard lesson, but I don't want our guys to have to learn the hard way. Oh, one other question. Where is the pre-positioned equipment out of Diego Garcia going?"

"It was supposed to go to Dhahran, but now we're thinking Muscat."

"That would be my vote. Truthfully, Norm, outside of Jeddah, I think Saudi is a write-off. Here, Horner wants to talk to you."

"Norm, how you doing?" General Horner asked once he was on the phone.

"I suspect a lot better than you are right now. What's the air situation?"

"Not good. The Iraqis are coordinating their air caps and close-air support missions and integrating the close-air into the ground maneuver plan really well. This is a vast improvement from what we were seeing in the Iran-Iraq war. They learned some lessons, but I think there's something else at play right now," General Horner said cautiously.

Schwarzkopf lifted an eyebrow at that last remark. Not that they could see or tell that he had. Still, he wasn't sure what his air chief meant. "Why don't you break it down for me, Chuck?"

There was a short pause on the line before General Horner spoke. "I'm sure you're aware the Iraqi Air Force has been sporting some new Russian-made aircraft. Some of it's stuff we haven't seen them fly, or at least not fly a lot of. I don't have anything official or anything, but these pilots seem to be a lot better than the Iraqi pilots we're used to seeing. I'm not saying these new aircraft are being flown by Russians, but it sure would make sense considering the level of skill and coordination they're displaying. It should also be noted the Russians have apparently lent or leased them some pretty high-end air-defense systems. Weapon systems designed to provide a fast mobile armored group with some pretty damn good protection against aircraft and helicopters.

"We're also seeing surges in different types of attacks. For instance, during two of the air raids, the Iraqis made heavy use of their Blinder and Backfire bombers. They really decimated the Saudi Air Force on the opening night of the war with their bomber squadrons and Su-25 Frogfooters. In the first wave alone, they took out all five of the Saudi airfields with dumb bombs and took out the aircraft with what appeared to be a copycat of our CBU-72 bombs. The overpressure was destroying aircraft, and the lack of oxygen and overpressure killed a lot of ground personnel and pilots attempting to take off. These were well-organized, well-coordinated attacks. We're going to need to really think about where we place our aircraft. Saudi is out, so that really only leaves us with Oman and possibly Egypt—and Incirlik, if the Turks will play along."

Schwarzkopf sat back in his chair with the phone receiver still pressed against the side of his head. *I'm going to need to get with General Powell and find out what the heck is going on with the Iraqi Air Force. Maybe Chuck is right about Russian pilots flying for them. In either case, we need to get the air situation sorted so the aircraft en route know where to go.*

Schwarzkopf concluded, "OK, Chuck, we'll get State going on this. Oman is the best bet at this point, or Turkey, but we'll see if State can work out something with Egypt. Tell John that there's a plane en route to get you guys out as well as the embassy staff. We'll meet you in Muscat shortly. Now get out of there. That's an order."

"Yes, sir."

184

Chapter Twenty-Five
Continue the Attack

6 August 1990
2nd Iraqi Corps
King Khalid Military City, Saudi Arabia

General al-Hamdani was rather pleased about staying in the set of quarters that had been graciously made available to him in King Khalid Military City.

So nice of the Saudi commander to have provided these accommodations for me, he thought privately as he chuckled. *Like he had a choice.*

After the complex had been seized, a surrender had been negotiated with the Saudi commander. He was smart enough to realize that resistance against two full divisions with air support would be futile. That night, General al-Hamdani got a good night's sleep, as did his entire force.

As he walked into the conference room, his division commanders looked equally refreshed. Also present was the commander of the IV Army Corps, which was the follow-on force to the 2nd Republican Guard Corps.

Lieutenant General Aryan bin Khalif was a fairly new corps commander, having commanded the 16th Infantry Division in the early days of the Iran-Iraq War. He had been wounded in an air strike while he led his division from the front. The IV Corps had followed the 2nd Republican Guard Corps and now sat north of King Khalid Military City at Hafar Al-Batin.

When al-Hamdani walked into the briefing room, he spotted his old friend. "Aryan, it's good to see you."

Republican Guard commanders always considered themselves a bit superior to regular Army officers of equivalent rank. Still, al-Hamdani knew he needed the regular army units if his Republican Guard units were going to be successful in the coming days.

Aryan bin Khalif smiled. "Likewise, General," he responded pleasantly but coolly. His lukewarm response did not go unnoticed among the junior officers present.

Al-Hamdani moved to the head of the table, where a map was spread out for them to look at. Picking up a pointer, he began to explain the purpose of the meeting.

"Well, let's begin. We have a lot to cover. Currently, the 1st Republican Guard Corps is moving to cut off Dhahran from Riyadh. They have taken the refinery at Al-Jubail and the oil shipping terminal at Ras Tanura, and they have isolated Dammam. The 45th Infantry Division is occupying Al-Jubail and the 49th Infantry Division is moving into Dammam. The 8th Mechanized Brigade of the 1st Hammurabi Division took control of the King Fahd Military Airport, and our air force has already moved elements there. They will commence operations, providing us with close-air support and attack helicopter operations tomorrow."

Al-Hamdani paused for just a moment to survey the facial expressions of the generals he was briefing. He then resumed, "Aside from token resistance at King Fahd Military Airport and some Marines in the Al-Jubail area, they have met no significant resistance. They would have moved faster had the roads not been clogged with people fleeing the area. We have captured the brigade minus the Saudi tanks and infantry here. The brigade at Tabuk is still in garrison according to our reconnaissance elements, and the brigade north of Yemen has not moved either. It may be the case that they have not been alerted as their communications are being jammed, or maybe they have lost faith in the King and decided to sit this war out."

Several of the officers laughed at his last comment.

"The Saudi Air Force was swept from the skies during the first few hours of the war. Most of their aircraft were destroyed on the ground at one of their five airfields. The few aircraft and helicopters not destroyed managed to disperse to some isolated airfields. I doubt they'll be a problem for us, and if they are, the air force will hunt them down.

"We are also getting reports that an American cargo aircraft was seen landing at the Riyadh International Airport and the Prince Sultan Military Airfield. Our eyes in Riyadh tell us the aircraft has probably been sent in to retrieve the American embassy staff and their families and anyone else who needed to be evacuated. We are under strict orders to avoid contact with the Americans for as long as possible. We do not want to give them an excuse to join this fight, especially since it is reported in the news that they told Saddam that this was an Arab-to-Arab conflict and they had no interest in being involved. So where does that leave us?" he asked, pausing long enough to take a sip of his tea, which he had not touched.

When no one spoke up, he continued. "It means we continue our attack. At 1800 hours tonight, we move to seize the crossroads in the vicinity of Al Artawiyah here, one hundred sixty kilometers to the south. Here we will control the highways to Medina, Jeddah and Riyadh. The 7th Mechanized"—al-Hamdani looked at Major General al-Karawi—"will attack to seize the town of Buraydah, which will protect the right flank and control the road to Medina." General al-Kaab nodded in acknowledgment.

"The 5th Division," al-Hamdani continued, looking at Major General al-Kaab, "will attack and seize the town of Al Majma'ah. Once you seize it, do not proceed any further south than Jalajil. Block the road to Riyadh, allowing no refugees to come north. Do you understand? I do not want our roads clogged with refugees. If they want to flee, they can go south out of Riyadh to Abha on the Red Sea and into Yemen."

"Understood, General," al-Kaab responded.

General al-Hamdani turned to General bin Kanh. "I would like your corps to come as far as Al Artawiyah and stop. You may be just lucky enough to win the prize of taking Riyadh, General," he said with a sneer.

Bin Kanh knew that there was no way the Republican Guard was going to allow that to happen. First, they wanted the honor, and second, it was too easy a target even if the Americans were still evacuating from the airport. He knew full well that if things got tough, his corps would be tossed into the breach as cannon fodder.

"Thank you, General, it would be a great honor for the Iraq Army to seize the Saudi Palace."

General al-Hamdani only smiled at the subtle reference to the Army as opposed to the Republican Guard. Looking back at the map, he continued, "Once we have secured these objectives, then Baghdad is going to have to make some decisions. 1st Corps has been told to push on to isolate the UAE and close in on the Saudi-Omani border. That means someone is going to have to take Riyadh, Medina, Jeddah, and Mecca as well as block the Saudi brigade at Abha.

"That brigade could cut up north along the coast against us. It could strike out northeast to flank the 1st Corps or make an attempt to retake Riyadh. If I'm to predict what Baghdad will do, I'd guess the mission to take Riyadh will fall to either IV Corps or IX Corps. Both of these corps are following 2nd Corps and 1st Corps respectfully, and with three armored divisions and an infantry division not committed yet, they'd be in a better position to nab Riyadh quickly. On the other hand"—here he looked at General bin Kanh—"you have six infantry divisions, a mech division and an armored division, all uncommitted. However, I feel that if we are to move to Medina and Jeddah, I am going to need your infantry divisions as the terrain is not very forgiving to armor forces. Therefore, I would recommend you be prepared to head to Riyadh."

General bin Kanh saw how his command was being whittled down to the point where he'd be left to capture and babysit the Saudi capital while the rest of the army trudged onward to greater glory. The general was suddenly aware of the other generals and colonels staring at him, as if waiting for him to say something. He said the only thing he knew was safe to say.

"Whatever Saddam orders, I will execute," General bin Kanh replied with a sarcastic smile.

General al-Hamdani then turned to General al-Karawi. "You, my friend, have a fine highway to follow, but I do not want your track vehicles on that road. Only wheeled vehicles are to use the highway, is that understood? Paved roads are hard to come by, and we need to keep them in good order for our follow-on supply forces."

Some of the generals grumbled at the order, which meant that their units were going to have to travel a lot more slowly across less-than-desirable terrain, but ultimately, they knew he was right and that this was a good call.

Al-Hamdani added, "I know this is going to have your lead elements moving slower across this wasteland, but that is fine as it is the same ground as al-Kaab will be traveling over. Our progress will not be as fast as before, but it does not need to be. This portion should be a drive in the country, as an American would say, nothing more."

Looking over at General al-Kaab, al-Hamdani clarified, "You will also find a paved road along your route. It's only two lanes, but the same rule applies. Keep your track vehicles off it. Understood?"

"Yes, sir," al-Kaab replied.

Al-Hamdani didn't need to remind General bin Kanh about this, as all his vehicles were wheeled vehicles except for some tanks, which were not the modern T-72s and were all loaded on the heavy equipment transporters (HETs), which were wheeled vehicles.

"Are there any questions before I dismiss you all?" the general asked as he looked around the room. Not seeing any, he moved on.

"The order of march is that 7th Division will be followed by 5th Division's combat elements. Leave your supply elements behind until we reach our objectives. I want the 7th to push out a reconnaissance element no later than 0400 to report on the road conditions, terrain, and enemy disposition. They are not to become decisively engaged. Understood?"

Chapter Twenty-Six
Recon the Route

6 August 1990
11th Motorized Brigade
King Khalid Military City, Saudi Arabia

First Lieutenant Muhammed al-Tikriti got to spend one night in King Khalid Military City before having to mount up and move out at 0400 hours. His scout platoon for the 1st Battalion of the 11th Motorized Brigade had enough time to refuel their vehicles and take on some rations before the battalion commander contacted him.

The battalion commander walked up to al-Tikriti, getting his attention. "Lieutenant, we've been ordered to resume the attack in the morning. You're going to be leading the brigade and moving as fast as possible to clear a path and identify any possible targets of opportunity. Your unit is to move along the highway from here to Umm Al Jamajm. It's imperative that you not get bogged down along the way. Your units need to stay on the move with speed and report any impediments to our movement. While your unit is on the move, the division wants to know if you come across any gas stations along the way, as well as the location and disposition of any Saudi forces of any kind, any topographic adjustments we should make to our maps, or changes in soil composition.

"Once you reach Umm Al Jamajm, report the condition of the population. Are they passive or are they going to resist? If you can drive through the town, do so, but do not become engaged. If you must, bypass the town and proceed southwest to Al Artawiyah. Again, determine the attitude of the populace. It is only twenty-five miles south of Umm Al Jamajm, so you should be there by 0800 hours. Once you've reached your objective, you need to halt in an overwatch position of the road from Riyadh and the road to Medina. The battalion will be about an hour behind you. Any questions?" his battalion commander asked.

Lieutenant al-Tikriti shook his head in the negative. "No, sir. I understand my orders." He'd been serving in this position for over two years with his commander, so he understood the man's intent pretty well by this point, as well as his own job.

"Good. After sunrise, if you need close-air support, the division's helicopters will be at your disposal. Call for them and they will be able to come to you quickly. They're being kept on standby at base roughly a hundred kilometers from our position. If you locate any sort of airfield of any kind between Umm Al Jamajm and Al Artawiyah, check it out and report if there is any aviation fuel there or any kind of support facilities. Maybe we'll get lucky and find a new forward base we can get the helicopters positioned out of. I like the idea of having them much closer to the front than where they currently are. Oh, and, Lieutenant—later in the day, I will know if we're being directed to proceed towards either Medina or Riyadh. Stay ready to move in either direction."

Lieutenant al-Tikriti smiled. "I hope it's to Medina. Then we'll be the ones to liberate the holy city of Mecca."

"Lieutenant, let's get to Medina first, and then we can think about going on to Mecca," the battalion commander responded with a smile. He liked the lieutenant's enthusiasm. He just hoped it didn't get him killed.

At 0400, the scout platoon rolled out of the gates of King Khalid Military City. The corps commander's flag flew over the central administrative building while infantry soldiers who appeared to be acting as security manned some of the street corners. Saudi soldiers and their families were instructed to remain indoors until further notice, and no harm would come to them. Most of the soldiers of the 2nd Republican Guard Corps had not entered the city complex as General Ra'ad al-Hamdani did not want any conflict between the forces.

He wanted to win over the Saudi forces and convince them to join with the Iraqi forces in deposing the King. He was particularly optimistic about getting the Saudis to provide them some insight into the new Saudi M1A1 Abrams tanks they had purchased from the Americans. The rumor mill said they were far superior to the Iraqi T-72s and much more technologically sophisticated.

Lieutenant al-Tikriti wasn't stupid. He knew General al-Hamdani would want his own soldiers to learn how to use this captured equipment as quickly as they could. Interestingly enough, al-Tikriti heard they had captured several American contractors when they'd captured the military city. Apparently, they were part of a larger group of trainers instructing the Saudi Army on how to use and maintain the new tanks. As of yet, these American contractors would not teach the Iraqis how to use them. Al-Tikriti figured they'd eventually come around, or they'd be made to come around at some point.

As the scout platoon proceeded southwest on the four-lane road, they met little traffic. This was a deserted portion of desert for seventy-two kilometers, with only an occasional home for a shepherd or a truck stop with fuel every twenty miles or so. The desert was lacking sand dunes but had plenty of hard-packed sand and rock outcroppings dotting the landscape—terrain features his men were annotating and making sure the follow-on units were aware of.

At each of the truck stops, they would purchase some sodas and snacks. They wanted to demonstrate to the locals that they were not conquerors but liberators. They also secretly—or in some cases, not so secretly—disconnected the telephone lines to make sure the locals couldn't phone ahead and report their positions.

As the sun rose in the eastern sky, foretelling a clear day, al-Tikriti had his unit disperse and pause for Fajr, the morning prayer. They were forty-eight kilometers southwest of King Khalid Military City, overlooking a truck stop with a mosque. In the distance, the call to prayer could be heard. Lieutenant al-Tikriti did not want to enter the mosque with his soldiers and their weapons, so they stayed four hundred meters to the northwest and faced Mecca. When Fajr was finished, they remounted their vehicles and continued on.

The desert area they were scouting was open, with little vegetation. While it was desolate, it was not always flat. The terrain rolled almost like the sea, with many deep cuts or wadis caused by rapid flooding in the very short rainy season that generally lasted just two days a year. When the rains did come, the ground did not easily absorb the water as it was baked hard from the sun. The result was the formation of rapid runoffs. The resulting wadis could be an impediment to vehicles attempting to cross them perpendicularly or an asset in concealing the movement of vehicles running in the bottom of them, depending on their width and depth. This was why their scout unit was out here. They needed to identify the potential hazards and opportunities the land presented in case they needed to use them.

Since concealment was not a concern right now, Lieutenant al-Tikriti kept his vehicles on the highway. He wanted to move rapidly and cover as much ground as possible while still fulfilling their mission. At an average speed of thirty kilometers an hour, his calculations said he should reach Umm Al Jamajm in roughly an hour.

Moving south, Lieutenant al-Tikriti became concerned as the terrain changed from the hard-packed ground and rock outcroppings to the soft sand and small dunes typical of most deserts. This kind of terrain, however, was not as easy for a large force to travel or fight on if it came to that. The fine sand tended to get into everything, to include the gears of tracks, the air filters for the engines, and other areas that caused problems for vehicles.

Continuing down the highway, al-Tikriti noted on his map where the terrain changed and how the follow-on vehicles would need to traverse it. The tracked vehicles wouldn't have a problem moving on the soft sand, but the wheeled vehicles would. This meant the ash-and-trash vehicles, or supply trucks, would need to stay on the highway while the tracked vehicles could fan out across the sand. Once he'd finished making his notes, he handed them off to his sergeant, who'd transmit the findings back to the battalion operations officer to distribute to the company commanders.

Continuing down the highway while his sergeant radioed in his notes, al-Tikriti just shook his head. *Why the hell wasn't this done long before now? These Russian maps are almost totally out of date. I wish we didn't have to rely so much on their help. The British and American maps are far superior. Why are we not using them?*

His thoughts were interrupted by the abrupt stop of his vehicle.

"What is wrong?" he asked his driver as he looked up, a bit startled.

The driver did not need to answer. They had just come around a slight curve in the road when they spotted it. Roughly five hundred meters to their front—a customs station. The first sign of possible danger they'd seen since the assault on the Saudi military base a few days ago.

Pulling his binoculars out, al-Tikriti scanned the area. The customs station had a building on the side of the road and several covered lanes on both sides of the highway to allow the inspectors to carry out their duties in the shade. This was typical of what you'd see along some of the roads not too far from the border. The station had four V-100 armored cars, positioned in such a manner that they blocked the highway altogether.

193

The terrain off to each side was open and flat for about three hundred meters on either side, but then the rolling sand dunes he had been traveling through for the past hour resumed.

"I don't think they spotted us, Lieutenant. What do you want us to do?" asked his senior sergeant.

"I'm thinking," was his immediate reply.

What are my options here? I could proceed and see if they will surrender to me. I could proceed and engage them, which may give them time to send out a warning and call for reinforcements. I do have some AT-3 Sagger antitank missiles I could use from a distance. We could also call for a helicopter gunship to dispose of them. But if we do that, it'll take time for them to spin up and get here, which means I'll lose several hours. No, I have to do this myself. After considering his options, he made his decision.

"Sergeant," al-Tikriti called as he dismounted the vehicle.

"Sir."

"Dismount the men. Get six of the AT-3 weapons and six teams to come with me. I intend to get off to the side of the highway and move down the shoulders to get us in range of the Saggers. If they are not paying attention, we may be able to get fairly close before we use them. I want you and the rest of the men to stay here with the vehicles while I take the teams forward. When you hear the shooting and explosions, come racing down the highway towards them. Use the guns and engage whatever is left. Any questions?"

The sergeant grinned. "No, sir. I like this idea. I'll get the teams organized and ready to go. Do you want to radio in what we discovered and what we're going to do?"

"I will. Now get the men ready and let's do this thing."

The sergeant turned and started issuing orders to the excited soldiers. They hadn't fired their own weapons yet, so the opportunity to engage in their own part of the war was exhilarating.

When the soldiers were ready, Lieutenant al-Tikriti briefed the soldiers. Three teams would proceed down one side of the highway as the other three teams moved with the lieutenant. As they moved, they'd look to utilize concealment behind the dunes as much as possible until they got in position.

Once they knew the plan, the six teams moved out. It took them half an hour to get in position. They'd managed to move within four hundred meters of the checkpoint when al-Tikriti motioned for his teams to start setting up their Saggers. It was time for their recon team to finally get in the fight.

Once the six teams had crawled to the top of their respective dunes, they started assembling the AT-3s. These were antitank missiles that would fly flat and true right to their intended targets. Since they were wire-guided missiles, it was important to have a clear line of sight so the gunner could fly the missile to the target.

Lieutenant al-Tikriti had once had the opportunity to see the American TOW antitank system with its optically guided missile, and he wished they had that weapon instead of the Sagger. It was much more accurate than their own. Still, he was confident in his men's ability and their training.

Since there were only four armored cars at the checkpoint, they'd only fire four of the six missiles they had with them. This way, if one didn't work or somehow missed, they'd still have two more ready to go.

"We're ready, sir," one of his sergeants announced.

Lieutenant al-Tikriti nodded, giving them the go-ahead.

Four loud pops and swooshing noises could be heard as the missiles leapt from their tubes and flew across the four hundred meters at lightning speed. There was almost no time to see the missiles as they flew across the space between them before all four of them impacted against the V-100 armored cars.

The four vehicles exploded in spectacular fashion as the warheads slammed into them. Several customs agents and soldiers standing nearby were thrown to the ground while a few others had limbs ripped from their bodies or were engulfed in flames. It was a horrific sight.

With the sound of the explosion, the reconnaissance platoon's BMPs and BTRs raced down the road towards the smoldering ruins. A couple of soldiers were manning the crew-served weapons and opened up on the stunned Saudi National Guard soldiers and customs agents.

While the vehicles were charging towards the station, Lieutenant al-Tikriti and his six missile teams left the launchers where they were and took off to join the fight. A couple of soldiers tried to fight back, firing their weapons at the Iraqi soldiers running at them. One National Guard

195

soldier positioned on the roof of the customs building fired his PKM machine gun at the lead BMP. His bullets just ricocheted off the armor and zipped off skyward. The turret operator fired a short burst from the 30mm gun, ripping the Saudi soldier and the customs building to shreds.

While this was taking place, at least two Saudi soldiers managed to jump into one of the customs vehicles and drove off as fast as the vehicle would go. A few of the BMPs and BTRs tried to engage them with their weapons, but the vehicle had managed to get around a slight bend in the road before their bullets could rip the truck apart. Lieutenant al-Tikriti was mad that some soldiers had managed to escape; still, they had done a good job of neutralizing the threat and clearing the way for the rest of the battalion, which was only a few hours behind them.

"Sergeant, use the BTRs and get these vehicles pushed off the road. Do your best to line them up along that side of the road. Then get the rest of the debris moved out of the way. I want these lanes cleared immediately. We need to be back on the road in twenty minutes, understood?"

"Yes, sir," came the swift reply. The men were in good spirits. They'd gotten to blow something up and shoot their rifles and lived to tell about it. What more could they ask for?

While the two BTRs pushed the blown-out vehicles to the side of the road, a squad of soldiers moved the dead as well. They didn't want to leave their bodies strewn about the road.

Once they'd cleared the area up, the convoy resumed its patrol. They'd reported the firefight to the battalion commander, who'd informed them he was only an hour behind.

Driving down the highway, they eventually caught sight of Umm Al Jamajm. It appeared to be a town of a thousand people, with most of them living on the western side of the highway. There was a tall communications tower on either side of the highway as well.

From their vantage point on the side of the road, al-Tikriti and his senior sergeant scanned the town and the highway with their binoculars. There was virtually no traffic to be found anywhere. A few people moved about on some of the streets and in front of a few stores, but that was about it.

It could just be too early for a lot of activity, but still, al-Tikriti wasn't sure if the town had been warned of their pending arrival. Some

196

of the shops that he would expect to be open were still closed. Then he spotted a man leading a couple of camels in the direction of his scout element. As they got closer, they didn't seem to notice or care that there were four armored vehicles sitting on the side of the road observing them. The man leading the camels nodded as he passed the soldiers.

Lieutenant al-Tikriti ordered his patrol to spread their vehicles out a bit, with the soldiers standing up through the top hatches in case of an ambush. They were going to move through the town with caution and report back what they found. He had to keep reminding himself his job was to report, not become decisively engaged or try to seize an objective.

Once they'd cleared the town with no outward signs of danger, the patrol picked up speed and continued to Al Artawiyah.

Proceeding southwest towards their next objective, the terrain became hard-packed sand and rock outcroppings again. They were also starting to go up in elevation. With the hard-packed sand, al-Tikriti had his vehicles spread out off the highway to acquire a better understanding of the terrain and the maneuverability of the vehicles over the ground.

Eventually they came to a road intersection that branched off to the west and into the foothills with an increased elevation. Two hamlets were at the end of this road, and neither looked to be significant. At this point, al-Tikriti reported the intersection and pushed on. Two miles further south, another hamlet appeared. The people in this little village appeared to ignore them and carry on with their normal business as the armored vehicles rolled on through. The small children of the little village were the only ones to pay the Iraqis any attention. Most just stood and watched; some waved.

As they proceeded south, the terrain became rockier and less sandy. Numerous wadis cut through the terrain, posing a potential cross-country mobility problem if they needed to get off the highway. Lieutenant al-Tikriti knew he was close to Al Artawiyah when he came across the airfield to the north of the town. He stopped and dispersed his patrol while two vehicles were sent to inspect the airfield and determine if it could be used to refuel aircraft and helicopters.

In short order, his team had determined the airfield was usable. Not only was it in decent shape, but it also had a five-thousand-liter fuel tank that appeared to be nearly full with aviation fuel.

197

Lieutenant al-Tikriti pulled his vehicles to the east side of the road, which positioned them on the high terrain, with vegetation overlooking the town near the airfield. The town center was six thousand meters away and very built up with one- and two-story concrete-block buildings, typical of the Middle East. The terrain to the east of the town was open, hard-packed sand. To the west was rocky broken terrain similar to what he was sitting on. To the west was the objective of the division and corps.

Lieutenant al-Tikriti was reluctant to move into the town because it was large and he could only observe a small portion in front. His follow-on mission after reconning the airfield was to proceed towards the corps's objective. To do that, he had to get to the southern side of Al Artawiyah. Instead of taking the direct route through the town, he elected to skirt the eastern side of the town across the open desert. This would give him plenty of room to maneuver and engage any hostiles should they encounter them.

Al Majma'ah was only forty miles to the south. The 5th Baghdad Motorized Division was to move to Al Majma'ah and then swing west towards the southern side of Buraydah. The 7th Adnan Division would pass to the north of Al Artawiyah and attack to the north side of Buraydah. Scout elements for the 5th would clear their route from Al Artawiyah to Buraydah.

By skirting the eastern side of the town in the open desert, al-Tikriti figured his scout element could travel around most of the town before he had to get on the highway again to cross a major wadi and some very rugged terrain.

In a way, it was good he was discovering these features and navigational challenges now. His people were able to annotate them rather than have a company of tanks encounter them later. When he called in to his battalion commander, he relayed what he'd encountered up to this point. His colonel seemed satisfied.

The closer his vehicles came to the choke point, which in this case was a deep-cutting wadi, the happier he was to be getting back on the highway. The terrain was becoming a lot harder for their vehicles to traverse.

There was one thing that really troubled him. It was nearing midday, and they had hardly seen any traffic. Given the size of this town, they should have seen some by now. The hairs on the back of his neck tingled as if somehow telling him something was wrong and he needed to stay on his toes.

As they proceeded down the highway, the road began to descend towards what appeared to be a valley. The division's primary objective and his secondary objective to recon lay right in the middle of this valley—the city of Al Majma'ah.

The major intersection that led to the west was six thousand meters in front of him, with scattered homes and pygmy palms scattered throughout the area. He ordered his patrol to leave the road and disperse to the west side of it. The hairs on his neck were speaking to him, and their message was one of caution.

Their vehicles started to pass the first grove of palm trees when suddenly a handful of birds in the trees a hundred meters in front of them took to the air like something had scared them. Their sudden movement was followed almost immediately by a small object that flew out of some bushes and slammed into the lead BMP.

In seconds, the BMP exploded in flame and smoke as the shaped charge in the RPG ignited some of the ammunition inside the infantry fighting vehicle. The air around them suddenly filled with the sound of buzzing from bullets and swooshes from RPGs being hurled at them.

Despite his cautiousness, they had somehow stumbled into a cleverly laid ambush. His turret gunner opened fire on something in front of them. The driver had stopped the vehicle and was rapidly reversing it out of the kill box, also firing off the vehicle's smoke canisters, trying to build up an emergency smokescreen in hopes that they might live long enough to escape.

Lieutenant al-Tikriti turned the crew-served weapon in front of him on a set of bushes he'd seen an RPG team firing from. He pulled the trigger hard and sent a stream of bullets into the position, shredding tree branches and debris around it.

Another explosion occurred somewhere behind him. He could feel the heat wave wash over him, and as he turned around to see what had happened, the BTR his platoon sergeant had been riding in erupted in flame and black smoke.

He instinctively ducked just before a string of bullets pounded the armor around the commander's turret he had just been sitting in. Then al-Tikriti saw a V-100 armored car firing on his vehicle. His turret

199

gunner sent a burst of 30mm rounds into the vehicle, causing it to explode. Moments later, the ground around them started to explode. Rocks, parts of trees, and dirt and sand erupted from the ground like geysers as the sound of 155mm artillery shells began to rain down all around them. The sound of artillery and pieces of metal slapping the sides of his vehicle was the last thing Lieutenant al-Tikriti heard before his world went black and suddenly became very quiet.

Chapter Twenty-Seven
Boots on the Ground

7 August 1990
Marine Expeditionary Unit
USS *Tarawa*, Red Sea

Miles away, three members of the Marine Expeditionary Unit stood on the hangar deck of the USS *Tarawa*, gazing out towards the port of Jeddah, seventy-five miles over the horizon. The group consisted of an infantry battalion, an aviation element of helicopters and a support element as well as a headquarters element, not exactly a large group. The MEU had previously been referred to as an MAU, Marine Amphibious Unit, but a name change had been introduced the previous year.

Since the creation of the Corps in 1776 at the Tun Tavern in Philadelphia, Marines had been aboard Navy ships, fighting alongside sailors in defense of the nation. They had a proud tradition of service both aboard ship and ashore. In 1805, First Lieutenant Presley O'Bannon had gone ashore with a Marine detachment and crossed over six hundred miles of the Libyan desert to capture the fort at Derna from the pirates of Tripoli.

The *Eisenhower* had sailed from the eastern Mediterranean Sea through the Suez Canal and arrived in the Red Sea. Earlier, the platoon leader had told them to get ready to go ashore. The platoon would be flying to the airport in two helicopters that were already on the deck. As this was just a basic rifle platoon, the young Marines were full of apprehension as to what it would be like in Saudi Arabia and what they were going to be doing.

"Jeff, you've been ashore here. What's it like?" asked Lance Corporal James Jones, or JJ for short, as he looked over his gear one last time.

"Nah, I've been ashore in Israel and Lebanon, but not Saudi Arabia. I understand they're a bunch of tight-asses when it comes to drinking and religion. Shit, they don't drink inside their own country but become raving alcoholics outside it. A bunch of hypocrites if you ask me," Corporal Jeff Holland said.

Holland had been a Marine for four years and loved it. Loved it so much he'd just signed his paperwork to reenlist for four more. He would probably make it a career and didn't mind the sea duty. He wasn't married and had no desire to get married, so sea duty was totally worth it, especially with the extra pay.

Lance Corporal Dave Kinnaird, one of the younger Marines in the detachment, asked, "Any idea of how far we are from those Iraqi forces the lieutenant was talking about this morning in the briefing?"

Corporal Holland shrugged. "As long as they aren't sitting at that airport, I could care less. Once we get to the airport and set up, they can come in if they want. They'll learn not to mess with us Devil Dogs. Oorah!"

"Talk is cheap until the bullets start flying, Corporal," JJ chided.

JJ had dropped out of college after his first year. His mother had had a shit fit when he'd joined, but his dad had supported the idea after JJ had promised that when his four years were up, he would go back to college.

"Do you think anyone else will be coming in here besides us?" Kinnaird asked.

"Who knows? We're the first, so I suspect some others will follow behind us. We just have to wait and see."

"Here comes the platoon sergeant. Guess it's time to load up," JJ announced as he picked up his rucksack and M-16 assault rifle along with everyone else.

"Alright, ladies, get in formation," announced their platoon sergeant.

As the Marines snapped into a platoon formation of four squads, the platoon sergeant started to speak. "When we get on the flight deck, first and second squad, take the first chopper with the captain. Third and fourth squad, follow me to the second plane. You know the drill. Two lines," Gunny Davis said and turned to start up the ladder well to the flight deck.

The deck of the *USS Tarawa* was probably the most tightly controlled orchestrated chaos on any ship. The six helicopters were on deck, their engines running, waiting to load up their human cargo.

Earlier, several F-14 Tomcats had departed the *Eisenhower* and were above the ship, providing a protective air cap. Once the Marines were seated, the rotor blades were engaged as the pilots got them ready to depart the floating air base.

Some of the Marines were all smiles. Their smiles quickly vanished as their helicopters lifted off over the blue sea. Once the aircraft was in the air, the pilots turned the choppers toward land as they flew under the cover of a pair of F-14 Tomcats. The flight was no more than thirty minutes from the ship to the airport, and so far, no Iraqi forces had been spotted in the area.

The Marines had been given one mission: secure the airport and be prepared to provide security to the arriving Air Force and Army elements until relieved. The Army elements were to secure the port and the airfield if necessary. It was hoped that Saudi police would take care of securing the port. Just securing the airport was going to stretch the Marines to the fullest. The perimeter of the airport was six miles long and five miles wide, so there was no way they were going to secure the entire place.

As a result, the decision had been made that the Marines would instead look to secure just the main terminal complex on the south side. As Army elements began arriving, one company would secure the ARAMCO terminal on the west side, north of the main terminal, and another would secure the north gate and deportees' lounge.

Once the choppers arrived, they landed by the control tower and main terminal building for the airport. In short order, the grunts exited the plane and started unloading their equipment. They hadn't brought a lot with them, but what they had brought would allow them to dish out some serious hurt on an enemy.

One squad of Marines took off to secure the control tower. They wanted to get a guard detail set up around the entrance and then a few observers up in the tower itself; this would provide them with a solid overwatch of the entire airport and the surrounding area. Another element took off to secure a group of hangars just south of the main building that connected in front of a large taxi strip. This area had been identified as an initial unloading and staging area.

When the Air Force eventually landed and started to bring in some heavier equipment, this was where they'd drop it off. Other companies of the MEU would head into the actual terminal.

The terminal was a large facility, and to the surprise of the Marines who'd just arrived, it was nearly packed. There were only three large commercial planes docked to the air ramps connecting the station. People were trying to flee the country ahead of the Iraqi Army.

"*Salam alaikum*," the Saudi colonel said as he approached the Marines.

"*Alaikum al-salaam*," replied Colonel Lightfoot, Commander of the MEU, to the astonishment of the Saudi colonel. Colonel Lightfoot was a short, stocky, square-jawed man, almost from the same mold as Chesty Puller. His Marines thought he was harder than a woodpecker's lips to work for, and he was.

"I have a lieutenant waiting to guide your men up to the control tower and help you secure the main hangars just as requested. If you'll come with me, I'll walk you into the main terminal. As you can see, it's a bit chaotic here right now," the colonel said as he waved his hand about.

"I wasn't aware people were still trying to use the airport to evacuate. Is there anything we can do to help?" asked Colonel Lightfoot.

The colonel shook his head. "No. Once these last three planes take off, my men will begin dispersing them out of the airport. Then we can start to get things prepared for the rest of your people to arrive. By the way, my name is Colonel Abdulaziz. I've been assigned by the Ministry of Defense to be the liaison officer to the American units arriving. If you or your men need anything, please do not hesitate to ask."

The two of them walked briskly towards the terminal with two squads of Marines following behind them. "Thank you, Colonel Abdulaziz. My name is Colonel Lightfoot, Commander of the MEU."

"Colonel, do you any heavy tanks with you?" Colonel Abdulaziz asked.

"No, but we will be having our amphibious assault vehicles and light armored vehicles coming ashore shortly. As you can see, we do have some attack helicopters that have an antitank capability, and some Harrier jets at our disposal.

"I am beginning to feel better already, Colonel," Abdulaziz said.

"OK, I'd like to have at least two of them block the entrance to the airport once they arrive. We want to start locking down who can come into the airport."

Abdulaziz smiled and nodded in agreement. "That is a good call. Your men up in the control tower should be able to direct the QRF team if they spot trouble. Last I was told, you have more soldiers arriving in a few hours, yes?"

Colonel Lightfoot didn't say anything right away. They had just entered the terminal, and it was abuzz with activity. When the rest of the Marines loaded down with their combat gear filtered into the terminal, it suddenly got very quiet as all eyes turned to look at them.

The people looked startled and a little concerned by the sudden appearance of Western soldiers. Not many people knew or were aware that the King had formally requested military assistance from the West and, in particular, the Americans. The sudden appearance of US Marines had certainly caught many of them off guard.

Nearly an hour went by before the three commercial aircraft had finally departed the airport. With them gone, true to his word, the Saudi colonel who had a small contingent of soldiers with him had emptied the terminal. He had also acquired six V-150S armored cars for his forces to use. Once they had their QRF established and a roadblock at the entrance to the airport, Colonel Lightfoot felt like they were ready to hunker down while they waited for the cavalry to arrive.

A naval officer and an enlisted man had traveled with them. They had set up in the control tower to shepherd in the C-5s en route to the airport. The enlisted man radioed Colonel Lightfoot, letting him know the Air Force planes were preparing to land. Lightfoot made sure his Marines knew the Army had arrived and to be prepared in case the Iraqis decided to do something froggy.

Colonel Abdulaziz was standing in front of the floor-to-ceiling windows with his hands on his hips, watching the first aircraft land.

The colonel tilted his head to the side slightly as he spoke. "It amazes me that an aircraft that large can fly."

Grinning at the comment, Colonel Lightfoot replied, "You should see how many soldiers will disembark from that thing and what other equipment it's carrying. These things are beasts." His curiosity getting the better of him, he asked, "Colonel Abdulaziz, did you study in England by chance?"

Snickering, the colonel replied, "You are curious about my British accent. Yes, I did study in the UK. My father was a diplomat, so we lived in London for ten years. Did you study Arabic? You seem to have a decent understanding of the language."

"I did while I was in college. But that was many years ago." Colonel Lightfoot reached for his radio and told the Navy guys in the control tower to tell the first C-5 to park closer to the terminal than the hangars. "Come, let's go welcome our relief," Lightfoot offered.

By the time they had both gotten to the flight line, the aircraft had stopped not far from the terminal. A Marine captain made sure the pilot was able to see him and a few of his Marines with him so they'd know it was safe. The aircraft wound down its large engines as they began to open its clamshell nose to reveal its cargo.

As the rear ramp lowered and the nose rose on the C-5 Galaxy aircraft, Lightfoot and Colonel Abdulaziz were surprised at what they saw. Instead of hardened combat paratroopers, Air Force personnel led by a female major deplaned. She immediately spotted Colonel Lightfoot and approached him. She also noted the Saudi colonel and rendered the proper salute.

"I'm Major Dickerson, and I'm in charge of the ALCE group. I understand this is going to be the offload area," she said.

"It's the planned location," Colonel Lightfoot said.

"Good, we'll get set up and will be ready to meet the next aircraft in one hour. Everything I need is on this aircraft," she indicated as three pickup trucks rolled out along a heavy-lift forklift and forty Air Force personnel. Then came three large ten-kilowatt generators and three large light sets.

"If you'll excuse me, I'll get my people organized and positioned to meet the next aircraft." And with that, she departed.

"Colonel Lightfoot, may I ask—are all your women this take-charge?" Colonel Abdulaziz asked.

Turning to face the colonel, Colonel Lightfoot said, "Sir, if they're in uniform, they probably are."

For forty-five minutes, Lightfoot and Colonel Abdulaziz watched the Air Force major organize her people. Then the next aircraft came into view as it set up for the final approach and landing.

Colonel Lightfoot looked at the colonel's face as he saw what was probably three hundred twenty soldiers begin the process of filing out of the aircraft.

Moments later, a lieutenant colonel walked towards the two of them. The paratrooper rendered a quick salute, which Lightfoot promptly returned.

"I'm Lieutenant Colonel Fitzgerald, the battalion commander for the 1st of the 325th Infantry Regiment of the 82nd Airborne Division. Are you the MEU commander?" asked the paratrooper, all businesslike.

Lightfoot nodded as the two shook hands. "I am, Colonel Lightfoot."

A second later, an Air Force colonel joined them. "I'm Colonel Gomez. I've got a team of air traffic controllers and airfield operations folks with me. Can I get some of your Marines to show my guys to the tower and then give us a quick update on the airport? We've got a very long gravy train of supplies inbound to this airfield, and we need to get things ready to roll ASAP. Do you know where Major Dickerson is?"

"Yes, sir, that we can do," Colonel Lightfoot said. He whistled and caught the attention of one of his junior officers. He told the sergeant to take care of the Air Force personnel and get them set up with Major Dickerson.

Colonel Abdulaziz stood there in awe as he saw how rapidly this civilian airport was transitioning to a major military airfield. He couldn't believe how large these monstrous aircraft were and how much equipment they could move.

While the Air Force contingent headed off with one of his squad leaders, a slew of the paratroopers were lined up outside the plane, pissing on the tarmac. Colonel Fitzgerald caught Colonel Lightfoot looking at them, "Don't ask, sir. Some POG back at the Pentagon thought it would be a wise idea for the soldiers to load up on water a couple of hours before we landed. Needless to say, these guys have been pissing nonstop since we flew over Egypt."

Colonel Lightfoot laughed out loud before he could catch himself. The Saudi colonel laughed as well. "Sorry about that. That just seems like something an REMF would say. If you'll follow me into the command post I've established, I'll get you and your officers up to speed on the facility and the location of the closest Iraqi unit."

Before Colonel Lightfoot and Lieutenant Colonel Fitzgerald started to leave, Colonel Abdulaziz said, "If you gentlemen will excuse me, I will see if I can find someone who has… how do you say… porta-potties, yes? I think we will need them."

Lieutenant Colonel Fitzgerald nodded in approval. "That sounds good, sir. Once we get inside, I'd like to discuss with you how best to use my men," Fitzgerald said.

The third C-5 parked near the second aircraft as the first C-5 had already departed. When its nose opened up, it revealed four M551 Sheridan airborne assault vehicles inside. There were also a handful of five-ton trucks fully loaded down with supplies the paratroopers would need. Lieutenant Colonel Fitzgerald looked at the number of soldiers getting off the planes and the equipment they'd brought with them one more time before heading inside the terminal.

These guys came ready to wage war…

Standing inside the command post, Colonel Lightfoot watched an additional C-5 aircraft as it opened up it's clamshell noses. Inside the aircraft were tons of communications equipment, ranging from vans and antennas to generators and powerful mobile light kits. Then a few K loaders, specially designed for the purpose of loading and unloading cargo, rolled off along with a handful of forklifts.

While the second and third C-5s had been dedicated to getting an initial group of soldiers and bare-bones equipment to the airport, the next two were filled with the initial Air Force equipment needed to make this a fully operational airfield. As each aircraft was fully unloaded, they quickly started heading back out to the runway and returned to Germany to pick up another load, making room for subsequent aircraft to land at Jeddah.

Colonel Fitzgerald announced, "The next two C-5s will be offloading the remaining elements of my battalion and our equipment. Should we need to, we're ready to bring the fight to the Iraqis until an element from the 24th Mechanized Division arrives in the wee hours of the morning. They'll be arriving with four M1 tanks, four Bradleys and a couple of APCs."

"That's good to hear. Colonel Abdulaziz was telling me the closest Iraqi unit looks to be around four or five hundred kilometers away, so plenty of time to get our forces built up," Colonel Fitzgerald explained.

Sticking a wad of tobacco dip in between his lower teeth and his lip, the paratrooper nodded in approval. "I think for the time being, I'm going to billet my battalion in the Haji terminal with your permission, sir. I suspect that will keep my boys away from the Air Force folks. Seems the Haji accommodations are unsat for the Air Force people," Fitzgerald pointed out, and Colonel Lightfoot agreed.

Colonel Abdulaziz had returned from ordering up a load of porta-potties and asked, "Why are the Haji accommodations unsatisfactory for the Air Force? Pilgrims on the way to Mecca find them satisfactory."

"Sir, us Army dogs would find them satisfactory too, as would the Marines, but since they only offer shade and sleeping on the concrete floor with no air-conditioning and portable toilets, that wouldn't meet the Air Force standard of comfort," Lieutenant Colonel Fitzgerald explained. He pointed to a number of the Air Force members who were taking over the Saudi Airlines international terminal. "They seem to have found the terminal the royals use while they wait for their flights and claimed it for their people."

The three officers laughed at the joke, though the Army and Marine officers knew it to be true. The Chair Force, as they were often called, tended to be the softer branch when it came to billeting. It was kind of an interservice joke between them all.
****

All night, C-5s, C-141s, and C-130s were landing one after another. They were bringing in a Patriot missile battery and its entire set of equipment along with additional missile pods and missile reloads. A company team of four Bradley fighting vehicles, three M113 tracks, and four M1 Abrams tanks arrived as the 24th Infantry Division's Rapid Reaction Force. A battery of 105mm artillery arrived from the 82nd Airborne Division. In addition to the vehicles being offloaded, pallet after pallet of food, water, medical supplies, and munitions continued to arrive and steadily began to fill the nearby hangars. By dawn, an additional six hundred soldiers had landed, bringing the total number of US forces on the ground to nearly thirteen hundred.
****

Dawn—Jeddah Airfield

209

As the aircraft came to a stop and it's nose began to open, the loadmaster started the process of loosening the chains on the two tanks the aircraft was transporting.

The tank crews seated upstairs in the back of the C-5 started moving down the stairs to assist in getting their vehicles offloaded. What everyone noticed immediately was that when the nose of the aircraft began to open, the cool air from the plane's air-conditioning was quickly replaced with an oppressive heat wave that felt like an oven. It was still dark, being only 0420 in the morning.

Almost wincing at the heat wave that washed over him, Captain Poggi was glad to finally link up with his first sergeant, 1SG Kenny Brown, and the infantry lieutenant for the four Bradley fighting vehicles, of which three had arrived on a previous aircraft along with two of the M113s. The fourth Bradley was on this flight with Captain Poggi. Three more C-5s would bring the rest of the tanks and company along with ammo and supplies.

1SG Brown usually rode in their M-113. These vehicles were typically used for resupply and medical evacuation, in addition to transporting up to eleven infantrymen. Captain Poggi led the company, riding in his own tank.

Normally he would have stayed back in Fort Stewart, pushing the rest of his company out the door. But this was a no-shit operation, and he wanted to be on the leading edge, leading from the front and not the rear. He had a competent executive officer and felt he could get the rest of the company deployed and link up with him over here.

His tank was the first vehicle to exit. He was excited as hell to be standing in the commander's hatch when they began to move forward. As the tracks touched the ground, the driver accelerated and moved the tank around to the left, heading towards a large open area. The gunner traversed the turret, moving the 105mm gun from its rearward-facing position during transit to the front of the tank.

"Renshaw," Captain Poggi called to his driver over the intercom system.

"Yes, sir," the young private responded excitedly.

"Do you see where the Bradleys are parked in that open area? Pull us in next to them," Captain Poggi ordered.

"Yes, sir," Renshaw replied as he turned the tank in a smooth, unhurried fashion. As they came to a stop, 1SG Brown climbed up on the tank.

The assistant gunner then climbed out, saying good morning to Top before going about getting their antennas put together and working with the gunner on getting a few other items on the outside of the vehicle readied.

"Morning, sir. Welcome to Saudi Arabia," Top said in a chipper voice.

"Thanks, Top. Has anyone met you yet that speaks English?" Captain Poggi inquired.

"Yes, sir. A Lieutenant Colonel Fitzgerald from the 82nd came by and told me to tell you that once we have everything sorted on our end, we're to get a move on and head over to the Haji terminal."

"Great, did he say where that was or how we get there?"

1SG Brown pointed. "Those shitty tent-looking things about a mile north. He gave me the GPS coordinates, and I plugged them in."

GPS was something new to the US Army, having only been released to the general forces less than three months earlier. Special Operation forces had been using the system for some time, but its introduction to the rest of the force was a huge leap forward in capability. A lot of people still didn't know how to fully use the system, but the ones that did were getting everyone else up to speed and exalting its greatness. The receiver was the size of a cigar box, which wasn't a problem for tankers or mech infantry soldiers. For light infantry who had to carry everything on their backs, it was added weight and a pain in the butt.

Top added, "Captain, the colonel wants us dispersed before dawn. He's concerned the Iraqi Air Force may pay this place a visit."

Captain Poggi grunted at the news. The last thing a tanker wanted to run up against was a ground-attack fighter—or, God forbid, a Hind. "Alright, Top. Let's get a head count and sensitive items check and get moving."

Once the remaining tanks arrived and were ready, their antennas set up, their radios loaded with their comsec, and their targeting computers warmed up, the company team started moving out in the direction of the Haji tents to figure out where they wanted them to head next.

Captain Poggi spotted a sergeant near the Haji terminal and stopped his tank near him. "Good morning, Sergeant," he announced loudly to be heard over the tank's engine. "Who's in charge here?"

Captain Poggi told the driver to turn the tank off for the moment as he climbed down to talk with the paratrooper. The rest of his vehicles did the same.

"Sir, I think the King is, but Lieutenant Colonel Fitzgerald could tell you better. I just called him, so he should be down shortly."

"Sergeant, I just spent eighteen fucking hours on a plane scrambling to get an armor company team all the way across the world. Cut the shit and try staying focused. We've got two corps of Iraqi Republican Guard units headed this direction. Got it?" Captain Poggi barked hotly. He didn't like the sergeant cracking jokes about the King being in charge. This was a US military operation, and that meant there was a US person in charge, not the King of Saudi Arabia.

The paratrooper looked like he wanted to melt away into the background but couldn't. He only nodded his head and went back to standing watch while they waited for Lieutenant Colonel Fitzgerald to arrive. *Wonder what got this captain's panties in a knot,* the young sergeant was thinking.

Sitting on the front of his tank with his feet dangling off the armor, Captain Poggi was amazed at the size of this place. The Jeddah airport was one of the largest airports in the Kingdom. During the Haj, it would service over eighty thousand people coming and going to and from Mecca. In 1981, it had been officially opened as the Kingdom's main international airport. Its formal name was King Abdulaziz International Airport, but the troops just called it Jeddah Airfield.

Maybe twenty minutes later, a Humvee pulled up and an American officer stepped out. Captain Poggi recognized the rank and saluted the officer. "Sir, Captain Poggi, A Company, 3rd of the 69th Armor, 24th Division. I was told to report to you."

The colonel returned the salute, then said, "Captain, we've been expecting you and are glad to see you guys have made it with your tanks. How many men do you have?"

"Sir, all told, I have seventy personnel," Poggi reported.

"OK, follow me and I'll show you where to park for the time being and where your troops will be staying. You need to be aware that you're

212

in Saudi Arabia, and there are some strict rules here that your soldiers must be briefed on. Their conduct must be no less than stellar," Fitzgerald explained.

"Yes, sir, I've had a talk with all of them, and they understand."

"Good, now follow me."

"Sir, this is my first sergeant, First Sergeant Brown," Poggi introduced his senior NCO.

"How do you do, First Sergeant?" Fitzgerald said, extending his hand as First Sergeant Brown saluted and then accepted the handshake. "I'll get you hooked up with my command sergeant major and you two can work out the sleeping arrangements while I take the captain here and show him our area of responsibility."

"Very good, sir. If you want, you two can get going and I'll find the command sergeant major. This is NCO business, and you two don't need to be involved," First Sergeant Brown said respectfully.

Fitzgerald turned to Captain Poggi. "I like this guy already. Very good, First Sergeant. Command Sergeant Major White is probably in the Haji area getting some coffee going," Fitzgerald pointed out.

The Haji terminal was the world's largest cable-stayed, fabric-roofed structure. The white fabric roof reflected heat, thus providing tolerable conditions during the day. The complex contained facilities for sleep (bare floor), food preparation, and various support services. To a soldier or a Marine, it was better than sleeping out in the desert, which they all figured was coming soon enough.

Lieutenant Colonel Fitzgerald and Captain Poggi climbed into Fitzgerald's vehicle and headed to the north side of the airport perimeter.

On the northwest side was the main entrance into the airport. One major highway entered off the 271 highway interchange and two secondary roads. The two secondary roads entered through what was known as Pilgrim Gate, so those could be controlled relatively easily. The problem was going to the major highway. A traffic control point would have to be established, and it was decided to place it under the overpass.

In the very north center was another road entrance that would require a control point. As the Saudi Aviation Investigation Bureau was there, they didn't think they could close this road off completely. Still, they'd ask the airport administrator and see what they could make happen. They

213

needed to get the airport fully secured before they brought in more aircraft and equipment.

There were also several other tertiary roads that entered the airport complex. Most terminated in what appeared to be vehicle storage areas enclosed in fencing. These would need to be closed off as well. In the northeast corner was a warehouse complex that probably couldn't be closed off. Fortunately, between the highway and the airport perimeter fence was a service road the track vehicles and the Humvees could easily move over.

As they drove around, they discussed a plan for the defense of the north side of the airport. The sun was beginning to come up as they arrived back at the Haji terminal, and so was the heat.

Most soldiers were asleep. Soldiers believed that you should never stand when you could sit, never sit when you could lie down, and never stay awake when you could sleep. Most were implementing that policy.
****

When Captain Poggi returned to the terminal, Lieutenant Colonel Fitzgerald introduced him to his other company commanders and began to outline their assignments.

"We have the mission to secure the northern perimeter of this airport. The rest of the division will be flowing into here, and I suspect a lot more than just our division will eventually make their way here. The Marines are going to secure the terminal, control tower and administrative building.

"We have responsibility for the north and screening along the eastern side, halfway down. A Company," he called, gaining the attention of the A Company commander, "you're responsible for maintaining the checkpoints at the northwest corner. That's the major highway off 271 and the checkpoints for the secondary roads. Put your checkpoint for the major highway under the overpass. Saudi police will assist you in checking individuals at those checkpoints. You are there to back them up. Understood?" Fitzgerald asked.

"Yes, sir. No questions."

"Bravo, you have the checkpoints at the Aviation Investigation Bureau entrance and the compound to the east of that area."

"Understood, sir."

214

"Charlie, you have from the Jeddah Northeast Substation east to the TALJV compound."

"Got it, sir."

"Delta, you have the TALJV compound to the end of the eastern perimeter fence, which includes the aircraft accessories and component compound."

"Roger, sir."

"Captain Poggi, I'm keeping you in reserve. I want your vehicles where they can quickly move to cover the major entrance to the airport as well as scan and conduct a screen along the eastern perimeter."

"Sir, I'll position two tanks with Company A and two in the vicinity of Delta, with my Bradleys acting as a roving patrol along that eastern perimeter if that's good with you?" Captain Poggi offered.

"Good. Now, the command sergeant major will get with your first sergeants and work out setting up the checkpoints. This is NCO business, so stay out of it. Rotate your guard mounts as you see fit. I'll leave that up to you, but I would recommend we don't leave people out more than four hours, and make sure everyone has plenty of water when out there. Be sure everyone has overhead cover of some kind to keep the sun off them," Fitzgerald said. Looking over at Captain Poggi, he asked, "How are the air conditioners in your vehicles working?"

"Oh, sir, they're working great," he responded with sarcasm dripping off every word. Armored vehicles had no air conditioners, and temperatures could easily reach 130 degrees in the tanks. Hatches were open whenever the vehicle was stopped and not in combat conditions.

"Alright, then, let's get to it. And be safe," Fitzgerald said as he concluded the briefing. Another aircraft could be heard making its final approach. They were landing at a rate of two jets every hour, if not more frequently at this point.

Chapter Twenty-Eight
Rolling Stock Deploys

7 August 1990
101st Airborne Division (Air Assault)
Fort Campbell, Kentucky

The transportation office at Fort Campbell had been working three eight-hour shifts for around-the-clock operations. They had to divide their time between getting loads ready for truck hauls, coordinating convoy clearances with the Tennessee and Georgia Departments of Transportation, and requesting aircraft for personnel and some immediately needed equipment in-country, as well as coordinating with CSX railroad to get them the needed flatbed railcars to transport the heavy equipment.

The office was manned by civilians who had worked at Fort Campbell for many years and had the process and procedures memorized. All that experience, however, still hadn't prepared them for the amount of work or pressure being thrown at them. In each unit, a transportation officer or coordinator was designated to ensure each unit's loads were ready and in the proper place to be picked up. The immediate priority was to get the Apache helicopters loaded on the C-5s that would ferry them across the globe.

"Sir, we're about ready to load those six birds now. Should only be another fifteen minutes," the maintenance officer told Lieutenant Colonel Cody. Dick Cody was the battalion commander for the 1st Battalion, 101st Aviation Brigade. His aircraft were Apache helicopters equipped with eight Hellfire missiles and a 20mm chain gun in the nose as well as two nine-shot rocket pods.

Six of his aircraft had already departed in a previous flight that had carried a mix of pilots and maintenance personnel. Their original destination was the airport at Prince Sultan Air Force Base, Saudi Arabia. That had changed due to the speed of the Iraqi ground war. It was now going to be Jeddah, reportedly one of the few air bases not heavily damaged in the air attacks by the Iraqi Air Force. From the reports they were receiving, they were concerned it might get hit by the Iraqis, though, making it unusable when they arrived.

"Dick, are we about ready?" General Sheldon, the Assistant Division Commander for Maneuver, asked. He would be traveling with Cody.

"Yes, sir. We got out six Apaches yesterday along with another plane holding three Black Hawks and a couple of OH-58s. I'll have six Apaches on this plane along with a couple more OH-58s. All told, I'll have all twenty-four Apaches, three UH-60 Black Hawks and twelve OH-58s loaded and out of here by COB on the seventeenth," he explained proudly.

"How about your support equipment and ammo?" the general asked next.

"Sir, that's leaving today as well and is going out on C-141 aircraft. We should be operational by the twenty-first or twenty-second at the latest," Cody said with some confidence.

There was no doubt in Sheldon's mind that Cody would meet his target operational date. General Sheldon was going to meet with General Luck and see what was in store for the 101st Airborne Division. In Army speak, he was going to protect the interest of the division. As the 82nd had already arrived, he didn't want the 101st relegated to just guarding the airport.

On the other side of the base, equipment was being loaded onto railcars. This included CONEX containers and MILVANs. MILVANs were the size and shape of a semitruck and were packed with most of a unit's equipment, everything from batteries to lanterns to medical supplies. Even toilet seats were loaded as some of the older guys remembered what it was like using slit trenches in Vietnam in the early days.

Heavy equipment such as bulldozers and graders was being loaded along with artillery pieces. The need for rail transportation was so acute that the division commander had to get on the phone with the president of CSX rail and discuss the situation. After that call, railcars began appearing on the base in record numbers. In another area, trucks were being assembled for the drive to the port of Jacksonville.
****

"Bill, have you got everything?" Colonel Cory asked his executive officer as he approached the sixty vehicles of his battalion. They were all

217

lined up in the unit motor pool area. Each had gone through a detailed inspection for the trip. Each had the battalion crest painted in the window so the vehicles could be quickly identified when it came time to retrieve them in Saudi Arabia, or wherever they were going to be delivered. Bill was the convoy commander and had two soldiers in the cab of each vehicle.

"Yes, sir, we're about ready to roll. Our SP time is 0900, and I figure it'll take twenty minutes for us to get on the interstate. From there, it's down I-24 to I-75 in Chattanooga and on to Fort Gillium outside Atlanta for the night stop. We should arrive in Jacksonville around 1700 tomorrow night. I understand they have three buses laid on to bring us home as soon as we turn the vehicles over to the port people," Bill said confidently as all was ready. "I'll be in the lead vehicle and Mr. Wooley will bring up the rear with the maintenance vehicle and wrecker."

"Have you got enough tow bars for the HUMMVs?" Colonel Cory asked.

"Every fourth vehicle has one, and we have one for every other deuce-and-a-half," Bill said. *Why is the old man playing twenty questions?* Bill was thinking. "Sir, you worried about something?"

"Nah, I'm just concerned that we haven't had enough time like everyone else to get ready. We pushed hard to get back from West Point. We've had, what, four days to get the vehicles ready for this trip to Jacksonville, and we still have a lot to do here to get the guys ready as well. Hell, we got over one hundred soldiers in over the summer that have never trained with their respective units. We need to get them in some live-fire exercises. We need to get some of these new lieutenants in some live-fire exercises too," Cory explained.

"Sir, you won't be able to do that—you have no vehicles to get them to the ranges. Can't carry weapons and ammo in POVs," Bill pointed out.

"Oh, yeah? Watch me. We're commandeering POVs, and I'll haul the weapons and ammo to the ranges in them if I have to. I will find a way. Hey, you best get going and have a safe trip," Cory said as he extended his hand to Bill.
****

In the port of Savannah, Lieutenant Colonel Rich Piscal watched as his tanks were unloaded from the flatbed railcars. The loading at Fort Stewart had gone smoothly, and this operation was going equally smoothly. As each tank was driven off the flatcars, a ground guide escorted the tank to the Ro-Ro ship to be loaded up. Ro-Ros, or roll-on, roll-off ships, were either military or civilian ships normally used for transporting vehicles from one continent to another. In this case, they were being used to transport tank or mechanized divisions from the United States to the Middle East.

Right now, Lieutenant Colonel Piscal had about one hundred vehicles to get loaded up. As the ship could only carry fifty-eight M1 tanks, the others would have to be loaded on another ship. Fortunately, he was able to get his entire wheeled vehicle fleet loaded on this one ship.

"Morning, Colonel, how goes it?" a gentleman in civilian work clothes asked. He was wearing a hard hat and had on a fluorescent orange vest.

"Morning, how are you doing?" Colonel Piscal said, looking over at the man.

"Good, these your vehicles?" the man asked with a lifted eyebrow at the number of tanks and assorted vehicles parked in front of the ship.

"Yeah, they's ma babies. Thought I would see them off."

"Well, we'll get them loaded and tied down nice and tight for their trip. Sure as hell don't want one of them rolling around in rough seas. Could make for a bad day."

"I take it you work on the ship," Colonel Piscal stated.

"No, sir, I'm a longshoreman. I load ships. Don't sail on them. Momma wants me home most nights. My crew and I heard they needed help. We drove up from Jacksonville, where we live and work, to help out. We'll head back home when you folks are loaded and gone."

"I hope you guys are getting a bonus in pay for coming up here and doing this," Colonel Piscal replied to the kind gesture.

"I wish, but no, we don't get extra pay. We're members of the ILA."

"The ILA?"

"The ILA, sir, means 'I love America,'" the gentleman said with a smile. "Actually, sir, it stands for International Longshoremen of America. We're the stevedores that load the ships. These Ro-Ro ships are pretty easy to load as your guys drive the vehicles on and we just have to chain them down. Not like the old days when you needed a crane to pick up each tank individually and swing it over the ship. This is so much faster. Bulk items are all loaded in MILVANs, so those are fairly easy to load as well. About the only thing that's palletized is ammo and items that can't fit in a MILVAN," the longshoreman said.

"MILVANs don't go on this ship, do they?" Colonel Piscal asked, looking at the upper deck of the ship.

"No, sir, they'll be loaded on another ship that'll be coming in tonight to start loading them. That one ship will take about half of your MILVANs here, and another ship is due in the day after tomorrow to pick up the other half. In the old days, it would take a week to load that much cargo. Now, it takes about twenty-four hours from docking to departure." As he spoke, he was constantly watching the loading process and holding a small transmitter/receiver radio in his hand.

"Sir, I have to go. Seems we have a problem on the ship. You take care and good luck," the longshoreman said, heading out toward the ship at a brisk walk.

The same scene was playing out in Galveston, Texas, as vehicles from the 3rd Armored Cavalry Regiment from Fort Hood began to arrive in the port area. Another civilian Ro-Ro ship had been quickly contracted and positioned to receive the vehicles. The 3rd Armored Cavalry Regiment was the reconnaissance element for the 18th Airborne Corps. Although their vehicles were being loaded and the soldiers alerted for deployment to the Middle East, no one was sure where in the Middle East they were going. They would find out soon enough.
****

4th Marine Expeditionary Brigade Headquarters
Camp Lejeune, North Carolina

Every logistician's worst nightmare was unfolding at the 4th Marine Expeditionary Brigade headquarters. They'd been given their deployment orders less than twenty-four hours ago, and as things stood right now, there was no way in hell they were going to make their deployment schedule. Amphibious Group 2 (PhibGru 2), which was designated to provide the transportation, could only muster nine amphibious ships instead of the twenty-four needed to move the entire MEB. They'd quickly figured out how to acquire four more, but that was still going to leave them eleven ships short.

Major Garcia was standing practically at attention as he tried to explain what was going on to the colonel on the other end of the phone line. "Sir, I know we were told we would have the MV American Eagle container ship for this move, but it's been diverted to the Army."

Holding the hand receiver away from his ear as the colonel shouted for all his worth, as if it would somehow change their current situation, Major Garcia thought, *Thank God I'm not in his office right now.*

"Major, do you understand that without that ship, we're not going to be able to deploy the 4th MEB without sufficient forces or supplies to sustain itself? Do you understand that?" the colonel screamed.

"Yes, sir, I do, and I'm talking to Military Sea Command about getting us a replacement ship right now," he replied, attempting to calm the colonel down. "We should have an answer by the sixteenth, sir."

There, that should make him happy.

"The sixteenth? The first ships sail on the seventeenth, for Christ's sake. You get on the phone and tell those people we need the damn ships now!"

Guess I might as well give him the rest of the bad news now, Garcia thought.

"Sir, we have another problem that you should be aware of as it's going to affect the loading. The amphibious ships will load at Morehead City and the MSC ships will be loading at Sunny Point Military Ocean Terminal in Wilmington," Garcia said and then pulled the phone away from his ear in anticipation of a new round of shouting.

"Those ports are a hundred miles apart! How the hell are we supposed to get men and equipment sent to both at the same time? Holy shit! Have you got any other surprises for me?" the irate colonel demanded.

In for a penny, in for a pound, Garcia thought as he dropped the next piece of information. "Yes, sir. You need to know that the MSC ships are not capable of supporting an amphibious assault and are not self-sustaining. In addition, they can't support in-stream offloading." Again, Garcia pulled the phone away from his ear as the colonel further melted down in fury at the situation.

221

"Oh, and one other thing, sir. We have limited dock space at Morehead City, so Amphibious Group 2 will be departing with three transit groups and each will have a different departure date." Again, the major quickly moved the phone away from his ear, only this time the phone line went dead.

7 August 1990
White House
Washington, D.C.

Colonel Atwell was in his usual position opposite the President, ready to begin as soon as the Commander-in-Chief walked in. Prior to the briefing, Atwell had taken some time to look over the slides and familiarize himself with its content before he had to brief it. What the various intelligence and operation groups had put together blew his mind. To see how fast the battlefield had changed in such a short time span was truly incredible.

As President Bush walked in and made his way over to his seat, Atwell could tell by the look on the man's face he was exhausted. The President looked like he hadn't slept in a few days. He told everyone to take their seats and nodded to Atwell to get started.

"Sir, in the past forty-eight hours, the situation in Saudi Arabia has changed dramatically. The King officially left thirty-six hours ago for his home in Spain, and most of the royals have likewise fled the country. The Sultan of Oman has offered to let the Saudi military establish their headquarters in his country at a location still to be determined."

Most of the military members in the room already knew this information, but to the civilian advisor, it came as a shock. Atwell could see the information hit the President like a punch to the gut.

He continued with the bad news. "Sir, this slide shows you the current disposition of Iraqi forces as we see them. The 2nd Army Corps in the west is fifty kilometers from Tabuk and hasn't met any resistance from the Saudi military. The 2nd Republican Guard Corps with the 7th and 5th Divisions has reached the cities of Buraydah and Unayzah, which puts them roughly six hundred and fifty kilometers northeast of Jeddah and just four hundred and sixty kilometers from Medina.

"Thus far, the Iraqis are running into some resistance from what appears to be a battalion of M-60A1 tanks and Saudi National Guard infantry equipped with V-100 armored cars. We believe the tanks are part of the armored brigade that was in Riyadh. That brigade appears to be conducting a fighting retreat along a stretch of highway that runs from Buraydah to Medina, some four hundred and sixty kilometers away."

"Jesus H. Christ!" the President blurted out angrily. "At this rate of advance, they'll reach the Red Sea in another three or four days. Maybe less. How in the hell is an army we've largely equipped and trained being systematically wiped out like this?" he demanded to know.

None of his advisors appeared to want to take this question, so Colonel Atwell resumed his brief. "Sir, we're receiving signals intelligence reports indicating a high level of street fighting taking place along the outskirts of Buraydah. A battalion of motorized infantry has placed several calls for additional support. An armored battalion was recently dispatched to assist them.

"Meanwhile, the 1st Republican Guard Corps's lead elements are now in the vicinity of Al-Hofuf on the eastern side of Saudi. The 45th Infantry Division of the Ninth Army Corps has moved into Al-Jubail and silenced any resistance there. The 49th Infantry Division, also of the IX Army Corps, is in the process of eliminating any resistance in Dammam. As of yet, we've seen no movement towards Riyadh. We expect to see the capital finally fall in the next twenty-four hours," Colonel Atwell explained, then paused to allow for some questions.

The President shook his head in frustration and disgust as he declared, "So if I'm hearing you right, Colonel, Saddam is going to overrun the place before we can even get anyone in there to make a difference. Is that about right?"

Before Colonel Atwell could answer the awkward question, General Powell intervened on his behalf. "Sir, we have the first brigade of the 82nd Airborne Division, which arrived yesterday and is even now continuing to arrive with all their follow-on equipment. We also have the lead elements from the 24th Infantry Division on the ground with a company team of Abrams battle tanks and Bradley fighting vehicles." The President nodded as he followed along.

Powell continued, "The MEU from the *Tarawa* is ashore at Jeddah securing the port and assisting in the security of the airport until the 82nd is ready to assume full responsibility. We have enough ground forces in-country to advance forward and stop the Iraqi Army's advance butt-cold along the mountain passes of Al Rathaya just north of Medina. With more air assets arriving in the area every hour, the Iraqi Army is about to get an ass-kicking the likes of which it's never experienced before."

President Bush laughed at the blunt assessment General Powell, his most soft-spoken general, had just given. His frown turned into a slight smile. "You always did have a way with words, General. I just hope you're right and it's not too little, too late. I fear if we don't send a message to these guys fast, they're going to keep gobbling up the country simply because they can."

"Sir, General Powell is right," General Dugan, Chief of Staff for the Air Force, interrupted. "We're on the verge of being able to give the Iraqis a solid punch to the face. We have the 71st Fighter Wing out of Langley laying over in Germany while we wait on figuring out where to base them. We also have the 42nd Bomb Group out of Loring that just arrived at Diego Garcia. With your permission, and if the Egyptians will go along, I'd like to get the 71st moved to Egypt. They can start interdicting some of these Iraqi MiGs and clearing the skies for other ground-attack aircraft. I'd also like your permission to send the 42nd Bomb Group in to plaster the ground forces heading towards Medina and Jeddah. If we can deliver a punch to the face to those forces advancing along that line, we might force them to pull back, or at least slow or stop their advance."

James Baker knew they were steadily moving into his lane as the reality of basing rights and air corridors was becoming increasingly important.

"Mr. President," the Secretary of State said, "I've spoken with the Sultan of Oman. He's genuinely concerned that Saddam may not stop with Saudi Arabia just like they didn't with Kuwait. It may be the Iraqis' intention to seize the entire Arabian Peninsula. So far, Saddam's forces haven't met any real resistance, so why stop? At least, that's the Omanis' thinking. As of right now, the Sultan has granted us basing rights and permission to stage out of his country and carry out defensive and offensive operations from their territory."

Jim paused for a second as he reached for a glass of water. He then carried on, "I spoke with Mubarak, and at first I thought I was going to meet a lot of resistance to our request to base our aircraft out of their country. President Mubarak told me personally that Saddam embarrassed and humiliated him in front of the Arab League when he went to bat for him to get financial and economic relief, only to have Saddam invade Kuwait and then further amplify that mistake by invading Saudi Arabia. He has officially given us permission to utilize some of their airfields."

"Whoa—this is big news," General Dugan exclaimed in surprise. "When were you going to tell my guys? I need to get teams out there immediately to start inspecting some of the airfields we've had our eyes on."

Baker turned to the Air Force Chief of Staff. "There hasn't been time, General. I literally just got off the phone with Mubarak moments before we all walked into this meeting. I think between the offers from the Sultan of Oman and President Mubarak, we should be able to mount an effective defense of Saudi Arabia and finally get into a position to stop the Iraqi Army while we build up a large enough ground force to push Saddam back into Iraq."

"Mr. President, please authorize my forces to go after the Iraqi air and ground forces. I believe it's highly likely the Republican Guard is going to go after the UAE. I'm all but certain Saddam is going to move his forces there next and gobble them up. Remember, Saddam has a score to settle with them as well. It was originally the Kuwaitis, the UAE, and Bahrain that refused to clear their debts from the war with Iran. My hunch says they're going to exact their revenge on them next," the Air Force chief said forcefully.

"Damn, do you really think he's going after Abu Dhabi and Dubai as well? All over their unwillingness to forgive his war debt?" the President asked, in shock at how quickly things were unraveling in the Middle East.

"Sir, it's our opinion that he's going to go all the way short of Oman in the Arabian Sea, to the Red Sea in the West," Mr. Scowcroft said. "His supplies and resources are going to cause a strategic pause very soon, as he'll have traveled a little more than five hundred miles from their border. His vehicles will be in serious need of maintenance at that point. It'll be during this period that he'll likely go on the defense, and we should begin to leverage our air power to go on the offensive and pound them from the sky while we continue to build up our ground forces."

The President sat back in his chair and absorbed everything being thrown at him. He wanted a moment to digest everything before he started throwing more questions out there.

226

The Soviets are at the end of their rope. Why would they be propping up the Iraqis? What game are they playing? What other nasty tricks have they given the Iraqis we haven't found out about yet? Bush hadn't had to think this hard in a very long time.

Leaning forward, Bush asked, "Does anyone know what the latest price of oil is?"

The question caught everyone off guard. No one initially knew, which meant one of the aides had to leave and find out. While he was gone, the steward refilled everyone's coffee cups and the pot for the room. The kitchen staff also brought in some breakfast sandwiches.

A moment later, the aide returned. "Sir, prior to the invasion, a barrel of oil was hovering at twenty-three dollars. Since the start of hostilities, it's shot up to thirty-seven dollars."

"Damn, if he does grab Bahrain, Qatar and the UAE, it'll likely push the price of oil well above fifty dollars a barrel. That's when he'll want to sue for peace. Once he has everything in his hands," Sununu chided.

Bush sighed at the news. He then turned to General Powell, asking, "Is there anything we can do at this point to slow down the Iraqi forces, or at least hurt them? Like maybe we hammer him with some Tomahawk cruise missiles or some precision-guided attacks?"

"Sir," Admiral Kelso chimed in, "we have one carrier group in the Arabian Sea that could launch strikes, but we have no contact on the ground that could direct the strikes. There are some Special Forces teams with the fleet. We could insert them if we knew where to put them. If we had contact with some Saudi forces or someone that could direct the strikes, that might help. I'd also like to move the *Eisenhower* out of the Med and get the 6th and 5th Fleets moved into the Red Sea."

Cheney tapped the admiral's sleeve. "Get with me after this and let's make that happen."

General Vuono was looking through some papers. "Sir, the 7th Special Forces Group has a team training with the Omani forces along the border with Yemen from prior to this mess with the Iraqis. We could pull them and insert them in Iraq or Saudi to adjust air strikes. We just need to have CENTCOM direct SOCOM to make the move," he explained.

"Let's run this by the Saudis and see if they'll buy into it. If we can, then let's insert them where General Schwarzkopf thinks they'll do the

227

most good and have them work with the Navy and that bomber group out of Diego Garcia to start hitting these guys. Let's see if we can't get our aircraft in Incirlik into the fray to throw the Iraqis off-balance as well," the President said as he looked at Mr. Baker.

"I'll get with the Turks and get that cleared," the Secretary of State replied.

The President then asked, "What has General Schwarzkopf asked for?"

"At this point, he's asking for the forces identified in OPLAN 1002-88, which include the 18th Airborne Corps, the full 82nd Airborne, and the 101st Airborne, and he wants them in the Jeddah area. In addition, he wants the 24th ID and the 3rd Armored Cavalry Regiment to set up shop in Oman as they aren't going to get there for two weeks at best and he wants to see how things flush out. He also wants those three divisions supported by the Marine 1st and 2nd Divisions. He's also asking if we're going to get any friendly nations to assist as well, and if we are, to try and position their forces in Oman. That's where he said our forces will likely break out from when it comes time to remove the Iraqis and throw them back into their own country," Powell said as he looked at Mr. Baker and then the President.

"I think we'll get aid from the British and Canadians as well as the Egyptians. I'll certainly ask the French and any others, but I wouldn't hold out any hope for their support," Baker answered. "Those requests will go out by close of business today."

"OK, we have the war fighters identified. Now how about the supporters? How do we move these forces and supply them? This is going to be a monumental move," the President stated.

"The pre-positioned ships in Diego Garcia sailed this morning. In four days, they'll be off the coast of Oman and ready to go ashore and start the offloading process. We have six Ro-Ro ships that are in ports on the East Coast. We can begin loading them as soon as we've identified which units to load first. The 24th is already in the port area, with Barry McCaffrey screaming to load. Other ports are Newport News, Jacksonville, and Galveston as well as Beaumont and Houston. Ammunition is loaded out of Sunny Point, North Carolina. Bulk container logistics can be loaded out of New York and New Jersey. Container ships are available as well, but the Ro-Ro are going to be the fastest to load. TRANSCOM has no units assigned but can request units to meet the needs of port operations as well as rail priorities. Moving bodies can be accomplished by activating the Civilian Air Reserve," Mr. Cheney explained.

"What's the Civilian Air Reserve?" the President asked with a raised eyebrow, not having heard of this group before.

"Sir, that's a fleet of commercial airlines that we have contracts with to provide planes and crews to the DoD in times of national emergency. Just about every major airline has committed a certain number of planes to this fleet, as have several charter companies, such as Tower Air and Trump Air, to name two. If you recall the Gander crash, it was a charter jet from Arrow Air. They've been excluded from the fleet since that crash," Mr. Cheney said. "Sir, in order to pull this off, we're going to need to activate some reserve and guard units. Most of our seaport operations are carried out by twenty-two port management reserve units. They work with the seaport managers and arrange the order of loading and scheduling as well as the go-to units that are deploying and help get the loads organized. There's no way around it, we're going to have to call them up. In addition, we'll need to activate a lot of the Air Force Reserve units. They'll be needed to augment the active force as we begin the process of deploying our fighter and bomber squadrons' assets. I know this may sound like a lot of forces, but I recommend we initiate a presidential call-up of at least one hundred thousand National Guard and reserve forces."

The President lifted an eyebrow at the number. "Really, you think we need that many?"

"Before this is over, Mr. President, you'll be looking at a partial mobilization of somewhere around one million for a two-year period," Mr. Scowcroft clarified.

General Powell quickly interjected, "Mr. President, this is about to become the largest deployment of American forces overseas since World War II. It's liable to be bigger than Korea and certainly larger than Vietnam."

The President grimaced at the mention of Vietnam. The country was still recovering from that war. He sighed and nodded. "Alright, but before we start calling people up, I'm going to have to brief congressional leaders and get them on board with this action. John," he said, turning to Sununu, "set up a meeting for them in my office as soon as possible. Tomorrow at the latest."

"Yes, sir," the Chief of Staff said and wrote down some notes.

"Alright, gentlemen, let's get with it," the President said as he stood. The meeting was over. It was now time to move the country to a war footing and begin the process of preparing the country for what was about to come.

Chapter Thirty
The Battle of Buraydah

7 August 1990
2nd Republican Guard Corps
Buraydah, Saudi Arabia

Colonel Jasmen Nassar was a battalion commander in the 7th Adnan Motorized Republican Guard Division. He commanded the 1st Battalion, 11th Brigade, and his was the lead battalion for the division at this point. He had pushed his scout platoons out early in the morning to gather information on what they might be facing as they moved towards the city of Al Majma'ah, the next major city they needed to pass through before they entered Riyadh. But so far, he hadn't heard anything from the scouts since they had reached the outskirts of Al Majma'ah.

That was not like his scout platoon leader, First Lieutenant Muhammed al-Tikriti. As Colonel Nassar's vehicles began to roll up on the town and the palm orchards at the outskirts of it, he now understood why he hadn't heard back. The smoldering vehicles with burnt and charred bodies told the story of what had happened.

They'd been ambushed, apparently by dismounted infantry and artillery. Nassar felt the loss of the young officer. He was a smart and determined officer. Nassar had no doubt the young man would have risen to the rank of general someday.

The battalion's vehicles moved on, leaving the exposed bodies as a reminder to those that followed that danger was always lurking nearby. Not wanting to get bogged down by a force left behind, Nassar had the battalion bypass the town. The order of the day was speed. He was under strict orders to let follow-on forces secure the town.

Colonel Nassar had pushed out from Al Majma'ah and was now sitting in Umm Hazim. He was starting to think he was fortunate, as there were several roads that led to their objective. The terrain in front of him dropped down from the town and then gave way to fifteen miles of rolling but largely open terrain. It was almost perfect for a motorized or tank force to use. The ground they were traveling on favored the attacker. The rolling hills did offer a defender some opportunities if they knew how to leverage them, but Nassar liked his chances.

The 12th Brigade would be attacking north of him on the better road and would be followed by the 21st Armored Brigade. One might think they were going to have an easier fight, but Nassar knew better. The enemy would have the bulk of his forces to the center and north. Nassar smiled as he thought about coming in through the back door.

It was late afternoon, and the corps commander had ordered a halt for the day. Patrols would go forth and probe, but rest and maintenance were the order of the night. Also, a dawn attack would put the sun in the defenders' eyes. They would be easy targets for the close-air support that was scheduled to lead the morning offensive.

Colonel Nassar and the 11th Brigade would have access to helicopter support should they need it. What did bother him right now was that he knew little of the force opposing him. From what he had seen of his decimated scout platoon, it was obvious the enemy had some artillery support and antitank weapons. But how much did they have? Was it just a company or platoon element? Was it something much larger? Not knowing was bothering him.

While his units conducted maintenance on the vehicles, Nassar and his operations officer developed their own plan in support of the larger brigade plan. The brigade plan was to attack from two different points to split the enemies' ability to counter their assault. The 11th Brigade would attack with his battalion on the north side of the road, while the 2nd Battalion would attack on the southern side. 3rd Battalion would follow and essentially act as their reserve force or bum-rush through a hole in the enemy position once they created one.

The goal was to have the brigades isolate these smaller towns along the way to Riyadh and not get bogged down in any potential street fighting. The 4th Corps was following behind them and would clean up any remaining pockets of resistance left behind.

When Nassar and the operations officer had finalized their plans for the intermediate objectives, they called the company commanders in and briefed them. Satisfied that all was ready, Nassar lay down for a couple of hours for sleep and ordered his commanders to grab some shut-eye as well. It was important for a commander to get sleep; otherwise, their brains would stop functioning properly and they'd be more likely to make stupid mistakes. Mistakes that cost people their lives.
****

232

Red Sea

Aboard the aircraft carrier USS *Saratoga*, time did not stand still. She had replaced the *Eisenhower*. The ship was plowing through the waters of the Red Sea, not far from the coast of Saudi Arabia. The sea around the carrier was both abuzz with activity and swarming with the frigates and destroyers of the strike group, which were screening for the carrier. Near the floating air bases were two *Ticonderoga*-class guided-missile cruisers, or Ticos. These sophisticated warships controlled the powerful AEGIS radar systems that would alert the battle group to any potential dangers.

If the Iraqi Air Force mounted any sort of attack on the carrier, the frigates and destroyers of the battle group would tie in their weapon systems to the Ticos' state-of-the-art targeting systems. As the ship slaved the battle group's collective defensive weapon platforms together, the advanced computing system would take over the defense of the battle group and begin prioritizing targets to engage, dispatching execution orders to the ships most capable of neutralizing the threat.

This was an incredibly powerful offensive and defensive platform the Navy would be putting to the test. The lesson of the *Stark* was still imprinted in the minds of the sailors. No one wanted to get sucker-punched like that again.

A whooshing noise was heard and then what sounded like a freight train raced across the ceiling above the aviators seated in the squadron briefing room beneath the flight deck above.

Captain Jose Arroyo was the Commander, Air Group for the *Saratoga*. As the CAG, he was the man in charge of all the aircraft aboard the ship. Fortunately for the pilots under his command, this wasn't his first rodeo. He'd flown nearly three hundred combat missions over Vietnam on three different carriers. He'd also been shot down twice, and in both cases, he'd been able to escape and evade long enough to allow the Combat Search and Recovery or CSAR units to retrieve him without being captured.

Looking at the pilots for the C-2 Greyhound and the four Tomcat crews sitting before him, Jose felt a twinge of jealously over the fact that he couldn't go with them. He cleared his throat. "Gentlemen, we've just

233

received an urgent tasking from our ground components near Jeddah. Apparently, the Saudi ground forces are getting steamrolled by the Iraqi Army and we've been tasked with doing something about it."

The CAG turned to look at his Greyhound crew first. "You're to fly to the Jeddah airfield and pick up an Air Force Tactical Air Controller Party and shuttle him and his team up to a Saudi air base near Buraydah."

The two pilots scribbled some notes on their maps but didn't say anything right off the bat. The CAG turned to his four Tomcat crews next. "You four will be flying escort duty. This is enemy-controlled space. The Saudi Air Force was largely wiped out on the ground during the first day of the war. What few aircraft and pilots managed to escape have been fighting a rather haphazard battle with the Iraqis. Whatever you do, do not underestimate these guys. Their Iraqi pilots are flying fully upgraded MiG-29 Fulcrums and MiG-25 Foxbats. Keep in mind that many of these pilots have already flown combat missions against the Iranian F-14s and F-4s from the Shah's air force. It's incumbent upon you guys to get that TACP unit to Buraydah. We can't start sending in CAS units to fuck up these Iraqi armor units until we have eyes on the ground, and it's your responsibility to get them there. Is that understood?"

The pilots in the briefing room all shared a few nervous glances with each other but wisely nodded in approval. They were ready for their baptism by fire to begin.
****

Jeddah Air Base

The rolled-up magazine hit the table with a thwacking crash, impacting against a fly that had to be the size of a US nickel. Brigadier General Ulysses Buckner used the magazine to brush the remains of the pestilent that seemed to plague this particular part of the world. Add in the inhumane heat of this place, and it was practically unbearable.

General Buckner had been on the ground all of six hours. In that short time, he had come to the conclusion that this hellscape was utterly unworthy of fighting for. However, he was a soldier—he'd fight on any piece of terrain he was ordered to fight on, and he'd kill any enemy his country ordered him to.

234

Reaching for his cup of coffee, he downed what was left in the cup, knowing he would need at least one or two more cups if he was to stay awake and make it through the next few hours. While his body was wide awake, his brain was all but ready to shut down and put him into a comatose state. Right now, he had two priorities that had to be accomplished. One was getting his coms people to finish getting their equipment put together so they could establish coms with their parent units still back in CONUS. The other was inserting forward air controllers into the Saudi National Guard units so they could direct air strikes against the Iraqi Army.

Knocking on his door, one of the staff NCOs interrupted his dour mood as he held up a fresh pot of coffee for the general.

"Oh, bless you, Jimmy. Just give it to me black. God knows I need the caffeine jolt. Oh, by the way—have you guys figured out who our FACs are from the Air Force?" Buckner asked as his staff NCO proceeded to fill his coffee mug up to the brim.

Jimmy smiled as he saw the general drink a quarter of the coffee he'd just poured. "Yes, sir, they did. A couple of them should arrive in a few minutes. I'll send them in once they get here," he explained before walking out to his desk on the opposite side of the general's makeshift office.

A couple of minutes later, Buckner heard a knock on the door and looked up to see a handful of soldiers wearing slightly different uniforms than the paratroopers.

"Ah, you must be my Air Force guys," called out Brigadier General Buckner as he waved for them to come on in.

Brigadier General Ulysses Buckner was the 82nd Airborne Division's Assistant Division Commander for Maneuver. At present, he was also the senior Army officer on the ground in Saudi Arabia. This placed him in a unique position—he was technically in charge of all ground forces in the country until someone higher up eventually showed up and replaced him.

Looking at the nametape of the man sitting across from him, Buckner announced, "Major Skooter, is it? I'm General Buckner. It appears the powers that be have determined that I'm the man in charge of all US forces in Saudi Arabia for the time being and I've got a special assignment that I believe is right up your alley."

The Air Force major, along with three other Air Force personnel—a first lieutenant, a master sergeant, and a senior airman—all looked to the major to see how he'd respond. It was clear they were going to take their cues from him.

"Well, General, I'm always up for a good mission. I've got a small team here with me, but I'm sure we could stir up some trouble for you. Whatcha got for us?" Skooter asked confidently.

Buckner smiled at the major. "I have a feeling you and I are going to get along just fine, Major. So, here's the deal. In about thirty minutes we've got a C-2 Greyhound inbound from the *Saratoga*, who's pulling figure eights in the Red Sea right now. When they land, they're going to pick your team up and fly you guys into some airport called Prince Nayef bin Abdulaziz Airport outside the city of Buraydah. It's about three hundred and seventy-five miles east of here."

Major Skooter raised an eyebrow at the news but didn't say anything.

"Once you get there, Major, you'll be met by an officer from the Saudi National Guard who'll be expecting you. It's my understanding that the Saudi National Guard in that area is a light infantry outfit. I was told they were equipped with V-100 armored cars, just to give you an idea of what you'll be working with. There is some good news. There are three battalions of M-60A1 tanks from an armored brigade that withdrew from Riyadh. That version of tank is equipped with the new 120mm cannon, so at least they'll be able to outshoot those 105s on the T-72s. But listen up, Major. Once you're on the ground, I need you to confirm the condition of the airfield. We need to know if we can refuel aircraft there if we opt to try and seize it. Once you've checked out the airfield, your primary job is going to be supporting the Saudis with air strikes from the carrier sitting off the coast."

Major Skooter smiled at the idea of raining death from above but then turned serious as he asked, "Sir, what do you want me to do if the Saudis fold and either retreat, fade away, or get themselves captured?"

"If they fold, then start making your way to Medina any way you can. If you can stay with the Saudis and send us missions, do so. If you have to E&E, then keep in touch and we'll send a helo to pick you up. If you can hunker down and let the Iraqis bypass you and still call targets, do so. With luck we should have more fast-movers from the Air Force

236

here tomorrow or the next day. Right now the problem is where to land all these aircraft."

The general sighed briefly as he shook his head in frustration at the situation. "The Iraqis have air superiority right now. We've got the Navy coming in with low-level attack aircraft, A-6 Intruders, but they're going to have to be on their toes as the Iraqis apparently have some pretty competent MiG pilots flying around the area. Until our Tomcats and Eagle drivers are able to sweep the skies clear of them, any air strike we call in will be going up against a contested airspace. So, I've given you a lot of information and basically told you what we're looking for from you—do you have any other questions or things you want me to clear up before we send you on your way?" General Buckner asked.

Major Skooter smiled and shook his head no. He'd trained for missions like this. He was a former F-4 Phantom pilot, so he had a good idea of what the pilots would be going through, and he knew the capabilities of the aircraft he'd be calling in for support.

"Alright, then, let's get you loaded up and on your way." General Buckner stood and held his hand out for Skooter and his team. The five of them shook hands, and the airmen left his office to grab their gear and get a move on.
****

Major Lane Skooter watched the C-2 Greyhound taxi towards them and eventually come to a stop. The pilot turned the engines off while a couple of ground crew ran towards the vehicle. They went about the process of getting the aircraft refueled and ready to get back into the air.

Turning to his guys, Skooter called, "Come on, let's get our gear loaded up and ready."

While they were loading their gear into the aircraft, one of the pilots came up to him. "Major Skooter, I'm Lieutenant Price. Is it just the four of you we're transporting?"

"Yeah, it looks that way. There were supposed to be some additional TACPs, but they appear to have been snatched up by some of the ODA teams. So, yeah, it's just the four of us."

One of the ground crewmen gave them a thumbs-up as he detached a fuel hose.

"Looks like we're ready to get back into the air. Why don't you get your team strapped in and we'll get going? I need to let our escorts know we're getting back into the air. They were topping off their tanks nearby. Hopefully we won't run into any enemy aircraft."

When everyone was on board the aircraft, they proceeded east-northeast for 375 miles. The airmen got comfortable in the airline-style seats, which faced backwards with a five-point restraining harness, and even tried to grab some sleep. Flying at midday and just above the ground for most of the time didn't exactly make for the smoothest flight. The heat radiating from the surface back up into the sky caused the aircraft to encounter some unique turbulence.

Eventually they found the airport they were looking for. Major Skooter breathed a sigh of relief as the pilot lined up to land. They'd managed to make it to the airport without encountering any Iraqi fighters along the way. Near as Skooter could tell from the pilots, the escorts hadn't encountered any MiGs either. That was a good sign as far as Skooter was concerned. The last thing he wanted was for the ground-attack planes he was going to call in to get nailed along the way.

When the Greyhound eventually landed, they taxied over to one of the hangars, where they spotted a pair of V-100 armored cars. Once the aircraft stopped moving, they lowered the rear ramp and started getting out.

Major Skooter tossed his ruck out of the plane and let it thud onto the tarmac. The others did the same, and in a few moments, they had their gear off the aircraft, ready to go. A couple of Saudis came towards them. They looked like aircraft ground crewmen. One of the Navy fliers got out and tried to talk with them.

While the flight crew was getting the plane ready to head back to Jeddah, the master sergeant and the lieutenant went about checking the runways, the taxi ramps, and the nearby buildings. They also tried to communicate with the Saudi ground crew. Luckily, one of them spoke English. He was able to answer a lot of their questions about the airfield's capabilities. For whatever reason, the Iraqis had left it alone.

Major Skooter made sure their initial assessment of the airport was hand-jammed and sent back with the aircrew to General Buckner. If the 82nd wanted to take the airfield once the rest of the division showed up, then he'd have done his part to aid in its capture.

At this point, a Saudi soldier had walked over to them, extending his hand. "Hello, I'm Colonel Faisel from the Saudi Army. I had spoken with Brigadier General Buckner. He told me he was sending a couple of forward air controllers who would be able to call in American air strikes to support our own forces," he said in fluent English.

Major Skooter smiled as he shook hands with the Saudi colonel. For the life of him he couldn't figure out how the guy spoke better English than half the officers and enlisted airmen he commanded.

"Hello, Colonel Faisel. I'm Major Skooter, the man in charge of the team General Buckner told you about. It's good to meet you. This is the rest of my team," he said, introducing the other three members. "Perhaps we should go meet with your commander and figure out how we can best help you guys," Skooter added, seeking to take charge of the situation and get things moving.

His guys reached down and grabbed their gear while the colonel motioned for them to follow him to one of the armored cars.

"I agree, let's get you loaded into the vehicles and head over to our command center. Things are a bit fluid around here. The Iraqis have been probing our perimeter all day. We anticipate another major push from them soon," the colonel explained as the group set out towards a building on the far side of the airfield. "Colonel Faisel, if you don't mind me asking, where did you learn to speak English? It's very good."

Chuckling at the question, Faisel explained, "Actually, I attended your Army Infantry School at Fort Benning and then Airborne school before I went on to your helicopter flight school at Fort Rucker."

"Wow, when was that?" Skooter asked.

"Nineteen seventy-five and seventy-six. I bought a house while in Columbus, Georgia. My wife and I make a habit of spending our annual leave there. We're both working on improving our English and making sure our kids learn the language as well."

Once their vehicles arrived next to a compound adjacent to the airfield, they parked, and everyone got out. Major Skooter noticed a few brand-new Toyota pickup trucks parked nearby as well.

Inside the building, a handful of Saudi officers were waiting for them as they stood around a table with a city map spread out on it. Skooter walked up to the map and saw it was marked up with the known positions of the Saudi infantry units and the locations of several tank companies. It also had some Iraqi unit designations and rough locations.

"Ah, the Americans General Buckner promised have arrived," Brigadier General Turki bin Bandar announced as he walked towards the four Americans. Major Skooter shook hands with bin Bandar and they exchanged some brief pleasantries before the general got down to business.

"Major, as you can see from the disposition of both my forces and the Iraqis arrayed before us, we have little hope of being able to stop their advance. At best, we can slow them down a bit and maybe buy a few more days. But ultimately they are going to break through."

The general then pointed to a couple of terrain features on the map. "The 425 highway is essentially a run around the cities of Buraydah and Unayzah to the south, with a river that separates the two. I've ordered my engineers to rig the bridges to be blown when we have to withdraw. I've also ordered some of my other units to establish additional ambush points along the major roads leading to Medina and Jeddah, so right now I'm focused on trying to buy those units additional time to get those ambush points readied. What I'd like to know, Major, is what kind of aerial support can I expect to receive from the Americans, and what are your thoughts on how we can slow or even stop the Iraqi advance?"

Major Skooter looked at the map as he thought about the situation. The general wasn't wrong—they were in a tough spot. He was facing multiple divisions with nearly an entire corps's worth of motorized and mechanized forces not far behind them. He had no friendly air support to count on and still had to deal with enemy air.

Looking at the general, he replied, "Well, first things first. We need to gain air dominance. Then we can start hammering the Iraqi formations. I'm going to work with the Navy on establishing air cover over the battlespace. From there, I'll see if we can get ground-attack aircraft to start making attack runs on the enemy formations. What I'd like to do is place one of my airmen with each of your battalions. This way they can start identifying what's specifically needed in their box. I'll stay here with you at your headquarters and work on acquiring the needed air assets and then assign them to the individual boxes."

Major Skooter then turned to Colonel Faisel. "Sir, does your artillery have FASCAM or RAAMS ammunition? If your artillery units are equipped with American hardware, they should."

"We do use American artillery. I'll get with the battalion commander and find out," Colonel Faisel said and turned to a major standing near him. They exchanged words, which Skooter didn't understand but figured they were probably working on finding him an answer.

"Colonel Faisel, the reason I'm asking if your artillery uses those specific types of rounds is because they can be used to lay antipersonnel and antitank mines. What we want to do is start saturating some areas with them to prevent the Iraqis from attacking you wherever they want. Our goal is to funnel them into specific kill boxes where your forces will be able to capitalize on your defensive positions. While you work on seeing if they have that kind of ammunition, I'm going to have Master Sergeant Rice work with you on where we want to employ them. Senior Airman Bottoms and I are going to get with our higher headquarters and start identifying what kind of air support we can get on the way here," Major Skooter announced.

For the next two hours, Major Skooter started lining up a series of air strikes that would start around 2100 hours this evening and carry on throughout the night. The USS *Saratoga* would maintain a continuous flight of F-14 Tomcats on station to keep the skies clear and engage any Iraqi fighters that tried to interfere. Next, a squadron of A-6 Intruders and F-18 Hornets would give it a go. He'd even been able to line up a single B-52 strike that would carry out a large carpet bombing mission along the main highway the Iraqi Army 4th Corps was traveling down.
****

3rd Squadron
King Khalid Military City, Saudi Arabia

Major Vitaly Popkov kept his MiG-29's radar off as he guided his fighter towards what the ground radar unit had identified as a flight of American B-52 bombers. For the life of him, he could not understand why the Americans had chosen to involve themselves in what was clearly an Arab conflict—and then to be so brazen as to think the Iraqi Air Force wouldn't be capable of defending itself.

Thirty minutes ago, his flightmates had been sitting in their dayroom at the newly acquired King Khalid Airfield when their commander, an Iraqi colonel, had walked in and said they had an emergency mission. When the briefer had said the radar station out of Prince Sultan Air Base had identified a flight of four B-52s heading towards Saudi airspace from Yemen, they couldn't believe their luck. The four bombers appeared to be escorted by a single EA-6B Prowler to provide electronic warfare support and two flights of four F-14 Tomcats from the American carrier *Saratoga* operating in the Red Sea. One flight of escorts was several kilometers in front of the bombers while the other flight was trailing in the four o'clock position.

While the Iraqis and their Soviet advisors were not one hundred percent sure where the bombers were headed, they had a rough idea given their trajectory and the Iraqi units in the vicinity. With this information, the air-defense command hastily threw together a mission to ambush the bombers and either force them to turn back or hopefully give the Americans a good bloody nose for interfering in what should be an Arab-only conflict.

Looking at his flight controls, Major Popkov was relieved to see his own aircraft was still making good speed and appeared not to have been detected yet. His flight of four aircraft was still moving fifty meters off the ground at a speed of six hundred miles per hour toward the Saudi city of Buraydah.

Glancing at his radar screen, he saw the two flights of four MiG-25 interceptors were continuing to approach the American formation from the east, just as they had planned. One set of MiGs was going to approach the Americans from an altitude of sixty-five thousand feet at a speed of roughly Mach 1.5. This would position the flight nearly ten thousand feet above the maximum ceiling of the Tomcats and would allow the Foxbats to dive down in an attack formation on the Tomcats and the bombers they were protecting.

The second set of MiGs was approaching from an altitude of fifteen thousand feet at a speed of Mach 2.5. The goal in this maneuver was to force the defenders to split their force up to go after the dual threats. Both flights were being guided towards the American aircraft by multiple ground radars, leaving the MiGs to fly with their own search radars off until they were within range to use their own missiles on the Americans. This would hopefully allow them to get in close before they'd be detected.

Nearly twenty minutes went by as the two sides' aircraft continued to close in on each other. Popkov suddenly spotted something on his passive radar. At the far edges of his scope, he detected the blip of what was probably an American AWACS aircraft. At first he wasn't sure if it was an AWACS. It was performing like one, but the electronic signature was slightly off from that of an American E-3 Sentry, the ones the US Air Force typically flew and that he was used to spotting over West Germany.

Then it dawned on him. If these bombers were being escorted by Navy aircraft, then chances were this was a Navy AWACS, which would make it an E-2 Hawkeye, the Navy's version of the E-3 Sentry.

Looking back at his radar scope, he saw the Tomcats had committed. One group had broken off to go after the high-flying group while the other had dived down to go after the second group. The fight appeared to be on. On the radio, the Iraqis were chattering away. He couldn't understand Arabic very well, so he had no idea what they were saying. All he knew was the pilots were flying the mission exactly how they'd been told.

Each group of four aircraft was being led by an Iraqi officer and a Soviet advisor. Of course the Soviet advisors were technically in charge, but the Iraqis had learned to trust their Russian friends. They should, after having spent the last seven months relentlessly drilling with each other prior to the start of the war.

Since Iraq was essentially a giant gas station, acquiring cheap fuel to fly maneuvers and practice a lot had not been a challenge. The Soviet pilots had taken full advantage of that. They'd put themselves and their Iraqi mentees through two to three hours of classroom instruction daily and at least three to six hours a day of flying. They practiced everything from nap-of-the-earth level flying to high-altitude attacks to straight-up dogfighting. The Soviet advisors had done the best they could to get the Iraqi pilots as ready as possible to support the ground force in the coming war.

Now they were going to face off against the Americans. Not another ragtag Arab air force, but a real honest-to-goodness professional air force that prided itself on its own rigorous training programs.

Steadily, the chatter on the radio became more disciplined. Popkov heard one of the Soviet advisors barking some orders in broken Arabic. Moments later, their search radars went active and they started engaging the Tomcats.

For Popkov and his pilots, that was the signal—it was time for them to rise up from their nap-of-the-earth position and start racing in for the American bombers. It wouldn't take long for a couple of the Tomcats to identify the new threat and break off their current fight to go after Popkov and his pilots.

Pulling up on his flight stick, Popkov felt the plane angle high into the sky. Next, he activated his afterburners, dumping raw fuel into his engines and boosting the power they were generating in seconds. He then flipped a switch and turned on his Phazotron Zhuk-ME radar. The electronic device made one sweep of the area in front of him before it populated his scope. In seconds, it showed him the four B-52s flying at an altitude of thirty-two thousand feet at a cruising speed of 430 miles per hour. His scope also showed a single EA-6B Prowler flying a few miles ahead of the bombers. Somewhere around fifty miles behind the bombers, he spotted the E-2 Hawkeye.

As Popkov turned his aircraft towards the first bomber, his radar screen went fuzzy before the blips on it disappeared. *Damn jamming. I'm going to need to get closer.*

Connecting himself to the rest of his pilots, he depressed the talk button. "This is Raider One. It appears the American Prowler is jamming our radars. I want everyone to accelerate to maximum military power and head towards the last known position of the bombers. Once we're able to burn through the jamming, I want Raider Three to take that Prowler out. The rest of us will focus on the bombers. Keep in mind we won't have long before those Navy Tomcats will be on our asses," Popkov explained rapidly.

After he accelerated to maximum speed for a few minutes, his radar started to burn through the electronic jamming and spot those big fat juicy bombers.

While Popkov was moving towards the bombers, he spotted two Tomcats break off from engaging the MiG-25s to deal with his flight of four aircraft. Knowing the 25s were about to blow past the Tomcats, Popkov angled away from the bombers and lined up an angle of attack on one of the Tomcats.

As he closed the distance, his RWR started blaring, letting him know one of the American aircraft was attempting to lock on to him. At the same time, Popkov activated one of his R-27 air-to-air missiles and waited until he heard the tonal change indicating the missile had locked on to the large American aircraft. Once he was sure he had a solid lock, he depressed the pickle button, sending the missile on its way.

His RWR also indicated he had an enemy missile heading right for him.

The missile was closing the gap quickly. It'd be on him in less than another twenty seconds if he didn't take immediate action.

Popkov continued to head right towards the missile. He didn't change his speed, but he did get ready to make a radical maneuver designed to shake the enemy missile and, if all worked out, leave him in a position to reengage the American if his missile missed.

In seconds, the American missile had closed the gap until it was nearly on top of him. In the blink of an eye, Popkov dumped his speed, opened his air brakes, and pulled up hard on his flight stick in a maneuver called Pugachev's Cobra. While he was performing this maneuver, he released a chaff canister to further confuse the radar-guided missile.

Popkov's aircraft's nose rapidly flared up as the plane stalled briefly while the chaff canister deployed its thousands of tiny aluminum foils to distract and deceive the American missile.

The missile flew right past Popkov's aircraft and into the ever-expanding chaff cloud before it exploded. Popkov then threw his aircraft back into the fight, lighting up his afterburner to get back up to speed and regain control of his now-falling aircraft.

The R-27 missile he'd fired at the Tomcat had missed its mark, but it had forced the American jet to break off his attack on Popkov. Lining back up on the American, he saw he'd now closed the distance to less than fifteen kilometers. He continued to give his engines more power as the larger, more powerful American plane deftly tried to maneuver out of his way. Popkov flipped one of his R-73 missiles, letting the infrared seeker get a solid lock on the Tomcat before firing.

He depressed the pickle button, sending the missile on its way. The American was no more than seven kilometers away at this point as he continued to turn hard into his position one moment, only to light up his afterburners the next moment and angle away from him.

What the American pilot didn't appear to realize was that he'd just launched a heat-seeking missile and not a radar-controlled one. The afterburners were only aiding the heat-seeker in finding him.

Moments later, the R-73 got within the required proximity of its target and detonated. It blew a shotgun blast of hot shards of metal right into the right rearward engine of the large American fighter.

The Tomcat's right rear engine blew out a puff of flame and then streamed thick black smoke as the pilot tried to stabilize the fighter while angling away from Popkov.

Having injured but not killed the American plane, Popkov maneuvered his plane back in behind the Tomcat and flipped from his missiles to his guns. At this point, he was closing within five kilometers. His targeting reticle activated on the guns as he centered it over the enemy plane. When his plane had closed the distance to less than two thousand meters, he depressed the trigger button for two to three seconds, sending a stream of 30mm rounds at the Tomcat.

He saw rounds walk up the back side of the plane, ripping into the left engine and the wing. Popkov had intentionally turned his plane to angle the bullets away from the cockpit of the plane so as not to hit the pilot or his back seat.

The American plane exploded in smoke and caught fire. Moments later, the pilot and his back seat ejected from the stricken plane, just before the aircraft exploded.

Popkov noted the location of the pilots and pulled his aircraft away. In that moment, he realized he'd been so singularly focused on his own aerial battle that he hadn't paid any attention to what else was going on around him. His radar told him all he needed to know. Five of the eight MiG-25s had been shot down; so had two of the four MiG-29s. His radar also confirmed three of the four B-52s were downed, along with the E-2 Hawkeye and three of the eight F-14 Tomcats. The rest of the American aircraft had turned away and were quickly leaving the battlespace. The three Foxbats were heading home. Now it was time for Popkov to link back up with the only Fulcrum left and head back to the King Khalid Military City.

They'd earned their pay today and shown the Americans that attacking the Iraqis wasn't going to be some walk in the park.
****

10 Kilometers East of Buraydah

In the hours before dawn, Lieutenant Colonel Jasmen Nassar moved his battalion out and started their movement to contact. The previous night and the early-morning hours had been tense. A number of aerial battles had taken place somewhere up in the night sky. No one knew for sure what was happening.

When Nassar's battalion left the high ground around Umm Hazim, they made their way towards the rolling hills and lower elevations that would lead them towards the enemy. The battalion bypassed the small village of Rawdat Al Hisu, then they passed Al Mithnab shortly before the sun started to rise in the east. As the Iraqi soldiers moved from one town to the next, they made sure to cut the phone lines to prevent people from warning the Saudis they were coming.

No one in Nassar's battalion paid the sheepherders that dotted the countryside any attention. What his soldiers didn't realize was that some of the shepherds were in fact Saudi soldiers, equipped with radios to let their commands know the Iraqi forces were steadily moving towards their trap.

When Nassar's battalion passed the small city of Al Mithnab, his battalion was to steer a more northern course to come up on the left flank of the 12th Motorized Brigade. This would give the units room to maneuver and help protect each other's flanks.

Nearing the 425 Beltway was Lake Aushazia. The natural barrier had separated some of the Iraqi units before they could reach the 425 Beltway that ultimately led towards their primary objective—the city of Buraydah and the Prince Nayef bin Abdulaziz Airfield nearby. Nassar's battalion needed to capture the airfield so it could be turned into a forward air base for the air force as they looked to march on Medina and then Jeddah. Once his battalion made contact with the 12th Motorized

247

Brigade, they would move in parallel lines opposite the 425 Beltway and try to split the Saudi forces.

Off in the distance, Nassar could hear the sounds of artillery. From the flashes in the northeastern sky, he suspected it was artillery from the 5th Mechanized Division. He wasn't sure what they were shooting at, but he was glad they were pounding some Saudi unit.

When Nassar's battalion neared the 425 Beltway, he ordered the battalion to cross the highway and set up on the opposite side. So far, they still hadn't met any resistance. While Lieutenant Colonel Nassar found that odd, he was also glad. He might have been a soldier, but that didn't mean he enjoyed the killing aspect of his job.

The part of town they were approaching was a built-up area, with plenty of potential places for a small unit to lie in wait to ambush an unsuspecting unit. Nassar ordered his battalion to change formations. They switched from a single-file line to a tiered wedge formation as he gave the order for his units to skirt the city instead of going through it. The more he looked at the built-up area, the more concerned he was about an ambush. He was also concerned about the civilian casualties that might result from a close-in fight like that. He didn't feel it was fair to position the civilians in harm's way if it could be avoided.

As his units skirted the edges of the town, the closest unit managed to get within fifteen hundred meters of the nearest buildings. When they crossed a row of apartment buildings, he caught his first glimpse of trouble. A couple of soldiers appeared just above the lip of the building. They quickly set up what appeared to be an antitank missile system of some sort.

In less than a minute, before he could warn the company closest to the threat, a missile streaked down from the rooftop and impacted against the side of one of his tanks. The tank exploded as the turret was ripped clean off the vehicle and flipped a couple of times through the air.

One of the BTR crews turned the turret in the direction of the missile crew and opened fire with the 14.5 mm KPVT heavy machine gun. The large projectiles shredded the roof of the building. The gunner adjusted his fire and then proceeded to rake the side of the building to make sure they had gotten the missile crew as the heavy rounds easily penetrated the walls of the cinder block structure. At this point, several of the BTRs and BMPs had dismounted their infantry, who moved to take up a defensive position around the rest of the armored vehicles.

A couple of light machine guns and rifles opened fire on the dismounted infantry, officially initiating the first battle of the day.

****

Captain Anatoly Turgenev had been eating dust for the past two days. He was not in the least enjoying the ride, either. He and three Soviet noncommissioned officers had been sent to 11th Motorized Brigade to teach the Iraqi soldiers how to operate the FlatBox radar on the SA-9 air-defense system and the ZSU-23-4. There were four of each with the 11th Brigade, and Turgenev was convinced the Iraqi soldiers would not grasp how to use the equipment without strict oversight by his men.

Sergeant Ivanov along with the other two NCOs were each riding with a battery commander of the air defense battalion.

"Sergeant Ivanov, have they put the radar in standby mode? I do not want to invite an antiradar missile until we have definite indications of enemy air activity," Captain Turgenev asked over his radio. with the air defense battery commander of the brigade.

"Sir, they are telling me they have not even powered the system up because they are being told that the Iraqi Air Force has complete dominance over the whole country. I have told them to power up the radar anyway, but they just ignore me," Sergeant Ivanov replied in frustration.

"I swear to Mother Russia, if I get out of here, I will shoot that damn company commander myself. He is letting this brigade roll along fat, dumb and happy and they could be hit at any moment," Captain Turgenev replied angrily. "Are they even dispersed?"

"Oh, they are in formation. Hi-diddle-diddle right down the middle of the road, as the Americans say. If an air strike would come, it would be an easy target for jets. They are not dispersed in the least," Sergeant Ivanov replied.

Captain Turgenev's blood pressure was going up. He had to find the brigade commander and get this straightened out.

As the armored brigade of the 7th Division pushed across the open area to their objectives, the sun was cresting the horizon as a bright red ball. The heat increased rapidly, and the tanks and armored vehicles had closed their hatches in anticipation of artillery fire. The heat inside the vehicles was stifling. The dust, which managed to come in through the smallest of cracks, was choking everyone, even with masks covering their faces.

As it was, none of them heard or saw the six A-6 Intruder jets coming at them from the south at low level. The air-defense units had not expected to see any aircraft attacking them as they had been told the Saudi Air Force was destroyed and that the only aircraft in the immediate area would be friendly Iraqi aircraft providing close-air support.

What they hadn't taken into consideration was the possibility of American aircraft joining the war on the side of the Saudis and launching an attack on them from the Red Sea. The American Intruder aircraft flew in a loose formation across the bunched-up Iraqi armor forces and released a series of CBU cluster bombs across the entire first formations of tanks and vehicles. Once they had dropped their cluster munitions, the aircraft banked hard to the south as they sought to gain altitude and distance between themselves and the scene of the crime. The aircraft were now going to beat feet back to the *Saratoga* and do their best to refuel and rearm for another attack run.

****

2nd Republican Guard Corps Headquarters
Vicinity of Buraydah

Lieutenant General al-Hamdani stood in the main room of the home they'd commandeered. He needed a place to establish his headquarters that wasn't too far from the front lines. His brigades were continuing to advance on the city of Buraydah and the nearby airport. Once he captured this city, he'd turn it and the airport into his regional headquarters and logistical hub for his corps.

Standing in front of the large table blanketed with maps of the local area, al-Hamdani ran his fingers across part of it, noting where some of his brigades had moved up to. The night before, he'd ordered them to fan out so they could approach the place from multiple vantage points. This would put a lot of pressure on the defenders to be in multiple places at one time. It also allowed his artillery battalion time to get their guns set up.

"Good morning, sir," one of his staff officers said as he handed him a cup of piping hot tea.

"Good morning, Major. Thank you for getting the tea going. It's going to be a long morning."

It was still dark out. The sun was a couple of hours away from illuminating the new day.

"I updated the map twenty minutes ago. As you can see, the 5th Division is approaching from the north, just as you ordered. The other brigades have reported they are in position and ready for the main attack. The 4th Motorized Brigade is positioned to pivot and exploit any breakthroughs in the Saudi lines. Likewise, the 5th Brigade is ready in the south to engage the known Saudi positions. The battalion artillery is ready to support their advance as well. Right here, I've noted the 6th Brigade is being held in reserve. They're positioned near the ring highway, so they'll be able to move around fairly quick should the call for reinforcements come."

General al-Hamdani interrupted to ask, "What about the 4th Brigade? I heard they had encountered some sporadic gunfire on the southern side of Al Hadyiah."

The major nodded. "They did. The fighting wasn't long or intense. When I spoke with the commander, he told me the attackers consisted of a couple of antitank missile teams who'd positioned themselves on the roofs of some buildings. He lost a single tank and two BTRs during the engagement. They eliminated the threat and managed to take eleven prisoners."

Al-Hamdani smiled and nodded in acknowledgment.

"There is one report that just came in moments before you walked in. Colonel Faisel's brigade reported their first real sign of enemy resistance. They've started their probing attack just as you ordered. During their initial probes, they encountered a handful of what appeared to be M60A1 Patton tanks in a defilade position along the 425 Highway. As Colonel Faisel's tankers moved to engage the Saudis, they were hit by a couple of volleys of airburst artillery rounds. A few of his tank commanders who'd been standing in their cupolas to spot for their gunners were unfortunately killed. The tanks buttoned themselves up and pressed home the attack," the major explained, recounting the first official battle of the day.

251

Finishing off his tea, al-Hamdani was eating the news up. He liked this particular major. He was a great staff officer and had a way of conveying the information in a succinct and precise way, but also in a manner like he was recounting a story. It kept your interest and made you want to hear more.

"Please, continue on and tell me how the rest of the engagement went," he beckoned as he refilled his tea.

Grimacing, the major reached for his notepad as he explained, "The rest of the battle was a mix of success and failure. Albeit, I think a lot was learned from it."

"Oh, well, now you must tell me what happened. Do not leave anything out. If he made mistakes, then I need to know so we can adjust our tactics."

"Yes, sir. As I was saying, when Colonel Faisel's armor units advanced on the Saudi tanks, the tankers buttoned themselves up. They unfortunately ran towards the enemy tanks without keeping an eye on their surroundings as well as they should have. When they advanced, they did not take into consideration the likelihood of Saudi tanks and missile teams lying in wait along the outskirts of the nearby town."

The major pointed to some spots on the map. "A few tanks had been hidden in some alleyways here. A few missile teams were positioned in these areas here, here, and here. Nearly half of a tank company was lost in the opening volley of the ambush. Within minutes, most of the company had been wiped out before they believed they were being attacked from the town. Colonel Faisel lost two more companies when they encountered a minefield and another set of tanks and missile teams lying in wait for them. Again, maybe five minutes before you came in here, he'd ordered his forces to withdraw. He wanted to regroup and figure out another way to deal with this enemy force besides throwing more units at them. All told, he lost around fifty vehicles. I did tell him the battalion artillery was finally up and running. If he wanted to call in for an artillery strike, that option was available. So are some air units out of the Khalid Military City."

Al-Hamdani grunted at the news. *It's too bad about the losses. I just hope these commanders learn their lessons sooner rather than later. If we do end up fighting the Americans, they're going to be a lot tougher to deal with than the Saudis.*

"Major, send a message to the Corps air-defense commander and let him know I want to speak with him immediately. Also, tell our air force liaison rep to join us as well. I'm fairly sure our brigade commanders will get things figured out and handle them appropriately. What I'm more concerned with is the air situation. Those air attacks throughout the night caused some serious damage, and that needs to be addressed," al-Hamdani explained.

The fact that American aircraft were now actively targeting and bombing his forces made the capture of Jeddah and Medina all the more important. They needed to prevent the enemy from establishing a foothold from which to bring in more ground forces.

Chapter Thirty-One
1st RG Corps Progresses

8 August 1990
1st Republican Guard Corps
Al-Hofuf, Saudi Arabia

It had taken some time, but the 1st Republican Guard Corps lead elements were finally through Al-Hofuf. The Saudi National Guard battalion had made a valiant last-ditch effort, but ultimately they couldn't stand against the 17th Armored Brigade backed up by helicopters and air support.

General al-Dulaymi, the 1st RG Corps commander, had assembled his division commanders at the Best Western Premier Al Ahsa Grand Hotel and Suites for a large-scale meeting. His headquarters unit had taken the hotel over as it had enough rooms to house his staff and meeting rooms from which to manage the rest of the war. Located on the edge of King Faisal University in Al-Hofuf, it provided adequate space to accommodate the corps staff with comfortable accommodations. Once the usual greetings had been exchanged between the assembled commanders and staff, al-Dulaymi called the meeting to order. It was 1900 hours. Everyone needed some decent food and a good night's sleep.

"Gentlemen, it is good to see you all in such good spirits. We have done well taking our objectives swiftly with little to no resistance. General al-Qadi, has the 4th Division secured the rest of Al-Hofuf?" al-Dulaymi asked. He already knew the answer. In fact, he generally did not ask a question unless he knew the answer beforehand.

"The 4th still has a few pockets of resistance from the Saudi National Guard remnants to clean out. It is a case of dealing with ones and twos with no organized resistance," General al-Qadi said.[9]

---

[9] In actuality, Major General Salah al-Qadi was executed by Saddam in the early 1980s, as was Brigadier General Juwad Asaad. I could not locate the names of the commanders of these units during Desert Storm.

Looking over at General Juwad Asaad, the commander of the 3rd Tawakalna Mechanized Division, al-Dulaymi asked, "General Asaad, has the 3rd Division closed into its assembly position of the night?"

"Sir, we will within the next hour and will commence maintenance and resupply operations. We'll be ready to move out in the morning," General Asaad assured him.

"Good. Now for a more pressing and disturbing matter," General al-Dulaymi said, which got everyone's attention. "I have just received a report that earlier today, while attacking the 10th Mechanized Brigade in Tabuk, the 2nd Army Corps was hit by an air strike. It is believed this strike was from a US aircraft carrier now positioned in the Red Sea. In addition, it is reported that the 2nd Republican Guard Corps was hit as well in the vicinity of Buraydah, but by a much smaller force. This attack was carried out by Harrier jets, so it is not clear if this was an American strike or a British strike. Intelligence reports also indicate that US forces have been seen landing at the airport in Jeddah." This brought murmurs from the assembled officers.

"Surely the Americans would not enter the holy city of Mecca," General Juwad Asaad said with some distress in his voice. "The 2nd Republican Guard Corps must get there quickly to prevent that."

"I am sure General al-Hamdani is well aware of his responsibility to do just that," General al-Dulaymi said in a calming fatherly voice. "Now, let us look to what we must do in the days ahead." Turning, he walked over to a map on the wall. "From here," he explained, pointing at Al-Hofuf, "we will attack south with the 1st Hammurabi Armored Division to seize Salwa and Nebak. Then I want them to continue along the coast to Al Bath." He looked at General al-Ujayli, commander of 1st Hammurabi Armored Division, who acknowledged him with a nod as he wrote down some notes.

"Once you have reached the coast at Al Batha, you are to proceed to secure Abu Dhabi." General al-Ujayli had trouble concealing his smile as he knew of the luxury that Abu Dhabi offered.

"General al-Tikriti, you have eaten enough dust on this advance. When General al-Ujayli enters Abu Dhabi, you will bypass him and proceed to Dubai and Sharjah and secure those locations. Notify my headquarters when you have secured the port area in Al Bustan and

255

Hamriyah so our Navy may come in and base from there. Any questions?"

There were no questions, though General al-Dulaymi could see a smile spreading on General al-Tikriti's face. He was happy with his new assignment after having driven through dirt and dust for the past few days.

"General Asaad, you will remain on the right flank of 1st Armored Division and guard their flank when the 6th Nebuchadnezzar Division heads south. Prior to reaching Abu Dhabi, you will pull away and head for Al Ain on the border with Oman. I will leave it to you to decide when you want to break off. Just make sure that when you do, you spread your forces out and create a screening force along the border. Begin evaluating how you want to defend that position should an enemy force advance from across the Omani border," General al-Dulaymi explained as he ran his finger across a few spots on the map.

"Sir, who would you expect to attack us from Oman? The Sultan has no real army of any size." General al-Tikriti asked skeptically.

"You are right, the Sultan does not, but the Americans do. I am concerned that we have seen two air strikes by them and American soldiers landing in Jeddah. The Americans could very well be planning to come to the rescue of the Saudi family. If they do, they will have to mount their attack from either Jeddah or Oman. The Empty Quarter protects our right flank strategically, so the only way they could come at us is through Oman and the UAE.

"We are closing the Strait, so that leaves only a few ports in Oman, most likely Muscat. If an attack comes, it will not be soon—at least not a ground attack. It will take the Americans some time to put a force together and move to this area. They are halfway around the world. By sea, that will be twenty days, and longer if the Egyptians close the canal. Once we arrive in the UAE, our priority must be establishing defensive positions that are well camouflaged and an active air-defense umbrella in conjunction with our air force." Turning to his operations officer, he added, "Have the regional air-defense commander come see me, along with the air commander for this region. I want to see them both in the morning."

Next he turned to General Dairi, commander of the 6th Nebuchadnezzar Mechanized Division. "You will continue south, passing through Al Harmaliyah, and then swing east to come on the right flank of General al-Tikriti. This will not be easy terrain for you, but I am confident that you will get through. When you reach the UAE border, there are some paved roads that will take you to your objective, which will be Zayed City, and south of there Arada, Taraq, Alyhyali, Sabkhah, Al Khis and Jereirah. Do not venture into the Empty Quarter except to push out reconnaissance elements. Nothing of any magnitude is going to attack out of there," General al-Dulaymi explained.

"Sir, what of the 9th Army Corps? Are they going to follow us into the UAE?" General Dairi asked for clarification.

"No, the 9th Army Corps will occupy an area outlined by Nadqan in the north, Ash Shalfa on the west and Al-Obailah on the east. They can continue to eat dust until relieved to go back to Iraq," al-Dulaymi said with a chuckle, which everyone quickly mimicked. "Once we have secured the ports at Al Bustan and Hamriyah, our resupply will come by sea, freeing up the highways to support the 9th Corps, who will be resupplied out of Dammam."

"Sir, what of the American Navy? Won't they be intercepting our ships with the supplies?" General Asaad asked.

"I would not worry about the American Navy. They will not be a problem in the Arabian Gulf after tonight," the general replied with a devilish grin on his face. He knew something was being planned to address this problem, and he was confident that it would curtail US Navy operations in the Gulf.

Chapter Thirty-Two
SF Is Committed

9 August 1990
5th Special Forces Group
ODA 5226

First Lieutenant Promotable Harris's team had been in Oman working with the Omani Special Forces when Saddam had invaded Kuwait. Actually, his ODA had been receiving some specialized training by the Omani Special Forces in desert survival. The two Special Forces groups were exchanging training techniques and experiences, with the Americans providing training on improvised communications in a desert environment while the Omanis taught them how to look for sources of water or food should one become stranded in the arid desert.

Lieutenant Harris was team leader. His second-in-command was Warrant Officer Three Myron Garrett. Chief Garrett was the team's intelligence officer and demolitions expert. He'd been in Special Forces for twenty-five years and served a tour as a buck sergeant with the 25th Infantry or Tropic Lightning Division in Vietnam before joining 5th Group, Special Forces and serving two more combat tours in Vietnam. One of those tours was with the infamous MACV-SOG before he turned his stripes in to be a warrant officer. He was the glue that held the team together. The team sergeant was Sergeant First Class Mike Weekly. He'd been in 5th Group for ten years, running the team with Chief Garrett like a well-oiled machine. Weekly was fluent in Arabic, which helped immensely; he was also the team's weapons expert. Staff Sergeant Donovan Fitzgerald was the team's communications NCO. His Arabic was passable, though his Hebrew was a bit better. Staff Sergeant Lance Cardwell was the team's medic; he spoke good Arabic and was fluent in Farsi. He was also the team's unofficial cook. Staff Sergeant Justin Lovett had been an artillery forward observer prior to joining SF. He'd attended the Tactical Air Forward Controllers' Course and was now in charge of coordinating air operations, in addition to being an assistant medical sergeant.

The team had been in the desert for the past month and were looking forward to getting back to Muscat for some showers, cold beers and a solid meal consisting of steaks and all the trimmings to go along with it. Good ol' Uncle Sam was nice enough to put them up in the Hilton Garden Inn on Dahat Al Adab Street in downtown Muscat once their training had concluded. Then they'd fly home and spend a couple of weeks with their families before they'd start the next training rotation.

When their vehicles had pulled up to the embassy, they'd started the process of unloading their weapons and other sensitive equipment that would be stored in one of the secured lockers on the compound. Once they'd done that, they'd head over to the Hilton and get ready for an evening of overeating and drinking too much. That was until a gentleman dressed in trousers and a button-down shirt called out, "Lieutenant Harris."

The soldiers all looked up at the stranger as he approached them. They could sense something was about to happen.

"I'm Lieutenant Harris. What can I do for you, sir?" Harris said, stopping what he was doing as the man approached him.

"I'm Colonel Wright, the military attaché here. Let's go for a short walk, shall we?"

The colonel headed toward an area of the embassy compound that was open and deserted. Lieutenant Harris trudged after him, wondering, *What the hell did we do wrong?*

The two walked for a few minutes in silence. Eventually they came around a bend and Harris's men could no longer see him. They had also approached a side entrance to the embassy that Harris hadn't noticed before. The colonel entered a code, and the door opened. They traveled down a corridor before they came to another room that had a heavy steel door with another keypad next to it. The colonel entered a code, and the door hissed slightly as it opened.

They'd just entered the embassy's Sensitive Compartmentalized Information Facility, or SCIF. The room had several classified radio systems set up and a *lot* of maps taped to the walls, all with various military units plotted on them. It took just a moment for Harris to recognize the markings. They were Iraqi Army units. What surprised him most was how far into Saudi Arabia they had penetrated. He'd been training in the desert for a month. Apparently, a *lot* had changed in that period.

As Harris stared at the maps, a voice spoke out from behind him. "You ready to go to work, Lieutenant?"

"Yes, sir," Lieutenant Harris replied before he turned around.

When he did, his eyes registered the three black stars on the officer's collar.

General Yeosock was a tall man, and although very friendly, he could be very intimidating the first time you met him.

"Good. That's what I like to hear. Are you aware of what's going on?"

"No, sir, my team and I have been in the desert for the past few weeks and just came in a couple of hours ago. That's when Colonel Wright picked me up," Lieutenant Harris replied.

"I was saving the good news for you to tell him, General," Colonel Wright said with a smile.

"Thank you, Colonel. I always like giving out good news," Yeosock chuckled.

Yeosock could see the lieutenant was getting nervous at this point. Turning to Harris, Yeosock took him by the arm and walked him over to a map board.

"Lieutenant, while you were out touring the Omani countryside, our friends in Iraq decided to invade Kuwait on the 2nd of August. But they got greedy on the 3rd and decided to go after Saudi Arabia too. Right now they're running down the eastern coast of the country, heading this way with at least one corps and probably two. In the northwest they have one corps heading to Tabuk and one corps heading to Medina and Mecca."

As he spoke, General Yeosock pointed at various Iraqi units annotated the map.

"Over here in Jeddah, we have a Marine detachment ashore and the first elements of the 82nd Airborne. The rest of the 82nd is flying in there as we speak. They also have an understrength company team from the 24th, but that's it. Are you following me so far, Lieutenant?"

"Yes, sir. I suspect you're about to tell me what my team and I can do to slow the Iraqis down," Lieutenant Harris said with a wry smile.

"See, I knew you were smart for a lieutenant. Where did the Army issue you your brain?" Yeosock asked with an equally mischievous smile. He liked joking around with some of the junior officers. It helped keep him young and reminded him that he used to be just like them.

"I was issued my military mind and brain at West Point, sir," Lieutenant Harris answered with some pride.

"Excellent, I'm glad they're still issuing above-average intelligence at West Point."

Getting back to business, Yeosock turned serious again as he pointed at the map. "You see this town right here, Salwa?"

Salwa was on the coast of Saudi Arabia and sat on a strategically important highway. It connected Saudi Arabia to Doha, Qatar, if you headed northeast, and if you followed the highway south and then east, it'd lead you into Dubai and the United Arab Emirates.

"Yes, sir. I would say it sits on some important road junctions considering those two major highways are the only paved highways in this part of Saudi that go anywhere. I'd suspect if the Iraqis are feeling really froggy, they might just go for the whole pie and take the UAE and Qatar, seeing how fast they've gobbled up Saudi Arabia. Do you have any eyes in that area that might be able to let you know if that's what they're doing, or maybe cause a little mayhem?" Lieutenant Harris asked.

Yeosock and Wright smiled as they exchanged looks.

"Lieutenant, you just named your poison. We're inserting your ODA in that area. I want you to find a spot and hunker down. We have satellites that can report movements, but what we don't have is someone that can designate targets for an air strike. We're going to have you guys bring a laser designator with you. Your top priority is to designate air-defense weapons and fuel trucks. We need to clean out the enemy's air-defense systems so our aircraft can get in there more easily. Fuel trucks are also important. Saddam's tanks aren't going too far if they can't stay fueled. I'll leave it up to you to select a hide position you want to use. In the meantime, I'll have you work with some of our satellite folks to look over the area and try to figure out decent hide locations from here. Have Colonel Wright sign off on it, so we have an initial idea of where you'll be. If things change on the ground, keep us informed so we always know where you are. We can't send you help if you go MIA on us. Got it?" ordered General Yeosock as he laid out the plans he had for Lieutenant Harris.

261

The general then reached in his pocket and retrieved a set of captain's bars, which he placed on the table. "Before I forget—your file says you're promotable. It says you're supposed to pin on captain in four weeks. Well, chances are you're still going to be in the field then, so I'm going ahead and promoting you now. Congratulations, Captain."

Harris smiled from ear to ear at the news. It wasn't every day you got promoted by a three-star general.

The general then added, "When you call for an air strike, it'll likely be Navy fast-movers. We're still working on getting the Air Force over here to join the fight."

"Air Force or Navy, they both drop stuff that goes boom. That's all that matters."

"Good, how soon can you be ready to go?"

"Sir, I need to replenish some equipment, batteries, ammo, MREs and a few medical supplies. If possible, sir, I'd like to let my team get a good hot shower, a solid two meals and then a nice long night's sleep. Once that's been taken care of, we should be ready to insert. I'd say this time tomorrow should be about right," explained Lieutenant Harris.

Yeosock smiled at his answer. *I like this young officer. He makes a point of taking care of his men over trying to impress a superior officer by overextending them. I knew I was going to like this guy.*

"How about we move your team tomorrow afternoon for a night insertion? Would that fit the bill and give your men the rest they've earned?"

The young officer nodded in approval. "Yes, sir, I believe it would. And thank you for understanding."

"No worries. A good officer knows to put the safety of his men above impressing some general. As to your insertion, the Royal Omani Air Force is going to insert you via two of their Lynx helicopters. They'll fly to Abu Dhabi and refuel. Just after dark they'll insert your team. Then the choppers will return here."

"Sir, those choppers can get us there, but they aren't going to have the fuel to get back to Abu Dhabi. What are they going to do?"

"Nice to see you're concerned for their welfare. Arrangements have already been made. A refuel point has been set up along the highway in some godforsaken stretch of desert. We're not in this fight alone, Lieutenant. Others have a deep interest in stopping Saddam. But enough of that. If there's nothing else, Colonel Wright will go over the rest of the details of your mission—call signs, frequencies, etcetera," Yeosock said as he held out his hand. "Good luck," he added with real sincerity before he turned and left the room.

****

That night, Captain Harris sat in his hotel room with Sergeant First Class Mike Weekly and Chief Garrett. The three of them started studying the map and terrain features of Salwa. They agreed they didn't want to be in the town as it would be a central magnet for Iraqi forces, both the lead elements and follow-on support elements.

Rear-echelon soldiers in every army were the same—find a building to sleep in and set up housekeeping and never leave. As they studied the map, they were looking for a location that would afford them visibility of both roads and provide a solid hide position for them to lie low for an extended period of time. The challenge they faced was that hiding in the desert was actually pretty hard, particularly when it was the flat, open, sandy type of desert. It was equally hard to hide in any place that offered shade, as those places were hard to find and were typically occupied.

"Look at this area here between the roads, south of town," Captain Harris said, pointing to a treed enclosure.

"Sir, that's the only treed area for God knows how many miles. Chances are some rear-echelon mothers will roll into there at some point," Weekly said, noting the obvious.

"Yeah, you're right," Captain Harris agreed and continued searching.

"Hey, sir, how about this area?" Garrett pointed at a mixed rocky and sand dune area further to the south but between the two highways.

Captain Harris looked at it intensely for a few minutes. "You know, that isn't a bad area. It's too rugged for any support vehicles to come nearby, and it's far enough off the highways that combat units won't come near it. If I'm reading this map correctly and those pictures are accurate, it appears there might be a couple of water holes nearby we can refill our canteens from," Harris explained excitedly.

Chief Garrett added, "It also has some high ground for observation and defense if we should end up needing it."

"How far from the roads is it?" Harris asked as a follow-up.

Sergeant Weekly started measuring it.

"It's dead center. Twelve miles from either road," he concluded.

"OK, we could set this area as our base. Strike out one direction one night and hide with the designations on one road. Come back after dark and switch off sending a team out to the other road to strike. Bouncing back and forth between the roads, they may think that the strikes are random and may not even look for us. We could even head up to town and designate some targets there to further throw them off," Harris explained.

"I think we've found our home for the next couple of weeks," Weekly responded. "Now can we go get a drink at the bar? Oh, you're buying, Captain. Congrats on the early promotion too," Weekly exclaimed as he slapped Harris on the shoulder good-naturedly.

Chapter Thirty-Three
Delay the 1st RG Corps

10 August 1990
Special Forces Team
Salwa, Saudi Arabia

Captain Harris and his team were inserted by the Omanis without a problem. Saudi Arabia was, after all, a very big country with a lot of open and deserted places. Once on the ground, it didn't take the team long to find some ground to their liking. The ground was rugged, broken terrain, not conducive to wheeled vehicle movement and far enough from the roads that tracked vehicles wouldn't randomly wander by. There was some scrub vegetation that would help hide them as well, and water was relatively close by. The only drawback was the tracks of animals. Likely sheep or goats the locals usually tended to. It was something they'd have to work around. The hide location was ideal, and they weren't likely to find many others like this one.

"Mike, let's dig under those boulders and set up a hide position for the CP. I want a separate hide site for each of us with mutual supporting fire," Captain Harris ordered as he dropped his rucksack and stretched his back. He was a young man, but the hundred-and-forty-pound rucksack still lacked comfort.

"Sir, I'll put our coms in the middle. We can set up our positions around it and the CP." Sergeant Weekly then turned to their coms guy. "Donovan, get your radio set up and contact higher and let them know we're on the ground and all is well. They're going to want a position report, so be ready to send that."

The team all knew what needed to be done, so long conversations weren't necessary. This was the way everyone liked it. They were all professionals and knew their respective jobs, as well as the other team members' jobs. As the sun began to come up, the team went to ground, ready and prepared for this mission.

"OK, it appears we're set. We'll have four-hour shifts while everyone else sleeps. I'll take the first watch. Let's stay down and out of the sun during the day. Tonight, right after dark, I'll set out with Sergeant Weekly and we'll set the first hide position. Tomorrow night, I'll take

Lovett with me and we'll spend the next day there and see what we can come up with. While we're there, Weekly will take Mr. Garrett and locate a second site on the eastern road. We'll alternate between the two roads for a couple of nights, but we don't want to set a pattern. Any questions?" Captain Harris asked. There were none. "OK, you guys get some sleep. Weekly, I'll wake you in four hours."

"Got it, Captain," Weekly responded and went about getting comfortable.

The day was uneventful, which was what everyone wanted. From their position, they could see some activity to the north around a farming compound at Al Sikak, but nothing threatening. There were three distinct orchards and agricultural compounds within a half mile of the crossroads that centered in Al Sikak. From the hide position, the main road to the UAE was four miles to the west and the main road to Qatar was ten miles to the north. As flat as the terrain was, moving to positions to direct air strikes would not be a tiring trek across the desert. However, if they were discovered, escape would be almost impossible as there was nowhere to hide.

Captain Harris was up as the sun set and contacted his higher headquarters. He wasn't sure who that was, but he suspected it was operating out of Muscat. All he had was a frequency and call sign. Who was on the other end wasn't really that important.

Leaving the hide location, he and Weekly only moved a couple of miles at the most, so they traveled light. As they moved across the desert, the landscape changed from the broken rocky hard ground to desert sand. It didn't take them long to find the perfect hide position to direct air strikes.

The spot was raised slightly above the surrounding terrain, but not high enough to attract attention. It was a little over a klick from the major highway according to GPS. That put them a klick from the road, which was what attack aircraft liked. The position took little preparation. Once they had gotten it ready for the next team to use, they returned to their base camp. They'd been gone for about five hours, so they still had a couple hours of darkness left.

Once back in their base camp, Captain Harris reported the location to Muscat and went to bed. Tomorrow they'd begin moving the laser designator and some other equipment to the overwatch position and then

266

identify their second position, looking at the other highway. Harris was hoping to be operational and ready to start calling in air strikes within the next forty-eight hours.

The following evening, Captain Harris and Staff Sergeant Lovett reached the hide position and got themselves set up. Today was going to mark the first day they'd call in air strikes. They'd also start sending regular reports describing the number and type of equipment they were seeing traveling down the roads and in which direction. All valuable intelligence at this point.

A few hours went by before they saw their first convoy. It was a military convoy, transporting what appeared to be some heavy equipment. They saw columns of HETs transporting T-72 main battle tanks, ZSU-23-4 anti-aircraft tracks, self-propelled artillery vehicles and long columns of 4x4 and 4x6 cargo trucks. There were also a lot of civilian buses traveling in the convoy. When they looked more closely, they could see they were full of soldiers. Likely the crews for the vehicles they were transporting. The lights on the vehicles snaked all the way north to the horizon. These guys clearly weren't anticipating an air strike being called on them. The vehicles were bunched up and they had their driving lights on. Not something a normal adversary would do during wartime. It screamed "attack me."

"Hey, Captain, Donovan says to tell you that an air strike has been launched and should be here in about ninety minutes. They'll contact us when they're ten minutes out to tell us when to start lighting the targets up for them," Staff Sergeant Lovett whispered softly.

"Tell Donovan to inform them that the enemy column is traveling with their headlights up. They won't need us to light anything up for them. It'll be like shooting fish in a barrel. They can't possibly miss this column," Captain Harris replied with perhaps a bit more excitement in his voice than he should have. He was about to participate in the killing of a lot of Iraqi soldiers.

When the air strike was maybe fifteen minutes away, a series of events unfolded down near the road, causing Staff Sergeant Lovett and Captain Harris to become concerned.

"Shit, it looks like something tipped them off. The air-defense vehicles are pulling off the road and getting themselves set up," Captain Harris pondered out loud.

"Sir, you think they might have picked up our transmission and know we're here?" Lovett asked with some concern.

"No, I don't think they picked up our transmissions. They would have reacted when we sent our contact report and request for an air strike. Besides, our radios are encrypted and transmit in short bursts to eliminate that likelihood. I think it's more likely one of the AA vehicles caught sight of the aircraft and sent an alert to the others. Or maybe one of the larger SAM systems in Salwa spotted the strike package coming in. In either case, let's start identifying the AA systems and tell the strike package to go for them first."

The two of them spent the next few minutes looking through their NVGs and binoculars for the AA vehicles. They found four ZSU-23-4 systems that had pulled off the road and activated their vehicles' radar. Four SA-9 anti-aircraft wheeled vehicles had also pulled off the road, separating themselves from the other vehicles and taking up a defensive position as their own radars started scanning the skies.

"How good do you think these Iraqis are at using this equipment?" asked Lovett out of curiosity.

Harris snorted at the question. "No idea, but I suppose we'll find out in a few minutes. Let's paint the SA-9s first and then we can go after the ZSUs," he ordered.

Lovett marked the targets with their laser designator, getting their exact locations so Harris could write them down. Once they had them plotted, they made contact with the strike package to give them a heads-up about what was waiting for them. They passed along the target coordinates for the SA-9s. The pilots thanked them and said they'd let the Weasels go in first and deal with the SAMs. Then they'd have some fun with the convoy.

"You know, both the SA-9s and the ZSUs are regimental weapons. That means these guys are likely part of the 1st Republican Guard Corps," Captain Harris explained.

As he continued to watch, he made notes on what he was seeing, to include number and types of vehicles. Overhead, he also noted the sounds of aircraft at altitude, although he couldn't see them. *Ours or theirs?* went through his mind.

Somewhere high above them, it sounded like a dogfight was going on. Harris stole a glance at the sky, and what he saw almost took his

268

breath away. There wasn't a cloud to be seen. Even with no real moonlight to speak of, there were millions of stars illuminating everything. A twinkle let him know something was up there. Harris saw a pair of them in one part of the sky and a different pair not far away. Both groups were moving erratically. Then one of them flashed. Likely a missile had impacted or blown up near them. Moments later, the light and little bits of flame trailed in the sky as it began to fall to the ground below.

They had no idea if it was an American or Iraqi aircraft that was falling to the ground. What they did know was the battle had started, and they had a front-row seat to it.

"Captain, Donovan says to paint the targets we want them to hit now," Lovett whispered in an urgent tone.

Just as Captain Harris shouldered the laser designator, a flash in the night sky caught his attention, followed shortly by the sound of an explosion. His concentration was broken only for a moment before he found the first target. It was one of the SA-9 launchers mounted on the BRDM six-wheeled vehicle. The laser beam wasn't visible to the naked eye but was clearly visible to the A-6 Intruder flying as a Wild Weasel ahead of the rest of the strike package.

A missile streaked through the sky, and moments later, the SA-9 exploded in spectacular fashion. Seconds after the missile system blew up, the other three SA-9s started firing their own missiles. Their 9M31 missiles flew after the American aircraft at a speed of up to Mach 1.8.

Harris realized the Intruders were using AGM054 HARM missiles, so there was no reason to lase the targets. Those missiles would ride the radar beam right back to the vehicle and explode. Rolling over to look behind him, he spotted the missiles rising off into the distance. One of the Intruders broke to the right as it dispersed a string of flares to throw off the heat-seeker warhead. Another aircraft pulled up and to the left as it also dispersed a series of flares.

Three of the six missiles fired at the pair of aircraft went for the flares. Two more missed entirely, while the sixth missile slammed into the belly of the A-6 that had pulled up and banked to the left. The Intruder blew apart in a massive fireball, and the wreckage of the aircraft started its return to the ground below.

Turning back to his front, Harris saw two more of the SA-9 vehicles explode. The remaining vehicle had backed up and was moving to another position when two missiles slammed into its previous position. The missile launcher on the vehicle turned towards the aircraft approaching it and fired off its remaining two missiles. Seconds later, the vehicle exploded as a third HARM missile found its mark.

Two F-18 Hornets flew in low and fast towards the column of enemy vehicles. The two Hornets released a stick of four Mk 20 Rockeye II each as they raced across the length of the convoy. Each Mk 20 would release two hundred and forty-seven Mk 118 Mod 1 bomblets across the enemy vehicles. Each bomblet weighed 1.32 pounds with a 0.4-pound shaped-charge warhead. At the point of impact, the bomblet produced up to 250,000 psi, which allowed each bomblet to penetrate as much as 7.5 inches of armor. Seldom did an armored vechicle have that much armor on top. It was a truly devastating attack. If the pilots properly timed their release, they'd be able to blanket as much as four miles of highway.

When the Hornets had reached about the halfway point of the convoy and effectively released their final Rockeye, two of the four ZSUs opened fire with their 23mm quad autocannons. The green tracers from the autocannons filled the sky in front of and practically on top of the two American Hornets. One of the Hornets flew into a string of bullets and exploded before the pilot even realized what had happened. Parts and chunks of his aircraft flew out in all directions and fell across parts of the convoy and the highway below.

The second Hornet had pulled up to get out of the way of the 23mm bullets now that he had released his final cluster munition. The remaining two ZSUs opened fire at this point. Their bullets had filled the sky as they chased after the Hornet pilot, who was jinking from right to left as he added altitude to try and evade the fusillade of bullets being fired at him by the quad cannons.

A string of green tracers somehow managed to connect with his right wing as he jinked to that side. In fractions of a second, the wing was sheared right off the plane, which arced upside down and started spinning out of control towards the ground at an alarming rate. The pilot ejected, his seat and body being hurled sideways away from the plane before his chute deployed. He was on his way to the ground, sadly very close to the enemy convoy he'd just mauled.

Four HARM missiles flew in and obliterated the remaining ZSUs, removing them as a further threat. With the last enemy air-defense weapons destroyed, two Hornets swooped in from the other side of the convoy to release their own Rockeyes on the portion of the convoy that hadn't been hit yet.

While that was taking place, the remaining A-6 Intruders dropped their sticks of Mk 82 five-hundred-pound bombs. The thunderous explosions ripped through the convoy, tearing apart many of the armored vehicles being transported on the HETs. The buses that had been packed with the crews of these vehicles were torn and burning, their human cargo unable to escape the fire and carnage that had been unleashed on them.

Captain Harris and Staff Sergeant Lovett couldn't believe the level of destruction, which was unlike anything they had seen before. They felt terrible about the loss of at least three aircraft, but the damage they had inflicted on the enemy could not be overstated. It was apocalyptic.

Harris turned to his partner. "Lovett, I think it's time for us to get the hell out of here."

Lovett didn't need to be told twice. The two of them did their best to get back to their hide position and put some distance between themselves and the scene of the crime.

Chapter Thirty-Four
1st Republican Guard Bloody Nose

11 August 1990
1st Hammurabi Armoured Division
Salwa, Saudi Arabia

"What in the name of Allah is going on?" Lieutenant General Majid al-Dulaymi asked as he walked into the 1st Republican Guard Corps headquarters. He'd been having dinner with the local mayor and leaders, explaining the facts of life as he saw it now that the royal family was no longer in power.

"Sir, it appears that the Americans launched an air strike against 1st Hammurabi Armor Division. It looks like the 18th Armored Brigade took the brunt of the attack. They were badly mauled, losing close a quarter of the entire brigade," the staff officer said, in fear of how the general might respond.

"Whoa—didn't they have air-defense vehicles with them? And what about the air force? Please tell me our people weren't asleep at their jobs when this all went down." General al-Dulaymi fired off one question after another before the first question could be answered.

The staff officer, a major, tried to respond to the questions as best he could. "Sir, the air force did detect the American fighters roughly one hundred and fifty kilometers out while they were forming up over Oman. What they did not detect until they were practically on top of them was the fighter bombers and ground-attack aircraft. It appears they had some electronic warfare aircraft flying with them and they were able to jam our radars until they got within forty-five kilometers of the 18th Brigade.

"When I spoke with a colonel from the air base responsible for protecting our forces, he told me they immediately scrambled fighters when they detected the American aircraft. He said they engaged and destroyed two F-14 Tomcats at a loss of four MiG-25s and one MiG-29. When I spoke with the 18th Brigade air-defense officer, he told me the four SA-6s attempted to engage both the F-14s and the ground-attack aircraft, but their radars were being jammed by an electronic warfare aircraft. They turned off their radars, since they weren't burning through the jamming, but two of them were still hit by enemy antiradiation missiles. The SA-9s and ZSU-23-4 of the brigade did engage the enemy and fared much better. The SA-9s managed to destroy two A-6 Intruders before they were destroyed by antiradiation missiles. The ZSUs destroyed two F-18 Hornets as they swept in to bomb the 18th Brigade's vehicles being transported on the HETs and the buses transporting the crews. All four of the ZSUs were also destroyed by antiradiation missiles, but not before they managed to damage another A-6 Intruder and one more F-18 Hornet.

"While we did sustain a lot of losses, General, our air-defense vehicles successfully destroyed four aircraft and damaged another two. The brigade commander currently has some units scouring the desert, looking for survivors from the air attack. They saw at least five parachutes deploy from the stricken aircraft," the major finished.

General al-Dulaymi stood for a minute thinking. *Damn those Americans. Why did they have to enter the war? This is an internal Arab conflict. Not something they need to meddle in. We'll have to change a lot of things around if we're going to have to fight off American attacks as well.*

Turning back to the major, he ordered, "Get me General al-Rawi on the phone. Now!"

The major left to get the general on the phone. A few minutes later, he came back into the room. "Sir, General al-Rawi's aide is on the phone."

General al-Dulaymi walked over to his desk and picked up the phone. "Colonel, put the general on the phone." He drummed his fingers on the desk as he waited for the general to pick up.

"Good evening, General. To what do I owe the pleasure of this call?" al-Rawi said, oblivious to why his superior would be calling to speak with him.

He hasn't been told yet, al-Dulaymi thought. *That or he's utterly clueless and incompetent.*

"General, I'm afraid this is not a pleasant call. About two hours ago the 18th Brigade of the 1st Hammurabi Armored Division was hit by what we believe to have been an American air strike. It's believed it came out of Oman directly or from one of their aircraft carriers in the Arabian Sea," al-Dulaymi said, attempting to control his anger.

"It would appear we had minimal warning for the air-defense service, and the air force made a dismal showing, losing five aircraft to shoot down just two of theirs. Worst, the air force was unable to engage any of the ground-attack fighters that mauled one of my divisions." The more he spoke, the more elevated his voice became. "If the air force cannot provide adequate air coverage, and if the air-defense force cannot provide protection to my corps, then we should call Saddam and tell him we need to surrender now and go. At the rate your force is performing, the Americans will be able to sweep us off the peninsula within a month!"

There was a moment of silence on the other end as General al-Rawi tried to figure out how to respond to the ass-chewing he was in the process of receiving from a subordinate commander.

"General, I was only recently made aware of the recent attack myself. I am still in the process of receiving what happened. First thing this morning, I'll be speaking with Muzahim Sa'b Hassan al-Tikriti, the Air Defense Commander, and General Hamid Raja Shalah al-Tikriti, the Air Force Commander, to find out what went wrong and figure out how we can make sure this type of thing doesn't happen again. Please allow me to work through this problem with my commanders first before we elevate this to the Minister of Defense or Saddam. This is a minor setback which we knew would eventually occur as it did in Iran. We will adapt and overcome this and continue to support your attack."

General al-Dulaymi heard some hurried conversations on the other end before al-Rawi continued. "We had hoped the Americans would remain on the sidelines of our Arab dispute. It is now obvious they are injecting themselves into a purely Arab affair. The world will condemn these attacks, and soon the Americans will be forced to back down as the rest of the Arab world rallies to our side of things."

Al-Dulaymi snorted at the general's optimistic assessment. He had known it was only a matter of time before the Americans got involved. He had hoped they would stay out, but what really angered him was how unprepared the air force appeared to be for their eventual intervention in this war.

"General, I pray to Allah that you are correct. In the meantime, I recommend we begin preparing our force now to deal with the Americans head-on. Right now, I need you to keep them off my back and let my Corps achieve its objectives before the Americans really get involved. Is that understood?" al-Dulaymi demanded in a very cold, insubordinate tone.

****

At the headquarters of the 17th Armored Brigade, the conversation was a bit intense. Reports were coming in from subordinate units wanting to know what was going on behind them. The 17th had not been in the kill zone at the time of the attack, having already passed through the area. Instead, they had heard and seen parts of the attack as it had unfolded while they were refueling their vehicles.

Sitting in his command vehicle, Brigadier General Ra'ad al-Hamdani was receiving updates on the progress of his forces as he sipped on his tea. "Sir, the 1st Battalion is two kilometers past Al Hudaid. 2nd Battalion is located eleven kilometers south of Al Hudaid at the road intersection and—"

"Tell 2nd Battalion not to worry about that cutoff road," al-Hamdani interrupted. "There is nothing out that way. And what about 3rd Battalion?"

"Sir, 3rd Battalion is held up on the side of the road. They are only twenty-three kilometers from the border. Thus far, they haven't made contact with anything, not even truckers or farmers."

"Good, I want 3rd Battalion to hold in place until everyone is able to close on him. When we cross the border, I want us to do it all together. Tell 3rd Battalion they can push out their reconnaissance units, but they need to stay out of sight. Also, I want a report on soil and topography conditions before I arrive there. I want to disperse our forces and not get caught with our pants down like 18th Brigade did in that air strike. We need to be better dispersed than they were."

Al-Hamdani paused for a second before adding, "Oh, make sure you talk directly to the air-defense commander. I want to make sure our air-defense vehicles have their radars turned on and are ready to deal with another air attack should we encounter one. When we advance, I want the 1st Battalion to take Alkwifriah Airfield. The 2nd Battalion needs to seize Al Batha, and then 3rd Battalion will drive on to seize Al Sila. From there, the 8th Mechanized Brigade will pass us on the right, followed by the 9th Mechanized Brigade. At that point we'll become division reserve. Do you have any questions?"

"Only one, sir. What about the 18th Brigade?" the staff officer inquired.

Al-Hamdani snorted at the question. "The 18th Brigade is going to remain in the vicinity of Salwa as it was too badly hit to be effective at this point. They will rearm and refit before joining us. You have the orders. Let's get them issued and get moving. I want to know everyone has reached the 3rd Battalion and is ready to move forward," he said with an uneasy feeling in his stomach. He knew if the Americans were going to get involved in the war, then their corps needed to finish securing its objectives and prepare to repel them once they began to land ground forces. This war was about to turn real ugly. Long gone were the days of easy victories.

Chapter Thirty-Five
Buildup in Jeddah

10 August 1990
XVIII Airborne Corps
Jeddah, Saudi Arabia

The C-141 and C-130 aircraft were dominating the airport in Jeddah. Coming in a close second were the civilian airliners the US military had pulled into service, ferrying battalion after battalion of soldiers from the US. Both the civilian and military aircraft were on the ground only long enough to unload before heading back to the US for another load. It was quickly becoming one of the largest logistical moves in decades.

Soldiers from the 82nd Airborne Division as well as support troops from the 1st Corps Support Command were arriving on an hourly basis. 18th Airborne Corps headquarters forward command post was finally on the ground. They'd officially taken over command of US Ground Forces in the Middle East until 3rd Army, the next higher-level command, arrived and was fully operational in Muscat. As more soldiers arrived, the Marines that had initially inserted began to breathe easier. They'd be relieved and sent back to the carrier group they'd originally been assigned to.

Brigadier General Buckner, the assistant division commander for the 82nd, was called in for a meeting with Lieutenant General Luck, the 18th Airborne Corps Commander. Buckner was an accomplished individual, having commanded a brigade in the 82nd Airborne followed by a one-year assignment in the Pentagon when he was sent back to the 82nd. The Department of the Army had no qualms about jerking brigadier generals around for assignments. It was a tough life as a brigadier general. You were often told to move or transferred to a new position with little if any notice. The Pentagon viewed brigadiers like sergeants, to be sent wherever there was a need for a division or XO position. Battalion commanders absolutely respected the man, as he had been a company commander in Vietnam and had distinguished himself under enemy fire. He was also an Army Aviator besides being a master parachutist and Ranger. Major General Pete Ford was the division commander for the 82nd and would be coming over in the days ahead.

Also attending the meeting was the commander of the Marine Expeditionary Force, Colonel Lightfoot. They were in the main terminal of the Jeddah airport, which was now closed to all civilian air traffic. A staff officer from the 18th Airborne Corps was about to give a briefing on the current situation.

"Sir, if you're ready, I'll proceed," Colonel Wagner indicated as he stood in front of a wall map of Saudi Arabia from the area of Tabuk to Riyadh to Al Lith some 150 miles to the south of Jeddah. Mecca was only fifty miles southeast of Jeddah. The map was a 1:500,000 scale and measured seven feet by twelve feet. The red symbols depicted the location of Iraqi forces while the blue symbols denoted the friendly forces. There were a lot more red symbols than blue ones.

General Luck nodded his head to begin.

"Sir, the current enemy positions are indicated on this map. These were their known positions as of 0300 this morning from a combination of satellite imagery and HUMINT[10] sources. In the north, the 2nd Iraqi Corps advanced on Tabuk with the 2nd Infantry Division coming down from the north, the 14th Mechanized Division coming from the east and the 7th coming from the southeast but having to turn north. It appears they were attempting not to destroy the agricultural areas as they converged on Tabuk. The 37th and 51st Infantry Divisions are in reserve and following the 2nd and the 14th Divisions," Colonel Wagner said, pausing to check his notes.

"In the east around Buraydah, the 2nd Republican Guard Corps with the 5th Mechanized Division and the 7th Motorized Division have seized the cities of Buraydah and Unayzah. Their lead elements are at Ar Rass at this time. These are the Iraqi ground forces currently in our AO. The 1st Republican Guard Corps is rolling down the eastern side of Saudi and the lead elements are poised to enter the UAE," Colonel Wagner continued.

Brigadier General Buckner shook his head while Colonel Lightfoot bit down harder on his unlit cigar.

"So let me see if I have this right, Colonel. You're saying that we're looking at seven Iraqi divisions coming our way?" General Luck asked.

---

[10] Human intelligence.

"Worst case, I would say yes, sir."

Looking at Lightfoot and then Buckner, he joked, "You guys think you can handle them?"

"Maybe with a little help, sir," Buckner replied, looking over at Lightfoot.

"OK, Colonel, now for some good news, please," General Luck said.

"Sir, on a more positive note, we do have some help. The 10th Saudi Mechanized Brigade at Tabuk was able to break out to the south thanks to our naval air strike that hit the 7th Iraqi Division hard. The 10th is currently moving south in company- and battalion-sized units over a series of trails, wadis and highways. Some of the company-sized elements have broken out platoons to set up ambush positions to delay Iraqi forces. The Iraqis, on the other hand, appear not to know about the trails and wadis, so their movement is much slower than the 10th's, which is being made more complicated by the delaying action by the Saudis."

"Where are the lead elements of the 2nd Iraq Corps now?" General Luck asked.

Pointing at the map, Colonel Wagner said, "The 7th is at Al Qalibah. The 51st passed them and is at Tayma. The 2nd is in Tabuk, with the 14th pushing west to Duba and the coast. This is real shitty terrain, forcing them to go pretty slow on a single-lane road. They had it easy when they left Tabuk, but the escarpments in this area will confine them to any existing roads. We're talking drops of one hundred to three hundred feet. Once they reach the coast, they'll have a much easier time of running south to Al Wajh and on down to here. The 37th Division is at Madain Saleh but is going to be getting into some rough terrain and will be confined to roads for the most part, or the wadis."

"OK, what does it look like for the 2nd Republican Guard Corps?" General Luck asked.

"Sir, the 2nd Republican Guard Corps has the lead elements of 5th Mechanized Division at Ar Rass and the lead elements of the 7th Division at Al Dulaymiyah. The Saudi National Guard Brigade, supported by elements of the Saudi Armored Brigade, bloodied their nose in taking Buraydah and Unayzah. We have a forward air control team with them, and our guys hit them with an air strike from the carriers

279

yesterday morning. The 7th Motorized is astride the highway to Medina with the 5th looking at overland travel on decent terrain to a point about eighty miles east of Medina, where there's a ridgeline running from north to south. For maneuver space, the 5th is probably in a better situation, as the 7th will be confined to roads in some areas. Either way, they both have pretty decent mobility terrain," Colonel Wagner explained as he showed them different parts of the map.

Looking at Lightfoot and Buckner, General Luck asked, "Your opinion, gentlemen?"

Buckner was first to offer his thoughts on the matter. "Sir, it appears that the 2nd Republican Guard Corps is the biggest threat as it can come at us the fastest. The 14th is further away and has some rough terrain to come through. What's going to cause us some major problems in defending the area is that we can't use Medina. It's one of their holy cities, and putting US forces in there will only strengthen the Iraqis' hand in turning the Muslim population against us. If we could get with the Saudi National Guard and that armored brigade, maybe we can have them break contact, pass through our forces and reestablish themselves around Medina since we can't. We can get some forces to replace theirs in fighting a delaying action. That would really help slow the 2nd Republican Guard Corps down. In the north, I'd say we find a way to hit the 14th before they get to the coast in those mountains. They won't have anywhere to go if we hit them in the mountains."

"I agree. If the 14th gets to the coast, they're going to come down on us fast. We need to hit them and hit them hard in those mountain gorges. Maybe we can even bottle them up in there or force them to withdraw. I can see getting a FAC team up there with the 10th Mechanized and hitting them with naval air," Colonel Lightfoot said, offering his own insight.

"That's about four hundred and fifty miles up there. We're going to need to fly them up with a helicopter and refuel a couple of times along the way," General Luck mumbled, thinking out loud about the possibility.

"Actually, sir, we can get a C-2A Greyhound from the carrier to come down here and pick up a team with a small security element and fly them back to the carrier. From there they can land with a couple of helicopters and be inserted. Once the air strikes are done, they can be

280

extracted by helicopters back to the ship and flown back here," Colonel Lightfoot explained.

"Colonel, you just laid out your next mission," Luck said. Turning to his operations officer, General Luck told him to get with Colonel Lightfoot and put the plan together.

"Now, what do we do about the 2nd Republican Guard Corps?" General Luck asked.

"Sir," General Buckner responded, "we have an Air Force TACP team with the Saudi National Guard right now. Let's coordinate with the Saudis for them to pass through our lines and become the reserve for us. I now have a full brigade that we can get out there to defend and delay along the highways and wadis. Off the roads and trails, the going will be very difficult. It's ideal light infantry country against mechanized and armor forces. We have the Cav squadron with their Sheridans, and the rapid reaction company from the 24th that will add some weight to our firepower. Toss in some TACPs and we should make a good showing of ourselves. By the way, any word on when the 101st will start showing up with its attack helicopters?"

"No word on them yet. But they should start flowing in fairly soon," General Luck said, looking at the operations officer. He did not need to say anything, as the operations officer was already writing a note to find out where the 101st was in their loadout.

"Let's not forget, sir, that I have attack helicopters, light armored vehicles and some Harrier jets at your disposal until I am ordered back to the ship," Colonel Lightfoot said.

"Oh, I had not forgotten, Colonel," General Luck said, "but I also have to keep in mind that I could lose you at any moment that MARCENT decides to pull you back. Having your force continuing to secure the airfield and port is sufficient for now. If we get in a bind, I can make a good case then for keeping you," Luck explained. His explanation seemed to satisfy Colonel Lightfoot.

"Alright, Buckner, get me your plan and I'll approve it and get you moving. It's a two-hundred-mile trip for your boys to get out there. I've been told that the King has ordered every bus, truck, and car that we need to be placed at our disposal. Gentlemen, we have a plan, now let's work the plan."

Chapter Thirty-Six
The Interview

10 August 1990
Republican Palace
Baghdad, Iraq

"We now bring you a report from Peter Arnett, who is on the ground in Baghdad. Peter, what are the latest developments?" the CNN anchor asked with deep concern etched on his face in light of this crisis in its tenth day.

"Good evening from Baghdad, where I just came out of a press conference with Saddam Hussein. He talked first about this conflict being a localized conflict between two Arab neighbors and said that the West should not be concerned with a reduction in the flow of oil, as that is not something they want to let happen. He wanted to emphasize that civilians, especially Western foreigners, were safe and protected within his country and the other Arab nations as well. To prove his point, he had with him Stuart Lockwood, a five-year-old boy whose parents are petroleum engineers here in Iraq." The screen left Peter and showed a small boy standing next to Saddam, who was seated. The child did not wear a smile but was rigid and almost trembling. His parents were not in the picture. After a minute, the camera came back to Peter.

"The other big development today is a joint message from Saddam and Hashemi Rafsanjani, the President of Iran. They are announcing that the Strait of Hormuz will be closed to all military vessels not flying an Iraqi or Iranian flag. Commercial traffic will be permitted with an appropriate pilot on board who knows the Strait. In addition, mines are being laid in the Strait to close it to military traffic. Iran is laying the minefield in the north and Iraq is emplacing the minefield to the south. Only one commercial ship at a time will be allowed in the Strait, according to my sources," Peter Arnett explained.

"Well, Peter, what is the impact of this action going to be in your opinion?" the anchor back in Atlanta asked.

"It is quite clear that the flow of oil is going to be greatly reduced if only one ship can traverse the Strait at a time. Currently about ten ships in a twenty-four-hour period pass through the Strait. Add to that the fact that some ships that must come through are not oil tankers but cargo ships, and the impact becomes very significant indeed."

In a voiceover, the anchor asked, "Peter, what has the response from the Western countries been?"

Peter raised his finger to his ear and looked down as he listened intently. After a short delay, he said, "This development has not had time to reach the capitals of the world yet. But we can be sure that some nations are not going to take kindly to these actions. The Iranians and Iraqis will be prioritizing which ships can enter the Strait. Currently the priority is set at China, Russia, and France. We have not had a response from Great Britain or the United States. However, we have received reports that US aircraft have bombed Iraqi forces in the area of Tabuk and Buraydah, but these reports have not been confirmed."

"Thank you, Peter, for this report," the anchor concluded.

"Back to you in Atlanta," Peter said and signed off.

Chapter Thirty-Seven
2nd RG Movement to Seize Medina

11 August 1990
7th Adnan Motorized Division
Al Petra, Saudi Arabia

General al-Karawi, commander of the 7th Motorized Division, was a bit surprised at the resistance the Saudi National Guard and the elements of the 45th Saudi Armored Brigade had put up in Buraydah and Unayzah. It definitely got his attention, and it was good for the soldiers to feel the sting of combat, which they had not yet experienced. Things were moving well now, with the 7th Division on the north dominating the highway and the 5th on the south over open terrain. The 7th Division's lead elements were approaching Al Petra, moving at forty kilometers per hour, a good pace, so the equipment wouldn't be stressed.

The 12th Motorized Brigade was the lead element with the 1st Battalion on point. The vehicles were in peak operational condition and the hatches were open to get some air inside the armored shells. The temperature was only 120 degrees today. The soldiers were hoping they'd be able to stop in Al Petra and hit the stores for soda and water.

They had just passed Nubayha and could see Al Petra ahead about ten klicks on their right with the beginning of the mountains on their left front. Unbeknownst to them, Major Skooter was observing their movement from his mountain perch. He and his TACP had withdrawn from Buraydah when the 45th Armored had; they would keep harassing the Iraqi units until they were relieved or captured.
****

Working with Colonel Faisel, they had planned a kill zone between Al Petra and Nubayha. One tank company from the 45th Saudi Armored Brigade was inside Al Petra, using the buildings to provide concealment for their nine M60A1 tanks with their 105mm smooth-bore cannons. The effective range for this cannon was four thousand meters, and the APFSD kinetic energy round could cover that distance in less than four seconds.

Two platoons of the company were located in the rugged mountains to the south and positioned in depth to both engage the kill zone and provide cover for the northern tank company to escape west. Added to this, Major Skooter had laid on a FASCAM minefield to be delivered by the Saudi artillery of the 45th Armored Brigade with their 155mm self-propelled artillery. And for added measure, while the Iraqis were dealing with all that, Major Skooter had a flight of four F-15s from the 71st standing by with a load of cluster munitions. If this didn't get the Iraqis' attention, nothing would, Skooter thought as he watched the Iraqi vehicles roll past Nubayha, heading westbound right into their kill box.

The ground was open hard-packed sand and limestone, so the vehicles were spread out, each attempting to avoid the dust from the vehicle in front. Between Al Petra and Nubayha was a north–south road that was the end of the kill zone. When Skooter saw the lead vehicle reach a point 1500 meters from that road, he called for the FASCAM mines.

The first indication of trouble for the Iraqis was the faint explosive airburst to their front, which they didn't realize was a FASCAM minefield being emplaced. The second sign of trouble was when airburst artillery exploded above them and showered the vehicles with shrapnel, cutting off antennas and killing anyone that was outside the vehicles.

After the first barrage of airburst artillery, the Iraqi track commander's buttoned up inside their vehicles which significantly reduced their visibility as they rolled right into the minefield and the prime engagement areas for the anti-tank weapons of the defenders. Once in the minefield, the tracks on the T-72s and the wheels on the BTR-80s and BTR-70s began exploding, stopping the vehicles where they were.

Now was the time for the Saudi tanks to engage. The thunderous sound of seventeen Saudi tanks firing their main guns reverberated through the area as their projectiles raced across the open terrain like red-hot comets. The Iraqi vehicles were still in the minefield as their tankers and armored vehicles began exploding.

Some of the turrets on the T-72s popped off from the explosions as if nothing was holding them on. The remainder of the tanks' ammunition tucked away in the chassis cooked off, adding more fire to the scene of the battle. The Iraqis attempted to conceal their positions by deploying the smoke grenades attached to their turrets, unaware that the smoke was utterly ineffective against the thermal sights of the M60A1 tanks, which continued to pick them off.

What no one initially saw was the four F-15 Eagles coming in low and fast from the mountains. As each jet passed over the formation, they released four Mk 20 Rockeye cluster bombs. The aircraft flew by at such a low altitude you could actually see the tail markings on the planes and the names of the pilots. The Rockeyes falling from under their wings would momentarily unsheathe their casings, allowing the casing to spit out the bomblets that would disperse themselves across the Iraqi armored forces.

While Colonel Faisel watched the death and destruction being unleashed on those who had invaded his country, his momentary excitement became short-lived. Unseen by anyone were two SA-9 Gaskin anti-aircraft vehicles following the 2nd and 3rd Battalions. They had picked up the F-15s once they'd come out from behind the mountains and had immediately begun tracking them. The F-15 pilots knew right away that they were being painted and started ejecting flares to throw off any missiles attempting to lock on to them.

As the aircraft twisted and turned on their bomb runs, they passed over the 1st and 2nd Battalions. The first two aircraft released over the 1st Battalion, while the two trailing aircraft released over the 2nd Battalion. That placed them within range of the northern-positioned SA-9. All four Stella missiles with infrared tracking were volley-fired and streamed towards the lead two F-15s. The first missile exploded on a flare as the aircraft jinked into a hard left turn, exposing his engine exhaust to the second missile coming at him. The missile locked on immediately, resulting in a fireball as the aircraft exploded and came apart. There was no parachute.

The second F-15 fared no better as its pilot saw the missiles fired at them with virtually no time to react or think. When the first two missiles appeared to go after his wingman, that gave him only a moment to turn sharp left and hit his own afterburner. This gave him only a few more seconds than his wingman had had before the missiles found his afterburner and zeroed in on it. The missile got within range and detonated, throwing chunks of shrapnel and metal into the side of his aircraft. It ripped one wing completely off and caused an engine fire. The aircraft was immediately thrown into a wild, out-of-control spin and splattered against the side of the hill.

"Fuck me!" shouted Major Skooter as he looked on in disgust.

He hadn't seen the SA-9 or the accompanying four ZSU-23-4s. They were normally associated with a brigade element, so he hadn't warned the fighters in advance before they had swooped into the tightly confined valley. They had no room to maneuver. He'd royally fucked up in not making sure they were cleared to enter the valley. He knew he'd hear hell about it from their squadron later. He was thankful the ZSU-23-4s weren't in range to engage the last two aircraft or it would have been a complete bloodbath.

"Colonel, time to get your tanks out of here. You hurt them, and you can be damn sure they're going to start hitting back with their own artillery. It's time to scoot and move to the next ambush point and reset," Major Skooter said.

No sooner were the words out of his mouth than the first artillery rounds started impacting on the southern hills. The two platoons of tanks weren't directly in the artillery's line of fire, but that'd change once the Iraqi forward observers started adjusting their fire. They needed to get the tanks out of there ASAP, or they could add them to the loss column with the pair of F-15s.

"They're moving now. They'll fall back to the next position and regroup," Colonel Faisel announced as he lowered a radio hand receiver.

He and Skooter climbed into their vehicles, but before the driver could start the engine, Skooter heard something that sent a shiver down his spine. It was the distinctive sound of the Mi-24 Hind helicopter. Worse, he was hearing not one but at least two more, and they were getting closer.

Looking over his shoulder, he saw two Hinds coming in fast towards Al Petra. The pilots had positioned themselves along the top of the ridge but just below the crest so as to not silhouette themselves against the sky. The Hinds weren't moving particularly fast, but they weren't sitting still while they carried out their attack. The first helicopter released a torrent of S-8 or 80mm rockets at one of the platoons of tanks. The entire area around the armored behemoths erupted in puffs of black smoke, flame and clouds of dust and dirt. More than one secondary explosion occurred amongst the platoon as a handful of the large rockets found their marks.

While normally a rocket couldn't penetrate the armor of an M60A1 Patton, this export version of the Patton wasn't as heavily armored as the American version. The second Hind had zeroed in on the other Saudi platoon. Instead of hitting them with a barrage of 80mm rockets, the gunner on this helicopter opted to engage the platoon with its 9K114 Shturm or AT-6 Spiral missiles. These were SACLOS radio-guided antitank missiles with a maximum range of five kilometers, giving them a decent standoff range. The Hinds could carry a total of four of the missiles—two on each wingtip. The remaining four inner wing pylons were fitted with four rocket pods carrying the S-8 rockets.

Colonel Faisel and Major Skooter watched in horror as the two Hinds took out six of the eight tanks in their first pass. Both helicopters were now turning in their figure-eight formation to make a second and probably final attack run to finish the last of the platoons off. They'd likely linger around the area a little longer as they looked for more targets of opportunity and took some time to scout ahead for the remaining units as they continued their advance. The American F-15s had done a real number of the brigade; now the Iraqis were getting their turn.

****

As the reports from the 12th Motorized Brigade came in, General al-Karawi felt his blood pressure going up the more he listened. They had only traveled fifty-four miles, and two battalions had been virtually destroyed. They still had another two hundred and twenty miles to go, and the ground was about to become much more rugged and restricted.

General al-Karawi called his staff together to determine what actions they could take. The current plan they had developed wasn't going to work given how fast the Americans had just smashed two of his battalions.

Looking at the map, it appeared the next major obstacle his force would have to overcome was thirty-nine miles ahead. It was a wide wadi with the highway crossing over a bridge. There was only a small bridge crossing the wadi. If the Saudis or Americans had already destroyed it, which was what he'd do in their shoes, they'd need to bypass it. Aerial photos showed some approaches into the wadi, giving them another way

288

to circumvent the destroyed bridge, but it also meant they'd have to move through it on only a couple of clear paths. Again, the Saudis or Americans would likely have some sort of trick or ambush waiting for them.

As he studied the maps and then the composition of his brigade, a new idea began to form. *Perhaps instead of having the 3rd Battalion lead the way and risking them getting mauled as well, I could take the remnants of 1st and 2nd Battalions and have them go ahead. If they stumble into another minefield or ambush, at least they'll be the ones to get hammered and not my tanks or heavy firepower units. I'll just need to make sure they are well supported. If we can smash the attackers like we just did those Hinds, that could change the entire outlook for my brigade.*

When his staff filtered into the room, he sat down and began to explain his idea. One of his battalion commanders suggested they make use of their Hip or Mi-17 helicopters to transport a company of airmobile soldiers. They could go ahead of the main force and look to clear the choke point of potential ambushes. The colonel also suggested they make use of their reconnaissance company and have them scout further ahead of the brigade to some of the other choke points along the way.

General al-Karawi was impressed with the idea and told his commanders to move ahead with it now that they had captured the Prince Nayef bin Abdulaziz Airport. The Corps had moved some of the division's aviation assets in. These consisted of the Mi-17 Hips and the Mi-24 Hinds to transport both airmobile and reconnaissance soldiers. The Hinds were also the division's main ground-attack aircraft. They had forty-two of them dispersed around the area. The air force had moved in a squadron of Su-24s, a squadron of MiG-25, and two flights of MiG-29s.

The air-defense commander informed him that by tonight, a battalion of the new S-300s or SA-10 Grumbles would be operational. All told, they were airlifting some twelve mobile vehicle launchers capable of holding four of the missiles aboard twelve Il-76 aircraft as only one launcher could fit in one aircraft. What made this system so unique was its ability to be built in a piecemeal fashion that allowed the defenders to tailor the system to meet specific needs.

289

In this case, they could disperse the launchers, making them harder to find and subsequently destroy. The radar trucks could also handle a multitude of different roles. In this case, the target detection radar had a range of up to three hundred kilometers. The target tracking and missile guidance vehicle could track up to six targets at a time at a range of two hundred kilometers. This gave them ample time to notify the alert fighters of what was heading their direction and give them time to figure out which missile launchers they wanted to engage the Americans and where they wanted to move other launchers for a better launch point. If this worked correctly in concert with the Riyadh system, it would give them an SA-10 line that would extend from the Gulf states to Riyadh to Buraydah to Tabuk.

Hearing the good news from the air-defense officer, General al-Karawi started to feel a little better. The Iraqi forces had advanced so quickly that they'd outpaced their air-defense systems. As long as they continued to operate under them, the American fighters shouldn't be able to cause them too much damage. Once he'd issued the new orders to get those airmobile troops moved forward along with his reconnaissance troops, he dismissed everyone. It was now time to let them do their jobs.

Chapter Thirty-Eight
2nd Army Corps Move to Tabuk

12 August 1990
2nd Iraqi Corps
Sakaka, Saudi Arabia

"This cursed terrain is sapping our strength. Behind us looks like a salvage yard at this point," General al-Douri fumed.

The terrain had proven to be much more difficult than they had expected. Attempting to move with three divisions abreast was proving to be difficult as the terrain was forcing units on the right flank to crowd south into the rest of the formation. Numerous times, units had become entangled, and each time it happened, it forced their movement to a stop to get it sorted out. The terrain further to the southeast offered easier mobility, but it also was cut with sand dunes and wadis that could stop a vehicle. To make matters worse, flint stones as sharp as knives were everywhere. They were slicing through tires left and right. The armored vehicles with tracks were not affected, but any vehicle with tires was having to stop to change tires anytime they got off the paved roads.

It had taken twenty-four hours to reach 256 kilometers inside Saudi Arabia to Sakaka. Now the divisions would commence a turn towards Tabuk, 384 kilometers to the west. When they did, the right flank had rolling open terrain that would improve his movement. The center also had hard-packed sand to move over and good mobility—at least it did at first, but then there was some rocky terrain that might prove challenging. General yai figured that at their current rate of movement, they would be in Tabuk in twenty-four hours. Of course all of that was dependent on them not getting mauled from the air by those traitorous Americans who had decided to get involved in this Arab-to-Arab conflict.

Once his division commanders were all present, he called the meeting to order and got down to business.

"Gentlemen, we have made the turn, but we are not out of the worst of the terrain except for you," he said, looking at the 2nd Division commander. "I want the 2nd Division to come at Tabuk from the north. As you come down from Bir Ibn Hirmas, please try not to destroy the crops in the area. These are fertile farms. We are here to liberate, not

291

destroy. The same goes for all of you. The 14th Division will have the most difficult time accomplishing this as you will be coming in from the east. Hold short of the cultivated areas and create a wide screen to prevent anyone from escaping to the east." The 14th commander nodded his head. They all understood al-Douri's desire for them to be seen as liberators, not conquerors.

"The 7th Division will attack from the south, seize the airport and block the roads south to Jeddah. We cannot afford to let anyone break out and move south. If we are to move south and join the 2nd Republican Guard Corps, we cannot be held up by elements that managed to escape from Tabuk. Does everyone understand this?" al-Douri asked.

They all acknowledged. None of them wanted to look the fool in front of their Republican Guard counterparts. In fact, they were eager to demonstrate that the army was just as good as if not better than the Republican Guard.

"Good, then let us continue our movement to contact, and praise Allah that he will show us his blessings, guidance, and protection as we move forward."

General al-Douri wasn't aware that only 153 miles west of Tabuk, the USS *Saratoga* carrier battle group had just entered the Red Sea from the Mediterranean. They had traversed the Suez Canal and would now take up station off the coast of Saudi Arabia to begin harassing his corps.
****

The USS *Saratoga*, CVA-60, had Carrier Air Wing 17 aboard. CVW-17 could easily be identified by the tail code AA. Subordinate to CVW-17 were several squadrons: VF-74, the BeDevilers, and VF-103, the Sluggers, who were F-14A fighter/interceptor squadrons.

Next were VFA-83, the Rampagers, and VFA-81, the Sunliners, who were fielding the new F/A-18 Hornets to which the Navy was looking to transition the fleet, away from the aging Tomcats. Their attack squadron was VA-35, the Black Panthers. They were flying the venerable and combat-tested A-6E Intruders. Flying alongside them were their kissing cousins, the EA-6B Prowlers, which provided the wing with electronic jamming aircraft, the VAW-125 or Tigertails as they were called. They had a small assortment of refuelers, AWACS and helicopters on board in a support role. All these aircraft working together created a powerful strike package with a total of eighty aircraft.

Commander Douglas Depouy[11] walked into the mission room and loudly declared, "Good morning, gentlemen! Take your seats and we'll get started. We have a lot to cover."

Compared to the rest of the pilots in VF-74, Depouy was an old man. Most of his pilots were junior officers with an average of five years of flight experience. None of them had combat experience, aside from a few squadron commanders like him who'd managed to catch a combat mission or two over Grenada or Panama.

Once everyone settled down, he got started. "Listen up. Today we're flying cover for a strike package flown by the Black Panthers. Seems the Saudis have asked for some help as their air force was taken out on day one by the Iraqi Air Force. The Black Panthers are going to hit some Iraqi tank columns in the vicinity of Tabuk and we're providing the interceptor cap.

"We may see some Iraqi aircraft as this will be the second strike against this particular Iraqi formation. It seems the F-15s out of Egypt from the 71st hit some Iraqi units yesterday morning in the vicinity of Buraydah. They made one pass and dropped everything they had before returning to Egypt. They weren't engaged by anti-aircraft fire, but they think it's because their attack surprised the Iraqis. A second flight of four F-15s wasn't so lucky. They hit two Iraqi battalions, and before they knew what happened, some SA-9s surprised them and flashed two of the four Eagles. Neither pilot was able to eject, either. It turns out one of the pilots killed was the 71st's squadron commander. You guys need to stay frosty. The Iraqis have been outfitted with some state-of-the-art Soviet SAM systems. These guys aren't messing around. As to enemy aircraft, they've been going after our Tomcats with a mix of MiG-25 Foxbats and MiG-29 Fulcrums. The Iraqis have managed to flash three Air Force B-52s, four Tomcats, an EB-111 Raven, an E-3 Sentry and two more F-15s. You can fantasize about the Iraqis being a second-rate air force all

---

[11] He would retire from the Navy at the rank of admiral after serving as the commanding officer of the USS *Abraham Lincoln* aircraft carrier from 2000–2002.

293

you want, but know that they've already shot down a number of our top-of-the-line aircraft. Do not underestimate these guys."

He paused for a minute to let some of that information sink in before he turned the rest of the briefing over to the next briefer. "Lieutenant Johnson will give you the mission brief and details. I'll see you guys in the air," he said and then left the room. He had other things he needed to check on before they got airborne.

Down the passageway, VA-35, the Black Panthers, had received their mission brief and were heading up the ladderway to man their planes. Several aircraft were loaded with twenty-eight Mk 20 Rockeye II cluster bomb pods. They didn't have any ground teams to lase targets for them, so they were going to do the best they could with the good old-fashioned dumb bombs.

For armored vehicle and soft vehicle targets, the cluster bombs were very effective. Other aircraft were armed with AGM-62 Walleye TV-guided glide bombs or GBU-12 laser-guided bombs. These precision weapons would be used against air-defense weapons as they identified them. It was critically important that they thin the SAMs out early on in this new war.

When all was set, the *Saratoga* turned into the wind and increased speed. Plane captains and deck crews never seemed to get tired of watching the aircraft launch into the air. Flight distance to the target was two hundred miles, which for the aircraft of CVW-17 was a short jaunt.

Earlier in the day, VAW-125 had launched one of its E-2 Hawkeyes as there was always one watching over the fleet to detect any aircraft approaching that could pose a threat. There were also a couple of F-14 or F-18 aircraft airborne, working with the E-2 to prevent any unfriendly aircraft from even getting close to the fleet. Today, VA-35 would be putting up twenty aircraft and VF-74 would be covering them with eighteen Tomcats. VF-74 took off first and went to a loiter point, waiting for the A6-E Intruders to get airborne and start their run to the target area.
****

General al-Douri was pleased at the progress in the past twenty-four hours. The 2nd Division had reached its checkpoint north of Tabuk at Bir Ibn Hirmas and its lead elements had turned south with no engagements. The 14th Division was east of the city and had paused outside the agricultural areas so as not to destroy any crops. They had spread out from the marsh area northeast of the town to the south for twenty miles. They were positioned between the agricultural lands and the rugged terrain they had just crossed. The 7th Division was the slow one today.

They had to cross the roughest terrain, and it had slowed their progress immensely. The one saving grace al-Douri had received in the last eighteen hours was that two battalions from the 8th As Saiqa Special Forces Division had been heliborne during the evening hours to capture and secure the Prince Sultan bin Abdulaziz airport just south of Tabuk proper. The Special Forces had been able to leapfrog ahead of al-Douri's force and took the airport with only minor resistance. Once the airport had been secured, a string of preloaded Il-76 and An-12 cargo planes descended on the airport in the wee hours of the morning.

The cargo aircraft had offloaded several SA-9 vehicles and a single battery of S-300s. The S-300 had a single passive search radar, one targeting radar vehicle for when they found a target, and four launcher vehicles, giving them sixteen missiles. If they were able to return the following evening, they'd deliver the next battery. Once the battalion had been fully delivered, they'd have established the first line of SAM defenses. Then it'd be a matter of building in the other redundant layers that would make attacking one or more of these hubs that much harder.

While al-Douri was looking at the various maps of the area and where his various units were located, one of his staff officers interrupted him. Practically out of breath, he blurted out, "General. The air-defense officer said to tell you we are about to be attacked from the air. It would appear another American force is looking to carry out a large raid on our forces. They'll be here within the next twenty minutes."

"Damnit, we're not fully ready yet to deal with the Americans. Tell the air-defense commander to do his best with what he's got and send a warning out to all the division, brigade, and battalion commanders to have their SAM and AA gun trucks up and running. Maybe we can still give the Americans a bloody nose if we're lucky," General al-Douri barked angrily.

I only needed forty-eight more hours and we'd have had enough SAMs to make this a very costly place to fly. I hope our guys can still protect us with what they have, al-Douri thought.

295

Walking outside his command track, he looked up into the sky, hoping he might catch a glimpse of the action. For the moment, the sky was relatively clear. Then he saw it. A smoke contrail from the ground, followed moments later by the sound of an explosion off in the distance as a missile was streaking its way into the sky, climbing higher and higher as it chased after something unseen. Then he saw a second and soon a third contrail heading into the sky. Whatever was taking place, it was well outside his ability to see it with his eyes. Instead, he walked back into his tracked vehicle and made sure the radio operator had the frequency switched over to the air-defense units. He wanted to listen in.

****

19th Air Defense Brigade Headquarters
Vicinity of Prince Sultan bin Abdulaziz Airport

Major Boris Gromov stood behind the Iraqi soldier manning the passive radar screen. The soldier, a lieutenant, was sitting erect, confident in his skills and ability to operate perhaps the most important part of the air-defense system. While in passive mode, they wouldn't transmit any electronic signatures that might give away their position. At the same time, they were able to collect a host of electronic information. It was then just a matter of crunching the data and determining what was of value and what was not. As they identified information of value, it was handed off to the targeting and missile guidance vehicle. They were the vehicle that would ultimately engage the hostile aircraft.

"You see this spot there?" Major Gromov pointed. "That is an American E-2 Hawkeye. He's running an active radar search to make sure none of our aircraft or other threats head towards the carrier. That blip right there is a second E-2. But the difference is he is starting to move. That means he is likely providing radar support to a strike package of aircraft heading towards us.

"Knowing this, do you think we should pass this information over to the alert fighters?" Gromov asked, wanting to see if the lieutenant would fall back on his training or get frazzled under the stress of it.

"I should send a message about what we're seeing to the brigade commander with a recommendation to launch the alert fighters."

296

Gromov smiled. "That's right. Good call, Lieutenant. Now, don't forget to pass the information off to the targeting truck. Once the aircraft are within two hundred kilometers, they'll be in range to start engaging them."

"If we engage from those ranges, won't the Americans be better positioned to evade them?"

Gromov nodded. "They will. But keep in mind, the American AGM-88 HARM missiles will need to get within one hundred and fifty kilometers to engage our launchers and targeting radars. Once the Americans start to engage us, we will switch them off and turn on our secondary targeting vehicle to continue guiding the missiles."

A couple of minutes went by with the lieutenant communicating with the other vehicle commanders and the brigade commander about what was happening. When they had observed the Hawkeye cross the two-hundred-kilometer mark, the active targeting vehicle turned their powerful search radar on. What Major Gromov saw caused his stomach to tighten. This wasn't a small raiding force heading towards them. This was a massive strike about to wash over them. The aircraft were showing as 140 kilometers away.

Seconds later, the launcher vehicles fired off their sixteen missiles. Once their ordnance had been expended, the launcher vehicles would relocate to another launch site, where they'd be reloaded and, if possible, they'd fire off another volley.

Major Gromov had done his work. Now it was time to wait for the results and hope the alert fighters might fare a bit better.

Chapter Thirty-Nine
Situation Room Meeting

12 August 1990
Situation Room
White House
Washington, D.C.

The phone call from Brent Scowcroft to the President drew everyone to the White House Situation Room. The President, the Vice President, SecDef, SecState, and the Chairman of the Joint Chiefs of Staff were present, as were the service chiefs. Even the SecEnergy, the White House Chief of Staff, and the Director of the CIA had rushed over to the White House to be a part of this urgently called meeting.

Lieutenant Colonel Atwell stood at his usual position during the start of these briefings and waited for the President to signal for him to start. The President gave his usual nod, letting Atwell know it was safe to get started.

Maintaining his serious face, Atwell nodded subtly in reply. "Mr. President, a lot has changed since the last brief we provided you, so I'll do my best to get you caught up before the service chiefs will expound on their sections. I'd like to get you up to speed on the air war, as that's where we've lost the most Americans thus far."

Holding a hand up, Bush interjected, "Colonel, I'd actually like to have General Dugan provide this if you don't mind, since it's primarily his domain."

General Dugan looked a bit caught off guard but quickly regained his composure. He flipped through the slide deck handout until he found the section detailing the air campaign.

"Mr. President, as you know—and as is currently being reported on the nightly news—the air campaign over Saudi Arabia has been a hotly contested battle. The Iraqi Air Force of the Iran-Iraq War is clearly not the same force we're facing right now. Since the end of that war, their force has improved significantly. Their pilots appear to be better trained and more aggressive, and their aircraft are in substantially better shape. As was mentioned a few weeks ago, the Soviets appeared to have lent the Iraqis many more MiG-29s, MiG-25s, and ground-attack aircraft.

298

This allowed them to maul and effectively destroy the Saudi Air Force on the first day of the invasion," General Dugan recapped.

"In the last five days of the air war, the Navy lost seven F-14 Tomcats, eight F-18 Hornets, and four A-6 Intruders spread across two carriers. The Air Force lost three B-52 bombers, two EF-111 Ravens, three F-111 Aardvarks, one E-3 Sentry and nine F-15 Eagles. I take full responsibility for our initial losses because we didn't fully understand or respect the capabilities of the Iraqi Air Force. This led us to sending in attack formations with fewer air assets than we would have if we were carrying out an attack against a similar Soviet target. I have personally spoken with my Air Force Commander, General Horner, who's there right now, and told him in no uncertain terms he's to hold off on launching any further missions until he can ensure he has enough air assets to perform the mission effectively without compromising the lives of our fliers or their aircraft."

General Dugan was clearly angered at the losses. He went on, "As a branch, we haven't sustained these kinds of losses since Vietnam. I can assure you we're rushing the deployment of multiple wings to make sure they do not occur again."

President Bush sat there taking the information in. It was a bit of a shock to say the least. He wasn't a man to watch TV, so he didn't really pay it much attention. But hearing about it directly from the man in charge of the Air Force really put the realities of this war into context for him.

"General Dugan, thank you for the summation of what's transpired these last five days, and thank you for identifying the problem and moving quickly to solve it. I appreciate it. I don't have any questions right now as it sounds like you're already on it. Keep us apprised of the situation." President Bush then returned his attention to Lieutenant Colonel Atwell. "Colonel, if you'll resume the brief, that'd be appreciated."

Colonel Atwell smiled briefly, then motioned for the slide manager to bring up the next image. "First, as we get our slides reorganized, I wanted to tell you about a piece of news that came out last night. At around 0200 hours Washington time, the Iraqi and Iranian governments announced in a joint statement the temporary closing of the Strait of Hormuz to all military traffic."

Some of the people in the room who hadn't already heard the news audibly grumbled. A few even muttered some curse words under their breath at the audacity of these two belligerents' announcement.

Atwell only paused for a moment; he knew there would be some grumbling, and he wanted to make sure their comments didn't interfere with the rest of his brief. "Sir, a satellite passed over their location just a few hours ago and provided us with some real-time data imagery of the Strait. It clearly shows the two countries are in the process of mining the Strait, with Iran mining the northern portion and Iraq the southern portion. In their statement, they said commercial traffic will be allowed to transit. They wanted to make it clear that the flow of oil will continue. However, there's a catch. They're prioritizing what ships are allowed to transit first. They want to ensure no ships accidentally hit a mine, so they're only allowing one ship to transit through the Strait at a time."

More grumbles could be heard. Some just shook their heads in frustration and disgust.

The Secretary of Energy then interrupted, "Let me guess. Their prioritization of who can transit the Strait doesn't include us or anyone that's supporting the Saudis or Kuwaitis?"

Colonel Atwell nodded. "That about sums it up. They've set the prioritization with Russia, France, and China in that order. Then it gets a bit murky as to who goes next. Right now, the US has no vessels in the Persian Gulf except our flagship located at Bahrain. There have been no moves against it yet, but that may change now that our aircraft have been actively engaging them."

President Bush asked, "What ships do we have nearby they could call on for support should it be needed?"

"Outside the Gulf, and currently located in Muscat, Oman, are three US Navy minesweepers. We also have the USS *Avenger* set to leave their home port in Norfolk to join them later today. The *Avenger* was recently commissioned and is our newest class of minesweeper. The three minesweepers in Oman are Vietnam-era ships."

Alongside Colonel Atwell, a picture of a sea mine appeared. It was your typical ominous-looking sphere with contact pins protruding all around it. "The Iraqis have an arsenal of approximately fifteen hundred sea mines. Most are World War II–era. However, they have some of the newer Soviet sea mines as well. The CIA has also reported that during their war with Iran, they began producing their own mines, the LUGM-145 Buoyant Contact mine. It has three Hertz horns and is packed with two hundred kilograms of explosives. These mines are attached to cables and anchors to allow the mine to float just below the surface, making them incredibly hard to find. The Iraqi tug *Jumariya* has been spotted off the coast of the UAE, towing a barge with approximately forty-five mines aboard. They've been seeding the south side of the Strait." The picture changed to show the Strait of Hormuz and the approximate location of the Iraqi minefield.

"The Iranians have approximately six thousand sea mines, which they developed extensively during the Iran-Iraq War. This slide also indicates where they're seeding the north side of the channel. These are both contact mines and influence mines—"

"Excuse me, Colonel, Mr. President, but what is an influence mine?" the Energy Secretary asked. The President nodded for Colonel Atwell to answer the question.

"Sir, an influence mine sits on the bottom and will be activated when either a metal object passes over it or cavitation from a ship's propeller and the noise of the ship set it off. With these mines, we rely on helicopters towing a sled to detonate the mine or on our minesweepers, which are built out of wood. The USS *Avenger*, which is the newest minesweeper in the fleet, commissioned in eighty-seven, has a wooden hull that's then covered in fiberglass, giving it a low metallic signature," Colonel Atwell said.

"Thank you," the SecEnergy said.

"Continue, Colonel," the President directed before taking a couple of long sips from his coffee mug.

"Yes, sir. Currently the British have the largest and probably the best minesweeper force in the world. They—" Colonel Atwell was interrupted by the President.

"Wow," he said, looking at the Chief of Naval Operations. "Admiral Kelso, what's the status of our minesweeper force?" The admiral knew this was coming and was not looking forward to the question.

"Mr. President, we currently have eleven minesweepers in the force, located throughout the world and home-based on the East and West coasts as well as Japan. *Avenger* is the newest of the ships, but the rest are pre-Vietnam-era ships, and frankly, our operational rate has not been good. With budget cuts and higher priorities, our minesweeper force has suffered. *Avenger* and three other minesweepers are being loaded on a transport ship and will be departing tonight for the Middle East. We have three ships in the Far East that we're dispatching as well to CINCCENTCOM and COMNAVCENT. They'll all be in the area of operations in approximately twenty days," Admiral Kelso said. "In addition, the USS *Tripoli*, a helicopter carrier, will arrive in that same time period to assist in mine-clearing operations and serve as the flagship for those operations," the admiral quickly added.

"So we wait at least twenty days before we can get in there to open the Strait is what you're telling me?" the President asked for clarification.

Secretary Cheney saved the CNO and took this question. "Sir, the Chairman and I have spoken to General Schwarzkopf about opening the Strait, and his concern is that we're liable to provoke the Iranians, drawing them in to support the Iraqis. He feels that until he has the forces in place, it's best not to poke that particular snake yet. In the meantime, we're tasking our satellite resources to continually follow the mining operation. This is allowing us to plot where they're being put down. When we're ready to move in, we'll know where they are with a high degree of certainty, so clearing them should be relatively quick and easy."

"If I may, Mr. President," the Director of the CIA, Mr. Tenet, intervened. Seated next to him was Vice Admiral Studeman, a quiet man and the Director of the National Security Agency.

"Go ahead," the President acknowledged with a raised eyebrow. If the CIA was adding something, then it was usually worth listening to.

"Mr. President, we have satellite coverage over the area with ninety-minute intervals between the passing of the two birds. We've been receiving priorities of coverage from multiple clients, each claiming a higher priority than the other. Sometimes we can accommodate two or more clients with each pass. However, requests for coverage over the Strait have only one client, the Navy, and only a small fraction within the Navy. Looking for sea mines doesn't rise to the level of a high priority unless CENTCOM comes up loudly on the net, and they have not," the Director explained. The President looked back at Mr. Cheney.

"Sir, General Schwarzkopf doesn't feel that it's a priority to expend time on the satellites looking for sea mines when there's nothing we can do about them at this time. He argues that this is why we have minesweepers and we should let them do their job when the time is right. The British also happen to have a larger fleet of these ships than we do, and between our two navies, they shouldn't have a problem clearing them. He wants the satellites to be focused on helping him track the Iraqi formations, which pose the greatest threat to our current and future operations. I hate to admit it, but he's not wrong about that. The Iraqi Air Force has also been surprisingly more effective than we thought they would be, which is another reason he wants more satellite time. The Air Force is having a hard go of locating where the Iraqis are moving their squadrons around, which makes it harder for us to engage them," Mr. Cheney said, explaining the crux of the problem in greater detail.

President Bush scoffed. "Well, I don't like it. You'd think after all the billions spent on defense over the last decade, we'd have been better positioned for a situation like this. At the same time, Schwarzkopf makes a good point. So here's what I want us to do. Get those U-2s operational and let's start having them provide us with continual surveillance of the Iraqi forces. Let's even see if they can help us watch where the Iraqis and Iranians are laying those mines."

The President then turned to his Secretary of Energy. "I want you to talk with our domestic oil producers and see if they can increase their production as high as they can get it. This crisis in the Gulf is going to put a huge crimp in the world economy if we can't fill in the oil shortage it's going to create."

The Secretary of Energy scribbled some notes down on his pad. He mentioned a few other things they could do to help the Europeans. The President agreed, telling him he had his marching orders for what his department should do next.

Bush returned his gaze to his Secretary of Defense next. "What forces has General Schwarzkopf asked for, and how soon can we get them in-country?"

"Sir, I have a list of his initial requests," Mr. Cheney replied as he signaled the slide operator to bring up his slide. "Oh, you'll see that we had initially called this Operation Desert Shield prior to the Iraqis' invading Saudi Arabia. Our goal was to get the Iraqis to back down and protect the Saudis. Clearly that didn't happen as they invaded before we could get any US forces on the ground. When the ground war commences and we go from the defense to the offense, the operation will change from Desert Shield to Desert Storm.

"On the slide is the initial force package Schwarzkopf has requested. This will likely change as the situation on the ground changes. We're still having to keep our eyes on Europe. East Germany is nearing its final days and will likely rejoin West Germany in a matter of weeks. But that hasn't deterred some of the hardliners in the Soviet Union from exerting their control in other Warsaw Pact countries. So while we're gearing up to fight this war in the Middle East, we need to stay ready for whatever the Soviets may try in Europe."

"I get it, Dick. We need to keep an eye on Europe and handle the Middle East. Give me a moment to look at the slide, will you?" snapped Bush, a bit irritated with the history lesson. He had used to run the CIA and had been Vice President under Reagan for eight years.

The President put his reading glasses on and looked at a handout of the slide rather than strain his eyes by looking at it on the wall. He mumbled a few times to himself and scribbled a note here and there. They read as follows:

Operation Desert Shield Initial Ground Force Package
82nd Airborne Division, Fort Bragg, NC
24th Infantry Division (Mechanized), Fort Stewart, GA
197th Infantry Brigade (Mechanized), Fort Benning, GA
Hq, XVIII Airborne Corps, Fort Bragg, NC
101st Airborne Division (Air Assault) Fort Campbell, KY
3rd Armored Cavalry Regiment, Fort Bliss, TX
1st Cavalry Division, Fort Hood, TX
1st Brigade, 2nd Armored Division, Fort Hood, TX
11th Air Defense Artillery Brigade, Fort Bliss, TX
III Corps Artillery, Fort Sill, OK
1st Corps Support Command, Fort Bragg, NC
13th Corps Support Command, Fort Hood, TX
12th Combat Aviation Brigade, Germany
3rd Armored Division Aviation elements, Germany
7th Medical Command, Germany
Hq, 3rd US Army, Fort McPherson, GA

When the President finished reading the slide, he looked up at Colonel Atwell. "Colonel, I see a lot of Army units on this request. But what about the Marines? Do we have them on the way yet?"

Atwell nodded. "Yes, sir. The 1st Marine Expeditionary Force out of California, the 1st Marine Expeditionary Brigade in Hawaii, the 4th Marine Expeditionary Brigade on the East Coast, and the 7th Marine Expeditionary Brigade in California's Mojave Desert were all given warning orders ten days ago and final deployment orders four days ago. Their equipment just finished being loaded and the ships are taking on their final provisions and munitions. They'll start loading the Marines tomorrow, with the convoys setting out in the next twenty-four hours. Again, it's going to take around twenty days for most of these forces to coalesce in the Middle East, which will give us time to finalize where we want them to disembark."

The President scrunched his eyebrows at the statement. "This all sounds great, Colonel. But we're talking about a lot of Marines and their equipment. Where exactly are we putting all these people? Is Jeddah still going to be the launchpad to liberating Saudi Arabia?"

"Sir," said General Powell, finally speaking up and joining the conversation, "the Iraqis have overrun almost every port in Saudi Arabia of any capability except Jeddah. That port really doesn't have the capacity to handle the size of forces needed for an operation like this. We're asking that we be allowed to use Muscat, Oman, for our staging base and port from which to liberate Saudi Arabia and Kuwait."

"Mr. President," Jim Baker said loudly to gain the President's attention, "I've spoken with the Sultan of Oman and he has opened the door for us to stage forces and use his ports and airfields. He is also allowing the Saudi government to go into exile to be located there. In addition, I've spoken to President Mubarak of Egypt, who is allowing us to use Egyptian air bases. If you call him directly, he just may be willing to commit ground forces to join our coalition. Mubarak is seriously pissed that he got Saddam and the Kuwaitis talking to avoid war, only to have Saddam stab him in the back and use those talks as a pretext to invade not only Kuwait but now Saudi Arabia, and look to invade the rest of the Gulf states."

"Is that the best we can do? Is there no place else for us to launch this operation from?" The President seemed skeptical about launching a liberation that would essentially have them march clear across the entire Middle East. Not an easy thing to do.

"Sir, at this point I'm afraid this is our best bet. We're going to look to open two sustained fronts. One from Jeddah, and one from Oman," Mr. Cheney explained. "As of right now, it looks like the Egyptians will join us if you call and ask Mubarak personally to join. Maybe we can even make him the head of the Arab coalition and he might convince others to join as well. Then we have the British, who have indicated they are going to commit forces but, aside from minesweepers, at this point can't say what else they will bring to the table. Unfortunately, the King of Jordan hasn't given us permission to stage out of his country or use any of his air bases. We don't believe he'll join our coalition, though Mubarak might be able to help persuade him. We're also negotiating with Turkey to see about opening a front via northern Iraq. The problem with Turkey is they have a large Kurdish population, and if we end up liberating northern Iraq from Saddam, then it's likely they may see a Kurdish uprising of their own. This is probably why the Turks aren't going to participate in any action against Iraq or allow us to stage a ground invasion either. They'll allow us to stage aircraft to attack Iraq, but that's about it. For the time being, Oman is our best bet."

The President looked at Jim Baker. "Jim, set the call up for me to speak with the Sultan to thank him for his support as well as Mubarak."

Chapter Forty
Extract SF Team

14 August 1990
Special Forces Team
Salwa, Saudi Arabia

Captain Harris's team had been in their hide position for three days. In that time, they had directed a total of six air strikes from the carrier in the Gulf of Oman, and the result was burning and destroyed vehicles stretching for miles across the desert. They had concentrated the strikes on air-defense weapons and fuel trucks but would target a tank if no AA or fuel trucks were present. Anything they could destroy would be of benefit in the upcoming conflict.

The sun was just beginning to brighten up the eastern sky when SFC Weekly and Mr. Garrett came in from putting in an air strike along the road in the vicinity of Salwa. Secondary explosions could still be seen. As they were dropping their equipment, Captain Harris approached them.

"I see you boys had a fun night," he said with a shit-eating grin on his face.

"Sir, they're making it too easy. Noise and light discipline doesn't seem to be in their vocabulary. The forward units may be tuned in to light discipline, but those rear-echelon dudes are clueless. We had no problem locating and targeting fuel trucks or air-defense weapons," Weekly replied jovially.

As the three reviewed the night's activities, Staff Sergeant Donovan approached.

"Excuse me, sir. We just got a flash message from higher," Donovan said.

That got everyone's attention as Lovett and Caldwell had joined the group as well.

"Sir, higher wants us to move out and head for Qatar for an extraction tonight. They sent the coordinates for a pickup point just across the border. The Qatar Air Force is sending a Sea King helicopter to pick us up. We'll be flown to Abu Nakhlah Airfield, where a civilian jet is waiting to fly us to Muscat," Donovan informed them.

"How far is the pickup point?" Cardwell asked. "I want to check everyone's feet before we take off. No time to come down with foot blisters."

"The pickup point is just across the border, about two and a half miles," Donovan said. "I plotted it out."

"Damn, that's close. I guess the Iraqis aren't going into Qatar just yet," Harris commented.

"Why do you think that is, Captain?" Cardwell probed. They'd been taking bets the last few days about when the Iraqis would invade the next country.

"Colonel Wright said that the UAE and Kuwait were pushing hard on Saddam to pay back the money he owed them for funding his war with Iran. He considered it a gift that didn't need to be paid back. They also refused to cut their oil production, which depressed the price of oil, which further deprived Iraq of money. Saddam was desperate for money. Wright said that Qatar didn't press him for repayment, offering to put the loan on hold for several years. Qatar also agreed to cut oil production to help Saddam. None of these concessions hurt Qatar's economy. As it is, they're sitting on the world's third-largest oil reserve and have huge natural gas resources on top of it. Wright thinks Saddam is just giving them breathing room. The more I've thought about it, the more I think Saddam might make a play to get them to side with him. Colonel Wright still thinks Saddam will hit them before this is over," Captain Harris went on to explain.

"OK, guys, it's going to be light soon, so let's get settled in for the day and be ready to move out right after dark. Steak and eggs for breakfast tomorrow," Weekly said, and everyone dispersed to settle in for the day.

****

Five hours later, Donovan said in a low voice, "Captain, you best wake up." He was lying on the ground next to the officer.

"What's up?" Harris croaked sleepily.

"Sir, we have company approaching," Donovan said and pointed to the north. Harris couldn't see anything from his hide position. He moved to get a better look at what Donovan was pointing at.

"Oh shit," he finally whispered as SFC Weekly crawled up next to him.

"What you got, sir?" Weekly asked as he poked his head over the hide position.

"What we have, Sergeant Weekly, is a patrol of what appears to be five guys walking this way. They seem to be lollygagging, but they just might come across our position," Harris replied as he handed his binoculars to Weekly. The senior noncom studied them for a moment.

"Sir, I think they're heading for the farm and orchard over there. I knew someone would wander over there before we got out of here. I don't think they know we're here, but best not give 'em any reason to suspect we're here either. I'll make sure everyone stays put, and we'll keep an eye on them and the farm," Weekly declared, confident that his plan would work.

For the rest of the afternoon, someone was on guard specifically watching the farm to the north of their position to see if the patrol would leave or stay. Once the Iraqi patrol had moved inside the farm compound, they hadn't seen any further movement.

To the east, the direction they would be traveling to reach the pickup point, traffic was moving on the road with approximately fifty meters between each vehicle. They were dispersing themselves better as they moved since the air strikes had started. They'd need to figure out how to cross the road after dark if the convoy was still moving through the area.

As darkness descended on the desert, the team gathered up their equipment. Footprints were the only thing they wanted to leave behind, and they would attempt to erase those as well.

Lovett took point and started moving to the east on the azimuth that Captain Harris had assigned him. He was followed by Mr. Garrett, who was serving as compass and paceman. GPS was starting to replace the need for a paceman, but old habits were hard to kill.

As they slipped past the back side of the farm compound, they could hear music playing on a radio or television. Hopefully it would hold the attention of whoever was inside. The real challenge was going to be getting across the highway. The closer they approached, the lower they crouched as they walked.

Thank God there's no moon tonight. It'll make this next part of our plan work out a lot better, Captain Harris thought optimistically.

309

When they got within fifty meters of a berm near the highway, Mr. Garrett gave the signal for everyone to get down in the prone position. Then he crawled back to Captain Harris, explaining, "We're in position to set the charges. I'm going to take Cardwell with me. I don't think it'll take more than an hour for us to get up there, rig it, and get back to you. We'll also figure out where we should hold up prior to us blowing this thing."

Chief Warrant Officer Three Garrett had explained this plan to him and Weekly before they'd left their hide position. He said that, during a SOG mission along the Chinese–North Vietnamese border, they had run into a similar situation. He told them how they'd handled that one and figured they could repeat it here.

"Good luck," Harris whispered and motioned for Cardwell to go with him. The two of them set off, crawling along the ground towards the road.

All the rest of the team could do at this point was stay prone and wait. Sometimes that was the hardest part. One's mind would begin to wander instead of staying focused on what was happening. Sometimes, sleep would come calling and attempt to lull one into pleasant comfort, or simply entice one to black out from sheer exhaustion. Other times, crawling creatures such as scorpions or camel spiders would decide to track across one's body. Occasionally, a desert viper might snuggle up to one to keep warm.

After what felt like an eternity but was actually only an hour, Chief Garrett and Cardwell reappeared.

"How did it go?" Harris whispered softly.

"We're good to go, sir. Nothing like leaving a going-away present," he whispered back. Harris couldn't see the man's face, but he was pretty sure it had a big grin on it. The chief added, "We spotted a small berm that runs parallel to the highway. It's fifty or so meters away. I suggest we move to it. It'll put us that much closer to the road once the festivities begin."

Harris grunted at the information. *I'm so glad this guy is on my team,* he thought. "That's a good idea, Chief. Let's get a move on, then. I want to get across the border and to the pickup point ASAP."

In the dark, the ODA crawled across the desert floor with their rucks on their backs and their rifles cradled in their arms. If anyone was looking in their direction with night vision goggles, they would have thought a family of giant Galápagos tortoises were moving across the desert. When they reached the sand berm, they stopped and rested. A few of the guys grabbed their canteens and proceeded to drink most of the contents down. Some grabbed for some leftover remnants from their MREs. Crawling fifty meters with one hundred and twenty pounds on your back didn't make for an easy trip.

As they lay there, one truck after another drove past their position. This was a particularly large convoy—that or the Iraqis had finally gotten their spacing down, because this thing seemed to drag on for a long while.

Most of the vehicles were running with blackout lights, so the drivers and any passengers could only see the road immediately in front of them. The team was betting that the drivers on these supply vehicles had not been issued night vision goggles. They lay there watching several cargo trucks with equipment or supplies roll past their position. Finally, Captain Harris spotted the kinds of trucks he was looking for with his night vision goggles. Two troop carrier vehicles were approaching, one following the other, and they appeared to have troops in the back.

He tapped Garrett on the shoulder and pointed. Garrett got the message.

The first troop carrier rolled past their position. When the second one approached, Chief Garrett flipped the switch on the detonator in his hand. Simultaneously, two explosions went off, taking out both vehicles in a giant fireball.

The vehicles to the front of this scene accelerated away and scattered across the desert. The trucks following slammed on their brakes and also began to scatter to the four winds. In that moment, they thought an air strike was happening, and the last thing they wanted to do was bunch up and give the Americans an even better target to shoot at.

In the kill zone, the two troop carriers were on fire as they ground to a halt. Some of the soldiers threw themselves over the sides. A few had stumbled out of the vehicle; some held their ears in pain. A few had their clothes on fire.

One Iraqi just ran down the road like a flaming Roman candle, screaming and flailing his arms about until he collapsed. Another soldier

311

who was on fire did the smart thing. He stopped, dropped, and rolled to put out the flames. Once he'd succeeded, he just lay there moaning loudly for help. In a way, it was a sickening sight to behold. To know they had inflicted this kind of suffering on their fellow man wasn't exactly something they felt proud of.

"Let's go," Harris shouted to be heard by his men. He jumped up and started moving swiftly in a hunched-over position. His body threaded between the two stricken vehicles.

Although they ran between two burning vehicles and a number of Iraqi soldiers spread out on the ground, some tending to their wounded friends, others just trying to figure out what had happened, no one questioned or stopped them. In these soldiers' minds, this had been caused by another air strike, and that was exactly what Harris and the team wanted them to think.

The team ran across the road essentially undetected amidst the chaos. Knowing that the Qatari border was only two hundred and fifty meters away, they picked up their pace and ran in a full upright position until they spotted the demarcation fence between the two countries.

When the Special Forces team approached the fence, Chief Garrett already had a pair of wire cutters out and in his hand. He was hard at work snipping link after link in the fence. He started at the bottom and worked his way up, then cut across, giving them a wide enough space to fit their bodies and their rucks. It took him less than a couple of minutes and he was through. He then motioned for the others to follow him through quickly.

When everyone was through the hole, the team maintained a tactical posture. Technically they should be safe, but a large Iraqi convoy was still only a few hundred meters away. Sergeant Weekly pulled out their GPS receiver and got their exact location. He then connected it to the anticipated pickup point and led the way. Fifteen minutes later, they'd reached the point and fanned out. They assumed a 360-degree perimeter, with everyone facing out and in a prone position. No one was taking any chances in case some Iraqis had followed them across the border. They were going to sit tight and wait until their ride out of this place arrived and they would be able to fly away.

Then they heard the most wonderful sound a grunt behind enemy lines could hear. The twin-engine helicopter was approaching totally

312

blacked out. Donovan activated one of their IR chem sticks and tossed it out away from their position. The helicopter spotted it right away and altered its approach, landing not far from the chem stick.

No invitation was needed. Once that bird was on the ground and the door opened, the ODA team ran aboard and took a seat. When the helicopter took off, Captain Harris saw two crew chiefs manning the side guns and a lone figure sitting nearby in civilian clothes.

Despite the whooshing of the air and the rhythmic thumping of the rotor blades, the man in civilian clothes spoke as he used his foot to shove a cooler down towards them. "Thought I would get out of the office and enjoy a little night flying, Captain. Would you like a beer?"

A grin spread across Harris's face. "Is that you, Colonel Wright?"

"You think some other colonel would jump on a helicopter in the middle of the night with a cooler full of beers? Of course it's me," replied Wright with a laugh.

Wright lifted one of the bottles to his lips. At this point, the other members of the team had all grabbed for a bottle and were doing the same thing.

Sergeant Weekly was the first man to spit the cold liquid right out of his mouth as he shouted, "It's fucking near beer, guys. Don't do it!"

This caused everyone to break out in laughter.

Wright laughed the hardest at the comment before shouting back to the Snake Eaters, "This is still a dry country. When we get you back to the embassy, we'll see if there might be a real one somewhere we can scrounge up for you."

Harris looked at Wright. "Thank you, sir, for coming to get us. I wasn't sure how much longer our luck was going to hold up there."

Wright nodded, then placed a hand on the young man's shoulder. "You guys did an outstanding job. But it was time to bring you in. We have big plans for you guys. It's time to get you rested up and ready for your next mission."

Chapter Forty-One
Third Invasion

15 August 1990
1st Republican Guard Corps
Al Batha, Saudi Arabia

The American Navy had launched several air strikes against the 1st Republican Guard Corps, but not enough to seriously cripple the forward progress. The only exception was in the case of the 18th Brigade of the 1st Armored Division. That brigade was now in Salwa, being refitted.

General al-Ujayli was confident that he could still achieve his mission of seizing Abu Dhabi with his remaining three brigades. There was an excellent highway from Al Batha on the border to Al Sila. It was a clear shot to Abu Dhabi, with several gas stations in the form of refineries along the way to refuel his vehicles without having to use his own supplies.

The towns along the route were small and would offer token resistance, if any. The soil along the northwest coast of Qatar was lithosol—rocky soil—which was only ten centimeters deep over hard underlying limestone. Lithosol soil is calcareous sandy loam, covered with rock debris and almost ideal for track vehicles. The decision was made that no track vehicles would travel on the paved highway as it was reserved for wheeled vehicles. Track vehicles tore up a paved highway, especially when the temperatures were in the 120-degree Fahrenheit range.

When the lead elements of the 1st Battalion moved out along the highway, General al-Ujayli was surprised that no resistance was offered at the Al Batha–Guwaifat border crossing point. He couldn't determine if it was a case of resigned surrender by the UAE customs officers or a welcome mat.

The 2nd Battalion's track vehicles were moving well on the right flank with the 1st Battalion on the left. He kept his 3rd Battalion in reserve following the 2nd Battalion a few miles back. He wanted his reserve unit somewhat close by in case they did run into some resistance.

Within the first twenty minutes, the 1st Battalion reported passing Al Sila and still no opposition. While the lead elements moved through the city, elements from the 3rd Battalion would enter the town to make sure no resistance was being formed to cause problems in his rear area.

General al-Ujayli knew the 2nd al-Medinah Armored Division would be following him several kilometers back but wouldn't interfere with his ability to maneuver should he need to. To the south, the 3rd Tawakalna Mechanized Division was moving towards the border with Oman. He could see the cloud of dust to his south indicating their direction.

Taking a deep breath in as he watched the formations of vehicles around him, General al-Ujayli wished he could be observing this from a helicopter. *From the air, this must be a wonderous sight. Four divisions moving in unison to seize a country. Maybe I can get up in a helicopter later today and observe this sight before it is gone.*
****

General Dulaymi, the 1st RG Corps commander, was already up in his helicopter observing the force below him. It always excited him to see his corps in a formation rolling across an open desert. He had positioned his helicopter behind the 1st Hammurabi Armored Division and ahead of the 2nd al-Medinah Armored Division. To his right front, he could observe the dust column rising from the vehicles of the 6th Nebuchadnezzar Mechanized Division as they began to pull further away from the 1st Hammurabi Armored Division.

While the 6th pulled away and headed for their objectives, the way was opening for the 3rd Mechanized Division to move to the Oman-UAE border and establish a screen line, serving as the Corps' covering force should anyone attempt to attack out of Oman. The road distance from Al Batha to Abu Dhabi was almost 320 kilometers. Dulaymi knew it would be difficult to make that distance in one day.

It would be tomorrow sometime that General al-Ujayli would reach his objective of Abu Dhabi and then another one hundred twenty-eight kilometers for General al-Tikriti to reach Dubai. The 3rd would have the most difficulty, as there were few roads and the terrain was high dunes. Fortunately, the dune pattern ran east to west, so it was possible for track and wheel vehicles to travel between the dunes and not have to traverse them perpendicular to their advance.

Fortunately, there was only one paved road that ran along the border between the UAE and Oman. This would make it easy to run patrols and observe the Omani side of the border. The 3rd would anchor its left flank in Al Ain, and the 2nd could cover the border north of there once it had secured Dubai-Sharjah. The rugged mountain terrain to the east, with only one or two passable roads, would preclude a force of any size coming from this direction.

Once his forces had seized Dubai, his reconnaissance units would find him a suitable place to establish his headquarters and sleeping quarters. Someplace nice, near a mosque, and maybe even with a pool. *Yes, that'd be nice*, he thought.

****

Brigadier General Juwad Asaad was not so optimistic about taking this next objective. His division, 3rd Tawakalna Mechanized Division, was a fast mobile division with tanks and infantry fighting vehicles. They were best suited to mobility warfare, dancing around an enemy force like a boxer moves between strikes. Asking them to transform themselves into an occupation force was a tall ask. His next objective, Al Ain, was a major city with several universities. It had a population of more than six hundred thousand, and while it was essentially an island oasis in the desert along the Omani border, it was also home to a number of ancient forts and archaeological sites, which could complicate his efforts to fortify the area.

General Dulaymi had discussed the importance of his men treading lightly with the locals. He wanted them to use kid gloves as much as possible. He also didn't want him to position a lot of his armor units within the city, if possible. The leadership back in Baghdad was emphatic about ensuring the Iraqi Army appeared as liberators and not conquerors. President Saddam believed if they came across as liberators, the population might ultimately support them, which would make forming up additional militia forces to work with their forces substantially easier.

In light of these restraints being placed on him, General Asaad decided on placing only a single battalion in Al Ain to work with local police and maintain a semblance of normality. The rest of the division would look to establish defensive positions along the Omani border and start preparing a defense in depth of the border. If the Americans planned to cross at his portion of the border, then his men would make them pay in blood for every meter of territory they captured.

When he'd needed to figure out where to establish his own headquarters, he'd decided on the Al Jahili Fort. It was centrally located in the city and easily defended. It was also close to the airport, out of which his aviation unit and air-defense systems would be operating. For the time being, it'd work. Beyond that, it was in God's hands now as to what would come next.

****

As the 1st Hammurabi Armored Division approached Abu Dhabi, it became obvious that word of their pending arrival had preceded them. Cars were parked, leaving virtually no traffic on the roads. Doors to shops and businesses were closed; some were even boarded up.

Children were absent from the streets, and so were the main street vendors. The propaganda machine had been throwing out false stories about Iraqi soldiers committing atrocities in Kuwait and Saudi Arabia as they approached the UAE. Al-Ujayli knew they weren't true; now they needed to show the people of Abu Dhabi they were lies being told by the West.

When General al-Ujayli's vehicle had finally stopped in a nearby park, he got out and stretched his legs. For the next couple of hours he wanted to use this place as his corps's headquarters until his people could find a more suitable location.

As he gazed at a couple of birds in a tree nearby, his thoughts were intruded upon when a staff officer called out to him. "General, you are needed."

Al-Ujayli turned to look at the major. "What is it?"

"Sir, we just received a request for your assistance from one of our lead elements as they reached the outskirts of Mohammed Bin Zayed City. The captain leading the unit said they've spotted a group of police cars displaying white flags as they blocked the road leading into the city. The patrol is requesting instructions."

"What do you mean they want instructions? Did they not ask for a meeting, or are a few police cars powerful enough to stop our tanks? Get back to him and ask for more details," al-Ujayli ordered, annoyed that

317

this junior officer appeared not to be taking the initiative to talk with the police officers and find out what was going on. *That's going to have to change if we are ever going to achieve greatness. I can't have platoon, company, and battalion commanders unable to think for themselves and improvise when needed*, he thought.

A few minutes later, the staff officer returned.

"Sir, they say the mayor of Abu Dhabi wishes to speak with you. He has had a tent and a meal prepared to sit with you," the major explained.

Al-Ujayli thought about this for a minute. *Why the mayor and not the Sultan himself, or at least someone from the royal family? This is almost an insult.*

"Alright, I will come and speak with him," al-Ujayli said as he climbed into his staff car.

"Sir, would you like to change out of that uniform into something more appropriate?" the major politely asked.

"No, I would not. I am a soldier here to do a soldier's duty. We are not here to coddle these people. We are here to govern. Now let's go."

While General al-Ujayli's vehicle drove through the city, he was pleased to see the discipline and professionalism of his soldiers as they interacted with the local civilians. He was also pleased to see the tracked vehicles were off the roads with their gun turrets pointing away at forty-five-degree angles.

His BTRs and other wheeled vehicles were on the sides of the road, allowing traffic to pass. As they started to enter a more suburban area, al-Ujayli noticed the police cars with white flags and a tent off to the side of the road. Several men in white robes, the typical attire in the UAE, were standing around waiting for him. His driver steered them in that direction.

When the vehicle stopped, he got out and approached the group.

"I am General al-Ujayli, commander of the 1st Hammurabi Armored Division. Who is the mayor here?" he asked in a loud and authoritative tone.

The group briefly exchanged looks before a middle-aged man stepped forward.

"*Allah wa Salam*, General." He extended his hand.

"*Salam Allah Mequam*. And who are you?"

"General, I am Sheikh Khalifa bin Zayed Al Nahyan. I am also the acting governor of Abu Dhabi. My father is the Emir of Abu Dhabi, but he is out of the country currently at our home in England. I can speak for my father. Please let us enjoy some tea and discuss our mutual interest," the young man offered as he motioned for the general to follow him into the tent.

The tent floor was a carpet so deep one sank at least an inch in the thickness. Several trays were arranged with fruit and cheese as well as cold milk and tea. A portable air conditioner cooled the interior to a comfortable ninety degrees. Large pillows were scattered about for the Sheikh and general to sit.

Damn, I should have changed into something more formal. I'm sure I must smell like a goat farmer right now, al-Ujayli thought privately.

Once comfortably situated, the Sheikh started the conversation.

"General, your army has traveled far and made an impressive campaign. But why have you ventured into my country? We have not demanded payment for the war you fought with Iran. We have even cut our oil production to assist in raising the price of oil, as your prime minister requested. What do you hope to gain by entering our territory like this?" The Sheikh's voice was very even and soft as he questioned the Iraqi general.

"Sheikh Khalifa, we are not here as conquerors. Our army is here to ensure that no outside forces enter your kingdom from Oman or the Persian Gulf. We wish to ensure that peace will prevail in the UAE now and into the future. We have no desire to interfere in your kingdom. Once we are assured that no Western forces will invade Saudi Arabia through your country, we will depart."

Al-Ujayli paused for a moment as he took a sip of his tea before looking at the Crown Prince. "We are all Arab brothers. But the House of Saud does not view all of us as brothers. They view themselves as the lords of the Middle East to govern and rule over us. Iraq believes we are all equal brothers in Allah. We do not wish to see the Saudis pressure you or any other Arab nation in the future as they have in the past. Our end goal is to unite all Arab brothers into one Arab nation to hold the Persians back and stop the West's attempt to seize more control over our lands and import their brand of morals and idolatry, corrupting our youth," General al-Ujayli said.

319

Sheikh Khalifa said nothing for a few moments as he thought about what the general had said. He reached for his own tea and took a couple of sips. Then he ate a single date before returning his attention to the Iraqi general.

"General, if I understand what you are saying, your army intends to stay in my nation for an undetermined period of time. Correct?"

General al-Ujayli nodded slowly. "Sheikh Khalifa, I am not going to try and deceive you or your father, the Sultan. I am also not going to pretend my force will only be here for a few weeks or a couple of months. I cannot say with certainty how long my force will be here. That will largely depend on the Americans and the West. As of right now, everything depends on what the Americans are going to do next. The Americans have already attacked my soldiers with their air force. However, I am hopeful that between our Foreign Minister and the Foreign Ministers of China, France, and the Soviet Union, we may ultimately be able to secure some sort of peace deal or cease-fire that will keep the West out of the Middle East."

He paused for a moment as the Sheikh took the information in before adding, "My forces will require some accommodations while we are here. In return, I would like to extend some job opportunities to your people who may be interested in working in our motor pool, servicing the thousands of vehicles in my corps. Our engineer brigade will also be looking to hire thousands of individuals to help us dig antitank ditches and berms in the desert and other facilities to shore up the defense of your territory from an American invasion."

Sheikh Khalifa nodded, acknowledging the request and the information before adding, "Yes, General. I fully understand and expected you to make a request like this before we met. If you will allow me"—he motioned to one of those standing nearby to approach them—"this man will coordinate your needs and assist in getting you and your soldiers suitable accommodations. In the meantime, you will stay in my home as my invited guest until we have found a suitable accommodation befitting a man of your stature."

"Thank you, Sheikh Khalifa. I am at a loss for words at your generous offer to have me stay at your residence while I am here in Abu Dhabi," al-Ujayli replied. "If you can show me where it is located, I will make sure my division commanders know as well. Perhaps your father won't mind us staying in his home since he is out of the country and likely won't be returning for some time, correct?"

The Sheikh suddenly realized the Iraqi general had just taken over a huge swath of his family's homes without so much as a word said in objection. Sheikh Khalifa did clumsily reply, "I am sure he will not mind. If you will give me few hours to move my family, I will meet you back here in four hours if that is satisfactory. He will accompany you"—he pointed at the coordinator that had previously been introduced—"and meet with our logistic officers so we may begin the process of getting your soldiers settled." Standing, the Sheikh waited for the general to stand and then shook his hand. He did not smile. "In four hours, General."

Holding a hand up to stop the Sheikh, the general said, "Excuse me. Please, do not move your family out of your residence. We will stay at your father's place because he is not here. But so long as you are here, we would not think of forcing your family to leave their residence. Please accept my forgiveness if it sounded like we were going to take over your residence as well."

The Sheikh's demeanor changed immediately, softening as he realized the general really was making a concerted effort not to appear like invading conquerors. Perhaps he had misjudged him.

"OK, General. Then we'll get things taken care of now and not bother with relocating my family. Thank you for that, I do appreciate it."

Chapter Forty-Two
Engage the 14th

15 August 1990
1-325 Airborne Battalion
Jeddah, Saudi Arabia

The three C-2 Greyhound aircraft landed at the Jeddah airport, keeping their engines running as they waited for the Marines and paratroopers to hop aboard.

The Marine Air Naval Gunnery Liaison Company from the MEU, or ANGLICO for short, had been detailed to provide a team to accompany the soldiers of the 82nd who would provide security. The ANGLICO team, consisting of two Marines with a laser designator, were still at the base and had briefed the soldiers from the 82nd traveling with them on what to expect when landing on an aircraft carrier. The young Marines had shared stories that succeeded in instilling the fear of God into the paratroopers.

When the C-2 Greyhound pulled up to the parking ramp and the waiting soldiers and Marines, the crew chief dropped the back ramp and signaled it was time for them to load up.

Walking into the crew bay, the Tactical Air Control Party or TACPs from 1-325th Airborne Infantry Battalion climbed aboard. The two consisted of the two Air Force personnel, Captain Harrison, and Master Sergeant James Kennedy. Harrison was an F-16 pilot who was now pulling a tour with the grunts before he was able to shift back to being a pilot again.

While Harrison was the team leader, he had a squad of soldiers from 1st Platoon, Company A, 1st Battalion, 325th Infantry to provide security for the TACPs and the ANGLICO team. The soldiers had just been notified that they'd be tagging along with the TACPs to provide security, which gave them only an hour to pack their equipment and get ready. Aside from Captain Harrison, no one had any idea where they were going or what they would be doing.

Once the Greyhound was loaded, it took off and headed straight for the *Saratoga*. The flight wasn't a terribly long one, but it was going to be the first time most of them had ever landed on a carrier. Once the

plane came to a gut-wrenching screeching stop, they all hoped it would be their last C-2 carrier landing. When the plane powered down their engines, the crew chiefs got the doors opened and the soldiers inside started bailing out, excited to still be alive. A flight deck member directed the soldiers to a nearby door that would lead them belowdecks.
****

Someone from the flight deck took them down a couple of decks and to one of the Navy SEAL team rooms. They were going to stay there until it was time for them to load up on the next transport.

Upon entering the room, Captain Harrison pointed to one of the walls. "Alright, set your gear down and get comfortable. I'm heading up to a briefing to get some last-minute instructions and then we'll figure out when we'll be leaving again. In the meantime, do a double check of your equipment. If you're missing anything, this is the last chance you'll have to grab it. So make sure you have everything you need. We're likely to be gone for a while once we leave."

When Captain Harrison left, Staff Sergeant Davis took over.

"Listen up, guys. I want you to double-check your water and weapons. This is the real deal. It's highly likely we'll end up seeing combat on this next mission and I'll be damned if I'm going to let any of you pukes get me killed because you failed to bring something I told you to bring."

Davis stared menacingly at his young soldiers as they did a quick check of their equipment. He'd laid out his own rucksack and LBE for them to look at and told them to make theirs look exactly like his. No exceptions. He wanted uniformity in what they carried.

Addressing the two young Marines, he asked, "Either of you been in combat with that laser designator?"

"Me and Corporal Doss have used it in training exercises with live ordnance but not in a combat situation," Sergeant Stevens responded.

"Well, I suspect you're going to be the first in your unit to use them in combat. Don't screw it up," Davis told them.

"Oorah," Sergeant Stevens and Corporal Doss responded in unison. Staff Sergeant Davis just rolled his eyes at the two young Marines.

"When we head out to the bird, you all will need to grab one case of water. Keep that water with you and make sure you bring it with you when we land. That water is more valuable than bullets right now, so don't fuck it up and accidentally leave a case behind. Understand?"

"Oorah," came the single-word reply from Doss and Stevens.

Turning to the assemblied squad of infantry soldiers and the two young Marines, Sergeant Davis said, "God knows what kind of camel jockey water might be around when we get there, so we're going to stockpile these cases we'll be bringing. Once on the ground, I want a fucking perimeter set up around the captain and his team until they've done what they need to do. You two jarheads stick to the captain like glue," Davis ordered pointing at Doss and Stevens. Continuing, "Remember, these are Chair Force rangers. They think they're hot shit because they can call in air strikes, but they ain't infantry like us. It's our job to protect them so the flyboys can lay the hurt on these hajis. Once they've completed their missions, the carrier is going to send some choppers to come fetch us and bring us back here. Once we land, we can gloat all we want to with these jarheads how many hajis we smoked, but until then, heads on a swivel, and try not to get me or these Air Force guys killed. Got it?" Davis bellowed at his soldiers.

"Hooah, Sergeant!,"the assembled groups responded with a couple of "Oorah" tossed in.

Specialist Ford, the one guy who had no fear of asking simple or stupid questions no matter how many times he got his ass chewed over it, asked, "Sarge, if we come back to the carrier, that means we have to have another ride in that Greyhound thing, won't we? Couldn't they just drop us off at some airport and let us fly from there?"

Specialist Ford was from Vidalia, Georgia. Oddly enough to his platoonmates, he wanted to be a fashion designer when his time in the Army was completed. His claim to fame with his squad was that he'd won the first Vidalia onion eating contest when he was in high school.

Staff Sergeant Davis laughed at the question. "Come on, Ford. Don't you like flying in the Greyhound?"

"It's not that I don't like the ride. It's that sudden stop that scared the crap out of me," Ford complained.

"Well, now, you have no need to worry about that because a helicopter will bring us back to the ship and the C-2 will fly us off," Davis answered with a smile.

"Oh, yeah, right. That won't be so bad, then," Ford said with a thoughtful look. Sergeant Stevens and Corporal Doss exchanged looks and shook their heads.

"Hey, dumbass," Jones spoke up, "how do you think the C-2 takes off from this thing? They launch it with a giant slingshot. You thought the landing was bad, wait till you feel the exit."

Ford just stood there with a lost look on his face. The other members just laughed at his expense. When the captain returned, he motioned for everyone to gather around.

"All right, listen up. We're being inserted by helicopter about thirty miles inland into some pretty nasty terrain. Our mission is to direct air strikes against an Iraqi division that's moving down the road to the coast. This area has very limited roads and routes, so once they're hit, they're going to be pissed."

Captain Harrison paused for a moment before he continued."There's another TACP team working out of Jeddah with me. They've been working with a Saudi armor brigade to fight a delaying action back to Jeddah while we keep bringing in more tanks. When they carried out an ambush and air strike not far from Buraydah, a major city and airport that straddles a major highway to Jeddah, the Iraqis called in a handful of Hinds."

Staff Sergeant Davis muttered a few curse words under his breath while a couple of other soldiers shook their heads.

"Needless to say, the Hinds tore the Saudi tanks apart and ripped the unit up pretty bad. The other TACP team barely made it out of there. I talked with the Marine detachment commander on board about this. He told me they do have a small number of Stingers on board. He offered two of his Marines who knew how to operate them. I told him I needed to talk with Staff Sergeant Davis first. Would you have a problem with two more Marines being added to the team?"

Grunting at the question, Staff Sergeant Davis looked at his squad, who all had grins on their faces. "Sure, let's add more jarheads. But they need to know they work for me when we're on the ground. No ifs, ands or buts about it, sir."

"Fair enough. Then let's go ahead and get our gear brought over to the hangar deck and load up. I'll tell the Det commander to send his two guys over. We leave in twenty mikes."

When they got to the hangar deck, some Navy guys had just finished loading the birds up with the cases of water and other supplies they were bringing. Everything was being spread out between the three MH-60S Knighthawk helicopters.

A couple of Marines then walked up to Staff Sergeant Davis and said they'd been assigned to join his squad. They looked just as young as the rest of his soldiers. Davis was starting to feel like an old man looking at all the faces of these Marines and soldiers. They looked like high school freshmen to his eyes. The Marines had their equipment ready and two Stingers slung over their shoulders.

"Staff Sergeant," one of the helicopter pilots shouted out to him as he walked over to the group of soldiers, "we're going to load the helicopters on the elevator to bring up to the flight deck. I want your squad to follow that helicopter as it gets loaded on the elevator. Once all the engines are spun up and ready, the flight deck personnel will tell you when to load up. We're spreading you guys across the three birds. Good luck on your mission." The Navy lieutenant then turned around to head back to his helicopter.

Thirty minutes later, the birds were in the air and flying fast over the water as they approached land. Sunset was rapidly approaching, which was fine with everyone involved who understood the limitations of night flight.

None of the Army guys understood those limitations, so they had to put their faith in the hands of the Navy pilots. As the helicopters approached land, the three aircraft took up a trail formation and tuned east towards the rough terrain they'd have to fly through. They crossed the beach at low level, two hundred feet, and flew towards a mountain range and canyon. Night vision goggles dropped down over the pilots' eyes as they deftly flew their aerial chariots. All the soldiers could see as the darkness began to envelop everything was the dimmed LED lights that bathed the cockpit in a warm green glow.
****

After an hour of flight time, Captain Harrison turned to those in his aircraft and held up two fingers, meaning two minutes to touchdown. As the aircraft slowed, the only thing visible outside it was blackness. Dust swirling around the aircraft and a hard bump were the only indications that the bird was on the ground. The soldiers knew what to do and started tossing everything and everyone out. As soon as their feet hit the ground, they lay down and pointed their weapons outward, ready to exchange gunfire.

Once the helicopters departed, stillness and darkness returned to the area.

Captain Harrison wasted no time, ordering, "All right, let's get a head count and sensitive items check, then we'll move out. Sergeant Davis, compass man, is to take a heading of zero-one-five for two klicks. This is not going to be a walk in the park, so we'll cache the water and supplies about halfway to the objectives. Everyone ready?" Captain Harrison asked as he looked around through his night vision goggles. "Alright, let's move out."

Staff Sergeant Davis placed Ford on point and Jones on compass and pace. He kept the two Marines towards the rear of his team as well as the two with the laser designators.

The terrain was mountainous and barren. Up one hill, down the back side, and then they'd face a bigger hill in front to climb. After four hours, they managed to reach the two-kilometer point.

"OK, let's take a break. Drink some water," Captain Harrison directed.

Everyone was soaking wet with perspiration. The desert fatigues were made of heavy canvas, so you would sweat, and thus your sweat cooled the body as it evaporated. Field soldiers thought it was a pretty good uniform. The rear-echelon office boys didn't like it and wanted a lightweight uniform. Of course, the rear-echelon office boys had air-conditioned offices or tents, so what did they know?

Sitting with his back against his rucksack, Captain Harrison called Davis over to talk. "Sergeant, here's our position. We'll now turn to a new heading of zero-three-five degrees for two klicks. That will put us in a good position to overlook this road and this road as well as that valley. That valley will afford some protection to our fast-movers as they come in low and fast."

Davis only nodded as he did his best to study the position with his NVGs on.

Master Sergeant Kennedy, who'd largely been silent during the last few hours, looked over the terrain and position Harrison had identified.

327

He'd been a TACP his entire career; this wasn't his first rodeo behind enemy lines. "I agree, sir. This looks like a good position to me. When is this division supposed to arrive in this area?"

"Don't know for sure, but I suspect we won't be lonely for long," Harrison explained. "Hey, just be sure everyone continues to drink water. We'll leave half the cases here and take the rest with us."

Davis then asked, "Sir, how long you figure on us being out here?"

"As long as it takes to destroy a division of vehicles," the captain answered as he removed his night vision goggles.

The group cached half their supplies and got back on the move. It took them a few hours, but they eventually reached the position Harrison had identified. Once there, the soldiers went to work getting everyone set up in a defensive position. The soldiers also started creating their hide positions to help protect their bodies from the sun that would surely bake them once it was up. They also made sure there wasn't anything reflective sitting in a position that might give away their positions. As the sun started lighting the eastern sky, they no longer needed their NVGs; they would be able to use the good old-fashioned Mark 1 eyeball.

Captain Harrison told Master Sergeant Kennedy it was time for them to get some shut-eye. He told Staff Sergeant Davis what they were going to do and recommended he start cycling his own guys through the same cycle. They'd had a long day and night; the men needed sleep. They also had no idea how long they'd have to wait for the Iraqis to start showing up.

Two hours later, Davis moved to Captain Harrison's position in a low crouch so as not to be silhouetted on top of the hill. The captain and his NCO were deep in slumber, and Davis almost hated to wake them.

Davis gently nudged the captain with his foot. "Sir, Captain Harrison, time to wake up, sir. We have company."

Instantly, Captain Harrison and his NCO were awake and appreciative of the fact that Davis held out two canteen cups of hot coffee for them.

"Thought this might help get the cobwebs out. Heated them up on some heat tabs we brought," Davis indicated, handing the coffee to them.

"Thanks, Sergeant. Everything quiet?" Captain Harrison asked.

"Up here, yes, sir. Down on the road, *hmmm*... not so quiet. Look." Davis handed the captain a pair of binoculars. From their position, they were overlooking a wide spot in the highway to the northeast. While some vehicles were moving on the road, it appeared the logistic tail was setting up a refuel point off the side of the road and numerous vehicles were already lined up to refuel. It also appeared that many vehicles had stopped for morning prayer.

This was just too good to let slide. Looking to the northwest, Harrison liked what he saw even more—the lead elements of the first formation of combat vehicles. Picking up his radio handset, Captain Harrison transmitted his first request for an air strike.

****

The attack aircraft from the USS *Saratoga* had launched and were loitering over the Red Sea as they formed up. VF-35, the Black Panthers in their A-6 Intruders, would make the ground attack with VF-74 and VF-103 in their F-14s providing a fighter cap. The Black Panthers would go in low-level, using the mountainous terrain to mask their approach while the BeDevilers and Sluggers maintained altitude to protect them from any attacking Iraqi interceptors.

An hour after placing his initial call for an air strike, Captain Harrison received word the strike package was finally formed up and ready to begin. While it felt like a long time, nearly an hour after he placed the call in for help, he had to keep in mind they didn't just keep strike packages loitering around indefinitely. Aircraft had to be refueled and, depending on what you phoned in, a particular set of ordnance had to be prepared.

With the carrier sitting just twenty miles from the coast, it wouldn't take long for the package to arrive once it was ready. They didn't have to fly through hundreds of miles to reach the target. The A-6 Intruders had already figured out the best approach to the target. They were going to fly a route through the mountains. It was a little more dangerous flying close to the ground and the canyon walls, but it also all but eliminated their radar signatures and would help protect them from ground SAMs that might be waiting for them. The F-14s at altitude, however, would be painted by the SAMs and would have to avoid the SA-6 and SA-9 anti-aircraft missiles, especially the SA-6s.

The route the Intruders had selected brought them from the south through a wadi between two mountains. From where they entered the wadi, it was three miles to the target, which was a road between two mountain ridges roughly two miles in length. The road was covered in a couple miles of wheeled and track vehicles from the 14th Division. They were sitting ducks and there wasn't a damn thing they could do about it once the bombs started falling.

Better yet, at the head of the target was a very narrow gorge the 14th Division vehicles had to pass through. With the right bombs, the road could be blocked, thus closing off the entire road. Aside from blowing up a bunch of vehicles, blocking that road was Harrison's plan for the first wave—crater the road or cause an avalanche of rock. The second wave would hit the vehicles that would be backed up on the road with nowhere to go until they found another way through the area. It'd be like shooting fish in a barrel.

This first strike wouldn't be an easy flight for the Intruders. The mountains would afford some cover from radar weapons as well as sighted weapons, but serious flying skills and advanced techniques would be required to avoid slamming into the canyon walls.

Their position was over a mile away, high enough on the ridge to observe most of the road but not the choke point. His only way of knowing the choke point was closed was when he saw vehicles began bunching up.

Captain Harrison got the call that the first flight of four Intruders was inbound from the southwest, following the road. They were going to fly low-level for as long as possible before they had to pop up and release their load on the choke point.

From his position, Harrison couldn't see them until they popped up. The sound of roaring jet engines zipping through the area nearly scared the hell out of the Americans. They barely had time to register the Intruders, who were flying fast as hell as they popped up and banking hard over the far ridgeline, heading north. Seconds after they completed this insane maneuver, a massive cloud of dust and dirt rose from the gorge to the northwest of Harrison's position. The ground rumbled and briefly shook from the ear-piercing thunderous booms of the explosions that rippled through the canyons. The sound waves seemed to echo and reverberate through the canyon walls.

Moments later, Harrison saw a flash in his peripheral vision as something whipped past his position. It was the first of four A6 Intruders

330

making a run on the vehicles. The lead aircraft was swiftly followed by the three others. The first aircraft released twenty-eight Mk 20 Rockeye cluster bombs as he passed over the convoy. An entire strip of vehicles and sections of the road blew apart. The second aircraft carried twenty-eight Mk 82 five-hundred-pound dumb bombs. The last two aircraft had a mixture of Mk 20 and Mk 82 bombs.

"Holy shit!" yelled Ford as the air was filled with flying bodies, vehicle parts and secondary explosions. Jones and Holloman sat there mesmerized by the destruction before their eyes, as was the rest of the squad.

"I sure don't ever want to be on the receiving end of that," one of the squad members said softly.

For the next hour, the small American unit stayed hunkered down, just watching the confusion unfolding before them. Finally, Davis crawled over to Captain Harrison's position. "Captain, are we going to stay here or be leaving anytime soon?"

"As soon as that dust settles and I get a good BDA, then I'll make that decision. Want to see if they have a way around this mess before we pull out. If they start bringing up road-clearing equipment, we may have to put in another strike today," Captain Harrison responded.

"Sounds good, sir. Just wanted to be able to tell the kids what we're doing. Otherwise, they're going to start asking and fidgeting," Davis replied. "Good strike, by the way. I take back anything negative I've ever said about the Chair Force. You guys sure know how to call in the pain when it's required."

Laughing at the comment, Harrison replied, "It's OK, Sergeant. It's a common misconception you grunts have about us TACPs. Most of you guys are oblivious to the fact that we're all Ranger-qualified, as well as HALO-, airborne-, and combat-diver-qualified. We're integrated into every SOF unit there is. Ironically, we hardly ever work with a line unit like yours."

Staff Sergeant Davis, who had no idea the Air Force guys his squad was protecting were actually Special Forces, wore a look of bewilderment. "Damn, sir. I've been a leg grunt in regular infantry units. I had no idea you TACPs were actually part of SOF. Here I was thinking you guys were just Chair Force. I owe you a beer when we get back to the world."

"Let's just get ready to sit tight for a little while and wait for the dust and smoke to settle a bit. If we need another strike, then so be it. If not, we'll get the hell out of here and relocate to another location or head back to the carrier."

****

Two hours later, the soldiers were burning through water. The heat of the day was really hitting them pretty hard despite them not being in direct sunlight.

"Man, I'm burning up," Specialist Ford lamented to anyone around him. "I could never get used to this heat. How do these people live like this?"

"This ain't so bad, man. This is what you call a dry heat. I'll take this any day over the humid heat of central Tennessee. Now that's hot, and terribly oppressive," Holloman countered.

Holloman was from Clarksville, Tennessee. When his hitch in the Army was done, he fully intended to return there and go into real estate sales with his father. His dad, mother, and older brother had built a very successful real estate company in Clarksville over the last ten years.

"How would you know?" Kinnaird asked. "You ain't from Tennessee, are you?"

"Yep, sure am," Holloman stated.

"You ever pick tobacco?" Ford asked.

"I worked with a friend on his granddad's farm picking tobacco in season. We used to chew on the leaves while we worked the field," Holloman explained.

"Interesting. The nicotine in the tobacco leaves can make you sick, can't it?" Ford asked.

"Don't know about that. But every day, about an hour into work, my head would hurt and I would be sick to my stomach," Holloman complained.

"Yep, that's the nicotine alright."

"Ford, how you know so much about it?" Jones asked skeptically. Ford wasn't exactly thought of as one of the smartest guys in the platoon.

"A while back I was stationed at Fort Campbell on my first assignment before jump school. I'm going back there to go to college at Austin Peay University."

332

"Alright, ladies, let's cut the noise and pay attention to what's out in front of us. Don't want any of these camel jockeys sneaking up on us," Staff Sergeant Davis chided them. He wanted them keeping an eye out on the enemy and not distracting each other with pointless idle chatter.

The TACP remained in place for the day, watching the activity below. It was obvious that the road was blocked as vehicles were stopped and bunched together. Trucks worked their way up to what appeared to be a casualty collection point and departed with wounded Iraqi soldiers. No engineer equipment was seen coming forward. By late afternoon, some explosions could be heard in the vicinity of the choke point.

Next to the small village to the east, it appeared that a refueling point was being established and a vehicle collection point as traffic flowed from the east, but nothing was moving west. After several hours had passed, several hundred vehicles were bunched together in the valley around the eastern village. Captain Harrison attempted to count but gave up and sent a report to his higher that he was looking at close to two brigades of combat vehicles just sitting together on the side of the road. The brass couldn't let this opportunity go to waste.

"Staff Sergeant Davis," Harrison called out.

Davis crawled over to the captain. "You called, Captain?"

"Yeah, we're going to put in a second strike on those vehicles down there"—he pointed at the cluster of them—"and then we're going to get the hell out of here. Have your people ready to move when I give the word. As soon as the strike goes in, we're out of here. I can all but guarantee the Iraqis will know that it's a recon team calling in air strikes on them. They'll be looking for us hard," Harrison told him as they looked at the vehicles arrayed before them. It really was a lot of vehicles and soldiers down there. Vehicles and soldiers designed to kill if you got to close to them.

"I like that idea, sir. We'll be going back to the original LZ we came in on for the extraction, right?"

Harrison pulled the hand receiver down from his face as he turned to face Davis. "You got it. I just got off the horn with the strike commander. He told me the first aircraft should be here in roughly one-five mikes."

"Roger, sir, I'll get them packing," Davis replied and moved off to get the squad ready.

As he moved about, he had to be conscious not to silhouette himself on the ridge to the enemy below. He moved around to each position and briefed his guys and the two jarheads that joined them. No one objected to leaving the mountain after they got to watch another strike.

The first indications they got that something was going on were the faint sounds of aircraft that sounded to be at some really high altitudes. The next indications were streaks of fast-moving smoke contrails zipping across the sky.

Twenty thousand feet above the soldiers, F-14s were engaged in a fight with MiG-25s and MiG-29s, with twisting, turning aircraft shooting missiles at each other. It was obvious to those on the ground the enemy was ready for another American strike. The soldiers on the ground also started climbing into their vehicles, doing their best to scatter as fast as they could.

Captain Harrison grabbed his binoculars, looking to see if he could spot any threats to the bombers coming in. He still had time to warn them if he spotted something.

He spotted two SA-9 mobile launchers that were traversing their weapons systems in preparation for the incoming aircraft. Likewise, the SA-6 was already starting to engage at least some of the aircraft. Two of their missiles had already been fired at something.

Then one of the SA-6s blew apart. One of the attack aircraft must have fired one of their AGM-88 HARM missiles and nailed the vehicle. Moments later, one of the SA-9 platforms exploded. The remaining SA-9 fired off its four missiles in a ripple fire in the direction from which the A-6 Intruders would approach. Davis looked over at Sergeant Stevens, who was all smiles as he lowered his laser designator. Davis gave him a thumbs-up.

Screaming loudly around the bend in one of the canyons, the first Intruder came in fast and low, leveling out just long enough to release its stick of five-hundred-pound bombs across a half-mile stretch of road. Trucks and armored vehicles started exploding from the bombs.

The second Intruder had turned and entered the stretch of the canyon to carry out its own bombing run, only to get slammed by two of the SA-9s missiles. The pilot and weapons officer didn't have a chance to react or even realize the missiles were headed right for them. The plane exploded and disintegrated, leaving flaming parts of it to be flung across

334

the ground. The remaining two missiles slammed into the canyon walls, coming up empty.

The last two Intruders zipped in quick and leveled out just in time to release their own sticks of Mk 20 cluster bombs. With each aircraft carrying twenty-eight bombers, it was a devastating attack. When the Intruders angled their aircraft up and out of the canyon, a ZSU filled the sky with 23mm rounds. Bright red tracer fire zipped all around the two Intruders until one of them had a wing ripped clean off. The aircraft caught fire and spun out of control. Fortunately, the pilot and his partner managed to eject before the plane eventually crashed to the ground.

The last Intruder managed to escape and looked to be heading back out in the direction of the sea. The lone SA-6 then fired off two more missiles at some unseen aircraft, adding more missiles and confusion to the area.

"OK, that's it! Let's get the hell out of here. We have a chopper to catch," Captain Harrison shouted to Staff Sergeant Davis and his soldiers.

He didn't have to say it twice. Each man grabbed his rucksack and weapon and set out in single file, moving to the south and away from the road. The pickup point was in the bottom of a wadi large enough for the aircraft to get into. It also offered protection from direct-fire weapons and a good egress route to fly out. It was a little over three miles away, but it was a downhill run. The only drawback was that it would be dark soon, which would slow their pace. The young soldiers didn't care. They were feeling pretty good about what they had accomplished this day. One thought kept creeping into each soldier's mind: *We all came together; we all go home together, even with a couple of jarheads along for the ride.*

Chapter Forty-Three
Move Out

18 August 1990
82nd Airborne Division
Jeddah, Saudi Arabia

General Buckner was drinking a cup of coffee and looking over the latest intelligence reports as well as the current boots-on-the-ground reports. The 82nd Airborne Division flag had been in Jeddah for the past seventy-two hours, and two brigades were now on the ground. The third brigade was stateside but would be coming over once the division tail had flowed in sufficiently along with the division commander, Major General Pete Ford.

Shooters are great to have, but if they don't have the supplies they need—the critical maintenance, the communications, and the fire support—then they're just in the way. Those items were flowing in now and were sufficient to support the two brigades he had here and now. Thanks to the Navy and the carrier battle group offshore, transport aircraft were flowing in unmolested by Iraqi Air Force interceptors.

"Excuse me, sir, but the staff is ready to brief you and the commanders," said Colonel Dobbins, the G-3 for the 82nd, sticking his head in the commandeered office in the main terminal.

"Good, I'll be right there." General Buckner finished his coffee and stood to leave.

He wasn't one for keeping people waiting. The walk to the conference room was short, but he made sure he paused along the way to speak with the occasional soldier he met in the hall who wasn't part of the everyday headquarters staff. He liked to get the pulse of the division from these guys not in the head shed. It was always interesting what you learned from these kids. They had no problem telling it like it was when their NCOs weren't around.

As he walked into the conference room, someone called, "Attention."

"Keep your seats, folks," Buckner said before anyone could stand. He moved quickly to his seat. "OK, Colonel, let's get on with it."

The briefing was always conducted in a set manner. The intel officer, G-2, was first, followed by the operations officer, G-3, then the G-4 supply officer. Special staff would coordinate ahead of time with the operations officer if they had something that needed to be covered. This was not the meeting to bring up routine administrative stuff. That was done with the assistant division commander for support or the chief of staff in his daily meeting.

"Good morning, sir," the G-2, Lieutenant Colonel McKenzie, said.

Buckner acknowledged him with a nod. Also present were the three brigade commanders with their battalion commanders, the artillery battalion commanders, the air-defense commanders, and the Cav squadron commander. Respective operations officers for each had also tagged along.

"Sir, as you know, the USS *Saratoga* hit the 14th Iraqi Division about thirty miles east of Duba in some very rugged terrain." He paused long enough to point at the map where the air strike had taken place. "Imagery shows that they brought down a mountainside that closed the road and cratered it in several places. It also looks like they destroyed or seriously degraded at least one and possibly two full battalions' worth of soldiers and equipment. It was quite the turkey shoot.

"That strike went in yesterday morning. A handful of hours later, in the afternoon, the vehicles got bunched up again once they'd cleared the obstacle, so the TACPs called in a second strike and hammered them again. Right now it appears the 14th Division is down somewhere around thirty percent strength and stuck. This morning we received a new satellite picture of the area. It looks like a large portion of the unit is still trying to figure a way around the choke point we've created. They're essentially stuck between a rock and a hard place, no pun intended."

General Buckner stopped him. "Colonel, what kind of losses did the *Saratoga*'s wing sustain, and is it possible for them to go back in and hammer the division again? I'd really like that group thoroughly beat up before they're able to come towards us."

"Sir, in the first strike, the Navy lost a single F-14 to an SA-6. Two of the Intruders took some minor damage but returned to the carrier. The second strike, they weren't so lucky. The Iraqis were ready for them this time around. The fighter CAP had to fight off a swarm of MiGs. They shot down two MiG-29s and four MiG-25s at a loss of four additional F-

337

14s. Two more F-14s were lost to SA-6s. Three of the four A-6 Intruders were also shot down during their bombing runs. The CAG on the *Saratoga* said it appeared only one of the crews from the A-6s was able to eject. They look to have landed near the Iraqis. Four of the six F-14 crews also ejected. No word on their whereabouts. The Navy tried to launch a CSAR twice but was forced to turn back on both occasions. As to additional strikes, the *Saratoga* says they need to focus on Wild Weasel missions for a few days and do more to regain air superiority before they go back in on another bombing mission. Since the start of the campaign, they've lost a total of eight A-6s and ten F-14s. The ship is down nearly forty percent of its air wing," the colonel explained.

"Damn. These Iraqi pilots and air defenses are a tad better than I think we first thought. OK, if the Navy isn't able to hit them, what about the Air Force? Let's get on the horn with them and find out if they can pick up the slack for us," Buckner said before he motioned for the colonel to get back on track with his brief.

"Sir, in the east, the 7th and 5th Republican Guard Divisions of the 2nd Republican Guards Corps are located with 5th Mechanized Division at Ar Rass, here"—he pointed at a location on the map—"and the lead elements of the 7th Division are at Al Dulaymiyah. They've paused after a combination of air strikes from the carrier in combination with elements of the Saudi Armor Brigade and Saudi National Guard. It appears that the 7th will be the main effort heading along Highway 60, this major highway to Medina, with the 5th conducting a supporting attack to the south. There are no major or secondary roads that lead to Medina, and the terrain is a combination of rocky, broken, hard-packed sand interlaced with wadis.

"However, it is ideal maneuver ground for vehicles until they reach a series of broken ground along this line from As Sumariyah in the north to Al Rathaya in the center and Hazrah in the south. The next line of defensible terrain is west of Medina and runs along a series of broken ridgelines from Shajwa in the north to Al Mindassah, Al Jafer, south to Alyutamah in the center to Al Seddah and finally Almwared in the south," the intelligence officer said as he traced a line on the map.

"Critical points along this line are at Almwared in the south and at Al Seddah and Al Bardiyah in the center. Almwared and Al Seddah offer easy access to the coast, but both are also defensible choke points by

338

light infantry, as is this choke point at Al Bardiyah. This is the line for the best defensible terrain east of Jeddah. Once past this point they're on the coastal plain and have an unopposed path to Jeddah," Lieutenant Colonel McKenzie concluded.

General Buckner leaned forward in his chair and studied the map for a few minutes without saying anything, appearing to be lost in thought. "What's the name of this ridgeline?" he asked.

"Sir, the Saudis don't have a name for it. To them it's just a ridgeline," the G2 said.

"From now on, we're going to call this ridge the Medina Ridge," General Buckner said.

"Roger, sir," Lieutenant Colonel McKenzie acknowledged.

"OK, let's continue," Buckner said.

"Sir, the weather for today and the next twenty-four hours is clear sky with temperatures reaching one hundred and twenty-five degrees later today. Tonight the temperature will drop to eighty-five degrees. The sun will rise in the east and set in the west," Lieutenant Colonel McKenzie said. It was a staff game to see who could make the most dramatic statement during the brief, and the general enjoyed it. He raised his eyebrows at this last statement.

"Good to see some things don't change, Mac," General Buckner replied with a slight smile.

"Sir, I will be followed by the G-3," McKenzie said as he stepped aside for the next guy.

"Aren't you always?" bantered back General Buckner.

The staff snickered as the G-3 approached the map, which was covered by a clear sheet of acetate with blue and red symbols.

"Sir, currently the Saudi National Guard units that were in Buraydah and Unayzah have withdrawn and are moving into Medina. Elements of the Saudi Armored Brigade, part of the 45th Armored Brigade, are conducting a delay action in front of the 7th and 5th Republican Guard Divisions. They're falling back towards Medina. Major Skooter, our TACP, is with them and has been calling in support from the 71st Fighter Wing.

"The Saudi 8th Mechanized Brigade that was along the Yemen border has moved up to and is occupying positions around Taif and guarding the approaches to Mecca. The Saudi 10th Mechanized Brigade

339

that was pushed out of Tabuk is withdrawing south and has set up numerous company-size ambushes through the passes in this area, delaying the forward progress of the 2nd Iraqi Corps. The two air strikes that have hit the 2nd Army Corps over the past two days have bloodied their nose and have them moving with more caution than they had been," the G-3, said pausing to check his notes. "Unfortunately, Iraqi air-defense systems have taken their toll on the Navy flyboys."

"OK, what about our current status?" General Buckner asked.

"Sir, we currently have 1st and 2nd Brigade completely on the ground, minus vehicles. The Cav squadron has one troop of Sheridans that were flown in. Div Arty has two battalions of 105s, and Corps artillery has one battery of 155 on the ground. We have a shortage of ammo for these weapons as well as a shortage of antitank ammo for the TOWs, which at this point are dismounted. Attached we have the rapid reaction team from the 24th Division with four Bradleys and four Abrams tanks. The flow is steady, with about one plane every hour bringing in the division, and we should close the division personnel within the next twenty-four hours. Vehicles are not expected for two or three weeks at the outside."

"So what you're saying there, Colonel, is we're supposed to stop two divisions from the east and three divisions from the north with two brigades of paratroopers and two companies of armored vehicles," General Buckner said, leaning forward in his chair, elbows on his knees.

"That's almost right, sir," the G-3 responded reluctantly. "18th Airborne Corps says the 10th Saudi Mechanized Brigade is going to take on the 2nd Iraqi Corps as it attempts to move south through this terrain. The TACP from 1st of the 325 is aboard the carrier and is being inserted with the 10th to direct air strikes from the carrier. We, on the other hand, get to play with the 2nd Republican Guard Corps heading to Medina. Corps says as soon as our last load is in, the 101st will commence flowing in, with their Apache helicopters being on the first plane."

Sitting back up quickly and looking about with a smile, Buckner said, "Well, looks like we have the Iraqis right where we want them. All around us. Now they're in for it. What's your recommended course of action?"

"Sir, there are three courses of action that we've developed. Option A"—the G-3 picked up a pointer and pointed to the north—"is for us to

340

deploy along a defensive line east of Medina, from Al-Malwi in the north to Al Nkheel in the south for our two brigades and from Al Nkheel to Ad Dumayriyah using the elements of the Saudi 45th Armored Brigade with our mechanized forces attached to them. It's a long distance of seventy-four miles, but the terrain behind them is really bad and we're accepting risk in this area. To the north, the terrain is crap for mechanized or armor forces, so the level of risk is low. They'll have to stay on the road and dismount their nfantry to move forward," the G-3 concluded.

General Buckner sat and studied the map. Grinning, he said, "OK, let's hear what your next course of action is."

"Option B, sir, is from Ad-Dulu in the north to Medina to Ad Dumayriyah in the south. This is some of the worst terrain in Saudi Arabia. It's mostly broken wadis with ten- to twenty-foot ridges, many of them with sheer drop-offs or walls. To make this work, we tie in the Saudi National Guard in Medina and we take the south side, offering support to the Saudis if necessary. Place the Saudi Armored forces in reserve on the south side in case the 5th attempts to flank to the south," the colonel said.

Again, the general leaned forward to study the map, then got up and walked up to the wall to get a better look. His fingers traced along a few points as he moved around the map, really studying the two options they'd presented him.

"OK, what else you got? I'm not sold on these two options," General Buckner announced.

"Sir, the final course of action we have for your consideration is to establish a defensive line west of Medina along this ridgeline, the Medina Ridge. It'd stretch from Al Mindassah in the north, south to Al Bardiyah, and continue to Alyutamah. This allows us to bottle up any wheeled or mechanized movements out of the Medina area and keeps them trapped in the mountains. This is essentially really good paratrooper country, given we don't have a lot of armor support ourselves. If we position our artillery right and build up some firebases and some really good defensive positions, we should be able to keep the Iraqis bottled up in this area for many months—at least until we're able to bring in some serious armored forces of our own. Once that happens, we'll be able to punch our way out of this area.

"You couple that with our Apaches and A-10 Warthogs for ground-support aircraft and we should be able to decimate these Iraqi divisions. I'll be the first to admit we're essentially losing a lot of ground early on. But we're the ones choosing the ground we want to take a stand on. We're also forcing the Iraqis to really stretch their supply lines incredibly long. This'll give our Special Forces and Ranger units some good opportunities to run hit-and-run desert operations against their supply lines. Kind of like the SAS Desert Rats did in World War II against Rommel," the colonel explained.

General Buckner stood and proudly placed his hands on his hips as he announced, "I love it. The chance to pretend to be a cross between Montgomery, Patton, and the SAS Desert Rats... wow is all I can say. You've sold me. Let's move forward with option C."

The officers all got a good laugh. It broke the tension and stress they'd all been under. Buckner quickly added, "In all seriousness, guys, option C is the better route. I hate giving up this much ground and potentially letting the Iraqis grab Medina itself, but the Saudis are never going to let us fight for it or fight around it. At least this option does allow us to really choose where we want to make a stand. Now I'd like you all to start identifying where we would place our artillery. The guns are going to be critical for our guys. Make sure we're factoring in how best to use the 105s and 155s so we have good overlapping fields of fire. If you have to, get on the horn back to 18th Corps headquarters and tell them you need a battery of 155s or a battalion of 105s sent to Jeddah immediately. Insist on them tasking a National Guard unit if need be. Sometimes they're more nimble in deploying than a regular Army unit. Just get creative in getting soldiers here."

"OK, sir. If you want to move forward with option C, then that concludes my brief. We really hadn't come up with an option D," the G-3 added.

Buckner laughed. "Well, I'm glad I liked option C, then. Let's get it all drawn up and present it to 18th Airborne Corps. I'll talk to General Luck and see if he can get us some additional artillery and munitions deployed from the States. I think General Luck and I would both feel a hell of a lot better knowing we could rain down some holy hell on the enemy when the time comes. Also, someone get Corps and find out if a couple squadrons of A-10s could be repositioned to Jeddah, and if not

342

there, then an Egyptian base across the Red Sea. We need those aircraft to help us go against all these freaking divisions if we don't want to get run over," General Buckner ordered as he gave several of his folks a hard stare. They knew what they had to do.

****

Arriving at General Luck's office in the main terminal building, Buckner saw the office door was closed and the aide was seated in the outer office.

"Afternoon, sir," the aide said.

"Afternoon, Major. Is the general in?"

"Yes, sir. I'll let him know you're here," the major said, standing and moving to the closed door. He knocked and opened it.

"Excuse me, sir, but General Buckner is here to see you," the aide announced, acknowledging the other officer with a nod.

"Damn good timing," General Luck said, then in a loud voice, "Buckner, get your ass in here."

As Buckner walked into the room, he noticed the other officer sitting in the overstuffed chair in front of General Luck's desk.

General Hugh Sheldon uncurled his six-foot-four frame from the chair and extended his hand. "Long time no see, Buck, how you doing?" he said.

"I'm doing a damn sight better now," Buckner responded, grabbing Sheldon's hand. They had served together several times over the course of their Army careers and had great respect for each other, even though they were in rival divisions. "When did you get in, and what toys did you bring?"

"Landed about two hours ago and I have part of one of our attack helicopter battalions with me. They should be operational by the twenty-first or twenty-second. Twenty-four Apaches with plenty of ammo," Sheldon declared with a wide grin on his face.

"Buck, I was just telling Hugh that I'm putting the 101st in at Yanbu up north a ways," Luck said. "There's an airport there that can handle the heavy aircraft, which will allow for some dispersion of our forces. It'll allow us to increase if not double our flow, and there's also a usable port there for offloading ships. The way things are shaping up, they may

343

be needed real soon. Best make it the twenty-first if you could," General Luck pressed.

"I'm sure we'll have a good portion of the aircraft operational by the twenty-first. Are you expecting company by then?" Sheldon asked with a raised eyebrow.

Snorting at the question as he tried to stifle a slight chuckle, Buckner countered, "Company? How about two divisions coming at us from the east and as much as four divisions from the north, all closing in on us over the next seventy-two to ninety-six hours? The 7th and 5th Divisions of the 2nd Republican Guard Corps are about to enter Medina. The 2nd Army Corps is coming down from the north with the 7th, 37th and the 51st Infantry Divisions. The Iraqis appeared to have left the 2nd Infantry Division in Tabuk and attempted to push the 14th to the coast. Unfortunately for them, we caught them in some really nasty terrain and chewed them up with air strikes from the carrier *Saratoga*. Opposing the 7th, 37th and 51st is the 10th Saudi Mechanized Brigade, and that's about all that's standing between them and punching us in the face. If the 7th, 37th and 51st link up with the 7th Adnan and the 5th Baghdad in Medina, we're going to have real problems holding the last line of defense. Add to the fact that the Iraqi Air Force seems to have improved to being a near-par to our own and we're in a world of hurt. Of course I'd never admit that in front of the troops, but it's just the three of us."

"Damn, what kind of trap did you guys drag my division into? What have we got right now to hold these guys off until more help arrives?" Sheldon said nervously as he looked the two paratroopers in the eyes.

"Currently we've got two-plus brigades of the 82nd. The rest should be here by COB tonight—a company team from the 24th who brought with them four M1 tanks and four Bradley fighting vehicle. We have the MEU from the *Tarawa* but don't know how long we keep them. In addition, we have the 8th Saudi Mechanized Brigade, which is moving north along the coast to join us," General Luck explained. "We also have remnants of the 45th Saudi Armored Brigade, which has been fighting a delaying action from Buraydah back to Medina. The sooner we can get your attack aircraft going, the better. Those Apaches may be the deciding factor between us holding the line and handing the Iraqis their first major defeat and us getting humiliatingly thrown into the Red Sea and summarily relieved of our commands and put out to pasture," General Lucky bluntly exclaimed.

"Sir, you sure paint a beautiful picture. Your namesake had better come true, sir," General Sheldon

"Sir," Buckner interjected, "that ridge, we're officially calling it Medina Ridge. My staff is presenting our plan for a defense along that ridge as we speak. We're going to turn that place into a meat grinder like nothing the Iraqis have ever seen. Trust me when I say we're going to stop them butt-cold along this ridgeline."

Luck grunted at the assessment. "Just make sure the plan your folks are drafting to be sent up the flagpole is rock-solid. I don't need to tell you gentlemen that a lot is riding on this plan and these next five or six days. Everyone knows about the unit's heritage during World War II. By the end of next week, the Corps will have a new heritage—whether it'll be one of an incredible and profound victory or an utterly humiliating loss and defeat. I'm telling you both right now, I'd rather die on that fucking ridge surrounded by a pile of dead Iraqi soldiers than live in defeat. Don't let me, the Corps, the Army, or the country down."

Chapter Forty-Four
Planning the Defensive Line

24 August 1990
82nd Airborne Headquarters
Jeddah, Saudi Arabia

The fight in Medina was winding down. It had been swift and brutal.

The 2nd Republican Guard Corps, with the 7th Adnan Division in the north and the 5th Baghdad Division to the south of Highway 60, had taken ten days to move from Buraydah to the outskirts of Medina. During that time, delaying actions by the elements of the 45th Saudi Armored Brigade and air strikes from US assets had mauled the 7th Adnan Division. The 5th was a bit more fortunate as this division was not using the highway and had thus largely not been tracked or monitored like the 7th had been.

For the past five days, the two divisions had been concentrating on capturing Medina. The Saudi National Guard forces were making it a house-to-house fight, especially against elements of the 7th Division. The 5th Division had engaged in the southern suburbs of Medina but had been ordered to bypass the city and get to the coast. It appeared that once the 5th had opened the passes to the coast, the 2nd Army Corps would follow and conduct a passage of lines and move to the coast to seize Jeddah from the Americans.

It had now been twenty days since the Iraqi Army had crossed the Saudi border, without much of a pause. They were running an absolute blitzkrieg of an operation—one that had stunned not only the Saudis but also the Americans and the rest of the world. This blitz across the desert, however, was beginning to show in the maintenance state of the Iraqi equipment. A pause at this time would be a smart play—a good opportunity to consolidate, refit and rearm before making the next lunge. However, Saddam and his generals weren't trying to play it safe. They weren't trying to play it smart. They were playing to win and gambling their entire army in the process.

****

General Buckner was feeling better about their situation now that he had all three brigades in-country and they were fully deployed to their sectors. The division artillery was in position, and two battalions of 105s and a battalion of 155s had been emergency airlifted to Jeddah by any and all mil air and commercial air transports available, along with at least two weeks of munitions for a heavy fight. Everyone knew the next five to ten days were going to make or break things in Saudi Arabia.

Buckner only wished he had more firepower. The air-defense battalion had also arrived in force. This was a welcome addition, although the towed Vulcan air-defense weapon wasn't nearly as effective as the Iraqi ZSU-23-4 or even the ZSU-57-2. The Stinger missiles were effective, but there just weren't enough of them. If they started to get hit by waves of Hinds, things could get really interesting for them.

During the last twenty-four hours, as the battle for Medina Ridge drew closer, he'd moved the division tactical command post or TCP to the center sector so he could monitor the battle as it unfolded. It quickly became evident that FM radio communication was going to be a problem at these distances and in this terrain. All of the brigade commanders were meeting with him this morning to go over their plan for the defense of their respective sectors. It might be one of the last times they all met together like this for a long time.

Colonel Joe Kinser had been a brigade commander for almost eighteen months. He was older than most brigade commanders, having been a staff sergeant. After a tour in Vietnam, he'd decided to make the Army a career and had gone to officer candidate school. His nickname among his soldiers was "Smoking Joe," and he was dearly loved by them. He could easily identify with his soldiers, and they really respected him as a man and an officer.

"Joe, why don't you start us off?" General Buckner said, looking at the man, who was several years older than he was.

"Yes, sir," Kinser said as he stood and moved to the map board, which was covered in acetate. He picked up a pointer and began.

"Sir, we're defending from Al Madinah in the north to this point in the south, as was agreed between me and Bob. Highway 340 is the major road through my sector with a few trails scattered throughout. I'm positioning the 1st Battalion 504th in the north along the ridge to this outcrop. He will cover the road connecting Highway 15 in the east to

347

Highway 15 in the west and Highway 8240. 2nd Battalion will defend from there to south of this unmarked highway. The 3rd Battalion will cover Highway 340 and Highway 60 and south, linking up with 2nd Brigade.

"Naturally, 3rd Battalion will be my main effort, and I've attached my engineer company to him for preparing that road. Priority of artillery fire is to 3rd Battalion. This is a wide sector, sir, but really the only places that we could expect serious trouble are in Al Mufrihat and along Highway 340. There are several foot trails through all the sectors, and all can be easily controlled. I have the Cav troop screening up Highway 15 to Buwat in the north. I'm feeling fairly confident at this point, sir. What are your questions?" Colonel Kinser concluded confidently.

"Sounds like you have it covered," General Buckner acknowledged. *I'll bet he's already played this battle over a million times in his head and accounted for damn near everything that's going to happen. I'm damn glad to have him here. He's going to be my rock this defensive effort will be built upon.*

Joe added, "Sir, the one concern I do have is Highway 15, which comes out of Medina and passes through Al Mindassah, going north to Tabuk. I'm concerned that I may find part of the 2nd Army Corps coming down that road about the time I have the 2nd Republican Guard Corps coming down on Highway 340."

Buckner chewed on his lower lip for just a moment before replying. He stood up and walked over to the map board to walk them through something. "That's a valid concern, Joe. It's also why I put the one troop from our only Cav unit and their vehicles on your flank. They'll be in constant contact with you. If they spot something, you'll be the first to know. They're more than capable of covering your flank, especially with Div Arty on standby. Let's not forget we also have the 10th Sudi Mech harrassing the lead elements of the 2nd Corps as they move south."

Surveying his commanders, Buckner smiled as he informed them, "I was saving this for the end of the brief, but now seems like a good time to tell you guys. An hour ago, I was informed by General Luck that the 511th Tactical Fighter Squadron out of RAF Alconbury in England arrived across the Suez twelve hours ago. Their pilots are resting up right now, but they'll be on standby to assist us, and only us, for the foreseeable future. A squadron of A-10s is going to make a big difference in this coming battle, guys. Does this alleviate some of your concerns, Joe?"

"Yes, sir, it does a lot," Colonel Kinser replied with a look of genuine relief on his face as he took a seat.

The rest of the briefing was more of the same, each brigade commander going over the disposition of their battalions and how they were going to handle the Iraqi formations arrayed before them. The outcome of this very war could be decided by what happened next.

Chapter Forty-Five
Battle of Medina Ridge

21 August 1990
1st Brigade, 82nd Airborne
Medina, Saudi Arabia

1st Brigade, 82nd Airborne Division had moved into positions on the eighteenth. Colonel Kinser had gone over the ground with his battalion commanders, and they had done the same with their company commanders, who did the same with their platoon leaders.

Leaders' recons, as they were called, were paramount in a successful defense. In this terrain, the problem wasn't so much going to be enemy armor as it was enemy infantry. The 5th and the 7th Republican Guard divisions weren't armored divisions, so each division only had seventy-eight tanks, although they had been upgraded to the newest Russian T-72s. Some had been lost in the previous days, but their numbers were still large.

This kind of terrain was going to restrict the tanks, but not the infantry. These divisions were packing many thousands of infantry soldiers, soldiers who'd be hell-bent on isolating the defending paratroopers and wiping them out.

The senior NCO manning the TOC had taken some time and built up a really nice sand table with the appropriate symbols and figures so the commanders could lay out their plan visually. The NCO was meticulous in building the terrain model as exactly as possible, with the appropriate roads, wadis and hilltops indicated.

"Sergeant First Class," Colonel Kinser said, getting the NCO's attention, "you should be a model builder for Disney Productions when you get out. This is a perfect replica of our sector."

"Thank you, sir. Glad to do it," the man said, feeling a lot of pride as all the battalion commanders were standing there.

"OK, 1st Bat, let's hear your plan," Colonel Kinser said.

Lieutenant Colonel Mike Walker stood and approached the sand table. Brigade and battalion boundaries were already marked on the sand table, with blue yarn delineating the battalion boundaries. Walker picked up three oval cutouts representing company defensive positions and placed one aside the two roads leading from Medina west and one in the back of his battalion sector where those two roads converged. He also laid down a symbol for his battalion mortars.

"Sir, in my sector I have two paved roads running east to west and one road, Highway 15, approaching from the north and splitting to run east and west of my positions. I'm accepting risk on my northern flank, as north of us somewhere are elements of the 10th Saudi Mechanized Brigade, and the one troop of the division Cav squadron is screening along that flank. In the east I've placed one rifle company across each road and my third company in depth, where those two roads intersect. Priority of fires is to the southern company, as I believe that's where the main threat will come, and it'll be the BTR-70s and 80s. I doubt they'll run their T-72 out front as this division doesn't have that many and will be holding them in reserve to exploit any breakthrough"—Lieutenant Colonel Walker cast a sideways glance at the 2nd Battalion commander, Lieutenant Colonel Ellison—"through John's sector."

Ellison had been a classmate of Walker's at West Point, and the two had been competing against one another their entire careers. West Point officers came in three profiles. The first profile was those that you could look at and just know they were destined to enter the general officer ranks. They were generally very focused but very good-natured. They were mentors to junior officers and compadres to any officers, regardless of where they got their commissions. Then there were the West Point graduates that were called "ring knockers" because they wore the huge ring and made it very obvious where they had gone to school. Some had never left the parade field at West Point, and their wives easily wore their rank. They would stab another officer in the back to get ahead, and some made it to general officer by climbing over the bodies of those they stabbed along the way. And then there were the incompetent officers. These guys might have been book-smart, but they were short on common sense. Definitely not general officer material, and they usually finished their Army careers before they could retire, or they retired as lieutenant colonels, having been passed over for colonel. Ellison and Walker fit the first profile.

John Ellison flashed a look at Walker and basically told him where to go without saying it. Profanity was something that Colonel Kinser did not approve of, so everyone was conscious not to use it around him.

351

"How are you going to use your engineer platoon?" Colonel Kinser asked.

"Sir, the engineer platoon is going to emplace cratering charges on this road coming out of Medina directly. That will steer any mounted force to the north or into John's sector. In addition, the engineer platoon is going to reinforce Bravo Company, which has responsibility for that road. The engineers are equipped with twenty M202 FLASH rocket launchers," Walker explained.

"Where the hell did you get those?" Colonel Kinser asked.

"Well, sir, it seems that there were a bunch of them in a bunker at the ASP, and the engineer company commander grabbed them all when they drew their basic load and deployed. I think every engineer platoon in the brigade has them," he said, looking at the other battalion commander, who acknowledged his statement.

"Remind me to give an attaboy to the engineer company commander when I get back to the brigade TOC," Colonel Kinser said to the brigade command sergeant major, Marvin Hill. The soldiers commonly referred to him as Marvelous Marvin, but not to his face. He was a hell of an NCO.

"OK, John, let's hear what you have planned," Colonel Kinser said.

"Yes, sir. I have the narrowest sector, being in the center of the brigade sector, and have positioned my companies in depth along the one road through my sector, with A Company on the south side and forward, while Bravo Company will be on the north side and slightly to the rear of Alpha. They'll be positioned so both companies will be able to engage in this area simultaneously. Charlie Company will also be positioned in depth to engage the enemy in this area at the same time, and I'm positioning my engineers with Bravo Company too. If we're paid a visit by any Hinds or other aircraft, my Vulcan section will be positioned with Charlie Company and, if need be, able to engage the enemy soldiers. I've got my scout section out to watch this hill for anyone attempting to flank Alpha. That concludes my brief, what are your questions, sir?" Pausing briefly, he snickered as he looked over at his friend Mike Walker. "Oh, sir—any forces that Mike and the 1st Battalion can't handle, they're welcome to send them over to us before my guys get bored."

Satisfied, Kinser turned to the 3rd Battalion commander, Lieutenant Colonel Hank Sabine. Smart as a fox, Sabine was an ROTC graduate from North Georgia Military and had all the mannerisms of a backwoods Georgia boy.

"Sir, my sector has 2nd Battalion on my north flank and 2nd Brigade on my south flank. Highway 340 and Highway 60 pass through my sector. I have positioned my scouts out front, watching both roads, and hope to identify the enemy main effort early. A Company on the north has an established kill zone and B Company on the south has set up a kill zone on Highway 60. Charlie Company is positioned in depth with one platoon across each highway and one platoon in the center positioned to react to either highway. We have emplaced mines in front of both of Charlie Company's platoon positions as well as along the flanks. The battery of 105 artillery is positioned to support the scouts' call for fires and the companies. In addition, if necessary he can lay direct fire on Highway 340."

"And your engineers, where are they?" Kinser asked,

"Sir, the engineers are concentrating on creating obstacles in front of Charlie Company's two platoons," Hank responded.

The banter and briefing went on for another hour as they went over their plans. They all knew this was going to be a tough fight. Sadly, they also knew a lot of their soldiers were likely to die over the next few days. It was a somber and great responsibility being a commander in combat. You were oftentimes issuing orders that would result in many of your men being killed or maimed. Yet those orders had to be given to win the day and protect your brothers in arms.

Before the meeting ended, Colonel Kinser informed them the 101st Aviation Battalion had finished establishing their operating base at the Yanbu Airport, eighty miles from their current positions. In addition, a forward rearm-refuel point was being established in the vicinity of Al Musayjid, only thirty miles to the southwest. This would place the Apaches substantially closer to the action and allow them to refuel, rearm, and get back into the fight a lot faster than if they had to fly back to Jeddah or Yanbu. Once the brief was over, the group had one final meal together before they broke to head back to their individual commands. They'd hope to eat together again once the battle had been won.

****

504th Parachute Infantry Regiment
Alpha Company, 2-504th

The night was cool for a desert environment. During the day, the temps had consistently hovered around 120 degrees. Now, with the sun shining bright on the other side of the world, they were left bathed in darkness. The moon had already started its transition across the horizon as the sun began to near its own grand entrance. The downside to the evenings in the desert was the dramatic temperature drops. The temp had decreased to eighty by the dead of night, a full forty-degree drop.

Staff Sergeant Allen Murphy had caught a couple of hours of sleep comfortably wrapped in his poncho, poncho liner, and shelter half. His feet with his boots on were tucked inside his waterproof bag, keeping toasty warm. Kind of an oddity given the temp of nearly eighty degrees, but his body had become accustomed to the 120 degrees of the day. As he slept, he kept his boots on, ready to run at a moment's notice. His gas mask had oddly transformed itself into a moderately comfortable pillow—not what the Army had designed it for, but a grunt makes do with what he has.

His company, Alpha, 2nd of the 504th Infantry, had spent the last seventy-two hours preparing their fighting positions along what had been dubbed Medina Ridge. They'd built a series of fortified gun positions along the ridge that would provide interlocking fields of fire. Their battalion commander was emphatic about making sure each platoon and company was able to interlace their fields of fire with each other. The ground along the ridge and most of the area around them was sadly bare of any real vegetation. This meant they had to get creative in blending their observation and listening posts, bunkers, and fighting positions.

When Staff Sergeant Murphy had built this position with his squad two days ago, he'd taken them out five hundred meters to their front. Turning around, he'd pointed at their position and told his squad, "This is what the enemy will see." They'd used that perspective to further improve their positions.

Stretching as he yawned, Staff Sergeant Murphy removed his poncho liner and stood up in the bunker he'd slept in. The machine gunner was still sleeping while the assistant gunner was already awake. Private Malady was using a heating tab to get some hot water going.

Murphy saw a handful of instant coffee and hot cocoa packs nearby along with a few canteen cup holders.

"Morning, Malady. You cooking us up some coffee?"

The young soldier looked up. "I am. I was going to surprise you and Specialist Arnold with a cup."

Murphy smiled at the kind gesture. "Thanks, Malady. I'm stepping out to take a piss. Why don't you go ahead and get Arnold up?"

Taking a few steps away from their fighting position, Murphy took care of the most important business of any day—emptying his bladder. While he was relieving himself, he looked off in the distance and saw some color starting to creep into the eastern sky. It was beautiful seeing the varying colors. This was one of the things he enjoyed about being in the infantry—sleeping outdoors and waking up to this kind of beauty each day.

Then he heard something that snapped his mind into sharp focus. Not sure if he was really hearing it, he stood waiting to see if it came again. When it did, the hairs on the back of his neck stood up. He moved silently and quickly back into the bunker.

In a soft voice barely above a whisper, he said, "Malady, Arnold, grab your weapons and get up!"

Specialist Arnold, who'd just woken up moments earlier, was about to protest when Murphy crossed the distance between them in the blink of an eye and placed his hand over his mouth. He held a finger to his own lips and pointed out the gun slit.

Malady and Arnold's eyes went wide as saucers as they realized what Murphy was trying to tell them.

The three of them heard another noise—the sound of some rocks sliding down the hill in front of them. Someone was approaching their bunker, attempting to sneak up on them.

Murphy grabbed for his night vision goggles. The twilight was starting to break through the darkness, but it was still just dark enough to cover whatever movement was taking place around them.

As he peered through the gun slit in the bunker, Murphy's eyes confirmed what his ears had heard and his mind had already concluded. He spotted two figures moving cautiously up the hill towards his position. They were still probably fifty meters away. They also didn't appear to have spotted the bunker through the terrain, rocks and other material they'd used to help conceal the position.

In the green light of the night vision goggles, Murphy couldn't see their uniforms, but the AK-47 was obvious. Both figures stopped and squatted down for some reason. Either they'd heard something that had alerted them to their presence, or they'd found what they were looking for.

Across the road, maybe three or four hundred meters north of their positions, Murphy heard a shot, followed by a second, and then a short burst from a machine gun.

Murphy didn't hesitate for a second. He already had his rifled leveled at the two enemy soldiers and fired.

Malady joined in with his own M16 while Arnold let loose a controlled burst from his M60 machine gun.

A swath of bullets raked the enemy soldiers, killing them both instantly.

"Stop shooting," Murphy shouted to his guys. "They're scouts. They're trying to find our positions so they can call in artillery on us. Specialist Arnold, go tell the others in the squad to stay ready and only fire if they hear us shooting or they spot an Iraqi heading towards them."

For the next fifteen minutes, sporadic shooting could be heard across the battalion lines as the Iraqis probed them. They were trying to assess where the forward edge of the battle area, or FEBA as the brass liked to call it, was, likely so they could begin plotting the American positions for their own artillery.

When the sun crested the horizon almost twenty minutes after the first shots had been fired, Staff Sergeant Murphy heard and felt the deep rumbling of artillery coming from somewhere behind their lines, likely from the 1-319th FA, the brigade's artillery battalion.

The friendly rounds flew over their heads to some unknown target. Minutes later, Staff Sergeant Murphy and his squadmates began to hear the air above them being pierced and shoved aside by the hundred-pound projectiles of the Iraqi 155mm howitzers in retaliation.

Murphy had heard from their platoon leader that the Iraqis had acquired several hundred, maybe even thousands of these South African G5 howitzers during their war with Iran. They were specially designed to operate in the dusty and sandy environments of Africa and the Middle

East. The G5s had a range of thirty kilometers with the use of a standard propellant. When a base bleed was used, that kicked the range up to forty kilometers, putting them well outside the Americans' ability to conduct counterbattery fire.

For maybe ten minutes, Murphy and his squad heard the artillery duel going back and forth. They had no idea which side was winning. What they could hear was a lot of explosions to the rear of their positions. Whatever was happening back there didn't sound good. Then the artillery fire shifted.

At first it was just a couple of shells, then it was dozens of shells landing all along the paratroopers' positions along the ridge. Murphy and his two soldiers had crawled down to the bottom of the bunker and prayed one of these hundred-pound shells didn't land directly on them or even close by. The ground continued to shake violently. Sometimes a round would land nearby and the three of them would bounce off the ground, only to be thrown back into it. The overpressure was awful. They felt like their ears were going to explode, or even their heads, with the constant pressure changes.

Murphy told them to keep their mouths open. It'd help.

Whatever was going on, it was obvious that the Iraqis were gearing up for a major attack. Murphy was hoping they'd have some soldiers and fighting positions left after this barrage finally lifted. He also had a brother over in Charlie Company. He hoped they were faring better than his company was. Suddenly, the artillery barrage ceased.

"Sarge, we got vehicles coming up the road," Malady said, climbing up behind his M60 machine gun and peering through the gun slit. Murphy was on the TA-1 field phone immediately, contacting his platoon leader to see if he knew what was going on.

Looking out the gun slit, Murphy nodded at Malady and then relayed what he was seeing. "Sir, this is position two. I have vehicles, BTR-70s moving towards my position on the road. I count six and—oh shit... I got five T-72s following behind them along with dismounted infantry," Murphy said and then hung up the phone. He had to get his guys ready to stop them.

"Arnold, hold your fire on those vehicles. I want to let the TOWs take them out. I'm going to check on the other guys. Malady, listen to Arnold while I'm gone." With that, Murphy half crawled and half crouched as he moved from one position to the next, checking on them after the artillery barrage and getting them ready for the fight of their lives.

****

"Sir, Alpha and Bravo have vehicles moving into the engagement area," the staff NCO said to Lieutenant Colonel John Ellison.

"I'm going to move to the western end of Bravo. Tell everyone to hold their fire until the lead vehicle hits the mines. Then I want every TOW to open up on them," Ellison directed. Turning to his fire support coordinator, he ordered, "Send a message back to the brigade artillery and let them know we're going to need a fire mission to those predetermined positions we talked about with them."

He then grabbed his helmet and headed to one of the observation posts connected to the battalion TOC. The OP was positioned just right, giving an observer a good field of vision on the western end of Bravo Company, two hundred yards away. As he reached the OP and walked up to look out over the scene unfolding before him, the first BTR-70 hit a mine. Once that lead vehicle blew up, the twenty TOW weapons of the battalion all fired on the primary targets, the tanks, BTRs, BMPs, and any air-defense weapons that were present.

The artillery started hitting the area with variable time-fused HE rounds, creating airbursts that were mutilating anyone that wasn't inside a vehicle. Confined inside the vehicles, the Iraqis found that their visibility was severely diminished. They shot wildly in any and every direction with greatly reduced accuracy.

When you added the smoke from burning vehicles to the situation, it was becoming a dire situation for the units. As Iraqi soldiers dismounted from their vehicles, the paratroopers in their prepared camouflaged positions opened fire.

The enemy soldiers started to panic as their officers and leaders were identified and cut down. Vehicles at the end of the column began driving backwards to get out of the engagement area. The road had become clogged with burning wrecks of tanks and APCs. Many of the soldiers inside the BTRs and BMPs, however, were dismounting their vehicles to rush forward to the aid of their comrades.

Turning to his operations officer, Ellison barked, "Tell Alpha and Bravo to move to alternate positions now. Make sure they grab their TOWs. I don't want those launchers left behind. The Iraqis are going to start hitting those positions with artillery any minute now that they know where they are. *Move now!*"

****

Staff Sergeant Murphy didn't need to be told twice when he got the word to beat feet back to their next line of defense. He shoved Malady and Arnold out of their positions and grabbed his weapon and the TA-1 field phone. He led his squad to new positions they'd finished preparing just the day before. No sooner had they dropped into the new fighting holes than Iraqi artillery began dropping on their old positions a second time.

This second barrage on their old positions was even heavier than the first. The whole area was being plastered by a mixture of ground and airbursts from the Iraqi 155mm howitzers. It was a devastating barrage, one the Iraqi soldiers thought would wipe the Americans out. They'd be in for one hell of a surprise when they reached the positions and found them empty. While the 2-504 was patting themselves on their backs for having stopped a major attack in their sector, the 3-504 further away from them was still in the thick of the fight.

****

1st Ground Attack Wing
Medina Airport

Major Nikolai Kamanin taxied his Su-25 Grach or Frogfoot towards the end of runway 18. This plan the Iraqis had come up with was utter lunacy. Then again, it just might work. God help them if it didn't.

Reaching the end of the taxi ramp, he waited for the other Su-25 to power up his engines and get airborne. That flight of four Su-25s was being led by an Iraqi colonel—a pilot Major Kamanin had actually grown to respect. He was a damn good pilot. Not that Kamanin would tell him that to his face. He was still a camel driver in Kamanin's eyes.

The Iraqi flight took off, their engines pushing them down the runway until they had enough lift to get airborne. Giving his own aircraft some juice, Kamanin moved into position. When his aircraft made its turn to get on the runway, he saw a lot of soldiers preparing a couple of SA-6 SAM systems. Other soldiers were preparing many other types of SAMs and AA guns around the air base. Most of these systems had arrived over the last couple of days. The Iraqis were doing their best to turn the airport into a forward air base to support their major ground campaign against the Americans. If they succeeded in the next couple of days, they just might be able to push the Americans clear out of Saudi.

Facing the runway, Kamanin looked at his wingman, a fellow Russian and veteran of the Afghan war. He saluted, letting Kamanin know he was ready. Returning the salute, Kamanin pushed his throttle forward, giving the engines more power. It didn't take long for his aircraft to get airborne. Even being fully laden down with ordnance, his two powerful Soyuz/Tumansky R-195 turbojet engines were more than enough to get him into the air.

He turned his aircraft towards the east, wanting to get situated first before they began their attack run on the Americans. The air base was less than forty kilometers from the Americans. Closer in other areas. Last night, the Su-25s had flown here from Riyadh with nothing more than drop tanks. They'd landed in the wee hours of the morning, and the fuel tanks were swapped out for munitions. Once loaded up, they were refueled and put right back into the air. They didn't want the Americans to realize they'd moved a squadron of Su-25s to the airport or they'd try to sortie some fighters of their own.

"Red One, Mohammed One. We are heading in. Good luck on your attack run," the Iraqi commander offered.

"Happy hunting, Mohammed One. We'll see you in an hour for tea," Kamanin replied.

"This is a crazy mission, Nikolai. We'll be lucky to get two missions in before the Americans catch on to what we're doing and send in waves of F-15s or those Tomcats to come shoot us down," his wingman said over their private channel.

"Shhh. You are not wrong, but let's not attract their attention with our chatter. You and I are going to pay that cluster of paratroopers on the ridge west of Medina a visit. I also want to sweep in behind that ridge and see what kind of units we can find back there."

The two of them turned their aircraft and headed towards the American lines. Even from their altitude and distance, they could see the battle unfolding below. It truly was an enormous battle. Maybe the Iraqis had been right to move their squadron this close to the front lines. If they could defeat the Americans here, they could push them out of Saudi Arabia.

Slung under each side of their wings was a single S-13 rocket pod, which carried five 122mm unguided fragmentation rockets. Next to that pod sat two S-8 pods. These carried a total of twenty 80mm fragmentation rockets. Kamanin's aircraft could hit the Americans with eighty 80mm rockets and ten 122mm rockets, thoroughly wrecking any kind of defensive fortification they had built.

Approaching the American lines, Kamanin was surprised his aircraft hadn't been painted by any ground radars yet. He realized this was likely because the Americans hadn't realized they had enemy fighters in the area just yet. Well, that was about to change.

"Follow me in. We're going to hit that ridge those Iraqi soldiers look to be preparing to attack. Let's hit them with two rocket pods, then we'll circle around to find another target," Kamanin said over their private channel.

His aircraft was currently sitting around twelve thousand feet—still pretty high up. Once he'd lined up on the ridge, he put the aircraft into a steep dive. The people on the ground looked like little ants or miniature people. The American side was shooting down the hill into the Iraqi side, who looked to be gearing up for a charge. They were starting to mass their numbers.

Then the Americans on the ground must have noticed him. His RWR started blaring. His aircraft was being painted by some sort of American radar. With his altitude now around twenty-five hundred feet, he depressed the trigger, firing off a volley of forty 80mm rockets across the American positions before he pulled up and began dispensing flares.

A warning alarm let him know at least one missile had been fired at him. The missile went for one of his flares and exploded harmlessly behind him—a not-so-subtle reminder of how quickly his life could be snuffed out.

Tracer fire started zipping around him. He felt a few rounds stitch his aircraft somewhere as he jinked and then gave the plane more throttle

361

to put some distance between himself and whatever was shooting at him. He instinctively fired a couple more flares and banked hard to the left, then dove. Unbeknownst to him, another missile had been fired at him. It connected with one of his flares and blew up.

Damn, that was close. These Americans know how to use their AA weapons a lot better than the Saudis.

Looking around for another target of opportunity, he spotted another cluster of Americans in some bunkers, foxholes, and other defensive positions. Turning his plane towards them, he switched over to his 122mm rocket pods. He angled his aircraft down just long enough to line up on their positions and release both rocket pods. Pulling up on the plane, he gave the engines more juice and now looked behind the ridgeline the Americans were held up on.

Turning to his right, he saw his wingman was still sticking to him tightly. Kamanin didn't bother looking back to see if his rockets had hit. It didn't matter. He wasn't going back there again. All he cared about was spotting the Americans and hammering them with some rockets, then looking for the next position to hammer. He knew if he hit enough of their positions, he'd create some holes the Iraqi infantry could hopefully exploit.

"Hey, boss. If I'm not mistaken, that looks like a lot of artillery. Perhaps we should pay them some love," his wingman called out.

Holy cow. That has to be a full battery of artillery. That is just too juicy of a target.

Turning his aircraft towards them, he saw the soldiers on the ground starting to scatter. Some raised their rifles and tried to fire at him. It was useless, as his aircraft was essentially a flying tank. Unless they had a 30mm cannon, they weren't going to harm him.

Flipping a switch to his final two rocket pods, he lined the battery of howitzers up and started firing rockets. He made sure to plaster the entire area as good as he could. Between him and his wingman, they'd hit the place with some eighty 80mm rockets. They saw a lot of secondary explosions intermixed with a lot of thick black smoke. They'd obviously hit something good. The question now was, how long would the battery be down? How many of their howitzers survived?

"OK, it's time to head home. Let's hope they will let us return to Riyadh before the American fighters show up," Kamanin said.

When they reached the airport, they saw the soldiers on the ground had gotten a lot more of the AA guns set up. That was good, but the SAMs were the real threat to the American aircraft. Kamanin also saw that the squadron of Hinds appeared to have arrived on the far side of the airport. They were being readied as well.

Once his aircraft was on the ground, he parked it in its designated spot. While he was climbing out of the plane, the ground crew was already running towards him. They had a set of fresh, fully loaded up rocket pods they were going to swap out his empty ones for. A couple of maintenance folks also started looking at the couple of bullet holes he'd taken, checking to see if anything important had been damaged.

When he walked over to look at the damage, it was clear he'd taken a few 20mm rounds. "Did they hit anything major?"

The mechanic looked at him. "You tell us, sir. How did she handle?"

Shrugging, Kamanin replied, "I was a bit busy dodging missiles and bullets and firing rockets to really notice. She got me back home."

The mechanic laughed. "OK, no worries, sir. We'll pull the panels off real quick and check it out. If it looks good, we'll put a temporary patch over it so you can get back in the air. Last we heard, this will be your last mission before they fly you guys back out of here."

Kamanin grunted at the news. It was the first he'd heard. Patting the mechanics on the shoulders, he headed into the building to find out what the Iraqis wanted them to bomb next.
****

Colonel Kinser held the radio hand receiver to his head as he listened to the report coming in from one of his battalion commanders. Judging by the panicked tone in Sabine's voice, things along his portion of the lines were not going well. "Sir, we have two columns of tanks and assorted armored vehicles hitting our front. One along Highway 340, the other along Highway 60, just like we talked about during the division brief with General Buckner."

Lieutenant Colonel Hank Sabine paused for a moment as he was receiving more information on his end. The sound of machine-gun fire and explosions could be heard over the radio. "Sir, both columns are being led by T-72s, lots of them. The infantry's also dismounted. They've moved on the roads and are now attempting to flank our positions while the tanks and the BMPs on the roads provide supporting fire with their main guns. Our TOWs took out a handful of vehicles, but more than a few of my guys have been taken out. Right now, in our current situation, my battalion is unable to withdraw to the alternate positions. The dismounted infantry has managed to get around our flanks. The brigade artillery is helping, but we need help with the tanks, sir."

Kinser had hoped they would be able to hold things together a bit longer before everything fell apart. *I can't have Sabine's unit getting surrounded and cut off from the rest of the battalion. He's got to break out of his current position and fall back with the rest of the brigade,* he thought. His mind was running a million miles an hour right now as he tried to figure out what he could do to help his battalion commander.

In the distance, Colonel Kinser heard the sounds of jet engines, followed by more explosions than he could count, all happening in a fast ripple sequence.

Holding the hand receiver tightly, Kinser shouted, "Hank, are you OK?"

There was a momentary pause. "Yes, sir, we just got hit by two Frogfoots coming in low and fast. I think my Vulcan may have gotten a piece of one. Sir, I need some help." Small-arms fire could be heard as well as the chatter of a machine gun, an M-60 or PKM.

"I understand, Copperhead Six," Colonel Kinser replied. Still holding the hand receiver, he turned to his assistant operations officer. "Get me General Buckner on the radio."

A few minutes later, Buckner came on the radio. Colonel Kinser didn't mince words. "Sir, we have a situation in 3-504 sector. Hank's receiving the main attack. It appears he's getting hit with too many tanks to handle. To compound the problem further, a pair of Frogfoots just plastered most of his lines with rockets. He's requesting a lot of medevac support. I'm going to move my reserves to his position, but we're going to need more help. Is there any way we can get some air or helicopter support? Hell, even more artillery support at this point would be a godsend."

"Joe, that's a negative on the arty support. I just got word a pair of Frogfoots laid a hurt on the division artillery. We just lost an entire battery, maybe more. As to air, I'll see where the tac air cover is and talk to Sheldon to see if his birds are up. Where do you need them most if I can get you some help?"

"Shit. They took out our artillery. Damn, this isn't good, sir, we needed that arty. Right now, I need whatever helo or tac air I can get along Highway 340 and 60 in the vicinity of Al Mufrihat. If we have a breakthrough, then they'll be in the vicinity of Al Furaysh."

"Roger. I'll get back to you," Buckner hurriedly replied and ended their call.

****

In the 3-504th sector, Lieutenant Colonel Hank Sabine was in a position to observe both engagement areas being with Charlie Company. What he saw was a commander's worst nightmare. His guys were in the middle of a fight to the death with a superior force and they were running out of ammo. His missile crews had laid a hurt on the Iraqi armor, destroying dozens upon dozens of tanks, infantry fighting vehicles, and armored personnel carriers. In the process, they'd chewed through their supply of TOW and Dragon missiles.

His paratroopers were now down to using their M72 Light Antitank Weapons or LAWs. The single-use 66mm rocket had an effective range of just two hundred meters, which meant his paras had to get close to their targets. They were also utterly ineffective against the Iraqi T-72s. The engineering platoons were using the M-203 FLASH, with devastating effect on the lighter, thin-skinned BTR-70s and BTR-80s. The more Sabine looked at what was going on in front of his battalion's position, the more he realized the Iraqis were likely to break through his lines any moment.

"Where's my mortars!" Sabine yelled to one of his staff NCOs.

"They're out of ammo, sir. Nothing more they can do right now other than join the fight with their rifles," the sergeant replied.

Sabine could see a look of concern on the man's face. He knew they were likely to get steamrolled soon.

Just as Sabine didn't think things could get much worse, he heard a terrible new sound. The unmistakable sound of a ZSU-23-4 entering the fray as they raked his company's lines with 23mm fire. The large-caliber slugs ripped one of his machine-gun positions apart. That gun position had been keeping the Iraqi soldiers at bay, preventing them from bum-rushing their lines. Once it had been silenced, a group of twenty or thirty Iraqis leapt up and ran towards the newly created hole in his lines.

A couple of NCOs saw the problem and were already on it. One of the sergeants had rallied a squad of soldiers to follow him as they tried to fill the gap.

Sabine got back on the radio to let Colonel Kinser know his position was starting to collapse. Once they were forced to fall back, the Iraqi advance on Al Mufrihat would be unstoppable. Looking down at his map, he tried to figure out how he could slow the enemy advance. At this point, there was only so much his boys could do.

Then he heard another new noise from somewhere overhead. He caught a glimpse of something zipping right over his head, making a swooshing noise, followed by an explosion.

The ZSU-23-4 truck that was tearing his lines apart was blown to pieces.

SWOOSH.

A second missile passed over his head and a tank blew apart, its turret somersaulting through the air. Suddenly the air was filled with missiles slamming into the armored vehicles. Looking over his shoulder, Sabine could see where the missiles were coming from, but he couldn't see what was shooting at them.

Then his peripheral vision caught some movement behind and to the left of him. He caught a glimpse of a OH-58 Kiowa helicopter. The observation helicopter had mast-mounted sight (MMS), which resembled a beach ball perched above the rotor system. This ball-looking device was feeding targeting data to a group of AH-64D Apache helicopters on either side of the Kiowa. As the scout helicopter found the Apaches' targets, they cut loose a missile.

With each Apache carrying sixteen Hellfire missiles, the eight helicopters were ripping the Iraqi attack apart. When they'd expended their missiles, the helicopters rose up in altitude and started using their 20mm chain guns. They packed twelve hundred rounds of ammo for the chin-mounted weapon. The gun was shredding the Iraqi infantry apart just as they were about to overrun the paratroopers' final positions.

The remaining tanks and armored vehicles started pulling back to find cover, or at least get out of the killing field of the enemy. Meanwhile, the Apaches continued to use their chin guns to go after the

366

Iraqi infantry and light-skinned vehicles, making sure they didn't leave any pockets of survivors alive. The remaining soldiers were retreating, exactly what the pilots had hoped would happen.

When Sabine was a young officer, he'd served two combat tours in Vietnam towards the tail end of the war. What he saw strewn about Alpha and Bravo Companies' lines and the roads leading towards them was unlike anything he'd seen in his life. The sheer carnage that had been unleashed on both sides was appalling. It made him want to throw up, but he knew he needed to be strong for his men. They were looking up to him. What concerned him most was that this was just round one. The first attempt by the enemy to root them out. They hadn't traveled across hundreds of miles of desert to give up after one attack. They'd be back. He just wasn't sure his battalion could do anything to stop them.

Chapter Forty-Six
Battle of Wadi Reem

21 August 1990
2nd Brigade, 82nd Airborne
Wadi Reem, Saudi Arabia

During the last two days of traveling across the brigade's sector, Colonel Allen could feel the tension, fear, and excitement among his troopers for the coming battle. His paratroopers were ready—they were eager to get this fight going.

Walking the company lines, Allen saw his soldiers constantly working on improving their fighting positions. Some were digging down, while others were improving the front or top protection of their machine-gun bunkers. They knew this fight was going to be a slug match. They weren't going on the offensive. The enemy was coming at them, and they were going to do so in numbers they couldn't even fathom.

What sucked about the terrain they were having to fight on was the soil and type of ground they had to work with. In most places, the ground was too hard to dig down more than a couple of feet. This meant there was a lot more emphasis on using sandbags to compensate. Each soldier and squad did the best they could with the cards they'd been dealt. The one major thing they had on their side was elevation. The enemy would have to assault their positions uphill. In addition to establishing their range cards for the crew-served weapons, they made sure to employ their Claymore antipersonnel mines properly.

A Claymore is a remote-command-detonated antipersonnel mine. When it's fired, it acts like a shotgun, blasting some seven hundred eighth-inch steel balls up to fifty meters in front of it. These were considered a last-ditch weapon you fired when your position was about to be overrun. The only thing lacking was rolls of barbed and concertina wire. There just couldn't get any of it when they needed it.
****

During the last few days, the volume of civilian traffic fleeing Medina was extraordinary. The civilians knew the Iraqis were coming, and they wanted nothing to do with them. Each vehicle passing through their lines was thoroughly checked to make sure they weren't inadvertently letting small elements of Iraqi soldiers from slipping into their rear area. Just the other day they'd caught several vehicles with a bunch of men masquerading as women. Had he not had a cluster of female MPs to check them out, these would-be Iraqi soldiers might have slipped past them and gotten into his rear area.

Having finally made some time to relax, Colonel Allen had been asleep for less than two hours when someone or something shook his foot.

"Colonel, Colonel, wake up," Captain Blumberg declared loudly.

Allen was a light sleeper and had dropped off as soon as he'd lain down. It was a policy in the brigade that leaders would only be awoken when it was something important. Leaders tended to push themselves into sleep deprivation, which could lead to stupid mistakes. Everyone, leaders and soldiers, needed sleep if they were going to think clearly.

"What is it, Captain? I'm awake," Allen said grumpily as he sat up and tossed his poncho liner off.

Allen didn't take advantage of his rank. He maintained the same sleep conditions as his soldiers. He ate the same chow, slept in the same foxholes, and used the same shitty shower stations they did. He needed to know the physical condition of his soldiers before he sent them into a tough mission, and he couldn't know that if he didn't live like they did.

"Sir, the ground surveillance radar team has picked up movement coming down the road from Medina. We think it might be a reconnaissance element from the 5th Division," Captain Blumberg said as he handed a steaming cup of coffee to the colonel. "1st Brigade lit up an Iraqi BTR-70 recon vehicle about an hour ago. They were apparently trying to scout Highway 340."

"OK, be sure that the battalions understand they need to let the reconnaissance element pass through the area and not engage them. We want the Iraqis to feel safe in sending their units through this sector so they fall into our ambush. Got it?"

Captain Blumberg nodded. He scribbled something down on his paper to handle it momentarily.

"Have we gotten any indications of the Iraqis deploying any biological or chemical weapons?"

369

The thought of WMD being released on them was the nightmare scenario no soldier wanted to face. Having to fight while weighed down in full MOPP gear and a gas mask was incredibly hard.

Blumberg shook his head. "No, sir. Our SIGINT guys at G2 said they've detected no chatter from the Iraqis about moving any of that stuff out of Iraq. According to the latest satellite and U-2 surveillance flights, the equipment and units responsible for deploying the rockets and artillery shells filled with the nasty stuff are still at their bases in Iraq. It's their assessment that the Iraqis aren't looking to employ any WMD, at least not at this point."

Allen nodded. "Makes sense. Why would they? They believe they're winning. No reason to turn the world against you when you're winning through conventional means. OK, I'll be in the TOC as soon as I drain my bladder. Have the FIST team meet me there. I want to be sure our artillery team is dialed in and ready to go. Also, make sure Captain Harrison from 21st Special Tactics Squadron is there as well. I suspect we'll see some Iraqi CAS and Hinds coming at us today."

"Yes, sir," Captain Blumberg said before departing and heading to the TOC.

****

325th Infantry Regiment

"Sarge, we have company," PFC German said as he looked through the night vision sight on the TOW weapons system. The thermal images clearly showed the heat signatures of several vehicles approaching.

German had recently been assigned gunner for the system but had never fired a live round. In training, they'd fired on a simulator—live missiles were expensive. The instructors had told them that the simulator was so good that they almost wouldn't be able to tell the difference. That was reassuring, but nothing substituted for the real thing.

PFC German had been in the Army for almost four years. Normally he'd be a specialist looking at possible promotion to sergeant, but he'd had a slight altercation with the MPs back at Fort Bragg. On more than one occasion, he'd managed to get busted down to PFC. The unit first sergeant had told him to just put Velcro under his rank because he put it on and took it off just as fast.

German's position was on the south side of Wadi Reem, looking right up the road coming from Medina. His range of vision with the TOW's optics was roughly five klicks. His weapon could reach out three klicks.

Sergeant Daily, his squad leader, crawled over to German and the weapon. "Whatcha got?" Daily asked.

"Looks to be a column of tanks and troop carriers. These aren't like that bunch we let roll through earlier. Those were recon dudes. These are heavies. I think this might be the start of the main body," German said.

"Let me have a look," Sergeant Daily said. German moved out from the weapon and let Daily get behind it to look through the optics. After he studied the column for a few moments, Daily said, "You just might be right. I'm starting to see more vehicles show up."

Daily eased back and reached for the TA-1 field phone. Cranking the handle, he waited for someone in the company TOC to answer.

"Sir, Sergeant Daily here. We have visitors. At least a company-size force of tanks and fighting vehicles approaching from Medina," he told the company commander.

"Roger, sir, we'll wait for it to start. Out."

"What'd he say?"

"He says to wait until the artillery starts landing. Then we're to join the fray and start taking those tanks out."

The two assistant TOW operators were listening in. When the time came, it'd be their jobs to change out the spent missile case with a fresh one so German could find and shoot another tank.

"Remember, German, you get a better kill on the side of a tank than on the front. From what we've been told, the Iraqis are running T-72s. What we don't know is if they're equipped with reactive armor. If they are, then that'll make it a lot hard to kill 'em. We don't necessarily blow the tank up. Hitting the side hull or at least taking out a tread and boogie wheel will disable them. Also, if you see an air-defense weapon, nail it. Those are to be prioritized even above tanks."

Five minutes later, at precisely 0437, the first artillery rounds sailed over their heads. It sounded like a freight train rushing through the air, making its own unique whooshing or screaming noise before the high-explosive projectile exploded in spectacular fashion among the enemy positions. The initial volley was only the 105 rounds. These were set for airburst to force the tank and armor commanders to button up, which would greatly reduce their visibility and impede their ability to react to what was coming next. The 105s were quickly followed by the heavier 155s, which were set to ground burst.

Fifteen shells exploded together at about two hundred feet above the Iraqi formation. The shrapnel from these rounds sheared off antennas, disabling communications in the tank formation. It also killed any tank commander or leader that wasn't buttoned up. Almost immediately from the north side of the wadi, the 1-325 Battalion's TOWs opened fire at their maximum range.

"Start picking your targets, German, and engage," Sergeant Daily shouted over the roar of the battle.

German fired at a tank he'd been tracking for a little while. Once the missile had ignited, he kept the targeting reticle aimed at the tank, guiding the missile right to it.

The TOW fired at a range of three thousand meters, which was a major factor considering that the T-72 weapon had an effective range of about eighteen hundred meters when firing the tungsten-core rounds. The 125mm gun on the tank could fire much faster than the TOW, but the TOW's accuracy couldn't be matched. At the three-thousand-meter range, it took the TOW missile about ten seconds to reach its target. In that ten seconds, the best the target could hope for was that they could move behind something or get out of sight before the missile impacted. German's target was not that fortunate, especially as he was in an elevated position, looking down on the open desert floor.

"Reload!" Sergeant Daily yelled as another round was inserted into the launcher.

"Target," German shouted excitedly. He'd just blown up his first-ever tank.

"Fire," Daily commanded, and another round exploded from the launcher.

From across the platoon in the four locations, missiles were streaking towards the armor formations. From four other locations, the other platoons of the company joined the action, sending their own missiles at the Iraqis. A total of twenty TOW launchers on the south side of the wadi were tearing into the Iraqi armor formations, with devastating effect on the enemy.

The Iraqi vehicles tried deploying smokescreens in hopes of throwing the TOW missiles off and giving themselves some sort of concealing cover as they pressed home their attack. Unbeknownst to the Iraqis, the TOW system was equipped with a thermal optical system capable of seeing the heat signature of the enemy vehicles. The vehicles stood out as a red glow in the gunners' sight given the heat difference at this early hour of the day.

As the Iraqi tanks were being cut down, the missile operators turned their attention to the BMPs and the BTR-70s and BTR-80s rushing the Iraqi infantry into the battle. These were considered the real threats to the paratroopers, as they contained infantry soldiers that could dismount and attack on foot. Once the infantry dismounted, then the close-in fighting would begin.

With so many wrecked and burning tanks and armored vehicles, the paratroopers heaved a sigh of relief. They'd succeeded in blunting the enemy advance. Now the battle would transition to an infantry fight—a fight that highly favored the Iraqis given their sheer numbers. This next part of the battle would get down and dirty as it became more personal.

****

Colonel Allen had moved to the sounds of the guns and was in a position to observe the events firsthand as they unfolded. The eastern sky was starting to get light, and he knew once the sun was up, the intensity of the battle would increase as the Hind-D helicopters and Su-25 Frogfoots started to show up. The enemy aircraft was a major concern of his.

His brigade had air-defense systems for incoming missiles and low-altitude aircraft, but they weren't sufficient to handle aircraft flying through canyons and hills. The Stinger missile system was OK but wasn't sufficient in quantity or capability compared to the air-defense systems the Iraqi Army had. His TOWs had taken out a couple of ZSU-23-4 weapons systems, but several more were on the battlefield, and they were accompanied by SA-9 Gaskins and SA-6 system further in the formation. Every gunner knew they were priority targets, even more so than the T-72s.

Allen watched as the first element of the Iraqi attack stopped and assumed hasty defensive positions. They were on the shoulders of the north passage into Wadi Reem and the south pass along the highway. The question was, which would the Iraqi commander attempt to breach through? When another formation of tanks showed up, Allen had his answer. They were going to move across the open ground and straight for the northern pass.

That makes sense. It's the larger of the openings, with more maneuver room than sticking to the highway. They'll break through the 1-325th at that point and roll right into the kill zone.

Colonel Allen turned to his engineering officer. "George, lay in the FASCAM minefield." Next, he turned to his FIST officer. "Dick, have the 155s lay in the minefield." The fire support officer or FISCO was the artillery's liaison officer embedded either with the tactical unit or at the brigade headquarters. The FISCO understood how to best use the artillery at their disposal and made sure the commanders did as well.

"Yes, sir!" the engineer replied as he grabbed for the field phone to send the word down. His crews had spent the last three days placing MOPM FASCAM mines along Highway 15 to the south of Wadi Reem. Now they'd activate those mines. The infantry companies had also been instructed on how to activate their respective suitcase minefields they'd deployed with. Each suitcase contained thirty-five antipersonnel mines and four antitank mines.

The 155mm Corps artillery would fire and place a brigade designated minefield in the kill zone in front of Al Ghzlan, effectively closing off the west end of Wadi Reem. In the haste to get ammunition to Egypt and Saudi Arabia, the logistic planners had overlooked deploying the Air Force CBU-89/B air-delivered mines in the initial force package. This entire responsibility had fallen on the shoulders of the artillery and the engineers for the time being.

Colonel Allen watched the Iraqi units go to work. A couple of their own engineering units had opened up some of the shoulder areas along the highway, creating a passage for the tanks and other armored vehicles to move down into Wadi Reem—just as his own engineers and experts had said they would.

When the first scout vehicles filtered into Wadi Reem, Allen saw his tactical air controller party rep radioing in for an air strike. The Air Force was going to provide his brigade with A-10 support while the division aviation unit provided their Apache gunship support to the brigades to the north of him.

Right on cue, as the Iraqi units moved more units into Wadi Reem and the different valleys and offshoots they could travel down, Allen's few units down there were making a big show of retreating. This was all part of their grand plan; they wanted the Iraqis to think they had the Americans on the ropes so they'd press home their attack, both spreading their forces out and thinning out their air-defense units' ability to be in all places at once.

For the next twenty minutes, Colonel Allen and some of his staff sat in their concealed perched position and observed what the Iraqis were doing through telescopic lenses. It wouldn't be long now until the Air Force arrived to begin drawing out the Iraqi SAMs. Once they were satisfied they'd gotten the ones they could, the A-10s would swoop in and massacre the enemy tanks.

"Sir, the Air Force is starting their attacks," one of his staff officers told him.

Flashes of light leapt from launchers on the ground as missiles took to the air, streaking after the fighters. A squadron of F-4 Phantoms from Germany had arrived the other day in Egypt. The Phantoms were resuming an old role they had played in Vietnam—drawing out enemy SAMs and then engaging them with their AGM HARM missiles.

Explosions rocked the area around the highway and further behind the Iraqi lines. Allen knew that was likely some of the SAMs exploding. The predawn sky then lit up with AA and Triple-A tracer fire. The Iraqis must have brought in some towed gun support to protect their units.

Somewhere high above them, the sounds of jet engines could be heard. While they couldn't see exactly what was going on as it was still somewhat dark, they knew the Iraqis must have sent some fighters in their direction. Chances were the Phantoms or maybe the Navy Tomcats were engaging them.

As the token American units fought a fighting retreat, the Iraqis pressed home their advantage, apparently oblivious to the trap they were rushing right into.

Then the American A-10 Warthogs made their grand appearance. The first pair of them swooped in from the east, placing them in the sun as it rose above the ridges, blinding the defenders. Still having some

375

range between themselves and the Iraqis, the pair of Warthogs unleashed their six AGM-65 Mavericks at the T-72s. The air-to-ground missiles were the perfect antitank missile to use against the T-72, even if it had reactive armor on it. The precision-guided missile allowed the A-10s to wipe out twelve T-72s in their first pass. On the second pass, they made use of their 30mm GAU-8/A Avenger rotary cannon, shredding additional tanks and armored vehicles. The gun made a unique ripping sound when it was fired—the unmistakable sound of American firepower during a battle.

The flight of three Warthogs was thoroughly tearing the enemy apart. Then a missile streaked down from a higher altitude and rapidly closed the gap on two of them. Both aircraft started spitting out flares and taking evasive maneuvers. The missile went for one of the flares and detonated harmlessly behind the two planes. At this point, the six Warthogs were scattering to the four corners. They were trying to get away from whatever was hunting.

Colonel Allen was fascinated—he'd never seen an aerial battle take place like this, the way the fighters danced around in the sky while they dispensed flares and chaff canisters and missiles flew around them.

Then a lone MiG-23 Flogger swooped in from higher altitude. It had set its sights on one of the Warthogs as it closed the gap between them. It fired off another missile, which closed the distance on the Warthog, leaving it no time to react. The right engine of the plane exploded in flame. The A-10 seemed to have stabilized itself and was able to stay aloft. Allen was sure this must have ticked the MiG pilot off as he probably thought he had a kill and wanted to go after another plane. The pilot must have switched over to his guns as he'd really gotten in close to the crippled American plane.

The space around the Warthog filled with 23mm tracer rounds. A string of them tore into the tail section of the A-10 and its remaining engine. Moments later, the pilot must have decided he'd had enough. He ejected in a position that would eventually land him over Allen's men.

The MiG pilot had already pulled away and started chasing down another A-10. Two of the Warthogs had circled around and fired their own nose cannons at him. The MiG jinked to the right just as a streak of bullets flew right where he would have been. The Iraqi pilot who had just used his guns on the other plane fired off a short burst from his own guns.

The 23mm rounds from the Iraqi MiG slammed into the cockpit and front section of the Warthog flying right at him. The Iraqi plane pulled up and applied speed while the American plane appeared to lose control and cartwheeled into the ground below. When the Iraqi pilot had turned around, three of the A-10s had already left the battlespace. One A-10 had remained, determined to take this MiG out. He somehow managed to get a lock on him with his Sidewinder missile and fired. Just as the Sidewinder left the wing of the A-10, the MiG fired two missiles at the A-10.

The Sidewinder connected with the MiG, forcing the pilot to eject. Then the pilot flying the Warthog ejected when both missiles from the MiG scored hits. Both pilots were now descending to the ground below.

"Damn, sir. That was a hell of an aerial battle," commented one of Allen's staff officers.

"Yeah, no joke. See if you can find out who that particular A-10 pilot is. He did a hell of a job battling that MiG. I'd like to make sure he gets some sort of medal for that."

"Sir, it looks like another battalion, maybe two, of mechanized infantry have entered Wadi Reem. They look to be heading right for our forces," the same staff officer informed him.

"Send a message to the battalion commanders. They need to make sure their guys continue to hold fire. They cannot spring our trap until the Iraqis are fully inside the kill box," Allen ordered forcefully.

"Yes, sir!"

The battle continued to unfold for another thirty minutes. The Iraqis eventually ran into the primary American defensive lines. When this happened, the battalions unleashed their TOWs. The wire-guided antitank missiles swooped down from their elevated positions and blew apart many of the remaining T-72s and BMPs. The Iraqi soldiers inside the BTRs started disgorging from their armored chariots. The infantry soldiers engaged with AK-47s and PKM machine guns at his soldiers' positions. It didn't take long for RPGs and grenades to be introduced into the fight.

Artillery rounds were impacting along the ridgeline and the tops of the ridges from which the American positions had finally launched their ambush. The Iraqi 155mm rounds were ripping the area apart. The infantry below commenced to maneuver to engage the paratroopers while under the cover of the artillery. While the Iraqis appeared to be making their first major push, Iraqi ground-attack planes entered the fray.

"Those Frogfooters have arrived. Where's my fighter cover!" shouted Colonel Allen as he looked at Captain Harrison, the Air Force TACP assigned to his brigade.

"I'm already on it, sir. We've got two F-16s inbound right now. They're five mikes out," the TACP replied while holding a hand receiver to his shoulder.

Allen nodded at the news. Maybe when the Air Force had learned they'd lost three A-10s to a single MiG, they'd decided to vector some fighters his way. In any case, he was glad they would be here soon.

The first Su-25 swooped down like a German Stuka pilot as he unleashed a torrent of 80mm rockets across the bunkers, machine-gun positions, and foxholes that dotted the ridgelines. When the first Frogfooter pulled away to gain some altitude, one of his soldiers must have seen this as his opportunity. A single missile streaked up from the American lines and gave a quick chase after the Iraqi pilot. The missile exploded near the rear left engine, causing a short burst of flame and black smoke. The Iraqi plane didn't blow apart and it didn't crash. Like its American cousin, the A-10 Warthog, it shrugged off the hit, having the ability to operate with just a single engine. The Iraqi plane did turn and head away from the battlespace, though, so at least it wouldn't hit them with more rockets.

That, of course, didn't discourage the other Su-25s. They swooped in, unleashing their own barrage of rockets. One of them made a decent strafing run across the American lines. More Iraqi soldiers joined the fray as they assaulted up the hill to get at the paratroopers. Fresh T-72s, BMPs, and BTRs continued to head towards this part of the fighting. They were acting like sharks when they smelled blood in the water.

When the Iraqi planes appeared to be coming in for a third pass on the American lines, one of the Frogfooters exploded in spectacular fashion. The pilot never saw what hit him. The fiery wreckage of the plane just fell to the ground.

An F-16 Fight Falcon zipped across the American lines as if announcing to the soldiers below that help had arrived. The remaining Su-25s peeled off from their attacks and dropped to the deck while lighting up their afterburners. They were going to try and put some distance between themselves and the scene of the crime as they flew back to their base.

Continuing to observe the battle, Colonel Allen figured they'd inflicted close to seventy percent casualties on the lead Iraqi brigade, the one that had charged forward and was currently engaged against his guys. The second Iraqi brigade looked like it had taken between thirty percent and forty percent casualties. The third and final brigade of the Iraqi division was pushing forward to support their comrades in their own attack.

It had finally come time to close the back door on this ambush they'd laid for this Iraqi division. Colonel Allen ordered his battalion on the ridge to fall back to their secondary positions. This would make the Iraqis believe they'd just broken through, leading the second brigade to dismount their infantry and spur on the third brigade to push around the wreckage of the first two. While this was happening, a vehicle and antipersonnel minefield was being laid behind them.

In addition to the minefield, elements from the 3rd of the 73rd Cavalry would help to close the gate behind them with their platoon of M551 Sheridans. They were backed up by the company team from the 24th Infantry Division. Once the gate was fully closed, the remaining two battalions of Allen's brigade would finally be unleashed, as would the rest of the division's artillery and the remaining A-10 Warthogs. It would now be a matter of how fast they could wipe the trapped division before help could arrive.

****

As the artillery fire began to hit its peak, Captain Poggi made the call to his unit. "All Panthers elements, this is Panther Six. Engage. Repeat, engage."

Turning his attention to his own tank, he called, "Gunner, Sabot. Two tanks, near tank first!"

Staff Sergeant Hernandez responded, "Identified!"

"Up!" said Specialist Dawson, the tank's loader.

"Fire!" Captain Poggi yelled.

Staff Sergeant Hernandez squeezed the trigger, and the main gun recoiled with a deafening explosion. Any dust that had settled was now airborne as the tank rocked when the main gun fired.

Staff Sergeant Hernandez was already aligning the gun for the second tank.

"Second tank identified!" Staff Sergeant Hernandez shouted as he had done so often in training.

Specialist Dawson immediately indicated, "Up!" having reloaded the main gun.

"Fire!" Captain Poggi commanded, and the process repeated itself.

All four M1 tanks were engaging the Iraqi rear-echelon units as quickly as they could. They were going to surprise the hell out of the Iraqi units as they busted through their rear area.
****

Lieutenant Kincade, the platoon leader for the Bradleys, had done his homework. When he'd examined the firing positions they would move into on the order to engage, he had worked out range fans for each vehicle. All were assigned overlapping sectors of fire and given the priority of targets for both the TOWs and the 25mm Bushmasters. The Bushmasters had a mix of ammunition, but mostly the M791 APDS-T[12], which could take out anything but the T-72.

The question was how much ammo each vehicle had. A total of nine hundred rounds were in each vehicle. The main gun, the 25mm chain gun, had a maximum rate of fire of three hundred rounds a minute. Knowing this limiting factor, Kincade told his vehicle commanders to set the gun's cyclic rate of fire to one hundred rounds per minute and to use controlled bursts when they did use the guns.

When a Bradley's main guns were dry, the reload time and process weren't exactly conducive during a battle. It required them to turn the turret in a particular position and unfasten a few things inside the vehicle to get at the ammunition box for the gun—something the vehicle planners clearly hadn't taken into consideration when they'd designed this beast. The platoon's gunners were well trained and knew it only took

---

[12] Armor Piercing Discarding Sabot with Tracer.

a couple of rounds to knock out a soft-skinned target like an air-defense weapon or a BTR-70.

When Lieutenant Kincade received the command to engage, he switched radios. "All Dog Breath elements, move out and engage. I want some scalps on the table for dinner tonight."

On that command, the four Bradley fighting vehicles, which had been situated on the north side of the wadi, left their concealed positions behind the small hills and moved the two hundred meters to their previously planned and prepared firing positions.

As Lieutenant Kincade's vehicle moved forward into position, he was overwhelmed at the number of targets appearing in front of them. His gunner didn't hesitate in the least. This was like a wet dream for a gun crew.

The first target his gunner found was a division level-one priority target. A damn ZSU-23-4 that was sitting station on the right flank of a cluster of thin-skinned BTRs and ash-and-trash vehicles.

No sooner had his gunner turned the ZSU into a flaming wreck than Lieutenant Kincade released his first TOW missile. He'd found a T-72 that had paused its advance and was in the process of rotating its turret to engage one of his Bradleys. Ten seconds later, the turret of that tank was doing somersaults through the air from the impact of the missile detonating against the side of the tanks.

In a T-72, the tank's ammunition was kept in a rotating jacket of sorts along the chassis and the turret. This allowed the autoloader to cycle in a new round after each shot or shift to a different section in the belt depending on the type of round the commander wanted to fire. This system meant the ammunition was left completely exposed to whatever happened in the turret, often resulting in it exploding or cooking off from the slightest of hits.

The defilade positions the Bradleys were firing from were well within range of the highway the Iraqis had been using to rush their forces forward. This gave Kincade's vehicles an exceptional field of fire from which to tear the enemy force apart before they'd have to withdraw to their next position. From their hide positions, they also had a good view into the southern approach to the highway and the backs of the enemy units assaulting the paratroopers right now.

381

Kincade had his Bradley gunners concentrating their fire on enemy air-defense systems as they found them, using the M242 Bushmaster 25mm chain gun. They'd also use the main guns on the BMPs, BTR-70s, and BTR-80s. For everything else, they'd wait and use their crew-served weapons. Kincade made sure his vehicle commanders knew to save the TOWs for the tanks.

Watching the tank rounds crisscross the distance between the two forces, Lieutenant Kincade couldn't believe how effective the depleted uranium rounds of the M1 tanks were. They just devoured the T-72s, causing massive internal explosions with each hit. The M1s were taking advantage of their extended range over the T-72s as much as possible. Still, some of the T-72s had gotten within range and were sending rounds at the Americans. When they did score a hit against an Abrams, the round would ricochet right off. Either they were too far away or they just couldn't muster the necessary kinetic energy to punch through the Chobham armor of the Abrams.

The combination of the ground-mounted TOWs of the infantry and the M1 tanks with supporting Bradleys was brutally mauling the Iraqi formations, and they hadn't even wandered into the minefields the engineers had left for them. In the first ten minutes of the brigade's ambush, more than half of the seventy-eight tanks in the Iraqi division were smoldering ruins. It was quickly becoming a turkey shoot of what was left.

****

Captain Blumberg practically jumped out of his seat as he was talking on the radio. He grabbed for his gas mask like his life depended on it. The others in the brigade TOC took notice and started grabbing for theirs without needing to be told.

With the damn thing on his face, he turned to look at Colonel Allen. "Sir, 2-325 just reported a chemical attack. He believes it's mustard gas."

Colonel Allen grabbed for his own mask and put it on. He hated wearing it, but being uncomfortable was better than being dead.

Fucking G2. Way to blow that intelligence, Allen thought angrily to himself. He was going to chew their asses out when this was all said and done. *How did they miss the deployment of the WMD from the Iraqi bases? They're under continuous surveillance.*

382

"Notify the battalions, but let the commanders decide if they need to go to MOPP 4. The wind is blowing towards the west, so that'll carry it away from most of our positions. Notify division, as they may get some residual, and notify the 8th Mech."

Allen continued to watch the engagement areas, concerned about a breakthrough along Highway 15. *If we only had more artillery—but we don't. I still can't believe those Frogfooters damn near wiped out the corps artillery*, he thought as he surveyed the situation.

The 71st Tactical Fighter Squadron was doing their best to keep those Iraqi Frogfooters off his soldiers. But damn if that South African artillery the Iraqis were using wasn't becoming an even bigger problem than the fighters. The rolling artillery barrages were taking a toll on his positions. Allen was on the radio with the squadron commander for the A-10s and the F-15s, desperately trying to get them more close-air support.

Hearing the sounds of jet fighters overhead, Allen looked up just in time to see a missile contrail from the ground eventually connect with one of the F-15s. A second later, the pilot ejected as the burning wreckage of his aircraft fell to the ground. The Iraqis had a pretty tight air-defense system. Those SA-6s were really becoming a nuisance.

"Sir, 3-325 is reporting some Hind-Ds coming down Highway 15. He said they're flying too low for their Stingers to get an effective lock on them," Captain Blumberg reported.

"What about the Vulcans?" Allen asked with a raised voice.

"They can't get a bead on them from where they're positioned," Blumberg called out.

Son of a bitch. Allen tried to come up with something to counter the Hind-D attacks. If 3-325 fell, then Highway 15 would be opened.

"Falcon Six, No Mercy Six, over," came over the radio.

Who the hell is this now? Allen pondered.

"No Mercy Six, Falcon Six India, over," Captain Blumberg transmitted on the Brigade Command Radio.

"Falcon Six India, No Mercy Six, flight of twelve Alpha Hotel Six-Four. Understand you have targets for me, over."

Colonel Allen grabbed the hand mike out of Captain Blumberg's hand. "No Mercy Six, this is Falcon Six Actual. We have Hind-Ds hitting us in the south along Highway 15. Can you take them out? Over."

"Roger, Falcon Six. I have them in sight. We're moving to engage, out."

Although Allen couldn't clearly see the highway from his position, he could see the Iraqi Hinds racing down the road, strafing everything in sight. As they entered the gorge to the south that was the key bottleneck in the traffic flow, the Hinds began strafing the hillsides overlooking the road and punching off rockets.

The Hinds were the kind of helicopters that liked to engage targets while flying. They seldom ever came to a hover to engage. However, the Apache helicopters normally attacked from a hover, and now they did so very effectively, firing six Hellfire missiles straight up the gorge. The Hinds had no place to hide and no time to react. The antitank laser-guided missiles slammed into the cockpits of each helicopter, causing a catastrophic explosion to take place. The burning wreckage of the giant helicopters fell to the ground below, further adding to the cauldron of death and destruction.

Once they were destroyed, the Apache flight still had another fifty-six Hellfire missiles between them to go hunting. In short order, they tore the remaining vehicles of the division apart. Even the dismounted infantry was starting to feel the wrath of the 20mm chain guns on the Apache helicopters as the platoons made contact and started using them for direct platoon-level support. By midafternoon, the paratroopers started to see small white flags begin to appear as the Iraqi soldiers had decided they'd had enough. The battle of Wadi Reem was over.

Chapter Forty-Seven
Degree of Certainty

22 August 1990
USS *Florida*
Gulf of Oman

"Con, Sonar," the speaker in the control room announced.

The tension in the control room was thick as they were practically on the bottom of the seafloor while they waited near the opening to the Strait of Hormuz.

"Sonar, what do you have, Simmons?" the captain asked, perhaps a bit more tersely than he had intended. The open microphone system allowed those in the control room to speak normally in response to the Sonar, Communications and Battle Management Center without the use of a handheld microphone from the old days of diesel boats. The open microphone system could also be heard in the wardroom, CO's and XO's cabins, and the chief's quarters.

Stay calm, don't take your stress out on the men, Captain Fletcher chided himself.

"Sir, I believe we found us a way in. I'm tracking a slow, loud clunky merchant ship heading towards the Strait. I think we should go for this one, Captain," Petty Officer Simmons said confidently.

Petty Officer First Class Simmons had been in the Navy for almost ten years as a sonar operator. In Commander Fletcher's eyes, he was the best sonar operator in the Navy. He was months away from making chief petty officer, and he would if Commander Fletcher had any say in the matter.

"Sonar, stand by, I'm on my way. XO has the Conn," Fletcher announced and was acknowledged by the watch officer, the helmsman and the quartermaster of the watch. The sonar room sat just forward and to the right of the control room. Almost immediately, Commander Fletcher was there.

Commander Fletcher, skipper of the *Florida*, relished this position. This was his command, something he'd worked for his entire adult life to achieve. Better yet, he was in command during a war, a real honest-to-goodness war. When he'd graduated the Naval Academy with a degree in nuclear engineering, he'd never thought he'd one day be in command of a guided-missile submarine. At six foot two, he wasn't exactly the typical image of a submariner. It was during his first cruise that the skipper of the boat had told him to respect the men under your command, and in return they'd respect you. Never treat them like they're beneath you, or just a stepping stone to your next promotion. You may command with the authority of the United States Navy, but having the respect and trust of the men below you will lead to a successful and gratifying command.

Entering the doorway of the very crowded sonar room, Fletcher asked, "Simmons, what you got for us?" Simmons was the senior petty officer and the section chief. On the ten waterfall displays on the bulkhead, Fletcher could see the sound waves of a ship's propellers. The four operators were focused on two screens each, and each display was focused on a certain type of processing.

"Sir, I believe we have a Russian freighter. The beat and blade rate are that of a turbine drive freighter with a blade rate of forty turns per minute. He's about ten thousand yards to the south of us and heading this way. It's a freighter, not a warship," Simmons explained.

"You're *sure* it's a freighter and not a warship?" Fletcher asked. A lot was riding on them getting this right.

"Yes, sir, this ship only has a single screw. It doesn't match any of the known warships we have on record," Simmons explained confidently. "If I had to guess, I'd say he's a Soviet resupply ship headed to Kuwait or one of the other ports the Iraqis recently captured."

"Good job, Simmons. Stay on this guy. See if you guys are able to identify any sea mines they may have planted on the seabed as well. If we do follow this guy through, I want you guys to do your best to plot a path for how we got in. We may need to follow that same path out or use it to lead others in. Got it?"

"Aye-aye, Captain."

"OK, let me see what Fire Control says about this," Fletcher said as he turned and headed for the control room.

"CO's in Control," the helmsman announced as Fletcher entered and walked over to the fire control officer.

"What do you make of this contact that Simmons has?" Fletcher asked.

"Sir, it appears to be heading right for the entrance to the Strait. The speed and direction are spot-on for an entrance."
****

Fletcher made his way over to the chief of the boat, Master Chief Jack Bridges, who was standing next to the plot table. Master Chief Bridges was a highly experienced submariner. He'd spent his entire Navy career serving in submarines. His first sub had actually been an old diesel boat before the fleet had converted to nuclear power. This would also be his last deployment in the silent service. He was retiring at the end of this cruise.

Lieutenant Higgins arrived just then. He spotted the chief, who'd called him up here, and made his way over to the two of them.

Lieutenant Higgins was the commander of SEAL Team One aboard the *Florida*. They had been in the Straits of Florida conducting training when the call had come to get to the Arabian Sea ASAP.

As a result of the SALT II treaty signed between the US and the Soviet Union in 1979, the US Navy had to remove four of its boomer subs from the fleet or convert them to non-nuclear missile boats. The Florida, an *Ohio*-class submarine, had her missiles removed and replaced with a pair of SEAL Delivery Vehicle systems located in dry dock shelters where some of her missile tubes used to be located. At periscope depth, SEAL team members would enter the dry dock shelters and then flood the shelters. Once flooded, the back hatch was opened and the team drove out.

Although the original launch tubes remained aboard as they were an integral part of the boat, the boat suddenly had a lot of empty space. Some of the tubes contained Tomahawk cruise missiles, but others were used as storage space, and a couple were converted into showers, something appreciated by the crew. One converted launch tube was even used as the ship's barbershop. Some launch tubes had been converted into quarters to house up to fifty SEALs and some of their accompanying support elements. This initial shakedown cruise was meant to determine the feasibility of converting a few more of the boomers into SEAL delivery systems and special warfare platforms. They had no idea their maiden voyage would actually see them engaged in combat.

When Lieutenant Higgins joined them at the plot table, Commander Fletcher brought him up to speed on the current situation. He told the SEAL commander they'd likely have a mission ready for them in the near future.

****

"Captain," First Officer Turgenev called out, knocking on the ship captain's door.

"*Da*, I am awake. Come in, what is it, Turgenev?" Captain Ivanov said as he rubbed the sleep from his eyes.

As captain of the bulk carrier *Kuzma Minin*, he could sleep when he wanted. He had three underling officers of the Soviet Navy to watch things while he slept. Captain Ivanov had served in the Soviet Navy his entire military career. This was his first command, however, of a "civilian" ship as it appeared to the American Navy. As such, he would not have to worry about being boarded by the American Navy unless something was seriously wrong—the American Navy would not suspect what his "civilian" vessel's cargo of "machine parts" really was. In fact, the entire crew of the *Kuzma Minin* were Soviet Navy sailors, though they wore civilian clothing.

Some of his sailors, after being out of uniform for too long, were starting to behave too civilian for Ivanov's liking. They were losing their military bearings and starting to get into trouble. He'd have to address this when they returned to Murmansk. Their loose lips at a bar in Singapore a month ago had ended shore leave for everyone. A KGB officer had made sure of that. The rest of the crew was not making life easy for the three offenders, not that Ivanov had a problem with that. At this rate, those three might not make it back to Murmansk. Sailors relished their shore leave. It was the one time these sailors got to see countries outside the Soviet Union and purchase Western goods—items that often sold for a small fortune when they returned to Mother Russia.

Swinging his feet around and planting them on the floor as he sat up, Ivanov looked at his desk. "What time is it?"

"Captain, it is 0430. We are approaching the Strait and the pilot boat is approaching with a pilot to take us through the minefields," Turgenev announced.

"OK, I am awake. I hope this pilot knows what the hell he is doing and speaks Russian. I am tired of having to struggle with the English that the Arabs speak. And I used to think the English that the British spoke was difficult. It is all English, and they all speak it differently. How they understand each other is beyond me," Ivanov grumbled as he reached for his pants and then a shirt. "I will be on the bridge shortly after I freshen up and get some coffee. Give me fifteen minutes. Oh, how soon until this pilot arrives?"

"Probably thirty minutes."

"Good, slow the ship to five knots so he can climb up. I don't want the fool falling into the ocean. What are the seas like right now?"

"Fairly calm with a moonless night. Maybe half a meter at best. Temperature is thirty degrees Celsius."

"Good, please tell the steward to bring me some coffee and I will be right up," Ivanov said as he dismissed Turgenev.

****

"Conn," Simmons said over the mic.

"Sonar, what you got, Simmons?" Captain Fletcher asked.

"Conn, a second boat is approaching the target. High-speed screws estimate thirty knots. I suspect it may be the pilot boat," Simmons said as Captain Fletcher walked into the CIC. He had been in the wardroom having breakfast.

Looking up, Fletcher saw a look of concern on COB's face as he stood at the ship control party, serving as chief of the watch.

"Sonar has a second boat approaching the target. He thinks it might be a pilot boat."

"Sonar, range to target?" Fletcher asked.

"Conn, range is two thousand yards."

Glancing at the clock, Fletcher saw the officer on deck, or OOD. "Mr. Whitlock, proceed to periscope depth," Fletcher directed. Mr. Whitlock was also the assistant navigation officer.

"Proceed to periscope depth, aye, sir."

Fletcher turned to the dive officer of the watch, or DOOW. "Dive, make your depth sixty feet."

"Make my depth sixty feet, aye, sir. Full rise, both planes, give me fifteen degrees up. Chief of the Watch, flood auxiliaries."

Chief Bridges stepped over to the stern plainsman and the helmsman/fairwater plainsman. "Take us up to sixty feet, fifteen degrees up on the bow. Heading three hundred and sixty degrees, reduce speed to three knots. Let's take this nice and easy."

Slowly the crew began to feel the rise in the bow as the *Florida* angled upward towards the surface from the seven-hundred-foot depth she had been sitting at.

"Sonar," Mr. Whitlock called out.

"Conn, Sonar."

"Report all contacts," Whitlock requested.

"Conn, the closest thing to us aside from the target is about twenty thousand yards behind us and moving at a speed of twelve knots. It's believed to be another freighter. We've designated it as Sierra 2."

"Roger, keep us posted."

Turning to the OOD, Fletcher said, "Mr. Whitlock, when we level off, I want you to eye the target and tell me what you see. I want to know when the pilot is aboard, and I want you to start paying special attention to exactly what speed he has the ship travel and where he has them make turns. We need to do our best to annotate everything that pilot has the freighter do from here on out. Is that understood?"

"Aye-aye, Captain," Mr. Whitlock responded with a grin.

Mr. Whitlock was a fellow Academy graduate, and Fletcher felt it was an unspoken duty of his to groom and mentor this young man, just as he had been mentored by his first commander, who had likewise been an Academy ring knocker.

Lieutenant Whitlock, serving as the OOD, was responsible for bringing the boat to periscope depth, and he was required to be on the scope at all times. At least once a day, he was required to bring the boat to periscope depth when underway. The new PERVIS system on the periscope would now allow everyone in the Control and other stations to see what he was seeing, to include the crew's mess on the big-screen monitor/TV.

"Conn, Sonar, Master 1 has slowed to five knots. Sierra 2 now appears to be alongside Master 1."

"Conn, Sonar, good copy," Fletcher said aloud, knowing Whitlock would have heard him on the open mic system.

Lieutenant Crawford worked the magnification on the periscope, which showed a clean image of the smaller vessel having come alongside the larger freighter. He zoomed in one more magnification level. This one gave them a real good glimpse of a lone figure scaling what appeared to be some sort of retractable ladder that had been dropped down to them.

"Damn, these new magnifications are something else," Whitlock commented to no one in particular.

"They sure as hell are," Fletcher said.

Fletcher then turned to his SEAL commander. "Lieutenant Higgins, we're going to piggyback our way into the Gulf via this freighter. Once we're inside the Gulf, I suspect we're going to receive some new orders from 5th Fleet. We'll keep you apprised of what happens. In the meantime, I'd keep your team ready to execute whatever may come our way."

Lieutenant Higgins nodded in approval as a wide grin spread across his face. "Yes, sir, my guys are ready for whatever the brass wants us to execute."

****

"Steady as it goes on this heading," the Iranian pilot said as the ship cleared the last of the minefields. At this point, the sun had started a slow descent in the western sky behind the mountains of Oman. The pilot turned to Captain Ivanov. "I was told to take you into Saqr Port. You'll be offloading your cargo there."

"That is correct. My orders are to offload and then depart immediately. If you have a crew standing by, as I was told you would, we should be out of there by morning. Will you be taking us back out?" Captain Ivanov asked.

The pilot shook his head. "No, another pilot will handle your exit." The pilot looked at his watch briefly before he returned his attention to Ivanov. "We should be dockside in a couple of hours. Once we near the port, a couple of tugs will be standing by to assist you the rest of the way in."

Ivanov was impatient. He wanted to offload his equipment and get out of this war zone as quickly as he could. One didn't survive this many years in the Soviet Navy by placing oneself in any more danger than one had to.

Wanting to see if he could glean some intelligence from their Iranian pilot, Ivanov asked, "I understand the Americans have launched air strikes against military targets in the area. Have they launched any attacks against the ports or commercial ships delivering supplies?"

The pilot shook his head as he lit another cigarette. "There have been attacks, yes, but so far they have only been against military targets, and only in Saudi Arabia. So far, the infidels have not carried out any attacks inside the UAE or against civilian targets or ships at any of the ports."

Ivanov snorted at the comment. He pulled a cigarette out of his breast pocket and held it in his mouth. He motioned for the pilot to lean forward so Ivanov could light his cigarette off his. "Well, that may be true. But I do not want to be in these waters when that changes. Mark my words, if Saddam does not return your armies to your borders, or at least to Kuwait's borders, all hell is going to be unleashed on you guys. As we approached the Strait, we saw several American warships to include one of their aircraft carriers taking up station in the Gulf of Oman."

The Iraqi pilot seemed a bit concerned by this information. He didn't appear to know a lot of what was going on around him other than what limited information he was being given.

Clearing his throat, the Iranian finally replied, "The Americans will not follow you into the Arabian Gulf. Of that I am sure. The minefields are not known to them, and the water depth is too shallow for them to risk it. The deepest point in the Gulf is only two hundred and ninety-five feet deep, and it's along the Iranian coast. The depths around Saqr are only thirty-four meters."

Ivanov lifted an eyebrow at that information. He hadn't personally made many port calls in the Arabian Gulf. "How are the port facilities at Saqr where we are headed?"

"The docking facilities are adequate. There are several berths with heavy-lift cranes that will be able to remove your machine parts quickly. I believe there is a company representative that will meet you when you arrive, along with a customs officer—not that they will give you any problems, of course," the pilot explained.

Looking at the pilot, Ivanov thought, *This fool has no idea what our cargo is or who we really are.* "I am sure the company representative will meet us along with proper government official," Ivanov said as he turned to find Turgenev.

"Mr. Turgenev, check that all preparations for docking have been completed and are in order," Captain Ivanov directed.

"As you wish, Captain," Turgenev replied with a slight grin on his face as he left the bridge. He was trying to stifle a laugh at their Iraqi pilot's complete obliviousness to who they truly were and what they were delivering to his government.

****

"Up scope," Mr. Whitlock stated confidently.

"Eighty feet, level on the bubble, ten knots," the DOOW indicated calmly.

As the scope came up, Mr. Whitlock positioned himself in front of the monitor. When the periscope broke the surface, using the gamelike controller in his hand, he quickly rotated the periscope a full 360 degrees to ensure there were no vessels in close proximity.

"No close contacts," he announced as he completed the scan. Since there were no close contacts, the scope would remain up and continue to execute a 360 scan. The ship they had followed through the minefield was seen moving away from them towards the port of Saqr.

"Mr. Whitlock, what was the name of that ship?" Fletcher asked.

From their vantage point, they could see the pilot boat, Sierra 2, departing the bulk freighter, Master 1, now that the freighter was under the guidance of a couple of tugboats from the harbor.

"Captain, Master 1 has been positively identified as *Kuzma Minin*, a bulk freighter home-ported out of Murmansk," their intelligence officer said.

"Thank you. I guess we wait and see what the brass wants us to do next," Fletcher replied.

Now that their sub had made it into the Arabian Gulf, it was a matter of watching and waiting to see what the 5th Fleet would have them do next. They'd managed to make it in; now the question was, what would the brass do with them next? They didn't have long to wait.

Florida's XO, Mr. Warren, entered Control with the TS binder in hand. Any classified message traffic would be logged in and placed in the TS binder. Only those with a need to know would be able to see the contents of the message.

"Excuse me, sir, we have a message from COMNAVCENTCOM," Mr. Warren said as he handed the TS binder to the captain. All eyes turned to the captain, who kept his calm demeanor as he read the message.

FROM: COMNAVCENTCOM
TO: USS *Florida*
SUBJ: Mission Tasking
RMKS: Proceed to vicinity Saqr Port, UAE. Russian Ship *Kuzma Minin* is believed to be carrying Scud missiles with potential Soviet WMD warheads or capable of carrying Iraq-made WMD warheads. These missiles and their launchers cannot be allowed to be transferred to Iraqi forces. You are hereby ordered to sink the *Kuzma Minin*. The USS *Florida* should then stand by for further orders, to include the possible deployment of the embarked SEAL team for deep reconnaissance operations.

No one on the Conn spoke for a moment. There was a lot to take in with that message.

Captain Fletcher turned to his XO. "Report Master 1."

The contact manager looked up at the BIG-1 Fire Control Systems. "Master 1 bears two-seven-zero, range ten thousand yards." What he was trying to determine was whether they could get a torpedo shot off and still hit it or whether the ship had already made the turn around the piers to get inside the port. He looked up at the captain. "Master 1 appears to be inside the harbor."

"Damn. OK, XO, muster the war council in the BMC. Make sure Higgins is there," Captain Fletcher said.

A few minutes later, Lieutenant Higgins, the SEAL team commander, joined the CO, XO, intel officer and department heads in the Battle Management Center to review the options.

"You called?" he said with a mischievous grin on his face. He knew a mission was in the offing.

Looking at the frogman, Fletcher explained the situation. The tugs escorting the *Kuzma Minin* would have the ship around the elbow in the port soon, which meant launching a torpedo was out of the question.

There wasn't enough time for the torpedo to travel the distance and hit the ship before they turned the corner.

The way the port was set up, it had a single entrance that led into a U-shaped design. This particular port wasn't a large one. It was designed to offload large shipping containers of construction materials and get them loaded onto either flatbed trucks or freight cars to be moved across the country via rail.

Lieutenant Higgins looked at the port and then the depth chart surrounding it and leading up to it. It was shallow waters, forty to sixty feet across most of it. Too shallow for the *Florida* to get them much closer than they already were.

Fletcher said, "I think this might be a good situation to test the deployment of your SDVs. What do you think?"

The frogman turned to Fletcher. "I was just about to suggest that. What better way to prove the concept than to use it in a real-world mission like this?"

The *Florida*'s original mission prior to the crisis in the Gulf was to test the concept of converting the original missile tubes into something new. Of the twenty-four tubes, two had been converted into lockout chamber for the SEALs, while the other twenty had been fitted with a reusable canister holding seven Tomahawk missiles. If the system worked, then the Navy would move forward with the multibillion-dollar conversion of the *Ohio*, *Michigan*, *Florida*, and *Georgia* into SSGNs.

"How long until your team can be ready to deploy? We need that ship destroyed before they're able to offload those missiles," Fletcher said urgently.

The frogman looked up at the ceiling above them, likely trying to think about the problem before responding. "If we're in position to launch right now, it takes two hours to get the SDV loaded up and flood the dry dock shelter and we should be ready to go. Judging by the distance to the target and the speed of our SDV, four knots, I estimate it'll take us roughly an hour to reach the ship. Then another twenty or so minutes to set the mines and then another hour to get back to the sub, twenty more minutes to get everything loaded back up into the lockout chamber. All told, I think we can deploy, travel and sink that ship and be back on board in, say, six hours."

Fletcher looked at his XO and the COB. Depending on how fast the Iraqis moved at offloading that freighter, that might be enough time. Then again, they didn't have a lot of options. "OK, Lieutenant. It's your show now. Get your team deployed and sink that ship. We'll move to deeper water and wait. Rendezvous back here in six hours."
****

Lieutenant Higgins locked the door in the chamber, sealing them in. Once it was sealed, the red light near the door turned green. This sent a message to the hangar supervisor behind the plexiglass wall in the chamber and to those on the Conn, letting them know they could start to vent and flood the chamber.

Looking at the three other operators in the tube with him, Higgins gave them each a thumbs-up and waited for each of them to give him one back. The two drivers for the SDV gave him a thumbs-up as well. Then the water started to come in. It came in slowly, replacing the air in the chamber until the entire chamber was filled. The divers moved to the outer hangar door, located at the rear of the dry dock.

Once the chamber was opened up, the SDV was slowly moved out of the chamber and made ready. As the pilot climbed on and his copilot got settled in, the four other SEALs got in. Each SEAL attached themselves to the onboard air system to conserve their own supply and then they were off.

Traveling at a speed of just four nautical miles, it was going to take them an hour and ten minutes to travel the five miles to get themselves positioned inside the port.
****

It was dark as the *Kuzma Minin* was slowly positioned along the outer dock of the port. The two tugs had done a good job of maneuvering them into position. As they entered the port itself, the ship was bathed in light by the massive floodlights that dominated the port and the cranes next to the docking ports.

Looking out the window of the bridge in the direction of the cranes, Captain Ivanov felt his blood pressure rise. The area below the cranes was empty. There should have been a small convoy of flatbed trucks ready to receive his cargo. Instead, no one was there.

Twenty minutes later, the ship was finally tied off and the gangway moved into place. Captain Ivanov was there, waiting to greet the port manager and start questioning him about where the truck drivers were at.

"Captain Ivanov, welcome to the United Arab Emirates. My name is Mohammed."

Of course his name is Mohammed. Everyone in the Middle East is named Mohammed.

"I have a couple of vans that will be here momentarily to take you and your crew to a nearby hotel where you can freshen up or grab something to eat," the port representative said, rather cheerfully considering the early hour of the morning.

"Excuse me, Mohammed. I was told when my ship came into port, the dockworkers would be standing by to begin offloading our cargo immediately! Why are no workers present?"

Mohammed bunched his eyebrows at the question before replying, "What do you mean?"

Ivanov wasn't sure if his poor English wasn't being understood by this Arab whose English was also poor, or if there had been a miscommunication about what would happen once his ship came into port.

Taking a deep breath in so as not to lose his temper, Ivanov countered, "Mr. Mohammed, perhaps you are not aware of what my ship is transporting. But it is vitally important that my cargo be immediately offloaded. The Soviet Union is taking a great risk in bringing this cargo to your country. It needs to be offloaded and dispersed now."

The Arab looked a bit confused by what Ivanov had just said. He pulled a radio out of his back pocket and jabbered away in Arabic for a couple of seconds. Looking back at Ivanov, he said, "My apologies, Captain. My supervisor informed me there must have been a mistake. Our dock crew is not due back at work until eight in the morning. My supervisor said the army will send some people over here to begin offloading your cargo. Someone should be here soon to talk with you."

Shaking his head, Ivanov turned around and returned to the bridge of his ship. If this was any port in Europe, the Americas, or Asia, a crew would already be here. *Only in the Middle East do they not run a twenty-four-hour operation.*
****

397

Approaching the port entrance, Lieutenant Higgins couldn't believe how much light was piercing its way down to their position. They were hugging the ocean floor, around forty-two feet in depth, and still the area around them was a lot lighter than it should have been. If the water truly was this clear, then he was certain they'd be spotted by a halfway attentive guard during the daylight hours. As it was, it was nearly three in the morning.

The pilot steering them pointed in the direction of their target—the Soviet freighter *Kuzma Minin*. He nodded and gave the pilot the universal thumbs-up. As they approached the large freighter, the SDV slowed until it came to a stop somewhere near the middle of the freighter.

Lieutenant Higgins motioned for his team to get to work. They didn't want to be down here any longer than they needed to be. They needed to place a couple of limpet mines on the belly of the freighter in strategic positions they knew would cause it to sink. Just to make sure, they placed a couple of extra mines for added effort.

When the SEALs had placed their limpet mines on the *Kuzma Minin*, they climbed aboard the SDV and made their way over to the only other ship in port. They had no idea what nation it belonged to, but if they wanted to make this little impromptu plan work, it had to join Davy Jones' Locker with the *Kuzma Minin*.

Looking at his watch, Higgins saw they'd been in the harbor for nearly sixty minutes. They were running late and they needed to get out of there. It was now a little past 0400 hours. They still had another hour back to the *Florida* and a bit of time to get the SDV positioned back in the lockout chamber. The sun would be up around seven in the morning. They'd be cutting it close as they tried to get back to deeper water, where they could hide.

****

Captain Ivanov looked at the minibus as it pulled up to the dock. When it stopped, half a dozen workers got out and started climbing up the massive cranes anchored next to his ship. A handful of the workers boarded his ship and made their way over to the deck. His crew worked with them, getting the tarps removed and the containers with the missiles in them ready to be moved.

398

Looking at his watch, Ivanov was ticked at how slowly these Arabs moved. His ship had been tied up in port now for nearly three hours, and they were only just now sending a crew to unload his ship. He was going to have a nasty conversation with the port manager once the missiles had been offloaded. The longer he was in port, the higher the risk of being discovered. With the war going, he'd bet his pension the Americans had every ship and port being watched by satellites to spot weapons being brought in to help the Iraqis.

No sooner had he thought about the Americans discovering what he was carrying than the ship across the harbor from his own exploded. At first the ship rose slightly out of the water. Then it was enveloped in flames as a series of explosions overtook the entire thing.

Seconds later, Ivanov felt something rumble under his own ship. In the blink of an eye he was thrown to the ground, a sharp pain washing over his body as a searing flash of heat and flame seemed to consume and melt everything around him. His brain didn't even have time to register the explosions that rippled across his ship as the Scud missiles added their own explosive power to the limpet mines.

****

Lieutenant Higgins looked at his watch. The only sign that the mines had gone off was the sound of some distant explosions in the water. They had just slid the SDV into the dry dock shelter on the *Florida* when they'd heard the first of a series of explosions. Knowing they needed to get the hell out of there, Higgins didn't bother sticking around any longer than necessary. Once the outer hangar door was shut and dogged, draining and pressure equalization commenced.

When the pressurization was completed, Higgins opened the hatch that'd allow them back into the *Florida*, where he was greeted by the chief of the boat and Commander Fletcher. They were there to congratulate him on a successful mission. The sonar room had reported the destruction of the ship. While Higgins and his men would now work on cleaning their gear and grabbing some hot chow and a fresh shower, the skipper would work on getting the boat moved to deeper water and going into hiding. They'd establish a routine for checking in for new orders. But other than that, their primary objective at this point was to do their best to disappear and pretend they didn't exist.

Chapter Forty-Eight
Wired

26 August 1990
Situation Room
White House
Washington, D.C.

Everyone on the President's National Security Advisor team was present, as well as some additional folks that could contribute to the conversation. The President was not happy. Everyone was exhausted from the lack of sleep and the gallons of coffee being drunk.

Once the President took his seat, he looked at Lieutenant Colonel Atwell. "Alright, Colonel, let's get started."

"Good morning, Mr. President. This—" Atwell did not get to finish.

"Good! What's so damn good about it? Tell me!" the President barked angrily.

Before Colonel Atwell could respond, the President broke into a wide grin. "Gotcha, Colonel."

Colonel Atwell's face revealed that the President had truly gotten him this morning.

"You did, sir," Atwell responded with a look that said he wasn't sure if he was happy or mad.

"OK, let's get started," said the President. "And no more long faces around this table. The world isn't ending. This too shall pass, and in the words of Captain John Paul Jones, 'I have not yet begun to fight.'" He recalled the quote from his training as a naval officer during World War II.

The last several days had been incredibly tough on the men in this room, and the country they represented. The stories written by a couple of reporters who had managed to get themselves inside the battlespace were truly terrifying. Some of the images they'd smuggled out only reinforced the terror of the battle that had been fought. The President felt it was important to try to change the tone of the meeting before it got going.

Colonel Atwell cleared his throat and began. "Sir, in the last forty-eight hours, some significant events have occurred. The 2nd Republican

Guard Corps continues its attack westward. Two days ago, the 7th Motorized Division finished capturing the holy city of Medina against the Saudi National Guard. They're claiming in the media that they have liberated the Islamic holy city from a corrupt King who has prostituted his country and his people to the West and is now begging the infidels to save him. Saddam is still trying to sway the Arab world into thinking he's a liberator and not a conqueror."

"Ha, fat chance of that," Mr. Sununu said. "He just took over the UAE."

Continuing, Atwell explained, "The 5th Republican Guard Mechanized Division, along with the 21st Armored Brigade, attacked the 82nd Airborne Division along its defensive line in two places. With the addition of the 101st Attack Helicopter Battalion and a *lot* of close-air support from the Air Force and the Navy, the 82nd was able to hold the position and destroyed a significant portion of the 5th Republican Guard Division in the process. Some elements of the 21st Armored Brigade attempted to slip south and bypass the 82nd but were soundly beaten back by the 8th Saudi Mechanized Brigade. Much to our horror, the 2nd Republican Guard Corps employed mustard gas against one of the paratroopers' positions. Thankfully, the paratroopers had prepared for this possibility, and while they weren't expecting it, they responded exceptionally well to it. As a result, they sustained very few casualties from the attack. With the battle over for the time being, the 82nd is doing their best to strengthen their lines and prepare for round two should it come," Colonel Atwell said.

"I still can't believe the Iraqis used mustard gas. It makes no sense to use it—and then use it in only a small area, so you don't even gain any real advantage from it. Putting that aside, what kind of casualties did we sustain during the battle?" the President asked as he looked around the room.

General Powell answered, "Sir, Lieutenant General Luck, the XVIII Airborne Commander, just sent us their initial figures a few hours ago. I must warn you—they are high. In the single-day battle, the 82nd Airborne and the supporting units fighting with them sustained three thousand, two hundred and forty-eight casualties. Of that number, one thousand four hundred and ninety-two are listed as killed in action."

No one said anything for a moment. They were trying to digest the magnitude of the casualties from the battle. It wasn't something they were prepared for or something they had expected.

"My God. Those are World War II kind of single-day losses," James Baker said softly.

The President, who seemed a bit taken aback by what Powell had just said, asked, "How could we have suffered so many casualties in a single day of combat?"

"Sir, you have to keep in mind that our single division with a few supporting elements was standing in the way of more than fifty thousand Iraqi soldiers. Had it not been for the enormous level of air support from the Navy and Air Force, we likely would have lost the battle and most of the 82nd. As it is, we need to have a tough conversation about the future of that division and whether we keep them there or redeploy them. They're not out of danger yet," Powell said.

"I...see," the President said, a bit more somber than before. Turning to Atwell, he said, "Please, Colonel, continue with the brief and bring us up to speed on things before we come back to this."

Nodding, Atwell explained, "Sir, in the northwest, the 2nd Iraqi Army Corps, with two divisions and possibly a third, is pushing down from the north with only the 10th Saudi Mechanized Brigade delaying it, along with air assets from the USS *Saratoga*. A US Tactical Air Control Party is with the 10th Saudi Brigade and has been hitting them hard, but they continue to move towards Medina. If they can link up with the other divisions, that'll place between eight and nine divisions in Medina. Our naval air assets have taken some heavy losses among the A-6 Intruder and F/A-18 Hornet fleets. The 2nd Army Corps is traveling over some open ground so they can disperse their forces better. They also have good air-defense coverage as well as a fighter cap. It seems the Iraqis have acquired a lot more Russian-made SA-6 systems than we had originally known about. We're seeing more of them than are usually found in a force structure for an Iraqi division. We're also seeing a lot more T-72s and BTR-70s and even BTR-80s than we would have expected."

The President turned to the Director of the CIA. "How does this square with your previous reports on the Russians supplying them with new equipment?"

"Sir, it's a matter of scope. The Russians supplied Saddam with some equipment to make up for what he lost in the Iran-Iraq War. And we monitored several Russian ships coming into the port of Um Qasr and offloading some heavy equipment, but it was all under wraps and our analysts weren't able to get a firm grip on the numbers involved. At this point we only know that it was a lot more than we previously thought," the Director said, not looking directly at the President but at his notes.

"I got a feeling you best tell your analysts to take another look at that," the President said in less than a joking tone. "Continue, Colonel."

"Sir, in the east, the 1st Republican Guard Corps is reinforcing its positions around Abu Dhabi, Dubai, Al Ain and Kayyam with a division in each location. One brigade which we were able to hit hard with air strikes from our carrier in the Arabian Sea is sitting in Salwa, Saudi Arabia, being refitted."

"Sir, if I may," General Powell interrupted, "it appears that they want to shut down the ports that the UAE could offer us and protect themselves from the most likely avenue of approach for our eventual counterattack. They've left the right flank open using the Empty Quarter as too difficult for us to traverse. They're—"

The President cut him off. "The what? What is this Empty Quarter?" he asked, his curiosity piqued now.

"Sir, that's the southern and southeastern portion of Saudi Arabia. Nothing exists out there except large sand dunes and one paved road that's covered the majority of time by shifting sand. The dunes are perpendicular to our advance and would be very difficult to cross over by any force, especially a mechanized or armor force. Our best avenue is to attack out of Muscat and Oman and through the UAE."

"Jim, are we still on track with the government in Oman to use their facilities?" the President asked.

"Sir, I speak almost daily with the Prime Minister and it's a go for us to use their facilities. I believe we have people en route currently to begin the process of identifying what facilities are available where and what we're going to need to stage out of there," Jim Baker said.

"Sir, General Schwarzkopf is in Muscat at this time with his logisticians, determining what those facilities are and where. That information will be sent back to the Joint Staff and we can get things moving in earnest," Mr. Cheney explained.

403

"What's the status of the initial package that General Schwarzkopf asked for?"

"Mr. President, forces are moving at this time. The 82nd Airborne Division has one hundred percent of the division deployed to Jeddah. The 101st Airborne Division has deployed one attack helicopter battalion and has thirty percent of its force in the air en route to Jeddah as well but will be moving to Yanbu, north of Jeddah. Future flights and ships for the 101st are being diverted from Jeddah to Yanbu. The 24th Infantry Division had some loading problems at the port in Savannah but has it sorted out now—"

"What kind of problems?" the President interrupted.

"Just a bit of a logjam at Savannah. We've worked it out. It just took more time than we wanted. They're at sea now with two ships, and more will be loaded," Cheney explained. No one wanted to relate another issue that had come up in the loading, and the President didn't need to know.

"Sir, the 3rd Armored Cavalry Regiment has moved by rail from their home station to Galveston, Texas, and is in the process of loading there. The 197th Infantry Brigade is moving by rail from Fort Benning to Jacksonville, Florida. Headquarters, XVIII Airborne Corps at Fort Bragg, North Carolina, is flying out to Jeddah. The 11th Air Defense Artillery Brigade from Fort Bliss, Texas, is moving by rail to Beaumont, Texas. Headquarters, 3rd US Army located at Fort McPherson, Georgia, will fly from Atlanta to Muscat, Oman, and their advance party is already in place.

"The remainder of the units he's requested have been alerted and are preparing to move. The other additional heavy units will flow into Muscat with only the 101st and 82nd in Jeddah and possibly the 24th ID. Right now, sir, the problem is finding ships to move all the competing parts. Military Sealift Command is just not equipped to move all the competing parts at the same time. TRANSCOM, the headquarters overall responsible for all the planes and ships to move stuff as well as coordinating with the railroads, is supposed to have a thirty-day planning window. We gave them two weeks. They're doing their best to make things happen—it's just going to take time," Cheney explained.

"Well, what are we talking about here, Dick? If we don't get some substantial forces over there now, the Iraqis will have kicked us out of the place," the President griped angrily.

"Sir, just in the first thirty days, we are estimating the movement of some thirty-eight thousand people by air, one hundred and twenty-three thousand tons of equipment and supplies by ships, and forty thousand tons of supplies and equipment by air,"[13] Cheney explained. "It's going to take time to spool up the airplanes and ships to move all this."

"OK, I get the picture," the President said defensively.

Cheney continued, "The Air Force assets in the fight at this time are the 71st and 511th Tactical Fighter Squadrons, presently located at Hurghada, Egypt, supporting the 82nd and 18th Airborne Corps. The 42nd Bomb Group, B-52s out of Loring, is currently at Diego Garcia. More squadrons are being called up. We'll have a more complete list to you at tomorrow's brief. General Schwarzkopf has also requested that the 4th Marine Expeditionary Brigade be assigned to Central Command as of the 11th, and like everyone else, we don't have the amphibious ships to support them completely just yet."

"How many ships do they need?"

"Sir, the 4th MEB requires two dozen ships, but only nine are available due to maintenance scheduling and competing factors. We'll get it worked out, Mr. President. It may not be pretty, but we will get them there," Cheney assured him.

"How soon can we see Marine boots on the ground in Oman? I don't want to have the Iraqis think that they can roll in there as well. We need the flag planted and fast," said the President.

General Powell answered, "The first ships departed Morehead City on the 17th. The Marines should be there in about two weeks. The amphibious fleet in the Red Sea will join them once they arrive. We're hesitant about putting them ashore just yet until things have stabilized in Jeddah. We're going ahead and flying the 7th Marine Expeditionary Brigade from California to Sohar International Airport along with the 1st Marine Expeditionary Brigade from Hawaii to Rustaq Airport outside of Al Mudayq, where the Oman Navy stages out of. Both brigades will land in Oman and join up with the pre-positioned stock from Diego Garcia, which will include their LAV and heavy equipment. We're coordinating with the Omani government as to where they will go once the

---

[13] Pegonus. *Moving Mountains, Lessons in Leadership and logistics from the Gulf War,* Harvard Business School Press, 1992 page 7.

deployment is complete. Oman has offered Masirah Island for a possible staging area for one Marine division. The other option is to be placed in some sort of blocking position near the Omani-Saudi border."

The Commandant of the Corps gave Powell the stink eye when he answered what obviously should have been his question. He didn't need Powell answering for him. Cutting Powell off before he could steal any more of his thunder, he interjected, "Discussions with General Schwarzkopf indicate that the first pre-po ships will offload in Liwa, Oman, and the Sohar Port. There's a major highway that comes out of Al Ain, UAE, through some very rugged terrain. The initial force will move to block that highway and prevent the Iraqis from attacking into Oman."

"Well, it sounds like we're moving in the right direction. Tell me, General Dugan, how is the Air Force shaping up for this?" the President asked.

"Sir, we currently have the 71st and 511th Tactical Fighter Squadrons in theater in Egypt along with the 27th TAC Fighter Squadron. The 336 Tactical Fighter Squadron is landing as we speak in Thumrait, Oman. We currently have five fighter wings in the process of deploying and thirteen other wings that have received alert notices for deployment. I expect by the end of September we will have approximately eighteen hundred aircraft operating in the theater, not counting what the Navy is bringing to the table or any aircraft from other nations supporting our position. At our next session, I'll have a slide listing all the wings by type of aircraft and a breakdown of the numbers," Dugan concluded and looked at his staff officer, who was writing notes and a tasking to get that slide made.

"Tell me about our losses, though. When I was reading over the summary of the brief during breakfast, I saw our air losses had been pretty high. What's going on, Dugan?"

Grimacing at the mention of the losses, Dugan replied, "Our pilots have been engaged in a lot of aerial battles. The Iraqi Air Force has been giving our pilots a real run for their money. We've also been encountering a very aggressive air-defense system. They appear to have a lot more SA-6 systems than we had previously known about." At that, the President shot a glare at the CIA Director as Dugan continued. "One real concern, however, was a recent set of reconnaissance photos a U-2 managed to capture around Riyadh. The Iraqis appeared to have acquired a Soviet SA-10 Grumble system. We're not sure how, but what we can clearly see on the photos is the missile system being deployed in various positions around Riyadh. We're now tasking our U-2s with trying to see if there are more SA-10s and, if so, where they are."

General Dugan leaned forward as he explained, "If the Soviets are now giving the Iraqis SA-10s, then we're going to have a real problem going forward. These are deadly SAMs. This kind of system will take a very concerted level of effort to defeat. We're talking Tomahawk cruise missiles and a lot of complicated Wild Weasel missions."

"Great, sounds like more fun stuff to deal with. Keep me apprised, General Dugan. How about you, Carl? You have more surprises for me like Dugan?"

General Carl Vuono, Chief of Staff for the Army, smiled as he shook his head. "Nothing we haven't already seen or run across. I have a list of additional assets Norm is asking for. Some of them are units in Germany, which may be a problem. I'm not sure if the Germans will want to see some of these forces be taken from NATO."

General Vuono motioned for a slide, having anticipated this question. "Sir, these units have been requested, and as soon as TRANSCOM can arrange the transportation, we'll start moving them to the respective ports.[14] We also need to see about where we'll be basing them in Oman," General Vuono explained. The slide showed the following units being requested:

---

[14] TRANSCOM, Transportation Command, centralized joint headquarters for allocating transportation assets to deploying units and supplies.

OPERATION DESERT SHIELD

INITIAL GROUND FORCE PACKAGE

82nd Airborne Division, Fort Bragg, Nc

24th Infantry Division (Mechanized), Fort Stewart, GA

197th Infantry Brigade (Mechanized), Fort Benning, GA

HQ, XVIII Airborne Corps, Fort Bragg, NC

101st Airborne Division (Air Assault) Fort Campbell, KY

3rd Armored Cavalry Regiment, Fort Bliss, TX

1st Cavalry Division, Fort Hood, TX

1st Brigade, 2nd Armored Division, Fort Hood, TX

11th Air Defense Artillery Brigade, Fort Bliss, TX

III Corps Artillery, Fort Sill, OK

1st Corps Support Command, Fort Bragg, NC

13th Corps Support Command, Fort Hood, TX

12th Combat Aviation Brigade, Germany

3rd Armored Division Aviation elements, Germany

7th Medical Command, Germany

Hq, 3rd U.S. Army, Fort McPherson, GA

"Do you think he'll be asking for more above this initial request? We have the 24th Infantry Division going, and I see the 1st Cavalry Division, but is that going to be enough heavy forces to kick the Iraqis out of Saudi and the Gulf states?"

"Sir, it's my opinion that he's going to be requesting additional forces before this is over. Probably going to see a request for the 1st Armored Division, the 1st Infantry Division and the 3rd Armored Division—unless of course Saddam comes to his senses, but I'm not going to hold my breath," General Vuono explained.

Without saying anything, the President looked at Admiral Kelso, who knew that was his indicator to start talking. "Mr. President, we currently have the USS *Saratoga* operating in the Red Sea supporting the 10th Saudi Mechanized Brigade. In the Arabian Sea we have the USS *Kennedy*. The USS *Midway* is in Yokosuka and is preparing to get underway, and the *Ranger* is in port at San Diego, also preparing. The *America* is on station in the North Atlantic and the *Roosevelt* is in refit but should be ready by the end of the month. Both battleships are in home ports on the East Coast and West Coast and are preparing to come out with their battle groups. With the *Kennedy* strike group, we have three cruisers, six destroyers and six frigates that are on normal rotational assignments right now and would likely need to be extended if we wanted to include them. The eight amphibious assault ships are either en route or loading and departing in the next twenty-four hours. As you know, we have thirteen boats at sea right now, with one in position to strike with Tomahawk cruise missile if so order."

"Let's hold off on hitting inside Iraq proper. I'm hoping that if our air and ground forces can do enough damage, Saddam may see the folly of his ways and pull them back to Iraq. Jim, be sure we're pounding the UN on this fact. Saddam has got to leave Kuwait, the UAE, and Saudi Arabia. No ifs, ands or butts. Have you heard from Mubarak about Egyptian ground forces, or from the Brits?" the President asked.

"I spoke to the Egyptian Foreign Minister before coming in here. The Egyptians have placed one heavy division on alert to move to the coast and will begin embarkation procedures in a week," Baker said, igniting smiles around the room. "As for the Brits, they're sending naval and ground forces. Sir Douglas Hurd, the Foreign Secretary, told me that

409

they're recalling Parliament on September sixth to put it to a vote. In the meantime, forces have been alerted for deployment," Baker said, again generating smiles and murmurs around the room.

Pleased with the news, the President turned to his Secretary of Energy, Retired Admiral James Watkins. "Admiral, how are we doing on energy?"

"Oil production is running at max capacity. The price of oil has also been on the rise since this started. There doesn't appear to be any panic just yet. Our strategic reserves are at acceptable levels. The North Sea fields are meeting the needs of most of Europe with a few exceptions for the time being. I don't foresee us having to go to a rationing program at this time. Our European friends are a bit worried, and the Russians have made some generous overtures to sell them oil—at our expense, of course. Alaskan crude is sufficient to meet the needs of Japan and the Far East. That's all I have, Mr. President," Watkins concluded.

"How is the presidential call-up of the reserves being received? I haven't heard any complaints in the press," the President said.

"Sir," Cheney said, "we have only one problem."

"And what is that?" the President asked in a resigned voice.

"We have more volunteers than we have positions to fill. We filled the one hundred thousand slots in about seventy-two hours with almost all volunteers, and plenty more are knocking on the door wanting to come on board. Our recruiters are having no problems filling quotas this month either. The nation has really gotten behind us on this one."

"If I may, Mr. President," said Marlin Fitzwater, the White House Press Secretary, nodding towards the television at the end of the table.

"Of course," replied the President.

Fitzwater nodded to an aide, who turned on the television. The Press Secretary's office had cued up a news story from CNN. On the screen, CNN anchor Bernard Shaw sat at his desk with a "Crisis in the Gulf" graphic over his left shoulder. He delivered his lead-in.

"Today in cities across the nation, support for our armed forces has achieved levels last seen at the end of the second world war. Robert Vito in San Diego, California, has more."

The scene flipped to a reporter standing in front of a building with a red Spanish tile roof that was ubiquitous in Southern California.

"This is Robert Vito, reporting from San Diego. In a scene that is playing out across San Diego and indeed cities across the nation, the line of potential recruits at this Navy recruiting station runs out the door. The influx of young men and women volunteering for military service is outpacing the ability of the recruiters to process them. While this outpouring of volunteers can't be boiled down to a single factor, we took the time to ask some of the men and women here at the National City Navy Recruiting Office about their motivation." Robert walked over to a young woman standing in line.

"Miss, why are you in line here today?"

"I just don't like what's going on in the Middle East. Kuwait and Saudi Arabia are our allies, and we can't let this Saddam push them around over there. I mean, if we're not going to stand up for our friends, what do we stand for?" Robert shifted the microphone to the next volunteer in line.

"And you, sir? Why are you joining the Navy today?"

The boy looked into his eyes, unsure how much to tell him. "My uncles both fought in Vietnam, and I always felt that if the time came, I'd join up to do my part too. This is the time, so I'm here to do my part."

The reporter stepped away from the line and addressed the camera.

"Support for our military efforts goes beyond this influx of volunteers. Just a few miles down the road, a massive rally of supporters has converged outside the gates of the North Island Naval Air Station, where the USS *Ranger* is preparing to depart for the Persian Gulf." The image shifted to the area just outside the Naval Air Station. A large crowd had gathered with signs that read "We Support Our Troops," "God Bless America" and "Wide Awake." The latter was a reference to President Bush's remark that the Iraqis had invaded Saudi Arabia while America slept. It had become an unofficial slogan of support for the military effort. The screen faded out.

"Mr. President," said Fitzwater, "we have people lining the interstates and cheering the convoys of military vehicles moving to the ports. Truck stops and rest stops are full of people serving coffee, soda, and food to the soldiers along the routes. We haven't seen support for a military action like this since 1945."

"What about antiwar protests? Surely we're seeing something there?" asked the President.

411

"Yes, sir," replied Fitzwater. "There are protests at the UN headquarters building in New York. About a hundred people asking us to give peace a chance. And there was a march outside the federal building in San Francisco, but nothing compared to the outpouring of support we're seeing."

"Well, that's good to hear," said the President. "The last thing we need is mass demonstrations like what we had during Vietnam. With that said, we need to keep the press on our side. If we keep taking losses like these"—he gestured towards the file in front of General Powell—"there'll be plenty of protests and we'll lose any goodwill we have from the media. Marlin, I need you to figure out how to break the news of these losses." The President stood and turned to look out the window over the South Lawn.

"We can't let this turn into another Vietnam, gentlemen. If we can't take the initiative in this battle, that's exactly what we're risking."

Chapter Forty-Nine
Knock on the Door

24 August 1990
Naval Air Station Oceana
Virginia Beach, Virginia

Virginia in the late summer was hot and humid. Kids were thinking about back-to-school shopping for school clothes but still getting in some beach time. Oceana Naval Air Station was relatively quiet as almost every aircraft had departed and joined the fleet. A few hangar queens could be heard throughout the day, but the noise at night was absent. Some news had gotten back to the families through the wives, rumors mostly being built on the nightly news. Nothing had been confirmed outside the nightly news broadcasts, which were providing broad stroke coverage of the day's events in the Middle East, but nothing specific.

Lieutenant Harry Morgan, an F-14 pilot with VF-74 aboard the USS *Saratoga*, had only been recently assigned to VF-74, having moved from Pensacola Naval Air Station. He had enough time to unpack boxes, hang pictures, and hook up the TV before he had to depart with the squadron to join the ship. Shortly after they were aboard, Saddam entered Kuwait.

His wife, Beverly, was getting settled into life at Oceana Air Station. They were fortunate to get on-base quarters with only a one-month delay. It was not uncommon to have to wait as much as a year to get base housing. The boys, Jordan and Dereck, aged seven and eight, had adapted pretty quickly to the neighborhood, which was typical of military brats. On day one, they had acquired three friends who would probably be in the same class as them at the Department of Defense Dependent School that was on the base. Beverly and Harry liked the boys attending the DoDDS as the school had money to maintain the buildings, provide quality education with quality teachers. The other thing they liked was the fact that the boys had friends of every race, creed, religion, and income level at the school. There was no discrimination among military brats. They were all in the same boat and they knew it.

"Mom, someone's at the door," Jordan called out as he and Dereck sat on the living room floor, glued to the Nintendo game *Super Mario Bros. 3.*

"Dereck, answer the door and see who it is. I'm fixing dinner," Beverly called from the kitchen.

"Ah, Ma!" Dereck sounded off.

"Dereck, don't make me come in there—answer the door!" Beverly commanded.

"Yes, ma'am." Dereck got up off the floor and went to the door. When he opened it, he saw two Navy officers standing in the door and a lady that he'd recently met but couldn't remember where. Her husband was in the squadron, but Dereck didn't know what he did.

"Hi, Dereck. Is your mom home?" the lady asked. "You probably don't remember me, but I'm Mrs. Lovett, your dad's commanding officer."

"Yes, ma'am, she's in the kitchen. Sorry, I remembered your face but not your name. Do you want to see my mom?" Dereck asked with some trepidation.

"Yes, could you ask her if we could come in?"

"Just a minute and I'll go ask her," Dereck said, anxious to get back to his game. He ran to the kitchen. "Mom, Mrs. Lovett is here and wants to see you," Dereck said, just knowing his brother was cheating in the game.

"Well, let her in. Don't keep her waiting," Beverly told him as she started to wash the flour off her hands. As she did, Dereck made a beeline to the front door and pushed open the screen. One of the officers took the door, and Mrs. Lovett entered first. Dereck headed into the living room as Beverly came out of the kitchen. She spotted Mrs. Lovett right away.

"Helen, to what do I owe…?" Her face changed from a smile to an expression of shock when she saw the two officers, one a Navy chaplain, the other another pilot.

"No, no, *no!*" Beverly yelled. Dereck and Jordan suddenly lost all interest in the Nintendo game and looked at their mother, who was now in tears. Helen quickly came over and hugged her.

"Beverly, it's not what you're thinking. He's missing in action and that's all we know at this point. Come, let's sit down," Helen said, guiding Beverly to the couch. "Boys, come over here and sit with your mom. We all need to talk, OK?"

As Beverly and the boys sat down, Helen began with introductions. "This is Chaplin Flanagan, our Catholic chaplain on base." The Navy

414

captain nodded, acknowledging the introduction. "And this is Commander Forest, the rear detachment commander for the ship." He likewise nodded. It was obvious that Helen was in charge at this point.

"Now, Beverly, boys, Commander Forest is going to tell you the facts as we understand them right now. Commander," Helen directed.

"Yesterday your husband's squadron was flying cover for an air strike going in over Saudi Arabia. The Iraqis engaged them with fighter aircraft and air-defense weapons. Reports indicate that your husband downed two Iraqi jets before his aircraft was hit. He ejected before the aircraft exploded. His wingman reported seeing two parachutes and both opened properly. It appeared he landed safely but behind Iraqi lines. A search was launched, but due to the air defense and number of Iraqi soldiers in the area, they couldn't locate him. There have been no communications on his survival radio either, which leads us to believe he may have been captured. Until his capture or death is confirmed, we are listing him as missing in action," Commander Forest explained.

"What do I do now?" Beverly asked between soft sobs, holding the boys tight to her sides.

"Mrs. Morgan, you don't worry about anything at this point," Chaplain Flanagan said. "The family support group has been notified. I will serve as your survivor assistance officer and take care of everything that has to do with the military. There is one thing we need to consider soon. As Missing in Action status is what your husband has now, his take-home pay is cut to fifty-five percent, with the remainder being held in a government account for him. If you need to increase that, we can, but we have to get some paperwork started for that. We can do that in the coming days, but you need to think about what you want to do," Flanagan explained.

"What? Why in the hell would the military do that?" Beverly asked in frustration.

"It seems that during Vietnam, wives of missing in action personnel received full pay. When former POWs returned home, they came to find that the wives had gone through all the money and filed for divorce. The husbands were left penniless. In at least one case, the wife even filed in the divorce for half the officer's retired pay and got it. Claimed he'd abandoned the family and the court bought it," Flanagan said.

415

"Beverly, don't you worry about a thing. We're all with you, and you won't be the only one, I fear," Helen said, patting Beverly on the knee.

Chapter Fifty
Duel in the Dark

2 September 1990
3rd Squadron
Western Saudi Arabia

The plan was simple. *But aren't they all?* The problem always comes down to execution. In this case, the plan called for a multipronged massive airstrike against multiple Saudi and American positions in hopes that some of the strikes would slip through the American air cover. For Major Vitaly Popkov and his squadron of sixteen MiG-29 Fulcrums, they would be flying cover for a squadron of Su-24s as they made a mad dash for the American buildup around the Jeddah international airport and a squadron of Su-25s looking to carry out some CAS missions along the Iraqi-American lines.

The Americans were still reeling from the previous days' ground assaults, so the Iraqi Air Force wanted to keep the pressure on. For his part, Popkov had broken his squadron down into eight flights of two. His thinking was this would force the Americans to have to divide their forces to try and go after his pilots. After the last month of aerial combat, he'd developed a handful of tactics and formations, all in hopes of gaining an advantage against the Americans. The last time Soviet pilots had flown against the Americans was during the Vietnam War. The number of Soviet pilots back home volunteering to be a part of this off-books expeditionary mission was through the roof. Still, it was dangerous work. The Americans had better support than they did.

Ten minutes into their flight, the Su-24s were now fifteen minutes from the target. As they got closer to the airport and the coast, their passive radars started to pick up an enemy E-3 Sentry. Its powerful search radars had found them. The only problem for Popkov was the damn things were flying a racetrack formation on the opposite side of the Red Sea with a carrier battle group between him and them. The damn Sentrys allowed the American aircraft to keep their active radars off longer, thus helping them get in much closer to the Iraqis before they knew they were even there.

Then his radio crackled to life. "Strela Leader, Strela Two. I'm being lit up by an E-2 Hawkeye near that American carrier. Requesting permission to go active with my radar," came the call from his lead element. He'd put his best pilots in the lead element, knowing they'd be the first to make contact with the Americans. If they were being painted by the E-2s, then chances were some fighters were being vectored towards them.

Depressing the talk button, he replied, "Strela Two, Strela Leader, understood. You are cleared to engage. Happy hunting, out." He switched his radio frequency. "Gonshchik Leader, Strela Leader. We're going active with our radars. Good hunting."

A moment later, Popkov heard two squawks on the radio, letting him know the Gonshchik teams were moving to engage. The Gonshchik teams consisted of eight MiG-25 Foxbats that would now rise up from fifty meters in altitude to around seventy-five hundred meters and go supersonic in their race out to sea. They were tasked with going after the E-2 and possibly even the E-3 if they could catch it. The threat to the American airborne early-warning aircraft would force them to divert some of their fighters to defend them, leaving fewer fighters to provide cover over the airport or the current front line. The Foxbats might even get lucky and get a few shots off with their long-range missiles and bag them. The supersonic interceptors were clumsy rockets, but they were damn fast and hard for the Americans to catch.

In the morning, hours after their duel in the dark, the ground forces would make another hard push to dislodge the American paratroopers and hopefully throw them into the sea.

Looking down at his own radar scope, Popkov saw two pairs of F-14s flying near Medina were attempting to give chase and go after the Foxbats. Additional F-14s flying over the carrier were now being vectored after the Foxbats.

The two pairs of F-15s flying over the Jeddah international airport were going after his lead aircraft. Then right on cue, Major Konstantin "Kostya" Ayushiyev's flight of four MiG-29s made their move to engage the F-14s as they diverted to chase the Foxbats.

The fight's on. It's time to earn our bonuses, Popkov thought as he gave his aircraft some thrust and started heading towards the F-15s.

Flying just fifty meters above the ground, the F-15s hadn't spotted him yet. They were busy engaging Strela One and Two. Just as he had engineered to happen. When he'd gotten within eighteen kilometers of the first F-15, he pulled up on his stick and angled his aircraft towards the trailing two F-15s flying cover for the two currently chasing down Strela One and Two. Popkov activated two of his R-73 infrared homing missiles, placing the targeting reticle on one of the F-15s just long enough for the missile tone to let him know it had a lock. Once it did, he pickled off the first missile, then the second at the same target.

In fractions of a second, the blackness of night around him momentarily lit up as the solid-fuel rocket engine ignited and took off after its intended target. The F-15 he'd just locked up and fired on immediately took evasive maneuvers, banking hard to the right as he started to pop off some flares in an attempt to throw off his heat-seeker missiles.

Popkov felt incredibly proud when, moments later his wingman, not hesitating in the least, had also pickled off two of his own missiles at the American's wingman. In seconds, they had four missiles racing after the American aircraft.

Giving his aircraft some additional power, Popkov dove to the right to give chase to the American he had just fired on. He saw his first missile get spoofed by the Yankee's countermeasures and blew up when it hit one of the flares. Not wanting to let this one get away, Popkov switched on his R-27 active-radar-homing missiles. He had to fight a little bit, but he kept the targeting reticle on it long enough for it to get a solid lock. He fired. Moments later his second R-73 missed the F-15 and flew off harmlessly from a brilliant maneuver the American pilot had pulled off. That miss only confirmed his earlier decision to fire a third missile at the F-15.

Then he saw a bright flash somewhere off to his eleven o'clock position. Looking in that direction, he saw it had come from one of the fighters. Which one he wasn't sure just yet. A handful of bright red objects zipped right past his canopy, forcing him to dive to the left to avoid whatever was shooting at him. Before he could react to whatever had just shot at him, his Beryoza or radar warning receiver started blaring in his ear, letting him know that some sort of missile was attempting to lock on to him.

Then his RWR shouted a new warning. A missile had been fired at him. Looking down at his scope, he saw the missile had originated from one of the F-15s. It was racing towards him quickly, almost too quickly.

Pulling back on his flight controls, Popkov attempted to gain some altitude, as he'd wandered a bit too close to the ground when he had chased after that other American fighter. A flash occurred somewhere to his right. It was in the direction of the fighter he had fired on earlier, but he wasn't sure if it had been his missile that hit it or if another fighter had blown up.

Warning, warning, warning, kept blaring in his headset. *That damn missile is fast*, he thought as he banked his aircraft to the right while dispensing a couple of flares.

Another flash occurred somewhere behind him. His aircraft was momentarily buffeted by the concussion of the blast. *I'm alive, that's all that matters*, he briefly thought as he pulled up hard on his flight controls and nearly cut his throttle.

His Fulcrum flared up almost vertically in a Pugachev's Cobra maneuver as it practically hovered momentarily in the air. Seconcs later, the F-15 that had just fired at him zipped right past him, with both its engines lit up as the pilot tried to put as much distance between them as humanly possible.

Popkov pushed his throttle to the wall, sending a rush of fuel to his engines, reigniting them with a renewed fury. He activated one of his R-73 heat-seeker missiles and while tracking the large American fighter visually, the missile's seeker gained a lock on the aircraft. He depressed the firing button on the side of his flight stick, firing his fourth missile of the morning.

His missile leapt from its rail and raced ahead of him after the two red-hot glowing Pratt & Whitney F100 engines still in full afterburner mode. Seconds later, the 7.4-kilogram warhead had gotten within its proximity range and detonated. It fired essentially an aerial shotgun blast of steel ball bearings right into the rear of the F-15s tail, shredding its left engine, vertical tail stabilizers and wing. A trail of

420

smoke and some flames followed in the aircraft's wake as the pilot was clearly struggling to maintain control of the stricken plane.

The American had turned the plane to head towards the international airport, likely in hopes of getting closer to friendly lines before he had to eject. Then the fire around the engine of the plane winked out, probably from the aircraft's internal fire suppression system. Popkov watched as the pilot deftly maneuvered his stricken plane towards the international airport, presumably wanting to save his aircraft. That was when Popkov knew he needed to finish this guy off. He wasn't about to let him land the wounded plane, only to possibly get it airborne again later to kill Popkov or his buddies.

Dropping in behind the F-15, he switched his weapon systems over from missiles to his gun system. With his 30mm autocannon activated, he lined up his gun sights on the one operational engine on the Eagle and depressed the trigger only long enough to send a handful of his hundred and fifty rounds into the rear of the aircraft. His goal wasn't to try and kill the pilot, who'd fought gallantly. He just wanted to remove him from being a threat.

When his handful of 30mm projectiles slammed into the plane, it ripped a couple pieces of metal from the aircraft. Then the plane suddenly burst into flames and exploded. This sudden eruption of fire and bright flash momentarily stunned Popkov. He hadn't intended on killing the enemy flier, only to force the pilot to eject.

Then his radio crackled. "Strela Leader, Strela Two. I think it's time for us to get out of here," came the voice of his second-in-command. "Congrats on the kill."

That makes eight...

"Agreed. We've done what we came here to do. Let's get out of here."

Turning to head back home, Popkov tried to do a quick head count. He'd started the mission with sixteen fighters. He was returning with nine. Talking briefly with his pilots, he learned they'd scored seven kills of their own. He'd check with the Foxbat commander when they returned to see how they'd fared. Seeing that the E-2 Hawkeye wasn't lighting them up meant they'd likely taken it out. How many F-14s they had managed to nail in the process was a different story.

Nearing the aerodrome, Popkov lined up for his approach and made one of the best landings he'd ever made. The adrenaline from this battle was still coursing through his veins. Once he'd parked his aircraft and was able to climb out, the first thing he did was walk to a nearby maintenance vehicle and relieve himself on the tarmac.

When he entered the operations center to begin his debrief, Popkov learned they'd lost a single Su-25s during the raid while three Su-24s were lost over the airport. As he sat in the debriefing room, it dawned on him that the Battle of Jeddah would likely go down as one of the largest aerial battles in decades. While he was feeling a bit euphoric over the results and his own aerial kills, he knew once the Americans were able to move more squadrons into the area, these kinds of battles wouldn't be as easy to pull off.

I hope the Iraqis can secure a settlement that benefits them soon, he thought. *Winning will be a lot harder once the American juggernaut starts moving in our direction. I just hope I can survive long enough for this war to end...*

Invitation to Continue the Action

We hope you have enjoyed reading *Project 19*. If you are hungry for more, you are in luck. The next book of the Crisis in the Desert series, titled *Desert Shield*, will be released November 9, 2021, and is currently available for preorder. Reserve your copy so you can continue the adventure.

About the Authors

Matt Jackson enlisted in the US Army in 1968 and served on active duty until 1993, when he retired as a colonel. In the course of his career, he commanded two infantry companies, one being an airborne company in Alaska. He also commanded an air assault infantry battalion during Operation Desert Shield/Storm with the 101st Airborne Division. Staff assignments with troops included operations officer in an air cavalry squadron, operations officer in a light infantry battalion, and executive officer of an air assault infantry brigade. When not with troop assignments, Matt Jackson was generally found teaching tactics at the United States Army Infantry Center or the United States Army Command and General Staff College, with a follow-on assignment as an exchange instructor at the German Army Tactics Center. His last assignment was Director, Readiness and Mobilization, J-5, Forces Command, and Special Advisor, Vice President of the United States. Upon retiring from the US Army, he went into private business. He and his wife of fifty years have two sons, both Army officers.

Matt Jackson has written three other books in the *Undaunted Valor* series: *An Assault Helicopter Unit in Vietnam, Medal of Honor*, and *Lam Son 719*. His next book will be *Undaunted Valor: Easter Offensive*, which will be released in 2022.

****

James Rosone started his military career in 1996 as a communications specialist with a self-propelled 155mm howitzer unit. He was later crossedtrained into becoming a forward observer for the artillery guns. James then transitioned from the Army to the US Air Force in 2004, where he went on to serve as a human intelligence collector. In this job, he worked as an interrogator throughout Operation Iraqi Freedom, interrogating senior-level Al Qaeda members and other terrorists, insurgents, and former regime members.

James would go on to work as a government contractor in intelligence for the Department of State and Defense in the Middle East, Eurasia, and Europe, continuing the hunt for Islamic extremists, transnational terrorists, and criminal organizations. In 2015, James began writing as a form of PTSD therapy, publishing his debut novel in 2016.

He has since gone on to publish more than twenty highly successful books in the thriller and science fiction genres. James's most current military thriller series is *The Monroe Doctrine*, which explores what would happen if China were to encroach on countries in the Western Hemisphere.

James now works to mentor other veterans struggling with PTSD through writing therapy, teaching them how to become successful authors so that they can write to support their families. You can learn more about James at his website,www.frontlinepublishinginc.com or join his mailing list to stay up-to-date on new releases or sales.

Acknowledgements

I would like to thank all the great leaders and soldiers I served with during Desert Shield and Desert Storm. There were so many, but I'd especially like to acknowledge the soldiers and noncommissioned officers of the 3rd Battalion, 327th Infantry. The Army authorized me to command the battalion, but they gave me the privilege of command. Great leaders provided guidance and mentorship throughout my time, and I am forever grateful to General Binford Peay, CG, 101st Airborne Division (Air Assault), and General Hugh Shelton, Assistant Division Commander for Operations, 101st Airborne Division (Air Assault). I would be remiss if I did not thank General Mike Oates, who was a major during Operation Desert Shield/Storm in the division. All are retired now, but still provide guidance and mentorship to today's leaders. Lastly, I would like to thank my wife who held up the homefront for the past fifty years, and my two fine sons that carried on the family tradition.

--Matt Jackson

CPSIA information can be obtained
at www.ICGtesting.com
Printed in the USA
FSHW021957151021
85526FS